The story of Josephine Cox is as extraordinary as anything in her novels. Born in a cotton-mill house in Blackburn, she was one of ten children. Her parents, she says, brought out the worst in each other, and life was full of tragedy and hardship – but not without love and laughter. At the age of sixteen, Josephine met and married 'a caring and wonderful man', and had two sons. When the boys started school, she decided to go to college and eventually gained a place at Cambridge University, though was unable to take this up as it would have meant living away from home. However, she did go into teaching, while at the same time helping to renovate the derelict council house that was their home, coping with the problems caused by her mother's unhappy home life – and writing her first full-length novel. Not surprisingly, she then won the 'Superwoman of Great Britain' Award, for which her family had secretly entered her, and this coincided with the acceptance of her novel for publication.

Josephine gave up teaching in order to write full time. She says 'I love writing, both recreating scenes and characters from my past, together with new storylines which mingle naturally with the old. I could never imagine a single day without writing, and it's been that way since as far back as I can remember.' Her previous novels of North Country life are all available from Headline and are immensely popular.

'Bestselling author Josephine Cox has penned another winner' *Bookshelf*

'Hailed quite rightly as a gifted writer in the tradition of Catherine Cookson' *Manchester Evening News*

'Guaranteed to tug at the heartstrings of all hopeless romantics' *Sunday Post*

ALSO BY

JOSEPHINE COX

QUEENIE'S STORY

Her Father's Sins
Let Loose the Tigers

THE EMMA GRADY TRILOGY

Outcast
Alley Urchin
Vagabonds

Angels Cry Sometimes
Take This Woman
Whistledown Woman
Don't Cry Alone
Jessica's Girl
Nobody's Darling
Born to Serve
More than Riches
A Little Badness
Living a Lie
The Devil You Know
A Time for Us
Cradle of Thorns
Miss You Forever
Love Me or Leave Me
Tomorrow the World
The Gilded Cage
Somewhere, Someday
Looking Back
The Woman Who Left
Jinnie
Bad Boy Jack

JOSEPHINE COX

Rainbow Days

headline

First published in hardback in 2000 by
HEADLINE BOOK PUBLISHING

First published in paperback in 2000 by
HEADLINE BOOK PUBLISHING

This edition published in paperback in 2005 by
HEADLINE BOOK PUBLISHING

12

ISBN 0 7472 5758 2

Typeset in Baskerville by Palimpsest Book Production Limited,
Polmont, Stirlingshire

Printed and bound in Great Britain by
Clays Ltd, St Ives plc

Headline's policy is to use papers that are natural, renewable and
recyclable products and made from wood grown in sustainable forests.
The logging and manufacturing processes are expected to conform to
the environmental regulations of the country of origin.

HEADLINE BOOK PUBLISHING
A division of the Hodder Headline Group
338 Euston Road
London NW1 3BH

www.headline.co.uk
www.hodderheadline.com

DEDICATION

For David; never formally one of the family, but with us for a long time. He wasn't perfect, but then none of us are. We won't forget you, David.

———◆———

I've just heard of someone who has fallen out with family, and vows never to speak to them again. I find that very sad.

For those of you who have a rift with friends or family, please don't let it get beyond repair. Life is too short for all that. Sometimes, pride has to take a back seat, and it's you who has to make the first move.

CONTENTS

PART ONE

1900

CATHLEEN

Chapter One

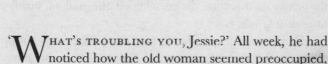

'WHAT'S TROUBLING YOU, Jessie?' All week, he had noticed how the old woman seemed preoccupied, as if there was something weighing heavy on her mind. Always independent, too concerned about hurting others to unburden her troubles on them, Jessie had a way of keeping her thoughts to herself.

Not today though. Today, she had a feeling that things were coming to a head and she needed to talk to someone before it was too late. 'It's our Cathleen.' Her soft Irish voice was lost against his mutterings.

'Look at that!' Irritated and impatient he gave the nail another hammering. 'Can't get the damned thing to hold!'

Jessie looked up from her sewing, watching Tom at work, and as always wondering what would happen to this lovely man after she'd gone. Moreover, what would happen to Cathleen? Young Robert too. Oh, but he was heading for a fall, that one.

Tom glanced at her. 'Sorry, Jessie. What did you say?'

'Nothing important. It can wait.' But not for much longer, she fretted. The matter of Cathleen would have to be addressed and soon.

'Damn it!' Plucking the nail out he moved it further up, to where the oak beam had sunk level with the wall; one swing with the hammer and it bit hard. 'That's better.'

Jessie followed his every movement: the hammer coming down, his eye intent on driving the nail home; the smile on his face as he wiggled the nail to satisfy himself it would hold.

Despairing, Jessie shook her head. She knew him all too well. When that task was finished he would start another. He never stopped. Rising at five to travel into Blackburn town and light the big ovens at the bakery, he never arrived home until the streets were shrouded in darkness. Even then he would find all manner of jobs to do about the house.

'What's that about our Cathleen?' Taking the picture he hung it carefully on the nail and stepped back to see how it looked.

Jessie didn't answer straight away. Instead she continued to observe him, noting how the long hard hours shovelling bread in and out of ovens had gently stooped his shoulders and weathered his face with a deep, warm glow. Tom was in his mid-forties, but seemed older. Yet even now he would have been a catch for any woman. Long of limb and dark of eye, he was still an easy-looking man. With no life outside of his work and his children, he was often lonely. He could have found himself a new wife without too much bother, but Jessie knew he never would. The plain truth was that Tom still loved the woman he had wed all those years ago. And though she was gone now, he wanted no other.

'What about our Cathleen?' he repeated. Turning from his task, Tom's dark eyes sought her face.

'I didn't think you were listening.'

'Sorry about that, Jessie. The damned nail wouldn't take hold.'

'I don't want you worrying, but . . .' Having started, Jessie had to go on, 'I've been meaning to have a word with yer, so I have.'

Sensing trouble, Tom put down the hammer and came to sit opposite her. 'Why? What's she done?'

'Nothing wrong, as I know of,' she answered. 'It's just that . . .' She shrugged her shoulders, trying to make light of it; already regretting being the cause of the anxiety betrayed on his face. 'Aw, sure it doesn't matter. It's just an old woman's ramblings.'

'Huh! I've yet to see the day when *you* take to "rambling",' he declared. 'Come on, Jessie. It's obvious you're concerned about our Cathleen. You'd best out with it!'

'I never said I were concerned!' she chided. 'I were just thinking . . . now that she's eighteen, and with not having a mam an' all . . . well, I reckon yer might need to have a talk with the lass.' Feeling uncomfortable beneath his curious gaze, she began to wish she had kept her worries to herself.

Frowning, he asked, 'What kind of a talk?' Cathleen

5

was the joy of his life. If there was a problem he needed to know. 'Jessie! What are you getting at?'

Changing her mind, the old woman shook her head. 'Aw, sure, it's summat and nothing,' she replied with a shrug.

'Let *me* be the judge of that, Jessie.'

'I were just wondering if you'd said anything to the lass . . .' Her mind raced ahead, thinking that the best thing was to change tack, at least for now. '. . . About the business, that kind o' thing?'

Crossing her fingers under her pinnie, she asked the good Lord not to strike her dead for telling lies.

Reassured, Tom gave a sigh of relief. 'By! I thought for a minute you were saying she'd got herself in trouble with some young fella. That bugger Lou Matheson comes to mind straightaway!'

She laughed. 'Lou Matheson might fancy his chances, but our Cathleen's never had eyes for him.'

Unsure, he searched her eyes looking for the truth then, suddenly leaning forward, he took hold of her hand. 'Look here, Jessie,' he said, 'I know you love the lass, and you've never been one for telling tales, but if ever there was anything worrying you, about Cathleen, in particular, I wouldn't want you to keep it from me.'

Shame and guilt filled her kind old heart, and now she was in a dilemma. 'I understand what yer saying, so I do.'

He kept his gaze locked with hers, a fond smile creeping over his manly features. 'That doesn't mean to say I don't trust you or anything, and I'd never want to hurt your feelings, Jessie. I love you like you were my own mother.'

Casting his mind back to the past, he thought of how things used to be. 'You've been an absolute Godsend to me,' he told her kindly. 'You were there the day our Cathleen was born ... then three years later when young Robert came along.' His eyes clouded over. 'You stood by us when their mam fell ill and were taken only days after.'

Swallowing his grief, he confessed, 'I fell apart after that, I let things go, God help me. I lost my work and my senses. But you were always there, for all of us. You saved my sanity.'

Jessie was special, he knew that. And he owed her more than he could ever repay. 'The day you persuaded us to come and live here with you in Pleasington, oh, Jessie!' He bowed his head. 'Throwing open your home to the three of us, well, it was a grand thing you did. Not many women would have done the same.'

'Aw, I'm sure they would,' Jessie answered. 'Where family is involved, a woman will always give that little bit extra.' A cheeky grin lifted her features. 'Besides, I didn't do it just for you!' she declared craftily. 'We've helped each *other*, so we have.'

Jessie had her own painful memories. 'When my Thomas went, he left behind a rundown bakery and a pile of debts. You took it on, and in no time at all the bakery was making more money than ever before, and all the debts long ago paid off.' She chuckled. 'I've even managed to save a shilling or two for me old age, so I have.'

Tom shook his head. 'However much you might dismiss it, you still saved my life, Jessie . . . mine *and* the children's. I know this much . . . if it hadn't been for you, I don't think I would ever have come through it.'

Remembering, Jessie nodded. 'Mebbe . . . mebbe not.' A great sigh rippled through her. 'There's no denying, it were a bad time,' she recalled. 'You lost a wife and I lost a daughter, but we were blessed with two little souls. We've a lot to be thankful for, Tom, you must always remember that.'

Taking a deep breath, he leaned back in the chair. 'I know,' he agreed. 'Sometimes, though, I wish young Robert was more like Cathleen.' He shook his head. 'I swear he drives me to despair.'

Jessie knew what he meant and agreed, but would never say so. Instead, against her own instincts she always found herself defending the lad. 'I'll not deny Robert is headstrong and rebellious, but sometimes that's the way it is . . . no two bairns are ever the same, any mother will tell yer that. He'll grow out of it, so he will. Sure, the lad's only fifteen, and o' course' – a familiar sense of sadness filled her old heart – 'from the day he was born the poor wee soul never had the love of a mother.'

She paused, thinking how Tom's only son did seem to have a streak of wickedness in him, but went on, 'For all his wild ways, he's still his mother's child, and his mother was goodness itself. So we mustn't despair.'

Suddenly, in the appealing way she had of turning a situation round, she began to chuckle. 'Matter o' fact, I were quite a handful meself in me young days.' Rolling her speckled brown eyes, she confided, 'I don't mind telling yer, *I* were a little divil, so I was!'

Tom couldn't help but throw back his head with laughter. 'I don't doubt that for a minute, Jessie Butler!'

Jessie's old eyes twinkled. 'I've allus loved the dancing.' She wasn't telling him anything he didn't already know. 'I reckon when I were born the good Lord gave me feet that wouldn't keep still. Me daddy told me I danced at the drop of a hat ... soonever the gramophone was wound up, sure I'd be off like a spinning top ... dancing all over the place and making everybody laugh. It's allus been the same so it has, the music starts and my feet begin to itch. When I were old enough to be allowed on the dance floor, I'd be the first one on and the last one off.' As she spoke her feet tapped a gentle rhythm on the rug. 'I were never short o' partners neither, though I wore the buggers out one after the other, so I did.'

Chuckling at the memory, she added mischievously, 'Sure, them other bonny lasses didn't like it at all, but that didn't bother me none. As long as I could dance, I was in me glory, so I was.'

'Sounds to me like you *were* a bit of a handful, Jessie Butler.' He laughed. 'I should think you drove your mam and dad to distraction.'

'Aye, that's what *they* said an' all.' She laughed with him, her heart happy at the memory.

Tom could imagine how she might have caused a stir as a young woman. With those beautiful hazel eyes and that long, thick hair, she must have turned many a young man's head. Now, at sixty-nine years old, she still carried a haunting kind of beauty; though the hair was plaited and streaked with grey, there was a mischievousness about her that gladdened the heart.

'You dance as if you were born to it,' he told her. 'Your daughter always said you should have a career out of it.' He smiled wistfully. 'I wonder what she'd say if she'd been here on Cathleen's birthday, and seen you dancing round the garden like some little pixie . . . wearing out everybody who was brave enough to try and keep up with you.'

'Oh, *Cathleen* kept up. She were still dancing when I sat meself down, so she were.'

'Aye, well, that's not surprising is it? 'Cause we all know our Cathleen is her grannie in the making.'

Feeling his loneliness, Jessie took hold of his hand, saying softly, 'You wondered what her mammy might have said if she'd seen us? Well, I'll tell yer . . . she'd have said how *you* should try dancing more often. She'd have said you needed to find yerself a woman, someone to spend the rest of your days with.'

Nodding thoughtfully, he conceded, 'Happen you're right, Jessie, but it's not likely I'll ever find a woman like my Mary, even if I wanted to.' Before the memories came flooding back, he shrugged off Jessie's suggestion with a smile. 'Besides, I'm not a dancing man,' he said. 'So, I'll leave all that to you and Cathleen, for you're two of a kind, and that's a fact.'

'Now you could be right about that,' the old woman agreed. 'She's got the feet for dancing, so she has, and a heart the same. And doesn't she love the outdoors an' all? Sure she'd spend her life like a gypsy on the road if she had half a chance.'

'She's a good girl, isn't she, Jessie?' It wasn't that he needed reassuring; it was just that, lately, Cathleen had seemed to grow up so quickly. She wasn't his little girl any more. She was a young woman, and very beautiful at that.

'Aye, she's a good girl, Tom. Our Cathleen will always make you a proud man, I'm sure of it.'

'And Robert?' He always felt anxious thinking about his son.

'Aw, the lad's young and headstrong. But so is every other lad at his age. So stop yer worrying why don't yer?' Though to her mind, Robert was a lost cause. 'Robert will come right in the end, mark my words. Besides, Cathleen keeps a wary eye on him, so he won't go far wrong, I'm thinking.' She prayed she was right.

'Oh, Jessie, I do hope so.'

Momentarily closing his eyes he pictured Cathleen's mother; slim and pretty, with vivid blue eyes and flowing fair hair, she might have been Cathleen herself.

Suppressing the image, he looked at the old woman. 'We seem to have got off the subject,' he chided. 'You were saying . . . about Cathleen?'

Having lied once, she did not want to do so a second time. Tom was a good man and deserved better. Besides, there was nothing to be gained by worrying him with her suspicions. 'I were just wondering about her future,' she confessed.

'Go on,' he urged. 'Tell me what's really on your mind.'

Jessie found herself edging towards the real issue. 'I've taught Cathleen all I know. She can read and write, she has a quick grasp of numbers, and a natural love for music and nature, but now that she's eighteen you need to be thinking about her future.'

Tom sat up, suddenly aware that he had been neglecting his parental duties. 'By! It never even crossed me mind,' he admitted. 'She grew up when me back was turned and now I'm not sure what I'm supposed to do.' An idea struck him. 'Look, Jessie, if the lass is good at figures like you say . . . happen we should take her into the business? She's already doing deliveries, and folk think the world of her.' His face darkened. 'I had thought our Robert might take over some day, but I don't think he has the spirit for hard work.'

'It's not a bad idea, Tom,' Jessie conceded. 'But I wouldn't want her weighed down with too many responsibilities, not yet anyway. She's of an age when her whole world is opening up. Many a lass of eighteen is already wed, with bairns running at her feet. For all we know, Cathleen could be setting her cap at some young man right now. If yer ask me, we should be guiding her in the right direction.'

'In what way d'you mean, Jessie?'

'I mean . . . if she were to fall for somebody not of her own station, it might cause the lass, and us, no end of grief.'

Alarmed, Tom sensed Jessie's veiled warning. He

finally understood what she had been leading up to. 'My God! That's what's been playing on your mind, isn't it . . . Cathleen and Silas Fenshaw.' He toyed with the possibility and rejected it out of hand, but when he looked up, neither his smile nor his voice was convincing. 'Surely to God she's got more sense than to entertain such an idea? They're *friends*, Jessie! They've *allus* been friends, and no more.'

Now that she'd stirred his suspicions, Jessie kept at it like a dog with a bone. 'Think about it, Tom,' she pleaded. 'They spend every waking minute together. Yes, to be sure, they've been friends since they were children and that's innocent enough. But friendship can change.'

'Not in *that* way.'

'*Yes*, Tom!' Forcing him to look at the possibility, she urged, 'Love can take a hold, and before you know it they're seeing each other through the eyes of grown-ups. 'Cause that's what they are. What's more, they've already got a head start on many another young couple who have fallen in love and found themselves in a tangle.'

'I still can't see that happening, Jessie.' To him Cathleen was still a baby.

'Then you'd best put yer mind to it, because she's *not* a bairn any more. She's a young woman with time on her hands, and you know what they say . . . the devil will surely find mischief for idle hands.'

'Silas Fenshaw has always been earmarked to wed the Turner girl, everybody knows that. Our Cathleen doesn't even come into the picture. It's all to do with business, and power.'

Jessie shook her head. 'There's nothing more powerful than love, and besides, no matter how desperately his father might want Silas to slip a wedding ring on Helen Turner's finger, it will never happen. Young Silas has no liking for her. You know it, I know it, and the whole of Lancashire knows it.'

'I think you're barking up the wrong tree, Jessie.' All the same, Tom's mind was made up. 'First thing Monday morning, I'd best make a start on teaching Cathleen the ins and outs of the bakery business. With your blessing o' course . . . seeing as we're partners.'

Jessie smiled. 'It don't mek no difference to me, son,' she answered. 'My half will come to her anyway, one o' these fine days.' Though she hoped that day was far off yet. 'But yer must ask *her* first, and see if that's what she wants.'

With that they each resumed their tasks, but their thoughts were of one mind: could Cathleen really have stepped out of line and fallen in love with Silas Fenshaw? If she had, then she had already taken the first step down a painful road, for while Edward Fenshaw might have accepted the baker's child as a playmate for his only son, he would never entertain the idea of her being one of the family. Never in a million years!

<hr>

D ESPITE THE HOT sun beating down on her head, Helen Turner made no move to find shade. Instead, she stayed by the verandah steps, hidden from sight and secretly observing the two figures below, her devious eyes following their every move.

Unable to tear herself away, she continued to watch them, hating their innocence, their obvious joy in each other. Oh, how she longed to run and tell them what she had discovered, and how because of it, she held both their futures in the palm of her hand. But, however much she wanted to, she could not tell them yet. Tomorrow would be soon enough, she thought bitterly.

Her hard features lifted in a smile. 'Enjoy each other while you can,' she murmured softly. 'It won't be long now, not if I have my way.' The smile gave way to a low, rumbling laugh. 'And as you should know by now, I *always* get my way.'

———⟫◦⟪———

U NAWARE THAT THEY were being watched, Cathleen and Silas ran through the spinney and on towards the lake, Cathleen in front, Silas in pursuit. Laughing like a child, her skirts held high above her knees, Cathleen tripped and fell. Lying there on the grass breathless and excited, she made no protest when Silas fell on top of her.

'You minx!' Grabbing her into his arms, he teased, 'Did you really think I'd let you get away from me?'

Reaching out, she traced her fingers along the curve of his mouth. 'I would never want to get away from you.'

His dark gaze mingled with hers. 'I do love you.' His voice ached with longing.

She smiled, a certain, wonderful smile that told him all he needed to know. 'Hold me, Silas,' she whispered. 'Hold me tight.'

When he drew her closer she confided, 'Sometimes I can't help but feel . . .' pausing, she looked away, '. . . afraid.'

Turning her face to his he asked worriedly, 'Cathleen, what is it? What are you afraid of?'

Looking up at him now, feeling his strong arms about her, she thought she would never be afraid again, but always there were doubts. 'What if others were to come between us?' she asked. 'What if you should ever stop loving me?'

'I could *never* stop loving you. Listen to me, sweetheart!' Cupping her face in his hands, he told her firmly, 'You're everything to me. I would have to lose my life before I'd lose you.'

Stretching up, she kissed him soundly on the mouth. 'I know,' she said. 'But you and me . . . the way we are.' Fear marbled her words. 'Sometimes I think it might be snatched away and we'll be punished.'

Drawing away from her, he frowned, his dark eyes troubled. 'You mustn't think like that! We've done nothing to be punished for.'

Scrambling up, she shook the grass from her skirt. When he took hold of her, she looked away, suddenly shy. 'I'm sorry,' she murmured. 'It's just that we don't really belong together. You live in a big house. Your father is a powerful, wealthy man.' She recalled the first time she had come to the Fenshaw house. 'He only allowed us to

16

play together in the first place because I ran and told him how the dogs were chasing you.'

Silas laughed. 'I saw you drop the bread-basket and run all the way to the house,' he recalled. 'You were so little . . . six years old, and as brave as a lion, and after Father got me down from the tree, I told him I wanted you to come to the house again – not just to deliver bread, but to play. And each time you went away, I pleaded with him to let you come back, again and again, until we were inseparable.'

Cathleen smiled. 'He only agreed because he was worried that if it hadn't been for me, the dogs might have eaten you.' A look of sorrow crossed her face. 'Remember how sad we were when he had them put down?'

'I've never loved anyone else, you know that, don't you?'

'Not even the other one?'

'*Which* other one?'

'Helen Turner.'

'My God, Cathleen! I hope you're not comparing yourself to *that* hard-faced bitch! Her father and mine are business colleagues, that's all. She means nothing to me and never has.'

'All right then . . . but we're *still* worlds apart and always have been. You went away to be educated by men of learning, while I sat on my grandmammy's knee to learn the reading and writing. You're being groomed to take over your father's empire . . . farms and cottages all over Lancashire. You know about things I could never hope to understand, and it will come between us, I know it will.'

'No, Cathleen!' Taking her by the shoulders, he gently shook her. 'They'll love you for what you are, a beautiful young woman created by heaven.' He sighed. 'And touched by hell, I think . . . you're bad-tempered and impossible . . . and I wouldn't swap you for the world!'

Tears gathered in her blue eyes. 'If your father knew how we felt about each other, he'd stop you from seeing me again.'

'*I* might have something to say about that.' Leaning forward to whisper in her ear, he urged, 'Marry me, Cathleen?' Stroking her long, fair hair, he waited for an answer, as he had waited all these years.

Thrilled, she gave a small, impetuous laugh. 'You've asked me that every year since I was six years old.'

'And I'll ask you every year until you're *sixty* if I have to.'

'You're a stubborn man, Silas Fenshaw!' Her blue eyes twinkled merrily.

'Only because you never give me an answer.'

'What makes you think I'll give you an answer *now*?'

'Because you're older and wiser.'

'You mean . . . I'm eighteen, so I should know what's good for me?'

'Something like that.' He grinned, a handsome, lopsided grin that made her giggle.

'What if I'm not ready?'

He shook her gently a second time. 'No teasing!'

he chided. 'Answer me, Cathleen. I could talk to your father this very evening, tell him how we feel about each other.'

She looked away. 'Maybe he already knows.'

'Answer me!'

'You'll have to ask me again.'

'You're tormenting me now, you devil!'

Her emotions in a tangle, Cathleen could hardly contain her joy. All she had ever dreamed about was being Silas's wife, but until this moment she had been too young to give such a promise. Now she was eighteen and ready to go to him, even though she still had misgivings, not about Silas or herself, but about the difference in their backgrounds. Yet it didn't seem to worry Silas, so she wouldn't let it worry her.

On waking that morning, with the sun shining, the whole world had seemed more alive than ever before; now she knew why. Silas was asking her to marry him, and it was the best day of her life. She felt wonderful and happy and cheeky, and wanted the moment to last for ever.

'Go on,' she teased. 'Ask me again.'

'Why?'

Wanting to laugh out loud with delight, it was difficult to keep a straight face. 'Because I'm not sure I heard you right the first time.'

'You *are* a devil!' He saw the look on her face and his heart leaped. 'Are you trying to drive me crazy?'

'No.'

Unsure of her, he waited for the laugh that might

follow. Instead, she looked at him, and he dared to believe she was serious. 'Tell me what you're thinking,' he murmured. 'Put me out of my misery.'

She was quiet, looking at him in a way that turned his heart over. In that precious moment, there was so much love between them, so much longing . . . mingled with fear. What if it all fell away? What if the joy they shared was suddenly to disappear, and they were driven apart. It didn't bear thinking about.

'All right then,' she cried suddenly, making off at a run, 'I'll give you an answer . . . but you'll have to catch me first!'

Laughing, he chased her through the undergrowth and on towards the lake. When he caught up with her, she was splashing barefoot along the water's edge. Keeping her in sight, he ran into the water, calling for her to come back. 'It's dangerous! There are reeds everywhere!'

Defiant, she ventured out a little further. 'Come on!' she beckoned. The water was up to her neck now, making her cough and splutter.

Fearing for her safety, Silas went after her. 'You're crazy, come out of there!' Lunging forward he took hold of her arm, but when she snatched it away and dipped under the water, he had to go with her.

They were both good swimmers, but only Silas knew how treacherous the reeds could be. 'Make your way back,' he urged when they resurfaced. 'Stay close to me.'

On entering shallower waters, and being already

soaked to the skin, they swam and kicked and splashed for the sheer fun of it all. A short time later, he took her by the scruff of the neck and hauled her out on to the bank, and they lay there awhile in the warm sun, excited by the thrill of the chase, and wonderfully exhilarated by the sting of cool water on their bodies.

Half laughing, half chiding, Silas told her, 'I'm not sure if I *want* you for my wife after all.'

'Why do you say that?'

'Because I don't know if I want my children brought up by a lunatic!'

'Aw, well!' Shaking the excess water from her clothes, she collected her boots from the bank. 'You'd best take me home then,' she sighed, a twinkle in her blue eyes. 'Being as you don't want to marry me any more.'

Suddenly she was grabbed from behind. 'I can see I'll have to take you in hand!'

'So, you *do* love me after all?'

Feigning astonishment, he asked, '*Love you*? Whatever gave you that idea?'

'Well, do you want to marry me or not?'

He turned away. 'Not if you were the last woman on earth!'

When he tugged at her skirt a moment later, she fell down on the grass, her long hair damp against her shoulders, and her wet clothes clinging. 'So, it's all over between us, then?' she said softly.

'Absolutely!' He could hardly contain himself.

'Whatever will I do without you?'

His gaze softened. 'You'll have to marry Lou Matheson.'

Biting her lip tantalisingly, she teased, 'He's not so bad.'

'I see.' He looked at her with adoration, his voice falling to a whisper. 'Let's make love, Cathleen.'

Her blue eyes darkened like the ocean. She couldn't speak, she was overwhelmed by the emotion that swept through her.

They lay there in each other's arms, unsure and afraid, until Cathleen thought she saw someone looking at them from the house. 'Let's go to the island,' she whispered.

'Are you sure?'

She nodded, her heart pounding as she slid her hand into his. In silence, they walked to the jetty where the boat was tethered, and he helped her clamber inside. As he rowed across the lake to the island, his dark eyes searched her face, watching for any sign that she wanted to go back. If she had asked he would have turned the boat around and taken her home.

Instead, she glanced at him and looked away shyly, and he loved her so much it was like a tight, iron band round his chest.

During the few minutes it took to reach the island, Cathleen felt as though she was embarking on a journey she had been waiting for all her life. She was nervous, but not afraid, not with Silas. She had known him too long to be afraid. He was gentle and caring, and even now, if she were to tell him she had changed her mind, she knew he would respect her decision. But she wouldn't change her mind. She had waited for this moment for ever . . . *dreamed* of lying in his arms and giving herself to him completely. She always knew that one day their time would come. And that time was now.

Discreetly, she looked up and saw how intent he was on rowing, his thoughtful eyes momentarily turned towards the island, and she had never loved him more than she did right now.

She continued to watch him for a while, his bare muscles flexing and tightening with each stroke, his long legs stretched out before him. Now, as the breeze played with his thick, dark hair, lifting it from his brow and flicking it across his eyes, he raised his forearm to push the straying dark strands away. Their eyes met and she knew his every thought.

He was so handsome, Cathleen knew he could have any girl he wanted. But he wanted her, and she was glad of that. She thought of where they were going, and why. There was no shame in her heart, only love, and such a powerful need to be his at last.

Trailing her hand in the coolness of the lake, she thought how special it all was; the sun shining on the water, sending out shards of silver on every ripple; the trees bowed low, dipping their heavy branches into the water, as if quenching their thirst; and overhead all manner of birds sang their late summer song. It was the loveliest July day, and today Cathleen had never been happier.

On reaching the island, Silas brought the boat in close to shore and, climbing out, tethered it securely to a tree. Afterwards, he helped Cathleen out of the boat and together they made their way up the bank to the old summerhouse.

'Remember the hours we spent in here as children?' he asked. 'Father called it my den, but it was more than that. It was *our* place. A special hideaway, where we could sit and dream, and no one could steal you away.'

Cathleen had never forgotten. 'And do *you* remember how we used to take the flag down when we were here, and haul it up when we wanted them to take us back? And how sometimes they'd come and fetch us anyway . . . because we'd been away so long? They were worried we might be in trouble, when all the time we were digging holes or exploring or swimming in the small pool beneath the trees.'

He nodded, his heart full. 'Or just being together . . . talking of how, when we grew up, we'd always be together.'

'I loved you even then,' she whispered.

Taking her in his arms, he held her close. 'You're trembling,' he murmured. But so was he.

She looked up at him then, and whispered softly, '*Now*, Silas . . . love me now.'

Tenderly, he removed her clothes one by one, and laid them in the hot sun to dry. Then he stood a moment, his wondering eyes roving her body, his whole being shocked by her loveliness: the long, damp ringlets of hair clinging to the curve of her waist; the perfectly shaped legs and the dark arc of hair between her small thighs. Her breasts were firm and round, with darker tinted nipples, erect and plump against her milk-white skin.

As she looked up at him with shy eyes, her slim young body still trembling in anticipation, he could hardly breathe. 'You're so beautiful!' Reaching out he took her to him, kissing her hair, her neck and mouth, feeling her against him . . . wanting her so much.

Poised on the brink of womanhood, Cathleen felt herself being gently laid on the ground. She looked up and saw how he loved her, with truth and honesty, and she knew she would be safe with him.

There, beneath the bluest sky, they made love. It was not frenzied, but warm and exciting, and when the actual moment came, it was incredibly tender . . . a wonderful memory she would cherish all her living days.

Half afraid, she clung to him, her arms around his waist as he pushed into her. At first there was pain, but the pain was short-lived, and in its place came something wonderful . . . as though her whole being had been asleep and now it was suddenly awake, vibrant and alive like never before. With her arms flung wide and her body open to him, she gave herself, hesitantly at first, then with a raging passion that swept them both along.

Afterwards, as they lay entwined in each other's arms, their bodies soaked in sweat, he told her he would never love anyone as he loved her. She didn't reply.

Instead she held him to her, and he dared to believe it would be that way for ever.

———❖———

LATER, NAKED AND free, they swam in the cool waters, diving and chasing, so incredibly happy.

When at last they emerged onto the bank, their clothes now dry, he took her in his arms again. 'No regrets?' he asked softly.

Cathleen shook her head. 'Never,' she answered, and he was content.

In the boat on the way back, they talked of their future together. 'Come home with me, Cathleen,' he urged. 'I want Father to know how we feel.'

'No.' The fear of losing Silas was too real. '*You* talk to him first.'

'Don't tell me you're afraid of him?' He might have laughed, but something in her eyes warned him not to.

She considered her answer well. 'I've known him too long to be afraid of him,' she said. Nevertheless, Silas's father was a formidable man. Big in stature, with a permanent scowl, he had often smiled at her, but she had never felt welcome in his presence.

Silas sensed her unease. 'He *does* like you, you know.'

'I wish I could be sure of that, but I'm not. I don't suppose I was too much trouble as your little playmate, but you mustn't expect his blessing when he knows you want me for your wife.'

Silas would have none of it. 'You're wrong, Cathleen. He *must* know my feelings for you.'

'We'll see.' Absentmindedly dipping her hand into the water, she let it trail for a time, watching the cool ripples as they trickled through her fingers. 'I'm not important to him and never will be. I'm the baker's daughter; my grandmammy is just one of his many tenants. We pay rent every week and supply free bread to your mother's kitchen, and for that we get to keep the cottage, an acre of ground, and the bakery in town.'

'That won't make any difference,' he promised. 'Trust me, Cathleen, I know I'm right.' He had been so certain, but suddenly her doubts were beginning to touch him. 'Look, it won't matter what Father says, I'll *still* marry you.'

'I don't want to be the cause of bad feeling between you and your father.' Families were important to Cathleen.

'It won't come to that, you'll see.'

Drawing her hand out of the water, Cathleen wiped it on her skirt. 'I'll tell Father and Grandmammy,' she suggested. 'You speak to *your* father. Then, tomorrow, we'll tell them all together.' Sensing his disappointment, she assured him, 'It's for the best, Silas. This way it will give them all a chance to get used to the idea.'

It only took a moment's consideration before he too was convinced. He laughed. 'You're right, I know, but I want to shout it from the rooftops!' Throwing his arms up in the air he almost capsized the boat. 'LISTEN TO ME EVERYONE! I LOVE CATHLEEN ROE AND SHE LOVES ME!' His voice sailed through the air above her laughter.

Suddenly a flight of geese took off from somewhere near the reeds, startling them both and making Cathleen cry out.

Throwing caution to the winds, he let loose the oars for the second time and came to where she sat, clinging on for dear life. 'Tell me what you were thinking a moment ago,' he said, 'when you were gazing into the water. You seemed . . . sad somehow.'

'Not sad, exactly.'

'What then?'

She shook her head. 'It doesn't matter.'

To her horror he began to rock the boat. 'All right!' she laughed. 'It's just that I can't help worrying about what your father will say; your mother too, though I reckon *she* might be pleased for us.'

'They will *both* be thrilled.' He followed his words with a hug, and a threat to throw her into the water if she didn't stop worrying, then he returned to his rowing. 'We should tell Father now, together,' he insisted. 'That would put an end to your doubts.'

'No, Silas. We've already agreed.'

He shrugged. 'Whatever you say, sweetheart. Besides, it's only a day. What could go wrong in a day?'

Cathleen thought on his words, and her fears were heightened.

Chapter Two

HELEN TURNER WATCHED as the couple came out of the spinney, her spiteful features betraying the jealousy she felt towards Cathleen and her lover. With all her heart she envied their togetherness. But then she remembered her plan, and her features relaxed into a smile.

She followed their progress along the wooded path and saw them pause to kiss. Again jealousy rose in her like a bad taste. Unable to watch any longer, she returned to the house.

Hurrying along the hallway, she heard the low buzz of voices. Good! The men were still talking. Excited, she quickened her footsteps and made her way to the closed door of the library. If her plan was to succeed, she must know exactly what was being said.

Glancing furtively up and down the hallway to see if there was anyone about, the sound of someone coming down the stairs made her press into the shadows, but then the footsteps died away and she was alone. Smiling wickedly, she crouched to the keyhole and listened.

The voices of two men issued from the library, agitated one minute, pleading the next. The row was fierce, then quiet, and sometimes the voices intermingled so she couldn't distinguish their words.

A few minutes later she stood up and turned away from the door, her face wreathed in a smile, her heart pounding with excitement. 'I *knew* there was something going on!' she whispered jubilantly. 'It may be bad news for Silas's father, but for me it couldn't be better.' There was no sympathy in her cold heart, only satisfaction in the knowledge that here was a situation which, if she was very clever, she could turn to her own advantage.

'Somebody is bound to get hurt,' she gloated, 'but it won't be me. I'll make sure of that!'

Taking a moment to observe her surroundings, she let her gaze wander down the hallway, with its beautiful panelled walls and tall, stained-glass windows; then on, to the wide, sweeping stairway and galleried landing above with its magnificent candelabra. From where she stood she couldn't see inside the rooms, but they were etched in her mind and heart. As a child she had been here many times, and knew it all . . . every curve, every picture, every ornament and rug, almost as though they were her own. The dark oak furniture, fashioned with deep carvings and big strong handles a man could get his fist round; paintings and sculptures, and deep chairs with pictures embroidered into the silken fabric. Every piece was a work of art, cherished from generation to generation. There was nothing in this house that surprised her, except the breathtaking beauty of it all.

She loved this place passionately. Her own home, the grandiose Kidalton Manor, seemed cold in comparison. Fenshaw House was full of beautiful objects chosen with love, and Helen's shrivelled heart craved to claim it all as her own.

Her glittering eyes were finally drawn to the front door. Carved from solid oak, with iron fittings and shaped hinges reaching across the wood like two protective arms, it echoed the nature of the house itself. The two stained-glass panels, arched on top and deeply carved with long green stems and cups of red roses, were particularly lovely. Even as she watched, the sun streamed through the glass, bathing the colours in a silhouette of silver light.

She lingered awhile, admiring it all. And the more she admired it, the more determined she became. 'I won't be content until it's mine,' she muttered.

A moment later, as she flung open the door and stepped out onto the porch, the blazing July sunshine made her blink. Shading her eyes with her hand, she peered into the distance, on the look-out for two familiar figures. A moment later she caught sight of them again, hand-in-hand, laughing together. She smiled, a slow, evil smile, satisfied that these were the last precious moments Silas and Cathleen would spend together.

'Enjoying the view, my lovely?'

Startled, Helen swung round. 'Father! I imagined you would be involved in the library for some long time yet.'

He shook his head. 'I've done what I came to

do,' he informed her sombrely. 'It was not something I enjoyed.'

'Can I ask you something, Father?'

'Hmm?' Preoccupied, he looked out across the lawns, his gaze falling on Silas and Cathleen. 'It's time we left, my dear,' he told her heavily. 'We're not welcome here any more.'

'I can understand why,' she revealed. 'I overheard your conversation with Silas's father.'

Surprised, he stared at her. 'You were not meant to. You know how I like to protect you from all that. I want you to be happy, my dear, not burdened down with things that shouldn't concern you.' He lied to her, as always. But then she deserved it.

'Would you do something for me, Father?'

His strong, plain features eased into a smile. 'Name it and it's yours. Ever since your mother chose a new man over the two of us, it's been my vow to give you everything possible.'

'Cathleen's grandfather!' she spat out the words. 'My mother – your wife! – ran off with Tom Butler, *Cathleen Roe's grandfather*. Why are you always afraid to say it?'

Ignoring her, he said, 'What were you about to ask me, my dear?' He thought she could not know the pain her outburst caused him; to find out that your wife preferred an older man to you, and one with little money to his name, was insult enough for any man.

Stepping closer, she gestured to where Silas and Cathleen were kissing. 'I want *him*!'

Shocked, he returned his gaze to her. 'Young Silas? I didn't know you cared for *him*.'

'You always said you would like to see me married with a family.' Cunningly, she played on his dreams. 'Maybe you don't consider Silas Fenshaw to be good enough for me?'

'Are you saying he's asked you to marry him?'

'No, but he will.'

Jack Turner gave a nervous little laugh. 'I imagined he might be in love with Cathleen.'

'Oh, I'm sure he is.'

'Then I don't understand.'

'I don't *care* about Cathleen' – Her name was like a bad taste in Helen's mouth – '*I want him for myself!*'

Beginning to sense her father's reluctance, Helen said piteously, 'Oh, Father, I've been so lonely since Mother left us. I know you've done all you can for me, and I'm grateful, but now I want a husband and children . . . grandchildren for you.' She felt him weakening and prided herself on being an excellent actress. '*Please*, Father. Do this one thing for me. You know Silas is a good man. He'll take care of me, and just think, you will need never worry about me again.'

For what seemed an age, he looked on this daughter of his, and he was ashamed. But he could not blame her, for she was what he had made her. After her mother had gone off with Cathleen's grandfather, he had spoiled and pampered her, all in the name of love, and like some grotesque monster, she had sucked his blood to the last.

'I know how demanding I can be,' she whispered,

'but when I'm married it will all change. You can hand me over to Silas and all your responsibilities will be gone.' Taking hold of his hand, she did not notice it flinch at her touch. Instead, she was arrogant enough to think he might even be sorry to lose her. 'I know you would dearly love to see me settled, Father. But I will never be settled, except with Silas.' Her soft, coaxing voice echoed in his ear, 'You can get him for me, I *know* you can. I heard you and his father just now. I know what he's done, and I know that because of it you can make him see sense.'

Her meaning was clear and, God help him, he hated her for it.

'If you heard what transpired between myself and Edward Fenshaw,' he said sternly, 'you must know he's been punished enough.'

Ignoring his comment, she whined, 'I'll never ask for anything again.'

'You just don't care, do you?' She never ceased to amaze him. 'It doesn't matter to you that I've just left a broken man in there. A man I called a friend as well as a business colleague.'

'For what he did he *deserves* to be broken!' Realising she mustn't show herself to be too spiteful, she softened her tone. 'Doesn't he, Father?'

He resented her spite, but had to agree. 'I suppose so.'

'Well then?'

Reluctantly, he nodded. 'I'll do it. Though it goes against my better instincts.'

'Wonderful!' Unable to conceal her excitement, she

34

kissed him several times. 'I'll be a good wife to him,' she lied. 'You won't regret it.'

Turning away, Jack Turner retraced his steps to the library, his thoughts in turmoil. He had pampered his daughter because he blamed himself for her mother going away. He had not been the best husband in the world, but he had vowed to be the best father. In doing so, he had created this selfish, cold-hearted young woman.

But, like she said, here was his chance to offload his self-made burden onto younger, stronger shoulders; even though Silas had done nothing to deserve such punishment. Hopefully, that fine young man could make of her what he himself could not . . . a decent, caring woman; someone they could both respect.

All the same, as he made for the library it was with a heavy heart. He gave a gentle tap on the door, and when there was no answer, he gingerly pushed it open and peeked in.

Edward Fenshaw was just as he had left him. Seated at his desk, he was leaning forward, head in his hands and a weariness about him that touched the other man's heart. Edward Fenshaw was a man of stature; with his shock of dark hair and strong features, he was fierce and formidable to look on, but soft and compassionate underneath. To anyone who didn't know him, he seemed a force to be reckoned with. Now, though, he was a shattered man.

'Edward?' Entering the room, Jack Turner quietly closed the door behind him.

On hearing the other man's voice, Edward looked

up, his eyes wide with surprise, fear, and a rush of anger that trembled in his voice. 'What do you want?' he asked sharply. 'Come back to twist the knife have you?'

Crossing the room, Jack stood before the desk, studying the other man's face. 'We need to talk.'

Edward Fenshaw gave a scornful laugh. 'Hmh! I should have thought we'd talked enough!' Breathing noisily through his nose, he banged his fist on the table, hissing, 'You're a hard man, Turner! I made *one* mistake . . . *one* lousy mistake in six years, and you can't wait to ruin me!'

Anger met anger. 'It was a mistake that could have ruined us both – you knew that,' Jack Turner shouted. 'Yet you ignored my advice. *I'm* the senior partner, damn it! It was my money that got the business off the ground . . . it was me who took all the risks. And now look!'

'So you *have* come to twist the knife!'

Already embarked on a course of self-pity, Jack Turner ranted, 'The first time I turn my back to travel all over Europe looking for opportunities, giving you proxy to look after our interests . . . I come home to find you've committed us to buying a quarry that was burnt out years ago. Whatever possessed you for God's sake? I warned you it was a bad bet!'

'And I happen to think it's a good buy. There is still a mine of sand waiting to be got out!'

'Even if there is – which there isn't – didn't you realise it would cost a fortune to bring it up?'

'There was a time when it was five hundred acres of

good farming land. Even without the quarry, I thought it had wonderful potential, I told you that.'

'And I told *you* it was too high a price to pay. For Christ's sake, Edward, I thought you'd got more business sense than that. And now you've sacrificed a valuable chunk of our capital, leaving us with even less bargaining power for acquiring other assets. Buy cheap and turn over quick at a respectable profit, that's always been my policy. You knew that, and still you went against me!'

'We've been through all this, Jack. If you mean to keep going over it, well, there's the door. You know your way out.'

'I just want you to know what kind of a damned fool you've been! You went against me, Edward, I never thought you'd do a thing like that. What's more, you've lowered our standing in the eyes of business colleagues . . .' Shaking his head, he dropped his gaze to the floor. 'Christ, we must be a laughing stock! And all for what, eh? Five hundred bloody acres of barren land that's neither use nor ornament.'

Humiliated, Edward leaned back in his chair, a defeated man. 'All right, Jack, that's enough. You've made it clear where I stand. The partnership is dissolved and I'm into you for a whole lot of money. God knows how I'll raise it, but I will, if it's the last thing I do. I'll sell everything I own and start again. I can do that, I'm not afraid of hard work.'

'Are you afraid of solicitors?'

'Go home, Jack. Send your solicitor's papers and I'll sign them. I'll admit to what I did and take my punishment. And now, if you've finished, I'd like you to go.'

Expecting the other man to leave, he drew a sheaf of papers from a drawer and pretended to work. But he had no work, not any more. Pride was all he had left.

'Listen to me, Edward.' Jack's voice came softly to him. 'There is another way out . . . if you have the heart for it.'

Intrigued, Edward asked warily, 'What game are you playing now?'

'No game, Edward.'

Unsure, Fenshaw looked into the other man's eyes and, for a fleeting moment, he saw there a desperation that shook him. 'Go on. I'm listening.'

Seating himself in the round leather chair, Jack took a long, deep breath. Summoning his courage, he said softly, 'It's to do with Silas.'

At once, Edward rounded on him. 'My son had no hand in what I did! I'll not have you bringing him into this, and I'll thank you not to let him know the trouble I've brought on this family.'

'Woa!' Putting up his hand to stop the other man, Jack told him, 'Take it easy! Look, I'm aware he has no idea what's been going on, and he'll not learn it from me, I promise you that, Edward. I owe you that much at least for what we've built together over the years, and for the friendship we've known.' He paused, his gaze resting on the other man's face. 'I'm sorry it had to end this way.'

Edward nodded. 'I'm sorry too,' he said in a choked voice. 'We had a good business and I've been a bloody fool; I've put you back years and cost you a small fortune by not thinking it through. I don't blame you for wanting out. I'd probably do the same myself if it was the other way round.' He had wondered about that. 'But, like I said, you'll get your money back, every penny of it . . . if I have to sell this house and everything in it.'

'That may not be necessary.'

'What are you getting at?'

'I have a proposition to make. If you go along with it, I'll wipe out the debt, and you can keep the five hundred acres; it's of no use to me. But the partnership is at an end, Edward. You understand I could never entirely trust you again?'

Edward quietly regarded his old friend. There was something not quite right about the generous offer he'd outlined. Yet, in spite of his wary instincts, his curiosity got the better of him. 'This proposition . . .' Leaning forward, he lowered his voice, 'You said it had to do with Silas?'

'You won't like it.'

'I already don't like it!' Glaring at the other man, he warned, 'Be careful, Jack. I've made one mistake; it will be a long time before I make another.'

For a minute, Jack wondered if he would do best to leave the matter there. But the thought of Helen outside, waiting for an answer, spurred him on. 'All right, Edward. Here's the deal . . .'

As he laid out his plan, Jack Turner saw the stricken look on the other man's face and he felt ashamed. Helen had made many demands on him over the years, and he knew she was hard-hearted, but this time she had excelled herself.

Relieved that it was out in the open, Jack concluded, 'So there it is, Edward, and I hope you have the good sense to consider it. As you know, my daughter has been fond of Silas since they were infants. Now it seems she wants him for a husband, and I must say I myself would be delighted!' Seeming proud and assured, he gave a wide smile. 'So, if you agree for them to wed, then the whole matter of this debt is wiped out, and no one is any the wiser.'

As his voice died away, the silence was impenetrable, until, in a shockingly quiet voice that shook with rage, Edward Fenshaw told him, '*Get out!*'

'*Think* about it, Edward,' Turner said hastily. 'It's a way to solve all your problems. I'll even be prepared to set Silas up with his own business, I can't be fairer than that. It's a damned generous offer and you know it. Nobody's the loser, not even Silas. My Helen will be a good wife to him. She'll make him happy, you see if she doesn't.'

'I told you to get out!' Grey-faced, Edward stood up, hands spread before him on the desk, his eyes boring into the other man's face.

'OK, Edward, I'll go!' Pushing back his chair, Jack stood up to face him. 'Don't be hasty, though,' he urged softly. 'The way things are, you just *might* have to sell this house and everything in it. Good God, man! It's been in your wife's family for generations! How could you ever bring yourself to part with it?'

Without meaning to, he hit on something that

had been playing havoc with Edward Fenshaw's mind. 'There's not just yourself to think of, is there?' he pointed out. 'What about Lucy? A good woman if ever there was one. I don't suppose she even knows about this whole business? How do you think she'd feel if she were made to leave this house? We all know she's not a well woman, Edward. This house . . . you and Silas . . . it's all she clings to now.'

With a speed that took the other man by surprise, Edward reached out and, grabbing him by the lapels, drew him forward. 'Leave my wife out of this, you bastard, or I swear to God I'll swing for you!'

For a long, painful moment the two men hated each other as they had never done before; theirs had been a strong friendship and never again would it be put to a test such as this. 'Get out! Go on! GET OUT!' Clenching his teeth, Edward threw him aside.

Straightening his jacket, Jack walked casually to the door, but not without a parting suggestion. 'You really should think about it, Edward,' he urged. 'It's the best deal you're ever likely to get.' With that he departed the room, leaving the door wide open behind him.

Edward sat by his desk in the quiet room. The minutes ticked away, and still he made no move. In all his life he had never felt lonely, always busy, always looking for the next mountain to climb, too preoccupied to feel isolated. But now, in the wake of Turner's remarks about his beloved Lucy, he felt as though he was the loneliest man in the world. Softly, he went across the room and closed the door.

Standing there, with his back pressed to the wood, he contemplated the chaos surrounding him; he was so proud of his son, Silas, and when he thought of that wonderful woman upstairs in her sickbed, his heart melted. But what could he do? The sheer hopelessness of it came home to him all at once.

His haunted gaze went to the desk, his mind leaping ahead, desperately searching for a way out. Moving across the room, he opened the desk drawer and, taking the small pistol from the secret recess, positioned himself in the chair and pointed the muzzle to his temple. With one finger bent on the trigger, he closed his eyes and started to pray.

Again the image of his wife came into his mind. Coward though he was, he could not leave her and Silas to face the consequences of his actions.

Slowly, he lowered the gun; he replaced it in the recess and softly closed the drawer. Then he covered his face in his hands and sobbed like a child.

When he was again composed, he stood up, tidied his clothes, secured his tie, and left the room with his head held high. He wasn't done yet, not by a long chalk! All the same, he had choices to make and none of them were pleasant. But for now, he must not think about it. As always when life seemed too much to bear, he needed to be with Lucy. He needed to see her face and hold her hand, and delude himself into believing that everything would be all right.

Coming into the hallway he went on up the stairs, his heart and feet taking him to her, his darling wife of thirty-four years; his best friend. Whenever he felt low he would go to her and she would listen, and afterwards he would feel content.

Today, though, it was different. He must tell her nothing of all that had happened. So, with an innocent smile and a mountain of love in his heart, he quickened his steps. To be with her and talk of other things; just to know she was there, was contentment enough.

Lucy was in her wheelchair, seated at the long casement window. Engrossed in watching the outside world she didn't hear her husband come in, so he took the opportunity to observe her for a time.

He thought her very beautiful; he always had. Small and delicate she was, like a precious china doll. With her long dark hair and soft brown eyes she had stolen his heart, and he in turn had captured hers, and never in all the years they'd been wed had he ever regretted it.

As he closed the door, he called her name, and when she turned to smile at him it was as though the whole room had taken on a special glow. 'Oh, Edward! I've been watching Silas and young Cathleen ...' Her brown eyes danced and twinkled, 'I think they might be in love.'

In the light of what had just been said downstairs, her words struck him deep. 'No.' He came to her, his eyes going to the window and the couple outside. 'You're just an old romantic, that's what you are.'

'I've seen it coming for some time,' Lucy insisted. 'They're not children any more, Edward. The way they are when they're together, well, I mean, it's not the same any more. They look at each other . . . oh, with such *feeling*. It isn't just friendship, it's *love*, Edward. Our boy and that lovely girl have fallen in love, I just know it.' Taking hold of his hand, she looked up, her eyes moist with tears. 'I've seen the way it is with them, and I've hoped . . . oh, Edward, if it were true, nobody would be happier than me.'

Deeply troubled he remained silent, careful not to betray his thoughts. Lucy had said that no one would be more delighted to see Silas and Cathleen in love. But she was wrong, for lately, he had come to value Cathleen. Now, he too would welcome the girl with open arms. Yet because of what had transpired between himself and Turner, and for the sake of Lucy . . . he might have to sacrifice both Cathleen and his son.

———◆———

JACK TURNER LOOKED at his daughter anew, at the pale, cunning eyes and tight-lipped mouth, and wondered how he could ever have thought her pretty.

'Did you hear me, Father?' Her whining voice invaded his thoughts. 'I said we should start making plans for the wedding.'

'Yes, Helen, I heard you.'

'Hmh! You seemed miles away,' she remarked curiously. 'What were you thinking about?'

He shrugged. 'Nothing important.' But what he was really thinking was how he pitied Silas, and how he would never want his own daughter for an enemy. Because, God help him, in his heart he believed she was wicked through and through.

Yet even now he was too much of a coward to deny her what she wanted. 'Make your plans,' he told her wearily. 'You said Edward Fenshaw had a choice, but you were wrong, my dear. I have put him in a situation where he has no choice whatsoever.' And may God forgive me for it, he thought sadly.

———⟫•◦•⟪———

BACK AT THE house, Edward promised Lucy he would take her into the garden. 'I'll get Maggie to wrap you up warm, and bring the wheelchair behind us.'

'Thank you, dear.' Reaching up, she kissed him lightly on the mouth. 'It's such a beautiful day, it's a shame to be cooped up here.'

With the touch of her lips on his, and his arm draped around her, he felt like a young man again. 'You're so pretty,' he murmured. 'You never change.'

She laughed at that. '"Pretty", is it?' She shook her head. 'I'm riddled with arthritis and my heart is giving out,' her eyes sparkled with mirth, 'but if my husband thinks me pretty, that's fine by me.'

'And are you sure you're well enough to be outside?'

'Stop worrying!' At that moment a movement outside caught her eye. 'Oh, look, Edward!' Excited, she pointed through the window. 'Cathleen's gone and Silas is on his way. Tell Maggie to hurry. I do so want to sit with our son in the garden.' Giving a cheeky wink she wondered aloud, 'He might even confide in me about him and Cathleen. Oh, Edward, wouldn't it be wonderful if they were already planning a future together? She's such a sweet, lovely creature – intelligent too. And so devoted to our son.'

Desperate to dissuade her, he said firmly, 'Don't get your hopes up, Lucy. It will only lead to disappointment.'

'You don't know that.' She gave him a sideways glance. 'Or is there something you're not telling me?'

'No.' God, he hated lying to her! 'I don't know how they feel towards each other, any more than you do. All I'm saying is, it doesn't do to surmise.'

'Away with you!' she chuckled. 'It's plain to see how they feel. Trust me, Edward. Those two young people are in love, and I've a feeling Silas is on his way to tell us so this very minute.'

Edward knew he must act fast. With a disarming smile, he said, 'I'd best go and get Maggie,' and before she could question him further, he was out of the room and going down the stairs two at a time.

He found Maggie in the parlour, preparing the table for the evening meal. 'Mrs Fenshaw wants to sit out in the garden for a time,' he informed her. 'I'll be up shortly to help her downstairs, and I shall expect you to follow with the wheelchair as usual.'

'Yes, sir.'

'Make sure she's well wrapped up. The sun is already dipping in the sky.'

46

Small and wick, the little woman gave a nervous curtsey. 'Very well, sir. At once, sir.' When he politely stepped aside, she scurried away as if the devil himself was after her; she knew he was not an unkind master, but it was still a frightening sight when his mighty frame filled the doorway and blocked her exit.

With Maggie on her way upstairs, Edward went straight to the front verandah, where he stood, legs astride, watching his son walk across the lawn and up the steps. 'Father!' Silas was breathless and excited. 'I need to talk with you and Mother,' he said, 'I have something to tell you.'

'Is it to do with Cathleen Roe?'

'Yes, sir, it is.'

Edward stood quite still, and in that odd yet familiar mannerism he had whenever he felt uncertain, he stretched out his neck and blinked his eyes to the heavens. 'I see.' He looked at the joy in his son's dark eyes and was mortified. 'Whatever it is you have to tell us, I must ask that you keep it to yourself for a little longer.'

Silas was puzzled. 'Can I ask why?'

'Because there are certain things you and I need to discuss before you talk with your mother . . . important things that may well have a bearing on what you have to tell us.'

'I'm not sure I know what you mean, Father.'

'Look, son.' Saddened, Edward knew there were serious decisions to be made, and right now he couldn't even think straight. 'Don't concern yourself about it for now,' he groaned. 'Let your mother enjoy her time in the sunshine. After dinner, you and I will withdraw to the library where we can talk.' Already he was dreading the prospect.

'All right, Father, if that's what you want.' For some inexplicable reason he had a bad feeling about what was to come.

'It is.'

There was no more time for questions, because Maggie was on her way downstairs with the wheelchair, bumping and clanging at a frightful rate. 'One of these days you'll end up in a heap at the bottom of the stairs,' Edward called up to her, 'you and that wheelchair both!'

'Yes, sir,' she grunted, red in the face and out of breath, and before either man could rush to help, she missed her footing and rolled all the way to the bottom, skirt flying and bloomers showing, the wheelchair bouncing after her. Landing safely, she sat bolt upright, hair tousled and a sheepish grin on her face.

'Ooh, thank you, Mr Silas, sir,' she gasped, when Silas hurried to her side. 'I don't know what came over me.' But she did! It was the sight of Edward Fenshaw looking through those bushy eyebrows at her, and the sound of his deep, booming voice.

Taking charge of the wheelchair once more, she limped to the back door and waited. As soon as the men had turned their backs she rubbed her sore buttocks and straightened her skirt then laughed at herself. 'Ooh, Maggie Martin!' she giggled. 'What must you have looked like, upending yerself like that, and in front o' *them* an' all!'

A few minutes later, after a slow and painful journey down the stairs and along the corridor to the back door, Lucy was made comfortable in her wheelchair. 'Why you insist on walking all the way to the door when Maggie could have the chair at the foot of the stairs is a mystery to me,' Edward nagged.

'I've told you before,' she gently chided, 'I need to force myself just that little bit further if I'm to keep my legs going.'

And, much as he worried about this darling woman, Edward knew there was no arguing with her. Sending Maggie off to the kitchen for a tray of cold drinks, he pushed Lucy down to the paved area in the rose garden. 'Oh, I do so love it here,' she told him happily.

'Oh, I'm sure there are other places just as lovely.' Fussing and fretting over her every move, he thought he could plant an idea in her mind. If only she didn't love this place so much. But then so did he. There was nowhere in the world he would rather be. But if circumstances demanded that he should tear himself away, then so be it; it was a fitting punishment for his foolishness. But not Lucy. She had done no wrong, and should not be punished. As Jack Turner so rightly pointed out, it would likely be the death of her.

Then there was Silas. Young and strong, he could no doubt make a life for himself, even with that awful Turner girl. But then, why should *he* pay the price for his father's mistake?

Edward's mind and heart were in turmoil. Which way should he turn? What other choice did he have?

Suddenly Lucy's voice was gentling into his mind. 'This is a lovely time of year, don't you think, Edward?'

Coming to sit beside her, he nodded, his troubled gaze roving the gardens; with their winding pathways, blossoming shrubberies and rose-covered arches, it was like a little piece of paradise.

'But then, it doesn't really matter what time of year it is,' she murmured. 'In summer, with everything in full bloom, the smells and sights are wonderful! In autumn the colours change to russets and golds, and the leaves begin to fall.' As she spoke, she clasped her hands together. 'I love the winter best,' she confided, 'when the snow hangs heavy on the branches and the creatures come to the kitchen door looking for scraps. Then March is here again and everything comes alive. Oh, Edward!'

Taking him by surprise, she grabbed his hand into hers and, looking up with shining eyes, told him softly, 'You've no idea the joy it gives me.'

Gulping hard, he tested her out in a cunning way. 'Well, now,' he replied light-heartedly, 'and here was I thinking you might like to move to a pretty cottage on the coast somewhere.'

Lucy shook her head, a slow, easy smile on her pretty face. 'Thank you, my darling, but no. I was born in this house and, God willing, I shall die here.'

At that moment, Silas arrived with a tray containing three glasses of cold sarsaparilla. 'I thought I'd save Maggie a trip,' he chuckled. 'After the escapade with the wheelchair, I thought she might be safer in the kitchen.'

Lucy laughed, 'Poor soul. In future, we must call Joseph from the stables, and get *him* to bring the wheel-chair down.'

While they sat together, listening to Lucy and enjoying her delightful company, Silas sensed his father looking at him. When he turned, unsettled, it was to look straight into Edward's troubled eyes. The two men held each other's gaze for a disquieting moment, before Lucy startled them both, crying out that the cat was about to snatch a young bird. 'Quick, Silas! Stop it!'

Chasing the culprit through the shrubbery he saved the bird and made his way back, at the same time taking the opportunity to study his father discreetly. There was no doubt that Edward Fenshaw looked more worried than Silas had ever seen him, but he appeared to have kept it from Lucy, who chatted and laughed and never once noticed that her husband wasn't even listening.

'There's something wrong, I *know* it!' Silas said to himself. 'But what could be so bad that he can't tell me in front of Mother?'

He recalled the distraught look in his father's eyes just now, and his earlier words, when Silas rushed home with his news. 'Is it to do with Cathleen Roe?' Then the sombre warning: 'There are things we need to discuss . . . before you talk with your mother.' Hidden by the trees, Silas paused at the edge of the lawn. In his mind, Cathleen's voice softly echoed '. . . the baker's daughter as a playmate is one thing . . . but don't expect his blessing when he knows you want me for your wife . . .'

Anxious to discover the reason for his father's behaviour, Silas was impatient for evening to come. But for now he must play a waiting game. With that in mind, he made his way back.

As they saw him approach, he raised a smile, but his heart was heavy, his mind filled with all manner of suspicions.

The smile was deceiving. It was for the benefit of his mother, who was ill. And because he believed that, like himself, she had no inkling of what was going on.

———◆———

CATHLEEN, MEANWHILE, WAS running barefoot across the hills, the wind in her hair and a song in her heart. Still tingling from her time with Silas, she was impatient to get to the cottage and tell her father and grandma the wonderful news.

Jessie saw her coming. 'Jesus, Mary and Joseph! Will yer look at the girl run!' Coming to the front door, she started yelling, 'Whatever's come over yer? And where the divil are yer boots?'

Laughing, Cathleen fell into her arms. 'I've got them here!' Producing the boots from behind her back where she'd been swinging them by the laces, Cathleen took hold of the old woman. 'Wait till I tell you,' she cried, 'you won't believe it!'

Jessie looked at Cathleen's shining blue eyes and the joy that lit her face like a beacon, and her heart sank. 'You'd best come inside,' she said, turning away. Curious, but unconcerned, Cathleen followed her.

Once inside, Jessie told Cathleen, 'Sit yerself down in the armchair while I make us a drink.'

But Cathleen was much too excited to sit down. 'Let me tell you my news first, then *I'll* make the tea.'

Fearing the news Cathleen had brought, Jessie rounded on her. 'For heaven's sake, child! Will yer do as yer asked?'

Taken aback by Jessie's stern words, Cathleen duly retreated to the parlour, where she sat in the big armchair and waited. What on earth was wrong? It wasn't like her grandmother to greet her in such a way.

A moment later, Jessie returned from the scullery. 'Now then,' she said, her mood having mellowed, 'drink it slowly . . . in sips, not gulps.' Placing a glass of clear liquid into Cathleen's hand, she sat down on the couch beside her, happily partaking of her own, much larger drink. 'Aah!' Smacking her lips, she told Cathleen, 'Go on then! You're turned eighteen so it's all right.' Cheered by the warming liquid, she chuckled, 'I'll not tell yer daddy if you don't!'

Taking the smallest of sips, Cathleen had a coughing fit. 'Ugh! What is it?'

'Mother's ruin!'

Cathleen giggled. 'It's *gin!*'

'Aye, just a wee drop, that's all, with a squirt o' gooseberry wine . . . to give it a little kick, if yer know what I mean.' Winking a cheeky hazel eye, she was as merry as Cathleen had ever seen her.

Cathleen took another sip, then another. 'Mmm, it's nice.' When she started giggling, Jessie snatched it away. 'That's enough! Yer not used to it,' and she promptly emptied the glass down her throat, before doing the same with what was left of her own. 'It warms the cockles o' yer heart, so it does!'

Cathleen was curious. 'Why are you in a bad mood?'

'What!' Jessie took a minute to study the lovely young face. 'Who is it says I'm in a bad mood?'

'You nearly bit my head off when I came in.'

'Ah, well now.' Placing the two glasses in the hearth, Jessie sat back in the chair and, looking Cathleen in the eye, she said quietly, 'That's because I know what you've come to tell us.'

'You *can't* know.' Sometimes Cathleen found it hard to fathom her, but, deep down, she suspected her grandmother's worries only echoed her own.

'Silas Fenshaw's asked yer to be his wife, am I right?'

Blushing at Jessie's directness, Cathleen explained, 'He's coming to see Father this evening, but I wanted to tell both of you first.' She wasn't surprised that her grandmother had guessed. She had an uncanny knack of knowing what was going through Cathleen's mind.

Jessie shook her head. 'I'm sorry child, but to my mind it's bound to cause all manner o' heartache.' The anger had gone now, and in its place was a kind of sadness.

Her heart sinking at the look in Jessie's eyes, Cathleen protested, 'I love him, Grandma.'

'Ah, sure don't I know that, child? Amn't I saying it to your father already?'

Kissing Jessie soundly on her weathered old face, Cathleen knelt on the rug beside her. 'Were you and Father talking about us?'

'Aye, we were.'

Embarrassed, Cathleen told her, 'I didn't think you knew about me and Silas . . . how we felt about each other.'

'Sure there's not much I don't know, child; not about you anyways.' Reaching into her skirt pocket, Jessie took out a small silver box. Opening it with great care, she gently shook it until the brown powder inside was nicely loosened, then, pinching a measure between finger and thumb, she drove it up her nose, first the left nostril then the right, until her eyes watered.

Impatient, Cathleen urged, 'How did you know?'

'I've seen it coming, child.' Blinking her old eyes, she sniffled hard and coughed even harder. 'That's some strong stuff, is that.' Plucking a crumpled hankie from her sleeve, she blew her nose so hard that her face turned a ripe shade of red. 'I told yer father: "Them two young 'uns are beyond friendship. If yer ask me, they're in love." That's what I told him.'

'What did he say?'

'Aw, sure he's a *man* isn't he? The poor divil couldn't even see what was afore his eyes.' Tutting loudly, she shook her head, 'I had to spell it out for him, so I did.' The old woman looked down on the girl, and her heart was sore. 'He thinks the same as me, lass . . . you and Silas Fenshaw . . . well, it's a bad thing.'

'You're wrong!' Cathleen was hurt and horrified. And she had thought it would be Silas's family who might come between them.

'Aw, now, don't you be angry with me.' Stroking Cathleen's long wild hair, Jessie lowered her voice to a murmur. 'Nobody's saying he's not a fine young man, because he is, and if things were different, I'm sure we'd all be dancing round the table right now at your news.'

Seeing the look of despair in Cathleen's blue eyes, the old woman was reluctant to go on, but there were things that needed to be said – for Cathleen's sake more than anything. 'I'll speak me mind and the divil with it,' she declared, wagging a chiding finger. 'You and Silas Fenshaw have grown up together; you've been the best of friends to each other and got on uncommonly well . . . considering. But now, with all this talk of getting wed and being part of the Fenshaw family, it's gone too far. You're not from the same side o' the tracks, my girl. It's just not right, and I think, deep down inside, you know it as well.'

She caught her breath, realising that every word was like a knife through Cathleen's young heart. 'Aw, sure you love each other, I *know* that. And I know how love can be an almighty powerful thing to deny, but deny it yer must, or as God's my judge there'll be heartache waiting round every corner.'

In spite of everything – even her own fearful instincts – Cathleen refused to believe it. Like her grandmother, she was not blind to the problems; hadn't she already told Silas the very same things this kind old woman was telling her now? But Silas had convinced her it could work, and she had to trust him.

'Well, child?'

Taking a moment to consider, Cathleen answered with quiet conviction. 'I know you mean well. And I know it won't be easy for us . . . not at first. But we love each other enough to make it work, and that's all that matters to us.'

'So, yer mean to wed him, whatever anyone says . . . including me and your father?'

There followed the slightest pause, but in the end, there was really only one answer Cathleen could give. 'I'm sorry, Grandma.' Tears of regret shone in her eyes, but her heart was defiant, 'I want to share my life with him.' She couldn't even *imagine* life if Silas wasn't around.

'I see.' With her mouth drawn tight, Jessie gave a slow, thoughtful nod. 'And what if yer father forbids it?'

Anxious now, Cathleen swallowed hard. 'I pray he won't.' Because if he did, she would have to defy him, and that would be the worst thing of all.

'Then there's nothing more to be said.'

'Please . . . will *you* talk to Father? Make him see how much I want to be with Silas.'

With an affirmative nod, Jessie gave a long, steadying sigh, 'I only hope the two of youse know what yer doing,' she murmured. 'I'd hate to see your heart broken, so I would.' Reaching out with both arms she drew Cathleen close, and for a time they stayed like that, each knowing the other would always be there in times of need.

After a while, Jessie held Cathleen away from herself. 'And what does Edward Fenshaw have to say about all this? Or doesn't he know yet?'

'Silas is telling him now.'

'Is that so?' Jessie suspected Edward Fenshaw would not welcome such an alliance, any more than she herself had. 'The young man is coming round later to speak with yer father, is that what yer said?'

Her excitement tempered by nerves, Cathleen nodded. 'I told him what time Father would be home. Afterwards, if everything is all right, I'm to go back with him to meet Mr Fenshaw.'

Jessie glanced at her eager face. 'We'll just have to hope everything goes to plan, eh?'

Though secretly, Jessie couldn't help but wonder what Cathleen's father would say when Silas Fenshaw showed up on his doorstep . . .

Chapter Three

Dinner had gone well, with both men entertaining the lady of the house, and the lady of the house enjoying herself more than she had done for a long time. 'It was a wonderful meal,' she told them, laying down her napkin, 'and even better company.' Stifling a yawn with the back of her hand, she apologised, 'But I am feeling very tired, so if it's all right with you two, I'll go upstairs now.'

Concerned that she seemed so pale and worn, Silas was on his feet at once and hurrying to her side. 'I'll take you up,' he said tenderly. Next to Cathleen, his mother was the light of his life.

'You go on up, my dear,' Edward told her. 'Oh, and I must say that blue shawl becomes you. It brings out the colour of your eyes.' He was an expert at complimenting her and, laughing like a young thing, she would lap it up like a cat at the milk. He kissed her goodnight and promised to be up later.

With Maggie following on with the wheelchair, Silas

helped his mother up the stairs and into her room. 'I'll sit by the window for a time,' she told him, 'I do like to watch the birds at their evening antics.' The garden was so lovely, it was a haven for wildlife.

'I'll come and say goodnight later.' With a kiss and this promise, he made his way across the room, only to find Maggie still struggling to get the wheelchair through the door. 'Here, let me help.' Taking it from her, he eased it into the room.

Maggie giggled. 'I can't never get the 'ang o' that contraption!' she moaned, and before he could answer, she was off down the landing and skipping down the stairs, and all the time Silas was fearful she might trip up and do herself a mischief.

Lucy laughed. 'She's worth every penny we pay her . . . for entertainment value if nothing else.'

'She's harmless enough,' he agreed, 'and this house wouldn't be the same without her.' Maggie had been with them a long time now; she was part of the family.

He would have gone then, but his mother called him back. Patting the seat next to her, she invited him to, 'Come and sit with me for a while, son.'

Doing as she bid, he glanced nervously at the door.

Lucy saw the gesture and was convinced there was something wrong. 'Are you in your father's bad books?'

'Not as far as I know.' And that was the truth of it. 'Why do you ask?'

'Oh, I don't know.' She had tried all evening to put her finger on it, but couldn't. All the same, she had the distinct feeling that there was something going on, and she was not a part of it. 'It's just that I sensed an atmosphere over dinner. You and your father hardly spoke to each other.' Giving him a sideways look, she asked pointedly, 'Have you seen Cathleen today?'

Silas's eyes lit up. 'Yes. We rowed over to the island . . . it never changes does it? So beautiful.' Making love with Cathleen had been beautiful too, he thought, the most beautiful experience of his entire life.

'How old is she now, son?'

'Eighteen.'

'Not a child any more then.'

He smiled, 'No, Mother. She's a lovely young woman, with a heart of gold and a smile to match your own.'

Lucy was startled to see how his eyes shone and his voice softened when he spoke of Cathleen. Carefully probing, she suggested, 'I expect some young man will come calling and she'll be off and married before we know it.'

He didn't answer, because to do so would have betrayed everything. And he mustn't do that, not until he and his father had spoken.

Taking her hand he held it in his. 'She's a lot like you, Mother. She laughs at the silliest things, and . . .' he smiled self-consciously, 'I'd better go. Father wants me to join him in the library.'

Lucy had seen the way his smile faded when she mentioned that Cathleen would soon have other young men calling. 'Silas?' Her voice was gentle and loving.

'Yes, Mother?' He had been miles away, first with Cathleen, then with his father, wondering what Edward wanted of him, and how he would react to the idea of having Cathleen as a daughter-in-law.

'You can always talk to me if you have a problem. You do know that, don't you, son?'

'Yes, Mother, I know that.'

'You'd best go to your father. You know how he hates to be kept waiting.' She raised her face for a kiss. 'Oh, and send Maggie to me, would you?' How she hated not being able to do things for herself.

Before leaving, Silas told her, 'I'll be going out soon, but I'll see you before you go to bed.'

'And I'll look forward to hearing what you and your father had to talk about.'

At the foot of the stairs, Silas was met by Maggie. 'The master sent me, sir. He says you're to go straight to the library.'

'Thank you, Maggie. And Mother would like you to go to her.'

'Right away, sir.'

He watched the maid make her way upstairs, then, without further ado, he hurried across the hallway and on towards the library. A quick tap on the door and a curt 'Come in!', and he was standing before his father who, slumped at his desk and looking haggard, seemed suddenly to have aged ten years.

'What is it, Father?' Startled, Silas wondered how such a transformation could have come about. 'You seem troubled.'

Straightening his shoulders, Edward looked his son in the eye. 'I *am* troubled,' he answered softly, his glance shifting to the door, as though he feared someone might be listening. 'I'm ashamed to have a son of mine know what a failure his father is.'

Silas could hardly believe his ears. '*Failure?*' He shook his head at the idea. 'You're no failure, sir,' he said sternly. 'You're a successful businessman . . . controlling land and property in all directions. Why, there's not a man in the whole of Lancashire who doesn't know you by name and reputation!'

It was a long, awkward moment before Edward spoke again, and when he did it was to say in a small voice, 'Sit down, son.'

Scraping out a chair, Silas seated himself opposite his father, his instincts beginning to warn him that there was more to be reckoned with here than just Cathleen and himself.

Easing his great frame out of his own chair, Edward walked back and forth, back and forth, until Silas thought he would go mad. Just as he was about to say something, his father confided, 'Jack Turner was here today.' He gulped a noisy intake of air before going on, 'He's cancelled our partnership.'

Unbelievable! 'Why would he do that?' Silas's father and Jack Turner had been partners a long time, and had made a lot of money into the bargain.

Now his father stood before him grey-faced, his eyes bloodshot and weary. There was desperation in his voice. 'Listen to me now, son,' he urged, 'and please . . . don't say a word until I've finished.'

Quickly, before he lost his courage, Edward launched

into a shamefaced account of what he had done, and how Jack Turner had acted within his contractual rights. 'Any other man might have sought to send me to prison. But we have been friends for a long time, and I suppose he thought he owed me that much at least.'

Silas was shocked at the revelation that his father had bought land that was not resaleable. What's more, he had bought it without Jack Turner sanctioning the deal. 'How will he recover such a vast sum of money?' he asked.

'From me.' He lowered his gaze. 'It's within his power to pauper me.'

'My God!' Leaping to his feet, Silas began to understand the implications of his father's irresponsible enterprise. Forgetting his place, he dared to ask, 'You have land and property – more than enough, surely?'

'No.' He had no choice but to confide in his son. 'I have debts.'

'So what will you do?' There was nothing else for it, 'I have money put aside from Grandfather's trust. I'll sign it over to you. It's not enough, but it will go some way to helping. Surely Jack Turner will be patient.'

'He's offered me a deal.'

Silas breathed a sigh of relief. 'What kind of a deal?'

Momentarily closing his eyes, Edward wished he was any place but here.

Silas saw the anguish on his father's face, and had to know. 'This deal, Father . . . what *exactly* does Jack Turner want?'

Edward hardly dared look at his son. 'He wants you.'

Wondering if he'd heard right, Silas leaned over the desk. '*Me?*' He gave a nervous half smile. 'What does he want with me?'

Still unable to look his son in the face, Edward took to pacing the floor again. 'The little cash I have is nowhere near enough to pay off the debt, so I'm left with three choices. Firstly, I can sell this house bag and baggage. Paintings, furniture – everything your mother loves.'

Taking a moment to pause, he put up his hand when he saw how Silas was about to protest. 'NO! Let me finish.'

Watching his father's every move, Silas waited.

Quickly composing himself, Edward continued, 'Secondly, I can "accidentally" fall under a train or step in front of a horse and carriage, then at least your mother will collect the insurance.' He wiped the sweat from his brow with the palm of his hand. Addressing Silas again, he looked directly at him, saying pointedly, 'Then there's the *third* choice. By which means we can clear the entire debt and your mother will be none the wiser . . .'

'And what is this third choice, Father?' Silas knew it involved him, though he could not see how.

'He wants you to marry his daughter.'

At first Silas stared at him, then laughed out loud, but seeing that his father was deadly serious, he shook his head in disbelief. 'Has he gone mad?'

'Somehow, Helen must have overheard our conversation. All her life she's only had to want something and Jack has given it to her; now it seems she wants you.' Now that it was out in the open, it was like a weight from his shoulders. 'If you agree, then the debt is honoured, though the partnership is ended.'

Realising the seriousness of what he was being asked to do, Silas walked to the window, where he looked out across the lawns and towards the lake, then beyond to the island, where he and Cathleen had consummated their love. In his mind's eye he could see her now, running across the grass, her skirt lifted to her knees and her laughter wonderful to hear. The smallest, saddest smile crept over his features. He was only ever truly happy when he was with her.

'I can't agree to it, Father,' he said. 'There has to be another way.'

'You already know the other ways.' Edward knew what was going through his son's mind, and his heart went out to him. 'I'm sorry, son, but I had to put it to you.'

Silas had an idea. 'I'll go and see Turner. Surely to God he must realise the enormity of what he's asking.'

'Don't you think I've already tried reasoning with him? He won't budge. That daughter of his has him where she wants him.'

'Then I'll talk to *her*!'

'Hmh! The arrangement was her idea. She's not likely to change her feelings.'

'It's worth a try.' And from that he would not be dissuaded. 'I'll go now, before the idea that she can buy me settles too deep in her warped mind.'

Edward took a step towards him. 'Earlier today, when you came home, you said you wanted to talk.'

He could only guess that it was about Cathleen. He too had seen the friendship turn to love, and now he dearly wished he had put a stop to it some long time ago.

Momentarily tempted to tell his father about his and Cathleen's wish to spend their lives together, Silas opened his mouth to speak. Then, realising it would only make matters worse, he decided against it. 'I do have something to tell you, Father,' he admitted, 'but it can wait until later. There are things that must be attended to first.' Like unravelling this unholy mess, he thought bitterly. Or his life wouldn't be worth living.

'I'll tackle Turner first,' he decided, 'and if I can't get any sense out of him, I'll speak to Helen directly. It shouldn't take long to make her see that what she wants is out of the question.'

'I hope you're right, but that still leaves me with a huge debt and no funds to clear it.' Edward was aware of how selfish he sounded, but during the past few hours he had come to hope that Silas might accept the idea of marrying outside of love, if it was to save the family name and their home.

Silas chose to ignore the remark. 'I'd best be going,' he said quietly.

First, however, he had to let Cathleen know. With that in mind, he ran up the stairs two at a time. In the privacy of his room, he scribbled a note:

Darling Cathleen,
My father has been locked in business discussions, so I
have not yet been able to talk with him, but I will . . .

either later this evening or first thing in the morning, after
which I shall come and find you.
But don't worry. You know how very much I love you.
It won't be too long before I see you.
Until then, think of me, and love me too.
                              Silas.

Folding the note into an envelope, he sealed it and carried it with him downstairs. Spying the new parlourmaid in the dining room, he called out to her while he collected his jacket from the cupboard, 'Edna, I have an errand for you.'

Putting down her feather duster, she came out in a rush. 'Yes, sir?'

'Do you know Fenshaw Cottage, on the other side of the valley?'

Screwing up her face in concentration, she asked in a shrill, cockney voice, 'Is that the one where Mr Roe the baker lives?'

'That's the one, Edna, yes.'

Her face creased into a lopsided smile. 'I know the place!' she exclaimed, obviously pleased with herself. 'Cathleen brings me old mum a whole batch of scones on a Sunday. Mr Roe fetches them home from the bakery for us every Sunday, regular as clockwork, since me dad died last year. He don't charge nuthin' neither, bless his heart. They're such a lovely family, and that old gran'ma, she's a real darling.' Winking, she confided in a whisper, 'Me mum says she's got a right bleedin' temper when the mood takes 'er.'

Anxious though he was, Silas had to laugh. 'I've heard Cathleen say the very same.'

Startling them both, Edward's voice suddenly boomed out, 'EDNA! GET ABOUT YOUR WORK!'

'It's all right, Father.' Silas was quick to defend her. 'Edna is just taking instructions on an errand I want running.'

'Hmh!' Disgruntled, Edward swung away and went back into the library, closing the door firmly behind him.

'Now then, Edna.' Handing her the note, Silas told her, 'Put it safe about you, and tell Mrs Jacob the housekeeper that I said you're to go straight away. It's very important.'

'Yes, sir. Straight away, sir. I'll not lose it.' To reassure him, she stuffed it down her blouse.

'Off you go then, and don't hand it to anyone but Cathleen herself – even if you have to go out and find her.'

'I'd best put on me running shoes then.' Edna had size ten feet, and an impish smile. 'Only I've got corns d'yer see, an' these shoes are only for poddling about indoors.'

'Quickly now, Edna!'

And off she scuttled, while Silas hurried across the courtyard to the stables. 'Saddle the bay gelding,' he told the stable-boy, 'as quick as you can.'

'He's a bit spirited, sir,' came the reply. 'I've not had a chance to exercise him for a couple of days.'

'Spirited, eh?' Pulling on his riding boots, Silas waited while the boy saddled the horse. 'He'll do.'

Mounting the animal, he set off at some speed towards the upper fields and the higher grounds which led to Kildalton Manor, from where Jack Turner presided over some of the finest land in the whole of Lancashire.

———◦◦◦———

USHERED INTO THE drawing room, Silas found Turner standing, legs apart, with his back to the fireplace, his face set in a hard, unwelcoming expression. 'If you've come here to plead on your father's behalf,' he said immediately, 'I can tell you now, you're wasting your time.'

As he spoke, he crossed to the dresser, where he placed two glasses side by side and poured two measures of whisky. Handing one to Silas, he went on, 'I've nothing more to add to what I've already said. The partnership's finished and I'm owed a great deal of money. How your father gets it together is none of my concern. I left him proxy while I was away – working, on both our behalfs I might add – all written and signed by your father, myself, and the solicitor.'

Swigging back his drink, he then poured another. 'It was quite straightforward. There were to be no deals, no risks, nothing of that sort. Just a signature for routine stuff, and instructions to keep the business out of trouble while I was away. Instead of which he squandered a small fortune on buying a quarry that nobody else wanted, and which very nearly bankrupted us into the bargain!' Jack's face was red and his voice had become strident.

'I'm sure my father acted on good faith.'

'Huh! Acted out of a sense of his own damned importance! In fact, he's fortunate that we've been friends and partners for some time, because if it had been anybody else, I'd have moved heaven and earth to have them put where they belonged . . . behind bars, and for a bloody long time.'

'You do know it's in your power to ruin him?'

'And it's in *your* power to save him.' Turner's smile was triumphant. 'You've known Helen almost all of your life . . . here in Lancashire *and* in London before your father agreed to move north. Well now, young Fenshaw, here's the proposition. My daughter has told me how she's ready to settle down and start a family.' His eyes shone with pride. 'I have long wanted her married with children, and there is nothing that would please me more than to have you as a son-in-law.'

'What you ask is impossible.'

Turner's smile slid away. 'Why "impossible"?'

'Because I don't love her.'

The other man laughed at that. '*Love!* What does love matter? Besides, I'm sure you could *learn* to love her.'

Silas was adamant. 'No, sir!'

'And why not?'

'Because I'm already committed to someone else. Someone I intend to marry.'

A look of disgust came over the other man's face. 'The baker's daughter?'

'Cathleen, yes.'

'Well, you're a bloody fool! Here am I, offering you a

young woman of handsome reputation and considerable means – and don't forget that when I'm dead and gone, everything I own will come to her.' He shook his head. 'I can't believe you would turn all that down for the sake of a pretty face.'

'No, sir. I'm turning it down, as you say, because it isn't right. The *reasons* for it aren't right. Even putting aside the fact that I don't care for Helen in that way, nor she me, if you were half truthful with yourself, you would see how a marriage between Helen and myself is bound to end in disaster.'

'Does your father know how you feel?'

'He does.'

'And what does he have to say?'

'That's between me and my father, sir.'

The older man studied him for a moment, secretly admiring this strong-minded young man. He was made to realise that Silas had principles that both he and Edward Fenshaw had long forgotten. Looking at Silas now, seeing how tall and proud he stood, and how determined he was not to be forced into a loveless marriage, he was filled with envy. Not for the first time, he found himself wishing with all his heart that he had behaved differently all those years ago, had loved his wife better, kept her happy and by his side. Life had not been easy for him; first a wife who had abandoned him, then a daughter who had grown cold and spiteful, and now, when Fate had given him a chance to be free of it all, here was this determined young man standing in the way. Edward Fenshaw was fortunate, he thought, to have someone who would fight a battle on his behalf.

Jack Turner was also determined not to let go, not to lose the opportunity. This was his chance, and he would not be deterred from it. Deciding on a different approach, he began to cajole. 'Look, I know Cathleen Roe is a real beauty, and I'm not surprised you want her, but think, man!' He winked knowingly. 'You can have any woman, any time you like . . . even *after* you're wed. Show me a married man who doesn't play around.'

Taken aback by his suggestion, Silas told him coldly, 'What you suggest is offensive, sir, both to me, *and* your daughter.' Squaring his broad shoulders, he added with quiet dignity, 'One way or another, Cathleen and I *will* be married, make no mistake about that.'

'Really?' Sneering, Turner laughed out loud, before taking on a grim expression. 'You're a stubborn bastard, I'll say that for you!' Exasperated, he swung away, reaching his two arms up to the mantelpiece. He gripped the timber edge until his knuckles bled white. 'So! That's what you came to say, is it? You'll not wed my daughter, but you'll wed some little nothing who brings neither name nor position with her?'

Realising the comment was meant to provoke him, Silas chose not to answer.

Muttering under his breath, Jack Turner continued to deride him, staring into the fireplace for such an age that Silas wondered whether he'd forgotten he was even there.

After a while, during which time Silas grew increasingly uneasy, the older man spoke, his voice trembling with rage. 'IT'S TIME YOU WENT!'

'I hoped there might be another way we could resolve the situation, sir.' Silas put forward the proposition he had been churning over in his mind ever since his father told him of the situation. '*I* could work with you . . . do my utmost to repair some of the damage. I've finished my commercial studies and now I'm ready to launch out on my own. I have five years of hard work behind me, and a fistful of good results to show for it. So you see, I'm not unfamiliar with business. Besides, I believe that that quarry has possibilities. I have an idea or two that might just work.'

'Oh! So you have an idea or two, have you? And what makes you think you know better than me, eh? To hell with your studies! It's experience on the ground that matters. I've forgotten more about business than you'll ever know. That quarry is burnt out, the land is worthless, good for nothing, finished! Just like the money your father squandered on it!'

'Well then, you've nothing to lose if you take a chance on me. All I'm asking for is a little time to recover your money and get my father out of debt.' Silas stepped forward, his dark eyes alight with excitement. 'Six months – give me that.'

For a moment it seemed as if Jack Turner was considering Silas's proposition. After all, he told himself, here was a fine young man, with values and standards that would either finish him in the first year or make him a force to be reckoned with. Look how he flatly refused to be used, even to save his father from disgrace, or worse! And see how he stood up to his betters . . . head held high and the look of a man who would not be beaten. All of these things Jack considered; it was a knife edge decision. But sadly the knife had already been turned by Silas's father, who had shown recklessness and disregard in matters of partnership and finance. These were dangerous traits that may or may not show up in his son. On top of that, how could he go along with the young man's suggestion, when the idea was for him to marry Helen and take that burden off his shoulders?

Contrary to what he had told Edward Fenshaw, Jack wasn't interested in the money; that was of little consequence to him. What *was* badly hurt was his pride, and his standing in the business world, and for that he wanted to punish the man responsible. Though he was tempted by Silas's proposition, he decided he could not, *would* not, settle for less than his pound of flesh. 'I'm not interested!' Advancing on Silas, he took him by the lapels and shook him hard. 'Go back to your father. Tell him he knows what I want, and I have no intention of settling for less.'

Silas snatched himself away. Looking the other man in the eye, he told him quietly, 'Father made a stupid mistake, which he will probably regret for the rest of his days. But *you* . . . ' Regarding Jack with sorry eyes, he shook his head. 'What you're asking of him, *and* me, is tantamount to blackmail. You shame yourself. He was a good friend to you all these years, made you a lot of money; he moved out of London to come north, because you wanted to expand the business . . . needed someone on the ground in order to grab the opportunities as they came up. You asked him, and against his instincts he moved up here bag and baggage. Not because he wanted to, but because *you* asked.' He continued to look on the older man with accusing eyes. 'And now, because of one unfortunate misjudgement, and because it cost you money, which incidentally he helped put in your pocket, you'd see him in the workhouse.'

Pausing, he searched Jack Turner's face for a semblance of regret, but there was none. 'I won't trouble you again.' His voice was quiet, respectful even, but his heart was hard and unyielding. 'Though I can promise you this much. I won't forget today, nor will I forget the callous man you've shown yourself to be.'

He turned to go, only to be called back, 'FENSHAW! You really don't understand, do you? You said a short time ago that it was in my power to ruin your father.' He smiled, a terrible, unforgiving smile. 'And of course, you're right, it is. But I take no blame for what happens from now on, because *you* have it in your hands to save the situation, and you choose not to. So, whatever happens now, the blame will for ever lie with *you*, not me.'

'You're a coward, sir. I was wrong in offering to work with you. The truth is, now that I see you for what you are, I could *never* work with you.' He made another promise. 'Don't worry about your money. We'll find a way to pay you back. My father is well known and respected hereabouts. There are friends in London too, who will help him, I'm sure.'

'Oh? You think so, do you?' Turner snorted. 'Respected or not, your father will have his work cut out. It's strange how "friends" disappear when they're asked to put their hands in their own pockets.'

'We'll see.' Knowing how he himself would help a friend in need, Silas refused to believe that his father's former partners would turn their back on him.

Ever persistent, Turner urged, 'Marry my daughter, that's all it takes. Good God, man! Surely it can't be such a sacrifice?' But it was, and he knew it, because when her mother went away, hadn't he sacrificed enough of his own life for that wretched girl, *and* lived to regret it?

Over the years he had twice found a woman he might have spent the rest of his life with, and twice Helen had driven her away. Another time he might well have overlooked Edward Fenshaw's misdemeanour, but he had seen it as a heaven-sent opportunity to free himself of his shrewish daughter. No other man wanted her, not even with a handsome dowry.

Now, with Silas about to walk away, he was seeing his one chance slipping from his grasp. 'Don't be too hasty!' he gabbled, 'I'll see to it that you never want. Your father will be out of my debt for all time. I'll deposit a considerable sum into your bank account, *and* build you a house the like of which you've never seen. Go away and think about it, that's all I'm asking.'

Silas shook his head. 'You've had my answer, sir,' he replied quietly. 'As you seem so hellbent on the idea,

I'll have to speak with Helen. Maybe *she* can make you see sense.'

'Hah! You can't know how obsessed she is with you. Good God, man, it was her idea!'

'Then you're *both* out of your minds!'

Striding across the room, he tried to shut his ears to the other man's abuse. 'Go ahead then! Marry the little peasant! Let your father go to the dogs, see if I care. Watch him lose everything. And what about your poor mother, eh? What do you imagine it will do to *her*, tell me that? It'll finish her, that's what, and you will have done nothing to save her!' Then, running after Silas, he bellowed from the doorway, 'Two good people broken! And all because they bred a selfish bastard like you!'

Pausing in the hallway, Silas turned to look at him for a long, agonising moment. There was no need for words. The look in his dark eyes said it all.

———※◇※———

Long after Silas had gone, Jack Turner ranted and raved, his mind confused by all that had been said . . . harsh words between himself and Edward Fenshaw's son, a fine young man who had always looked on him with respect and liking, and who now looked at him with such loathing that it stuck in his craw like a wedge of stone.

'It wasn't *my* doing,' he consoled himself. '*I* was the one wronged, and I have a right to compensation!'

Pouring one drink after another, he began to feel

righteous. 'He *will* come round to my way of thinking,' he smiled, convinced that he had won the day. 'Oh, yes. He'll search for a way out, and there'll be times when he'll wish he'd never been born, but in the end he'll have no choice, and I'll be rid of the little vixen at last. He'll marry her all right. For his mother's sake, if not for his father's.'

To celebrate, he poured himself another measure, then another, which he raised to his daughter's portrait hanging on the wall. He stared at the narrow features and small, piercing eyes, the thin smile that gave her a certain cold attractiveness. 'To you, my dear,' he saluted her. 'And the poor bastard who will rue the day he ever clapped eyes on you.'

Swallowing the large whisky, he poured himself yet another in an attempt to cover his feelings of self-loathing. He kicked the waste-paper bin and tripped over the leg of the desk, then fell into the chair and threw the remainder of his drink down his throat. 'He'll be back!' he groaned. 'You see if I'm not right.'

Staggering out of the chair, he went to the dresser and grabbed the whisky decanter, which he carried back to his desk. 'Jack Turner . . . father-in-law,' he grinned. '*Grandfather?* Maybe . . . if she melts long enough to let him lie on her.' He gave a shuddering sigh. 'I'd rather him than me!' But he drank to it all the same, three times over. Then he slumped across his desk and was out like a light.

When Helen returned from her ride, it was to discover that he had ensconced himself in the den and was snoring enough to frighten the dead.

She couldn't know the things he had said or the way he felt towards her, nor how, because of the pride and dignity of that young man, his own shame seemed tenfold. Nor did she realise how much he had come to hate her . . . his own flesh and blood. And, even if she had known, would she have cared?

Chapter Four

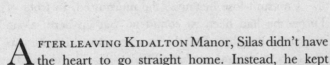

AFTER LEAVING KIDALTON Manor, Silas didn't have the heart to go straight home. Instead, he kept riding, through the valley and on, towards the higher ground. There was a place he knew where the world seemed never-ending and where the heart could be at peace. Whenever he had need of solace, this was where he would go.

Urging the horse onward, he climbed high above the valleys and woods, until he stood on the highest point. Dismounting, he tethered the loyal animal at a safe distance to graze. Striding out to where the lip of the hills hung like pie-crust over the lands below, he sucked in the fresh air, filling his lungs like a desperate man. 'The edge of the world,' he murmured, his eyes and soul drinking in the awe-inspiring beauty.

From where he stood he could see the land stretching away for miles; woods and spinneys, the lake of Fenshaw House shimmering like a vast dark jewel against the green land. Night was drawing in fast and, as always at this time of the evening, the mist was cradling the island in a ghostly halo; incredibly beautiful, and haunting too.

'*My* island. Mine and Cathleen's.' A warm, secret smile covered his handsome features. She was only ever a heartbeat away. Now, when he closed his eyes, her face gentled into his mind. He felt her nearness, saw her smile, and his heart was warmed. She had trusted him, given herself eagerly to him, and he knew that even if he lived for ever, nothing in his life would ever compare.

'I mustn't lose her now,' he murmured. In front of Turner he had been so confident, but up here, alone with only thoughts of Cathleen to comfort him, he was not so certain, and yet he told himself, 'There *must* be a way to satisfy Turner without losing my soul.' But he didn't know, not for sure, and it was that which gnawed at him.

Lifting his gaze to the endless, darkening skies, he got the feeling that he was not alone. 'I don't know what to do,' he whispered. 'If I lose Cathleen, I lose *everything*.'

The idea was unthinkable, and yet in spite of his bravado before Turner, he was forced to consider it, because of his mother, and because he feared, as Turner had so cruelly pointed out, that 'friends disappear when they're asked to put their hands in their pockets'; Turner himself had shown how a 'friend' could so easily become an enemy.

He stayed a while longer, then made his way home. Later, knowing that Cathleen was waiting to see him, he would go to her. His mood darkened. 'She'll have to know what's happened,' he muttered. 'There must be no secrets between us.' It was not an ordeal he looked forward to, but there was still hope. He would make it his business to see his father's old colleagues. Surely once they learned of Edward Fershaw's troubles, they would *want* to help?

For the moment, however, and with Turner's warning echoing in his mind, he didn't want to dwell on it too much.

T HE RIDE BACK seemed to take an age. By the time he got to the house, the night was thick and black, pierced only by the stars and distant lights.

Looking ahead, he saw that his father's house was lit up like a beacon, with lights glowing from almost every room, including his mother's. 'That's strange,' he mused. 'Mother's usually asleep by this time of night.'

As he came up the drive, he noticed the small black carriage outside, recognising it immediately as belonging to the doctor.

Fearful, he urged his horse into a canter. 'Come on, old fella!' There *was* something wrong; he felt it inside, like a hard fist in the pit of his stomach.

Entering the yard at the gallop, he loosed the horse and, calling out for the stable-lad, Joseph, ran into the house. His father was in the hallway, and standing beside him was Dr Leighton. Both men wore solemn expressions.

Anxious, Silas addressed the doctor. 'It's Mother isn't it?'

Matthew Leighton answered immediately: 'I was called out to your mother, yes, but she's quiet now, and much better.' Turning to Edward Fenshaw, he said, 'The sedatives I gave her are already taking effect. She should soon be asleep.'

Donning his hat, he noted Edward's ashen face. 'And I suggest you too need your rest. You'll be of no use to her half asleep.' He paused, his head gently shaking from side to side. 'I'm sorry, I know how you must feel.'

Dropping his gaze to the ground, Edward Fenshaw acknowledged him with a nod of his head.

'As I explained, I'll be back in the morning with my colleague, Dr Copperthwaite. Meanwhile, just follow my instructions.'

Edward Fenshaw promised he would. 'Thank you again,' he answered wearily. 'In the morning then.'

Addressing father and son in turn, the doctor bade them goodnight and left for his own, warm bed.

After seeing the doctor out, Edward Fenshaw came back to find Silas pacing the floor, his worried gaze turned upward to the landing. On hearing his father come into the hallway, he swung round. 'What happened?' Wanting to see his mother, yet loath to disturb her, he forced himself to be patient. 'What did he mean, "I'm sorry, I know how you must feel"?'

At first it seemed as though his father either had not heard or did not want to. In any event he remained silent, his glazed eyes fixed on the floor.

'Father!' Unsettled by the doctor's comment, Silas took a step closer. '*Please*, Father!'

'Sorry.' Raising his eyes to the upper landing, Edward noticed Edna coming out of his wife's room. 'You'd best come with me, son.' Before Silas could reply, he led the way into the library at a quick pace, as though wanting to escape.

The news was not good.

'Your mother's condition has worsened,' Edward revealed. 'The rheumatism has crippled her beyond repair. All these years tearing at her body, wearing her down – she's been in constant pain, as you know. Tonight, though, she was taken ill.' He looked into his son's dark eyes and saw the anguish there. 'She couldn't breathe, you see . . . oh, you've no idea.' His voice breaking, he glanced away and his eyes filled with tears. 'I thought we'd lose her, but thank God she's quiet now.' He took a deep breath. 'Her heart won't stand much more, that's what the doctor meant.'

'This Dr Copperthwaite, who is he?'

'He's a specialist.' In a trembling voice, Edward told his son everything. 'Your mother's heart has been dangerously overworked these past years. Without a second opinion we can't be certain, but it seems there's been some damage.' Swallowing hard he went on, his voice almost inaudible. 'She's got nine . . . twelve months left at the outside, that's what the doctor said.' Seeming to crumple, he sat down, his head in his hands. 'So little time,' he whispered. 'I can't take it in, son.'

Stunned by the news, Silas remained by the door, his back to the wall and his eyes closed, all manner of emotions raging through him. His mother had been ailing for years, but he had never thought . . . never realised . . . until now.

Suddenly he heard his father sobbing like a child. Opening his eyes he saw him, arms stretched over the desk, his head turned to one side across them. 'It's all over, son,' he groaned. 'Nothing matters now.'

His grief turning to rage, Silas strode across the room and, wrenching his father into an upright position, demanded, 'What sort of man are you? It's *her* you should be thinking about, not yourself! What do *you* matter, eh? What do *I* matter? Besides, we haven't lost her yet and, God willing, the doctors have been known to be wrong.' Though he felt instinctively that this terrible news was final.

Edward would not be consoled. 'Leave me be!'

'Oh, don't you see, Father, we should be looking at ways to make her remaining time more enjoyable. Enjoy her beauty and her laughter the way we always have. Be there for her when she needs us. Help her to forget the pain, if we can.' Gently shaking his father he said, 'Show her how much you love her, and don't ever let her know how you're suffering inside.' The enormity of what was happening began to overwhelm him too. 'We owe her that much.' He could say no more, because the words clogged his throat and tears blinded his eyes.

When Edward Fenshaw finally looked up and saw the devastation on his son's face, shame engulfed him. 'You're right,' he said. 'But you're stronger than me. You always have been.'

Gripping his arm round his father's bowed shoulders,

Silas told him with a smile, 'We'll be strong together, for her sake.'

Calmer now, Edward leaned into his son's grasp, and that was how they stayed, father and son, understanding each other for the first time in their lives.

After a while they were able to talk and plan, putting Lucy first in all things. Yet there was another issue that had not gone away, and which affected her more than ever now.

When Silas told his father how Turner would not be persuaded from his mad idea, and that it seemed Helen was even more immovable, Edward answered, 'I've been giving it some thought. I have friends, old colleagues in London, who I have a mind to go and see. I'm sure they'll help. I didn't want to go cap in hand begging, but neither can I let you ruin your life on account of me.' He gave a small laugh. 'Besides, your mother has already paired you off with Cathleen.'

'There isn't much gets by her, is there?' Silas said fondly.

'Not much.'

Returning to the subject of Turner, Silas suggested, 'You stay here with Mother, she needs you. If you think me capable, *I'll* carry your messages to London.'

Edward considered for a moment. 'Of course you're capable,' he said. 'And you're right, I should be here. Turner gave me one week to get back to him, so we have a little time yet.'

It was agreed. First thing in the morning, Silas would travel to London, where he would call on certain gents who in the past had received favours from Edward Fenshaw. 'They owe me,' he said. And Silas could only hope they were of a different calibre than Jack Turner.

While Edward set about writing his letters, Silas went upstairs to look in on his mother.

Edging open the door, he expected to find her in a deep sleep. When she called out, 'Come in, Silas,' he was pleasantly surprised, though concerned that she should still be awake and possibly in pain. 'I thought the doctor gave you a sedative?' he chided as he came in. 'Here was I thinking you'd be fast asleep, and here *you* are, wide awake, looking beautiful as always.'

In the golden glow of the lamp, with her hair loose about her shoulders and her soft brown eyes smiling up at him, she looked like a child. 'You mustn't worry, you know.' Taking hold of his hand she drew him down beside her. 'I'm in no hurry to die.'

Shocked by her candour, Silas replied light-heartedly, 'Shame on you. What a thing to say!'

'Oh, I know you men,' she laughed. 'The merest *sight* of a doctor brings you out in a sweat.'

'We worry for you, that's all.'

'There is no need. I had a bad attack and now it's over and I'll be right as rain in the morning.' She laughed, 'Besides, I've so much to look forward to. Your father and I have been planning to travel to Europe this autumn. I've always wanted to see the Eiffel Tower, and Venice is so beautiful you want to go back again and again.' She clapped her hands with delight. 'So, I mustn't be ill again. I have things to do.'

'It *sounds* like it. You make me breathless just listening to you.' It was obvious that Lucy had no idea how close she had been to losing her life, and Silas was thankful for that.

Tugging at his hand, she chuckled. 'Besides, I want to see you married,' she confided. 'I want to hold my grandchildren.'

'Steady on!' Silas objected. 'I expect you've even chosen my wife, haven't you?'

Smiling secretly, she told him, 'Oh, I think *you've* already decided that.'

'Really?' It was like a little game, and he went along with it for her sake.

'I saw you and Cathleen together,' she said at last. 'The two of you seemed so happy.'

'You mustn't jump to conclusions, Mother.' In view of what had happened, and because he had not yet got security from his father's old friends, Silas's instincts warned him to be wary.

'Oh, well, I could be wrong,' she said, hoping he might enlighten her. 'Perhaps your father's right and I shouldn't read things into an innocent friendship. Still, it's a shame. I can see Cathleen in this house, with hordes of children running around.'

Her pretty eyes moistened. 'I love this house, Silas. It's been my life and your grandparents' life before me. My own mother was born here, then myself, and then you, and who knows how many other generations of our family will come after us? Over the years, there have been many children running through this house, bringing *such* happiness.'

Reaching up, she stroked his face. 'You're all I have,' she murmured, 'you and your father. All I want is for you to marry some young woman who will love you as you deserve to be loved. I want to believe that when I'm gone, this house will be handed down to your children and their children after that.'

Silas prayed his visit to London would go well. 'And all *I* want is for you to be here for a very long time yet, so let's not have any more talk of "when you're gone", because, as you so rightly put it, you have a lot to do, and one of the things I absolutely insist on is that you're around to teach my children how to be as gracious and delightful as you are.'

'Oh, they'll be that already.' There was a twinkle in her eye. 'Because they'll all be little images of their grandmother.'

'You're incorrigible.'

'But you love me?'

'You know I do.'

'Then stop keeping me awake, young man! Don't you know I've had a bad day?'

'It doesn't show.'

'Liar!'

'Goodnight, Mother.'

'Goodnight, son.' Stretching her arms up to him, she held him for a moment. 'Go to your father,' she whispered. 'Tell him I'm stronger than he thinks.'

'I'm sure he knows that already,' Silas lied. 'But I'll tell him anyway.'

'And get Cathleen to come and see me,' Lucy said sleepily. 'She's such a happy little soul, I do love having her around.' When he wagged a chastising finger at her, she sighed, 'There I go again, poking my nose in.'

'Oh, but what a pretty nose.' Which he cheekily kissed, before quietly leaving. When he glanced back from across the room, she was already sound asleep.

'Trust me,' he whispered sadly. 'Whatever happens, I won't let anything hurt you.'

———◆———

S ILAS AND HIS father sat talking downstairs for a long time. 'You mustn't worry,' Edward told him, 'I'm sure everything will turn out for the best.' Yet, even as he spoke, his mannerisms told another story; nervously fidgeting and unable to sit still for a minute at a time, it was obvious that, like Silas, he was on edge, unsure and afraid of the outcome. 'If only the bank hadn't turned me down when I went to see them yesterday,' he fretted.

'I expect they know about the partnership being dissolved, and it's made them nervous.'

'That's partly it,' Edward confirmed. 'The other reason is that I borrowed against the house when Turner and I formed the partnership. As you know, I'm a southerner, born and bred, but your mother's heart was always in the north, and, understandably, she did not want to move away permanently. So I borrowed money against this house to buy the other, smaller house in London. When we came back to stay, the London house was sold and somehow the money was all eaten up. Consequently, the bank loan was never paid off.'

As before, Silas was a little taken aback. His father rarely confided matters of finance to him, and there had been no reason why he should. But now, and against his better feelings, he was made to wonder whether his father was the shrewd businessman he had been led to believe.

As though anxious to justify his actions, Edward muttered, 'Of course, I'm not altogether without income, dear me, no! I'm still entitled to any future monies that might come from joint ventures between myself and Turner . . . nothing big I don't expect, but enough to tide me over until I get started again, I dare say.'

'So, is there no capital left at all?'

'Not too much, no,' he admitted reluctantly. 'The land agency hit on hard times a few years ago and hasn't really picked up since. That's why Turner went to Europe, where new opportunities are opening up. It's also why I took a risk with the quarry land. I honestly thought it would come good, but it seems I made a bad choice.'

'I see.' What he *was* beginning to see was that his father had somehow not only squandered his own money, but had tapped into the partnership money while Turner was away touting for work. 'I had no idea things were so bad.'

'Ticking over, like I said . . . just ticking over, waiting

for the right opportunity.' His bright smile was deceiving. 'I was so sure the quarry was it, but there you are, son, it was not to be.' His smile became a broad grin. 'Things will turn out for the better once you've taken word to London.'

'You seem very sure.'

'And why not indeed!'

Taking a deep breath that swelled his chest and put a smile on his face, he reminded Silas, 'Long before I took up with Turner, I held down a very responsible position in the export industry. Although I can count the number of "true" friends on one hand, I'll tell you this: I know they won't let me down. Any more than I would let them down should they ever need me.' As though desperate to convince himself, he began muttering, 'Good men every one. They'll want to help, I know they will.' Restless, he began pacing the room for the umpteenth time. 'I only wish I'd gone to them before.'

Struggling with his own doubts, Silas watched his father. 'Stop torturing yourself,' he told him. 'I have your letters safe, and I'll be away before first light. We'll know the outcome soon enough.'

Pausing in his frantic pacing, Edward regarded his son with gratitude. '*I'm* the one who should be going, but how can I? Your mother knows my every move. She's *bound* to ask questions.' Lowering his voice, he begged Silas, and not for the first time, 'She must never learn anything of this, especially now, when . . .' He couldn't bring himself to say it, and so he merely pressed his chin into his neck and fell silent.

Seeing his distress, Silas's heart went out to him. 'Go to bed, Father,' he urged, 'we can neither of us do anything until the morning.'

Exhausted by the day's events, and with the constant threat of losing everything, Edward offered no resistance. 'I can't deny that I am tired,' he said hoarsely. 'And of course you're right. There's nothing we can do tonight.' He gave a wry smile. 'I'll be interested to see what friends I have in my time of need.'

'We'll know soon enough.'

Moving across the room, Edward said that he would just look quietly in on Lucy and make sure she was sleeping.

'You heard what the doctor said,' Silas reminded him. 'It's important that you get some rest yourself.'

'Will you wake me in the morning?'

'If you like, but there's no need.'

Edward gave him a strange look of condemnation. 'There is *every* need!' His voice was harsh, his manner the same. 'Do you imagine I could lie in my bed while you set off for London on a shameful errand, brought about by my own irresponsible actions?' He shook his head so vigorously that the flabby jowls began to shiver. 'Oh no! Seeing you away safely is the very *least* I can do.'

Silas nodded. 'All right, Father,' he conceded, 'I'll wake you in plenty of time before I leave.'

'Did you instruct Joseph to have the carriage ready?'

'It's all done. He knows I'll be wanting to leave no later than four-thirty.'

'Hmh!' Edward Fenshaw had always known he was

blessed with a decent son, but at this moment in time his admiration of Silas had never been greater. 'I'm sorry, son,' he murmured, 'I know how difficult this is for you, and I want you to know I'm very grateful.'

Silas had never known his father be so open about his troubles, and it stirred deep emotions in him. 'Don't be grateful,' he chided. 'I'm doing it for you and Mother, yes, but don't forget I have my own reasons for wanting to see it settled.' Both his and Cathleen's happiness depended on it.

A curt nod, then a timely warning. 'Nevertheless, you have a long, hard drive ahead of you. I'm not the only one who needs to get some rest.'

'I'm sure I won't be far behind you.'

'Goodnight, son.'

With his hands behind his back, Edward trod heavily across the room and out the door, and when it clicked to behind him, Silas leaned back in his chair, a thoughtful remark issuing from his lips. 'I pray to God your friends are made of better stuff than the one who would see you in the workhouse.'

Long after his father had gone to bed and the whole house was quiet, Silas remained in the chair, thinking of Cathleen, and agonising over what to do for the best. 'Should I tell her the truth?' he wondered aloud, 'or would that be too cruel, especially when there might be a chance that it will all come right?'

Though he had never wanted to keep anything from her, this might be the one exception; it would be kinder than making her suffer, even for the short time it would take him to get to London and back. 'I'll keep it from her for now,' he decided. 'At some time in the future, when we're older and wiser, I'll be able to tell her how close I came to losing her for ever.' The idea was unthinkable, so he thrust it away. 'Father's right,' he mused. 'Amongst all his old colleagues, there must be *one* who will want to help.' They were none of them short of money; he knew that from what Edward had told him: 'successful businessmen every one', that's what he'd said.

Silas glanced at the clock, Cathleen strong in his mind. 'Almost eleven. She's bound to be in her bed.' But he couldn't sleep. Not yet. He needed to breathe the cool night air; he had to walk and clear his mind, and think of Cathleen. Putting on his jacket, he made his way through the kitchen to the back door.

There were two iron keys hanging on the wall inside the narrow passage. He took one down and unlocked the door to let himself out, then locked it behind him and slipped the key into his jacket pocket. 'They won't even know I'm gone,' he told himself.

A chill had come with the evening so, pulling up his collar, he fastened his buttons and strode out in the direction of Fenshaw Cottage. He didn't expect to see Cathleen at so late an hour, but somehow it made him content just to know she would be there.

———◦———

As SILAS WAS making his way to the cottage, Cathleen was lying sleepless in her bed, tormenting herself as to whether Silas had told his father about them yet. She wondered how the conversation had gone between the two men, and what the outcome had been. She expected the worst and prayed for the best, and now her mind wouldn't lie still, any more than her body.

Since early evening she had waited for him, and when it became clear he wasn't coming, she began to think about her grandmother's warning; what if Silas's father had forbidden him to see her again? What if he had persuaded Silas to forget her, told him that she was not good enough for him, and that a marriage between them was impossible? What if Silas was easily persuaded? What if he hadn't loved her the way he said he did? What if? What if?

So many questions – with one in particular that would not go away. What was the truth behind the note he'd sent? Silas had never lied to her before, but she felt he was lying through those few words he had hastily scribbled. There was a sense of urgency about the note that worried her; though when she mentioned it to her grandmother, she had tutted and sighed and told Cathleen, 'You've too strong an imagination, that's yer trouble!' Then she too had fallen silent, as if mulling over what Cathleen had told her.

So, all Cathleen could do was wait until he came to her. But waiting was a worrying game, and she had waited too long already. Now, at almost half an hour past midnight, she lay in her bed, turning one way then the other, tired to the bone yet unable to rest. Time and again, she would close her eyes and try to blank out all thought, but it was no use. Her mind was full of Silas. 'I was sure he'd come and see me tonight,' her quiet voice echoed the burning thoughts inside her head. 'There's something's wrong, I *know* it!'

Clambering out of bed, she shivered when her bare feet touched the cold lino. Summer or winter, the floors in the little cottage always struck cold. But the walls were thick and the rooms warm and, even with the window partially open and a cool breeze blowing in, the rest of her body felt uncomfortably hot, and she was so thirsty her tongue felt as though it was stuck to the roof of her mouth.

Slipping her arms into the sleeves of her gown, she drew it about her before going softly out of the room to make her way downstairs. She was especially quiet as she passed her grandmother's room; the old woman was a light sleeper, and these days it seemed to Cathleen she couldn't do anything or go anywhere without her grandmother worrying about her.

She needn't have bothered creeping past the door though, because Jessie was wide awake. The walls around the cottage were fortress thick, but inside they were paper thin. Consequently, having the bedroom next door to Cathleen, Jessie could almost hear her breathe; Cathleen only had to turn over and Jessie turned over with her.

Knowing that her grand-daughter had gone downstairs, Jessie too got out of bed and put on her dressing-gown. 'Worrying herself sick because he hasn't been to see her, I dare say,' she muttered. 'Men! What do they know?' Slipping her feet into her raggedy shoes, she shuffled across the room and out the door. 'Look at the time!' Her red eyes stared at the wall clock on the landing. 'Twenty to one of a morning, God love and save us!'

Seated at the table with her head bent forward over a tumbler of sarsaparilla, Cathleen didn't hear Jessie when she first came into the kitchen.

'Will ye look at the state of youse!' At the sound of Jessie's voice, Cathleen almost leaped out of the chair with fright. 'Anybody would think it were the end of the world, so they would!' It was a long time since she herself had been a young woman in love. All the same, Jessie understood how Cathleen might be feeling.

'I didn't want to wake you,' Cathleen told her. 'Sorry, Grandma.'

'Ah, it's all right.' Jessie laughed. 'It's not as if I need me beauty sleep, is it, eh?' With a smug little smile, she rolled her eyes and flicked her plaited hair. 'Sure aren't I lovely enough already?'

Having brought a smile to Cathleen's eyes, Jessie went to the cupboard where she took out a tumbler and, filling it from the sarsaparilla jug, she carried it to the table. The minute her bottom touched the cold wooden chair she gave a shrill little cry. 'That's a shock to yer arse, so it is,' she joked. 'Serves me right for not putting me bloomers on.'

'Do you want me to fetch you a cushion?' Cathleen couldn't help but laugh at the old woman's antics: she looked a comical sight. 'We don't want you catching cold.'

'I'm all right now,' Jessie assured her, though goose pimples stood out proud on her flesh. 'It's *you* I'm worried about.' Taking a deep drink of the dark liquid, she smacked her lips together. 'D'yer want to talk about it?'

'I couldn't sleep, that's all.'

'Huh!' Taking another swig of her drink, Jessie declared, 'I know *that*!' Bloodshot and tired, her eyes stuck out like hatpins. 'Didn't yer wake me from a deep sleep with yer walking up and down half the night? And don't I already know why the two of us are sitting here, half asleep and me with me arse still shivering from the shock of a cold chair?'

Knowing there was no use trying to fool her, Cathleen voiced the question that had been playing on her mind. 'Why didn't he come and see me?'

'Didn't he already tell yer that in the note he sent?'

'He said his father was tied up with business and they hadn't had a chance to talk.'

'Ah!' Jessie had wondered about that. 'And yer don't believe him, is that what yer saying?'

'No, I'm not saying that.'

'So, what *are* yer saying then?'

Cathleen didn't quite know how to explain it. 'I just feel that he didn't tell me everything.'

'Aye well, yer know him better than I do, so I can't argue with yer feelings, lass. You'll just have to wait and see what he has to say when yer next meet up with him.'

'He said he might come and see me in the morning.'

'There yer are then.' Peeking at Cathleen's downcast face, she asked, 'There's summat else on yer mind, isn't there?'

Jessie was right. 'There *was* something about that note,' Cathleen confided. 'What if Edward Fenshaw dared him to marry me?'

Jessie turned it over in her mind. 'If that is the case, and we can't be sure that it is, then there are only one or two things Silas can do.' Pursing her lips while she thought it through, she explained, 'As I recall, Silas Fenshaw is twenty-four years of age. So the fact that he feels the need to talk to his father is out of a son's regard for his parents. He doesn't *need* anyone's permission to wed you, though o' course he would rather have it than not, I dare say . . . his mother's blessing too, I imagine.'

Laying a comforting hand over Cathleen's, she said, 'Yer really love him, don't yer, lass?'

A softness came into Cathleen's eyes and Jessie had her answer. 'Yes, Grandma,' she murmured, 'with all my heart.'

'Aye, I can see that.' Squeezing Cathleen's hand, she said, 'Yer know how against it I was? Well now I've come to believe you two belong together, like you allus have. But yer still have Edward Fenshaw to deal with, and the truth is, if he or Lucy Fenshaw are dead set against their son putting a ring on yer finger, then that young man has to make some serious decisions. Either he weds you and loses favour with his family – and if he does that, it's likely he'll also lose any money that might have come his way . . .'

All of this, Cathleen had already realised, so she finished the sentence for her, '. . . Or he turns away from me?' Even the thought of it sent her heart to her boots.

Jessie nodded. 'Aye, it's as simple as that, lass. Unless o' course there's summat he's not telling yer?'

Cathleen didn't think so. 'We've never had secrets from each other.'

'Well, there's allus a first time.' Jessie had to say it. 'Yer so unsure about the note he sent, I reckon yer must already be thinking he's keeping secrets. Yer even said it yerself: "I feel he didn't tell me everything." Isn't that what yer said, lass?'

And, albeit reluctantly, Cathleen had to agree.

⟞•◦•⟝

OUTSIDE, HIDDEN FROM view, Silas waited. Through the open curtains he could see Cathleen and Jessie talking. Twice he began his way to the cottage, where he meant to stand by the window and attract Cathleen's attention. Twice he decided against it.

Standing there in the dark, he might frighten the two women. Besides, if Jessie saw him there she might call Cathleen's father from his bed, and there would have to be explanations. It was Cathleen he wanted to see, Cathleen who had a right to know what was going on. But, for now, she was out of his reach.

He waited a while longer, his stricken gaze focused on Cathleen's face, his heart aching to be with her. Yet the old woman showed no sign of leaving her alone so he could not make his move. Hopeful, he waited another half hour, then ten more minutes, and longer, until his body was chilled to the bone.

Disillusioned, he turned away, his heart heavy as he made his way home across the fields. 'Trust me, Cathleen,' he murmured. 'I promise I'll do all I can.'

A few hours' sleep, then he would be on his way to London, where his and Cathleen's fate would be sealed.

Chapter Five

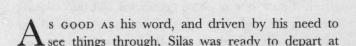

As good as his word, and driven by his need to see things through, Silas was ready to depart at four-thirty the next morning.

'My God, man, you look dreadful.' Having been called from his bed fifteen minutes earlier, Edward Fenshaw had availed himself of the smallest measure of whisky, which he now sipped thoughtfully while quietly regarding his son. He noticed the hollowed eyes and the look of despair, and knew he had done that to him. 'You look as if you haven't slept in a week!'

Glancing up from fastening his jacket, Silas regarded his father in the same way. 'That makes two of us, I think.'

Placing the glass of spirit on the dresser, the older man walked with Silas to the door. 'Safe journey,' he said, and wished he could go in his place.

With Cathleen on his mind, Silas was anxious to get away. 'The sooner I'm gone, the sooner I'll be back,' he told his father as he climbed into the waiting carriage.

Edward Fenshaw was anxious. 'Have you got the letters?'

Silas patted his breast pocket. 'I have them safe,' he said.

'Are you sure of the address of the most important one?'

'Trench Exporters. Main office. Sixteen, Baker Street.' It was etched in his brain. 'I'm to ask for Frederick Carstairs or, if he's not available, Mr Thomas Lawson.'

Smiling broadly, Edward Fenshaw shook his son's hand. 'Either one of those gentlemen will do.' Closing the door, he spoke through the carriage window. 'If *they* can't help me, nobody can.' At the last comment his smile faded. 'Good luck, my boy. I'm afraid it's all up to you now.' Stepping back, he put up his hand and watched the carriage roll away.

'Make for Fenshaw Cottage,' Silas told the driver, 'and cut through the back lanes.' He knew his father would be watching from the house, and didn't want him to see the carriage turn to the left off the main road.

'Right you are, sir.' Jack of all trades, master of none, Bill Trimble was getting on in years. He valued his work at Fenshaw House, so he minded his own business, and what he saw and heard never went beyond the four walls of his own room over the stables.

The lane was rough and, as always, the wheels of the carriage seemed to search out every rut and bump. 'Sorry, sir,' Bill called back to him, and Silas told him not to worry, but to take his time. 'Don't turn into the cottage,' he advised, 'stop some way down the lane and let me out.'

Finding a smooth area of land, Bill drew the ensemble to a halt. 'Here we are, sir,' he told Silas. 'The cottage is just beyond that hedge.' Pointing to a tall blackthorn hedge, he got down from his perch with the intention of opening the door for Silas. Silas, however, had never fussed over such trivialities and was already jumping to the ground. 'I'll only be a minute,' he said, and, quickening his steps, was soon down the lane and out of sight.

Going up to the two fine horses, Bill gave them each a bite of his apple. 'What a to-do, eh?' he mused. 'That poor young divil seems to have the world on his shoulders if you ask me. What with his mam on 'er last legs and his dad up to his neck in debt, I feel sorry for the lad. He's like his mam though, kind and considerate, with none of your fancy airs and graces. Treats a man like an equal he does, and that's why he's well liked hereabouts.'

Checking to make sure Silas wasn't on his way back, he leaned forward to confide in the nearest horse. 'They say Edward Fenshaw is close to bankruptcy, and I'm not surprised after buying that quarry land. Acre upon acre of huge great holes in the ground, and nothing worthwhile left to dig out 'cause it's all gone. Used up, finished and good for nothing. By! He must want his head tested, buying summat as nobody else would touch with a barge-pole.'

Tutting loudly, he took another bite from his apple and wiped the juice from his chin. 'So long as *I'm* not thrown out on me ear, that's all I care about, and that's why I have to watch me Ps and Qs with old man Fenshaw. At my age I wouldn't get no other work, that's for sure.'

Scratching his stubbly chin he wondered aloud, 'By! D'you know, I would never a' thought Edward Fenshaw were so gullible . . . paying good money on summat as is worth nothing at all. But then, ain't it true what they say. There's no fool like an old fool, eh? I mean, look at me. There's nowt I like better than watching the girls turn a pretty ankle down at the market. Meks me feel young again.'

Sighing longingly he gave a cheeky little chuckle. 'For all me whistling and winking, if one o' them pretty lasses were to tek a fancy to me . . . which is 'ighly unlikely . . . well, I'd not know what to do with meself. It's gone, you see . . . all gone, long since.' Laughing aloud, he declared happily, 'Still, I've managed to hang on to me own teeth, so at least I can enjoy a juicy apple. Here!' Thrusting the core forward he let the horse take it out of his hand. 'Teeth or not, I don't fancy crunching through no core.'

Taking a minute to wipe the slaver from his shirt, he stood on the steps of the carriage and peered over the hedge. 'He's been gone a long time,' he told the horse who pricked up its ears in anticipation of another juicy titbit. 'Ooh, hey up! Here he comes.' Wagging a finger he warned the animals, 'Not a word, else I'll tell the ostler not to give you any hay when we change you.'

Muttering as he clambered back on his perch, he

sighed, 'I expect he's been trying to catch a sight of his young woman. Poor bugger!' He was glad he wasn't young again. 'It ain't much fun being in love,' he murmured, ''specially when the world and his father seem to be agin you!'

Striding towards the carriage, Silas seemed a million miles away. Bitterly disappointed because he hadn't been able to see Cathleen, he climbed back inside. 'All right, Bill,' he said, 'it's London all the way. As quick as you can.'

———————————⋙•0•⋘———————————

IN THE COTTAGE, Jessie stayed by the window for a time. Waking early, she had seen Silas standing by the gate, and later had heard the carriage leave. Now she wondered if she'd done wrong in not getting Cathleen from her bed. 'Where will it end?' she wondered. 'Somebody's heart's bound to get broken, or my name's not Jessie Butler.'

She stared at the spot where Silas had stood, her mind going over the heartfelt conversation between herself and Cathleen last night. 'Funny,' she mused, 'how you can see a storm brewing a mile off, and there ain't a blessed thing you can do about it.'

Then, hearing Cathleen come down the stairs, she hurried to the stove, where she began breaking eggs into the frying pan. 'Yer father'll be down any minute,' she said. 'You sit yerself down.' She beckoned to the chair. 'Breakfast won't be two minutes.' Glancing down at

Cathleen's bare feet she chided, 'Where's yer shoes? Go an' put 'em on, afore yer get a chill . . . yer like a gypsy, so ye are, going barefoot at every opportunity.'

Yawning, Cathleen went to the window. 'What were you looking at?' she asked curiously. Just now, as she came into the room, she imagined Jessie looked guilty.

'I weren't looking at nuthin',' Jessie answered cagily.

'You must have been looking at *something*!' She peered through the window. 'Was it that fox again?' she asked. 'Dad said he was here yesterday. He reckons we'll have to cage the chickens tonight, in case that old devil goes on the rampage.' She looked at Jessie suspiciously. 'But it *can't* have been the fox you saw, because he only ever comes out at night.'

Breaking the last egg, Jessie wiped her hands on her pinnie. 'I told yer, I never saw nuthin'.' Tutting impatiently, she came to the window and stood beside Cathleen. 'Well, all right,' she confessed. 'Happen I *did* see somebody, I'm not sure. I expect it were some old vagabond looking for a free breakfast.' Embarrassed, she felt the colour run up her face. She wasn't a good liar at the best of times. 'Come away from the window, lass.'

One glance at her grandmother's face and Cathleen knew. 'It was Silas, wasn't it?' Excitement heightened her voice. 'Tell me the truth, Grandma . . . *Silas* was here, wasn't he?'

Realising she couldn't fool the girl, Jessie confessed, 'Aye, 'e were there, lass. He hung about for some time, just looking. He seemed worried like. I were sure he'd come up to the cottage, but he didn't. He stayed for a few minutes, and then off he went.' Tutting, she put her hands on her hips and, shaking her head, remarked, 'For the life o' me, I can't understand what he were doing out there at that time of a morning.'

Cathleen's heart leaped at the news. 'Why didn't you tell me?'

Jessie answered slowly, 'I didn't call yer 'cause I thought you were fast asleep, and what with being late to bed an' all, I just . . .' She faltered. 'I'm sorry, lass.'

Cathleen was frantic. To think Silas had been here and she hadn't even known. Why so early in the day, and why didn't he come up to the cottage? She had to see him, to put her mind at rest. 'Which way did he go?'

'That way, I reckon.' Pointing to the right of the cottage, Jessie recalled, 'He were in a carriage, wi' Bill Trimble driving. They went off in that direction. Going like the clappers, they were!'

She was only halfway through her sentence when Cathleen fled across the room and out the door. 'Cathleen, come back, lass! He's gone, I tell yer!' she called frantically.

But Cathleen didn't hear her. Barefoot, her hair flying in the wind, she ran across the fields, taking a short cut to the main road. 'Silas!' Her voice sailed through the air. 'Silas . . . *wait for me!*'

Away from the cottage, she could see the carriage in the distance. 'Silas!' Running until her heart was almost bursting, she sped along the ridge and down towards the road, her feet cut and bleeding from the rough bracken and stones beneath, but she didn't notice. The only pain she felt was the pain of having lost the man she loved, for she felt as if he was already gone from her. 'Silas, look round . . . *Please* look round.'

If he had, he might have seen her. But he was already out of her reach and for some inexplicable reason she felt afraid.

Reaching the road, she caught her last sight of the carriage as it swung away, round the wide bend. Exhausted, she fell against the bank to catch her breath. There was no point trying to keep up. From here the road went steeply up; the horses would take it in their powerful stride, but she had run as far as she could. She had no more strength left in her.

Looking down, she saw that her feet were covered in blood and scratches. And with the realisation came the pain. Knowing the brook was too far away, she squared her small shoulders and, with every step an agony, she began to make her way back to the cottage.

When Tom found her hobbling along the road, she was bent double in pain. 'Oh, lass!' Careering to a halt he jumped down from the wagon and ran to her. Lifting her effortlessly into his arms, he carried her to the cart. 'Whatever were you thinking of, running away barefoot like that?' he chided. 'Have you taken leave of your senses?'

'Silas came to the cottage,' she said. 'I needed to see him.'

'Is that so! And what was so urgent it couldn't wait?'

Setting her gently down on the seat he examined her

feet. 'Dear God, they're cut to ribbons.' Pointing to the storage area behind the bench, he drew her attention to a large hessian bag. 'Jessie made me bring your shoes, but from the look of your poor feet, you wouldn't even get them on.'

'They're not as bad as they look.' Though they hurt like the very devil, she would never admit it. Especially not when he was already annoyed with her.

'If you say so.' Clambering up beside her, his concern gave way to anger. 'Jessie had no right letting you run out like that! She might have known you'd no chance of catching up with the carriage. By! You'd need a fast horse and five minutes' start, and even then you'd be lucky.'

Cathleen knew he was right, but all she said was, 'Don't blame Grandma, it wasn't her fault. When she told me Silas had been there, all I could think was that I *had* to see him.' Now she was made to voice her fears aloud. 'I've a feeling he was there to tell me something bad.'

'I don't like the sound of that.' Giving her a worried glance, Tom demanded, 'I reckon you'd best tell me just what you mean.'

Cautious now, Cathleen evaded the question. 'Now I come to think about it, it couldn't have been all that important after all, could it?' she answered. 'Or he would have come up to the cottage, don't you think?'

'Hmh!' Shifting in his seat her father gave her another wary look. 'I'm sure I don't know *what* to think. You young 'uns are a complete mystery to me. First he turns up at the cottage, then he goes away without saying anything to anybody, and here's you, running your feet raw to catch up with him.'

'I needed to see him, that's all.' She daren't say too much, at least not until Silas came back and she knew how things had fared with his father.

'Aye, so you keep saying.' He had the reins in the air, ready to flick them onto the horse's rump, when he suddenly caught his breath, his eyes widening with horror. 'Jesus, Mary and Joseph!' Startled by his own thoughts, he dropped the reins and caught hold of her. 'I want the truth now, lass! That young bugger's not got you in trouble, has he? I mean you've not been . . .'

'NO!' Cathleen knew what he meant, and was torn by guilt. 'If I was in trouble . . . like *that* . . .' Remembering their time on the island, she felt her face burning, '. . . you know I would tell you.'

'Aye, an' I'd strip the skin off his back, so I would!'

'He's a good man.'

'He's *young*, that's what he is. Young and rich, and too far above your head for you to get any ideas about him.' Tom's mind was made up. 'I don't want him at the cottage any more. It might belong to him in the long run, but while I pay rent, *I* decide who visits and who doesn't, and I say he keeps clear of us. What's more, I forbid you to go anywhere near the Fenshaw place from now on!'

When she lowered her gaze, he persisted, 'D'you hear what I'm telling you, our Cathleen? You and that young man together spell trouble, and I'll not have it.'

Cathleen continued to keep her gaze downcast, and he gave her a sharp shaking. 'Look at me!' She raised her eyes and his heart plummeted at the sadness there, but after seeing how she had run after Silas Fenshaw without any thought for herself, he knew he had to stop it here and now. 'Did you hear what I'm telling you?'

'Yes, Father.' But she could not obey him. Not if it meant sacrificing a lifetime with Silas.

Seemingly satisfied, he nodded. 'Right, lass. So long as you know I'll be watching you like a hawk from now on.'

Silenced by his outburst, Cathleen settled back. After a moment she couldn't resist asking, 'The road back there – it goes to Preston, doesn't it?'

'Aye.' Tom didn't glance back. He was too preoccupied, training the cart wheels on the bumpy road ahead, and praying that his decision to ban young Fenshaw would not ruin his good relationship with this lovely daughter of his.

'After Preston where does it go?' Her emotions were calm now, but her determination as strong as ever.

'It goes to London, or so they tell me. I've never been that far meself, so I can't be sure.'

His answer did nothing to reassure her. What if Silas *had* gone to London? Why would he go all that way without telling her? Not for the first time that morning, Cathleen felt miserable and worried. And desperately alone.

'How are your feet now, lass?'

'All right.'

'I'm sorry I was harsh with you about young Fenshaw.'

Tom's voice hardened. 'But I take none of it back. I meant every word.'

Wisely, Cathleen led the subject in another direction. Apologising because he had had to come after her and miss his breakfast, she went on, 'I don't want you to be late on my account, so I'm glad we're going straight to the bakery. When we get there, I'll tend my feet with salt and warm water and they'll be good as new.'

He laughed. 'You sound just like Jessie. "Warm water and salt" is the answer to everything where she's concerned.'

'Well, she's never wrong, is she?'

'No, lass,' he admitted with a grin, 'she's never wrong.'

'So you're not to worry.'

'All the same, if they don't look no better after you've tended them, it's in the cart with you, and back to Jessie before you know it.'

When all was said and done, the lass hadn't come to any real harm though, he thought gratefully. 'Right! The road's levelling out now so we can shift on a bit.' At which he urged the horse faster. 'Let's be having your best, you old bugger,' he told the elderly cob. 'We've ovens to fire and bread to be turned out, and soon there'll be customers knocking at the shop door.'

Glancing sideways at his daughter, he saw how her wild, wavy fair hair was bushed out by the breeze, giving her the look of a small child. 'Jessie sent your clean work-apron,' he told her. 'And some other bits and pieces too . . . your hair-brush and such.' Glancing at her unruly hair he said, 'She's popped in a ribbon to tie that mop of hair back an' all. By! I swear you look like some wild thing outta the woods. And we don't want any stray hairs in the dough, do we?'

While Tom negotiated the way she brushed her hair and tied it back, and set about tidying herself up. Soon they were coming towards Blackburn town at a fine pace.

Normally, Cathleen enjoyed riding through the countryside, watching for the early morning creatures and waving with a smile to anyone who passed. But not today. Today her mind was with Silas. Her heart too.

Tom had his mind on Silas Fenshaw. After the events of this morning his eyes were open. What had been an innocent friendship between two youngsters had become a dangerous matter.

Sensing Cathleen's curious gaze on him, he turned to her. 'Comfortable are you, lass?' Glancing at her feet he was pleased to see the swelling already subsiding.

Cathleen merely nodded. She so much wanted him to accept her and Silas together, but now she knew he never would.

Tom, though, seemed to sense her thoughts, because now he was telling her, 'Look, lass, I've nothing *personal* against young Fenshaw. But he isn't right for you, and never will be. If you ask me, you'd do well to look amongst your own kind.'

Subdued by his comments, Cathleen said sadly, 'I expect Silas's father has already said the same to him.'

'It doesn't matter whether he has or he hasn't,

because *I'm* saying it to *you*, and as far as I'm concerned, that's an end to it.'

Glancing sideways, he saw her downcast face and his heart sank to his boots. 'You'll soon forget him. You're a good-looking lass.' He gave a half-hearted chuckle. 'Oh, I'm not saying you're perfect . . . far from it! You can be defiant and stubborn, and at times you have me at me wits' end.'

Pausing to smile on her, he softened his voice with affection. 'But you're a loyal little thing. You've a kind, loving heart and you're easy to be with. Ey, lass! You've no need to cast your net further than your own backyard. Not when there's a certain young spark who'd give everything just to walk down the street with you.'

Cathleen knew who he had in mind, 'You're talking about Lou Matheson, aren't you?'

'Aye, lass, I am.' Tom's grin was broad and proud. 'He sees the stars in your eyes and the moon in your smile, and whenever he has a word to say, it's allus about you.'

'Lou's a friend, and I do like him, you know that.' Cathleen had known Lou almost as long as she'd known Silas. 'But I don't love him . . . not in that way.'

'Happen you don't, and I'm sorry about that. Yet he's a fine bloke all the same,' Tom insisted. 'You'd not do better in my opinion. He works like a Trojan . . . up at the crack of dawn and still going strong when I've run outta steam and am itching to go home. Lou Matheson could run that bakery with his eyes shut, and not put a foot wrong. I'll tell you summat else an' all, he's ambitious. The lad has a mind to make himself a fortune. It wouldn't surprise me if there didn't come a day when he has a whole chain o' baker shops right across the country.'

'Oh, I'm sure he will.' Knowing Lou's capabilities, Cathleen could well believe it. 'I'm also sure he'll make some lucky woman a good husband one day. But it won't be me, I can tell you that.'

'An' are you sure about that, lass?'

'Never surer.'

'Then it's a great pity.' There was a determination about her that made Tom afraid.

He would have had just cause to be afraid if he could have read her thoughts, which were that, if she couldn't have Silas, she didn't want anybody.

'All I can say is, give yourself time an' you'll soon see him in a different light.'

'I don't think so, Father.'

'I see.' In fact, he didn't see at all. The truth was, he couldn't understand why she didn't snap up young Lou before another girl came along and did so. 'I'll tell you this though; you'll look long and hard for a partner, but you'll not find better than Lou Matheson.'

Knowing he meant well, Cathleen humoured him to a point. 'You don't have to convince me that he's got a kind heart,' she said, 'because I know it already. I also know he's ambitious, and I believe he'll do well.' She didn't want to hurt him, but couldn't see how it might be avoided. 'I'm sorry, Dad, but I don't see Lou as being anything other than a good friend.'

It was painfully obvious to Tom that Cathleen had set her sights on young Fenshaw. 'All the same, Lou's been a Godsend,' he persevered. 'If he hadn't befriended young Robert, there's no telling *where* the lad would have ended up.' Giving her a sly, sideways glance, he declared, 'He's been a real good influence on the lad, and I reckon we should *all* be grateful for that!'

The mention of her wayward brother came as a relief to Cathleen, not only because it took the spotlight off her, but because it also gave her a chance to change the subject. 'Robert didn't come home again last night,' she said. 'Did he tell you where he was going?' She didn't recall seeing him last evening, or this morning.

'He stayed at Lou's house,' Tom told her. 'I'm surprised Lou's mam hasn't sent me a bill for the food he eats. By! I've never seen a lad tuck away so much grub.' He grunted, his mood darkening. 'I only wish to God he had the same appetite for work!'

At once, Cathleen was on the defensive. 'Robert's not all bad.' Yet, like Jessie and her father, she worried about him.

'Mebbe not. But he'll be sixteen soon and still hasn't any idea what he wants outta life!' Tom had tried every which way to bring young Robert into the fold, but it was proving very difficult.

'He's still young, Dad.' There were times when she could strangle her brother for the heartache he caused, but she could never give up on him.

Tom's good humour was restored. 'Young, is it?' he chuckled. 'And I expect *you* consider yourself to be old?'

'*Older*, yes.'

He looked at her then, at the proud set of her pretty features, and he knew in his heart there was no comparison between her and her brother.

'Aye, you're right, lass,' he murmured. 'There might be three years an' such between you, but you've more common-sense and guts than he'll *ever* have! You've earned my respect, I'll tell you that, lass – aye, an' the respect of them as know you. What's more, the customers have nowt but good things to say about you. Tekken to you like ducks to water they 'ave. By! You do me proud. You've a quick mind and you're not afraid of hard work, an' I've allus been able to count on you for anything.' Snorting with disgust, he groaned, 'It'll be a fine day when I can say the same about that daft, lazy bugger!'

'Be patient, Dad,' she pleaded. 'He'll come to earn your respect before too long, you just wait.' Oh, and wouldn't it be wonderful if he did so, she thought.

'Well now, I've been giving it some serious consideration,' he mused. 'I reckon if I were to give him more responsibility, it might help him to grow up.' His voice quickened with anger. 'I'm telling you, lass, if he doesn't knuckle down soon, I'll not be able to control the young devil!'

'I think he might take to more responsibility,' Cathleen agreed. 'Besides, it'll help to keep him off the streets and away from bad company.'

'We shall have to see, won't we, eh?' Having an idea was one thing, he thought, putting it into practice was quite another.

For the last part of the journey, the two of them lapsed into silence. Tom's mind was on his rebellious son, while Cathleen's was on Silas. She wondered where he was at that very minute. Maybe he was only a few miles away, maybe he was far off, she had no way of knowing. Wherever he was, she would have gone to him, given the chance. Still, he would see her tonight, she was sure of it, and the thought made her heart leap.

When Tom stole a glance at her a moment later, he saw how she had leaned back in the seat, her eyes closed, her soft voice quietly humming a song. More than anything else in the world, he wanted her to be happy, and he believed she never could be with the likes of Silas Fenshaw.

Soon they were passing through Blackburn town centre, then on towards Ainsworth Street and into Penny Street where the bakery was situated.

'Morning, Tom!' The brewery wagon was out already, the two draymen perched high on the bench, one holding the reins, the other checking the delivery list for the day. As always, they looked smart in their flat caps and uniform. 'You're looking pretty as a picture,' the older one told Cathleen. 'I've a good mind to send me old missus packing and tek you instead.'

'Hey!' Tom called back light-heartedly. 'Watch your tongue, Amos Tanner, or I'll let your missus know what an old bugger she's got for an 'usband!'

Close by, the milkman overheard and laughed out loud. 'I think you'll find she already knows!'

Tom and Cathleen joined in the ensuing laughter,

their cares forgotten for a moment. Somewhere along the journey, Cathleen had convinced herself that, later that evening, Silas was sure to seek her out. She felt content, eager to start work, and as always the sight of the old bakery raised her spirits.

It was a grand old building. Two storeys high, with numerous small windows, it was set in a cobbled yard. The yard was enclosed by four low walls, and the whole property secured at the pavement by a pair of high, black iron gates. Like the gates, the warehouse was past its best; 'It'll last another two hundred years, though,' Tom would say, and Cathleen was inclined to believe him.

'Look at that.' Tom gestured to the entrance. 'The gates are open. Looks like Lou's already here. Got the ovens up and running as well, I shouldn't wonder.'

As he manoeuvred the cart through the gates, Tom called her attention to the young man crossing the yard; of sturdy build, with fair hair and kind brown eyes, Lou Matheson was almost bent double beneath two great sacks of flour.

At the sight of Cathleen, his face lit up. Quickening his steps through the bakehouse door, he hurriedly offloaded his burden and was out again before the cart even came to a halt.

'Morning, Cathleen.' Lou had always addressed her by her first name, and Tom had never seen just cause to correct him. 'You look bonny.' His admiring eyes swept over her.

'Away with you!' Cathleen was used to his flattering comments, because didn't he have a different one for every occasion? 'I'm windswept, red in the face and my feet look like two lumps of half-baked dough.'

It was only when Tom hurried to lift her down from the cart, that Lou noticed her sore feet. 'Whatever have you been up to?' he asked, concern written all over his homely features. 'And where's your shoes?'

Tom came to her rescue. 'Stop naggin' the lass,' he chided. 'Put the pan on, and see if you can find that big enamel washing-up bowl. Part-fill it with hot water and top it up with cold. Oh, an' you'd best put a scoop o' salt in the water an' all.'

While Lou hurried away, Tom carried Cathleen to the office. 'You don't have to carry me, Dad!' Embarrassed in front of Lou, she protested, 'I *can* walk, if you'll let me!'

Ignoring her protests, Tom put her down on the black horse-hair sofa. 'Stay where you are.' He wagged a finger at her. 'You're not to move until your feet are bathed and you can get your shoes on.'

'All right,' she conceded. 'But there's no need for you to stay with me. There's nothing wrong with my feet that a few minutes' soaking won't put right.' Suddenly uncomfortable, she began shifting about on the sofa.

'Hurting you, are they, lass?'

'No, Dad, and stop fussing! It's this awful sofa,' she complained. 'The horse hairs are pricking my bare legs.'

'Oh, so it's *that* again, is it?' Rolling his eyes to heaven, he recalled her having something to say about the sofa every time she sat on it. 'You've never liked that sofa, have you? It's comfortable enough for me, though,' he declared. 'And what's more, I gave two bob for it from the sale rooms, and I still haven't had my money's worth. So if you're after me getting rid of it, you can think again. I am *not* selling a good sofa, and that's an end to it.'

'You can afford a *proper* one now,' she coaxed. 'One with soft cushions and springs that don't attack you every time you move.'

Deliberately ignoring her, he called out for Lou. 'Where the devil are you with that water!' Whereupon Lou came rushing through the door, bowl in hands and a frantic look on his face.

'About time too!' By now, Tom was not in the best of moods. 'Set it down there.' Pointing to the floor directly beneath Cathleen's feet, he waited until Lou had set the bowl down. 'Make sure it's not too hot afore you put your feet in it,' he warned Cathleen. 'I'll go and get you a towel. Then me and Lou will have to leave you to it, while we get on with the day's work.'

As he knelt to place the bowl by her feet, Cathleen caught Lou's uplifted gaze. With a smile she thanked him. 'You can go now, the two of you.' She turned to her father. 'I'm more than capable of taking care of myself.'

'Women!' Shaking his head, Tom went off for the towel, while Lou remained at her feet a moment longer.

'They look bad,' he said, tenderly cupping his hands round her two feet. In a quiet, serious voice, he asked, 'How did you do this?'

'I was running.'

'With no shoes on?' He had seen how the soles of her feet were cut and bruised, and his suspicions were roused.

Realising he meant to wrestle the truth from her, Cathleen was wary. 'Don't ask too many questions, Lou Matheson!' she chided. 'Thank you for your help, but I can manage now.' To prove her point, she wiggled one toe in the water and, seeing how it was lukewarm, slithered both feet in with a huge sigh of relief.

Lou was in no hurry to leave. Instead, he kept his hands gentle about her feet, his senses excited by the sight of her flesh.

Made restless by his touch, Cathleen suggested, 'You'd best go.'

Instead, he ran his hand over her ankle and on towards her calf, his loving gaze never leaving her face, his voice soft and persuasive. 'You were running through the bracken, weren't you? What were you chasing, Cathleen? *Who* were you chasing?' he asked pointedly. The smile left his face. 'Was it *him*?'

Snatching her feet from his grip, she winced with pain.

At once he was mortified. 'Oh, I'm sorry! I didn't mean to hurt you, I was just . . .' He hung his head. 'I was plain jealous, that's all.'

Angry now, Cathleen scowled at him. 'You've no right!'

'I know.' His smile was boyishly appealing. 'Forgive me?'

Turning her face away, she told him impatiently, 'You'd best get back to work.'

At that moment, Tom returned. 'You're a wild and wilful creature, and should be kept in a cage!' he told her good-humouredly. 'And you're right to send Lou back to his work.'

Both Cathleen and Lou regarded him with concern, unsure whether or not he had witnessed the scene between them.

Dropping the towel and her shoes onto the sofa, he told Lou, 'Come on then, leave her to it. If she's no more sense than to go running barefoot on the hard ground, she doesn't deserve to be cosseted.' As he went to leave he gave Cathleen a sly little wink. 'Soonever you think you're ready for work, lass. The wagon will be loaded for off, and Robert alongside to give you a hand.'

'Ten minutes,' she answered, 'and I'll be ready to do the rounds.'

Lou didn't look back, but then she didn't expect him to. Recalling how sorry he was, she chuckled to herself. 'Poor Lou! Can't blame him for trying.'

Once they'd gone, she sat forward on the sofa, wiggling her feet and splashing the salty water over the cuts and scratches. 'It's all your fault, Silas Fenshaw!' she said fondly. 'If only you'd have come up to the cottage.' It still puzzled her.

After a few minutes of bathing her feet in the salty water, the soreness eased and the skin was less angry. She leaned back and let them soak for a while, before lifting them out one at a time and blotting them dry with the towel. Next she tried on her shoes. At first they felt tight, but once she had them laced up, they were only slightly uncomfortable. 'Come on now, lass!' Mimicking Jessie, she sounded just like her. 'You'll not die from sore feet!' A few wary steps across the floor confirmed it.

Out in the yard, Tom was making the cart ready for the rounds. Lou was inside the bakehouse, taking trays of bread out of the oven. 'Stack them near the door,' he told Robert, a slightly-built lad with dark hair and sullen green eyes.

Carrying the trays to the door he stacked them where Lou had instructed. 'You like our Cathleen, don't you?' he asked slyly.

Swinging round with another tray, Lou answered guardedly, 'You know I do.'

Taking the second tray, Robert carried it to the door where he stacked it on top of the other one. 'But she don't like you, does she?'

This time Lou glared at him. 'And what would *you* know about it?'

'You'd like to wed her, wouldn't you?' There was a kind of wonder in his voice.

'Yes, and I will too.' Pausing in his work, Lou thought of Cathleen, her soft skin and those full, pink lips, and his appetite was whetted.

'You ain't got a cat's chance in hell. Not when she's got her sights set on Silas Fenshaw.'

Lou smiled at that. 'Your faither will never let him near her!'

'Oh? And d'you reckon he'll let *you* near her?'

'Why shouldn't he? I'm clean and presentable, aren't I? I've allus been hard-working, and one day I mean to have my own business.' His voice softened. 'On top of that, nobody could love your sister like I love her.'

'Silas Fenshaw does.' Enjoying the banter, Robert goaded, 'He's *allus* loved her.'

'He ain't her type. Give her time and she'll find that out.'

'Let's hope she don't "find out" about you.'

'What the devil d'you mean?' Enraged Lou went across the room at a run to grab Robert by the scruff of the neck. Dragging him into the shadows, he pushed his face close to the boy's. 'You little snot!' Eyes bulging and voice trembling, he warned, 'You'd best shut your trap, else I might tell your faither what you've been up to.'

Robert made a feeble attempt to push him away, 'I ain't been up to nuthin'!'

'Oh no?' Smiling now, he gave the boy a shaking. 'Hiving off twenty loaves a day, with barmcakes and muffins into the bargain ... got a nice little earner going there, ain't you?' Through the window he saw Tom approaching, and quickly let go of the boy. Eyeing him warily, he hissed, 'Remember what I said! Keep your trap shut or I swear to God I'll have to tell him how you've been robbing him while his back's turned.'

'You wouldn't dare. Because if you did, I might be forced to tell Cathleen about them other women ... them as come to you every week with money they've earned on the streets.' Knowing he had him on the run, he grinned wickedly. 'Silas Fenshaw or no Silas Fenshaw, she'd not look at you twice if she knew that.'

Under threat of betrayal, Lou had a choice. He

could either shut the kid up by fair means or foul. Or he could play along with him. 'Look, kid, we're friends, aren't we?'

'Not if you tell my dad about me stealing from him.' Not only would he get a leathering, he would lose a good little income that Tom knew nothing about.

''Course I won't tell him! We understand each other, you and me. A man's got to make his business where he finds it. The girls do what they do, and I put a customer their way now and then.' He winked. 'Nowt wrong with that, is there?'

The boy didn't answer because Tom was at the doorway. 'Right!' He looked from one to the other. 'You, Robert, finish loading the trays onto the cart. Cathleen's all ready for leaving. You're to go with her – and don't let her do any running round.' When he hesitated, Tom raised his voice. 'Go on, lad. Move yourself!'

When Robert was gone from the bakehouse, he instructed, 'Lou, open the shop, will you? There's customers waiting. I'll get the new batch of dough in and then I'll give you a hand.'

They always followed a tried and tested routine; load up the cart with newly baked goodies, covered over with upside-down trays and big white muslin cloths, then open the shop for the locals and, once they were satisfied, clean out the ovens ready for the next batch of baking.

Hearing the cart draw away, he went to the door and looked out. 'Mind you sell the lot,' he called, laughing aloud when Cathleen promised there wouldn't be a crumb left on the cart when they got back. 'That's what

I like to hear,' he told her. 'Now be off with you. Time's money!'

Swinging round, he was surprised to see Lou craning his neck to see her. 'She's a bonny lass, your daughter,' Lou told him.

Tom winked. 'Aye, she'd mek some lucky man a bonny wife an' all.'

'I'd be right proud if she were *my* wife.' Another time he would never have been so bold, but wanting made a man desperate.

Tom said something then that set him thinking. 'I don't mind telling you, son, if she were to smile on *you*, I'd throw my cap up in the air, so I would.' He then gave Lou a friendly slap on the shoulder and, whistling merrily, went about his work.

Behind him, Lou was flushed with pleasure. 'Now that I've got her faither on my side, who knows?' He sneaked a look at Cathleen as she guided the cart skilfully on to the street. 'Well, my beauty,' he murmured, 'it seems I might just have a chance at you after all.'

Chapter Six

THE MINUTE HE set foot in the office, Silas knew he would not find a friend here. The other man *appeared* glad to see him; his quick, ready smile and charming manner, together with the concerned way in which he asked after Silas's father, were all meant to convey an interest.

Silas, however, found the true signs easy to read; the smile that didn't quite reach the eyes; the weak handshake; and the way the other man hurried to sit behind his desk, as though putting a barrier between them.

There followed a long, uncomfortable moment when each quietly regarded the other, the big man looking at Silas and thinking what a handsome young man he was, and how much stronger in character than his father.

Beneath the man's probing eyes, Silas kept a steady gaze. He didn't flinch or look away. Instead, he waited, knowing he was bound to leave this office empty-handed, yet prepared to do all he could to rescue his father and, in turn, find a solution to his own terrible dilemma. Loving

Cathleen, wanting her always near was uppermost in his mind every waking minute.

Taking a cigar from his waistcoat pocket, the big man bit off one end and lit the other with a match taken from a box on the desk. Another aggravating moment while he savoured the taste, then a smile at Silas, while he stretched out in the chair, his frame swamping the cushion beneath him. 'Right then, state your case,' he instructed. 'You haven't come calling for the good of your health.'

Silas took a deep breath, while discreetly surveying the other man; he was not a pretty picture by any means. Frederick Carstairs was huge of stature, with piercing blue eyes, a fearsome beard and a nature to match. He admired success and frowned on failure. Silas had come to see him only because he knew his father and Carstairs had done much business together in the past and Edward believed that this man owed him a favour.

'I'm here on behalf of my father,' he began.

'You don't need to explain why you're here.' He seemed to look right through Silas. 'I know all about your father's unfortunate circumstances, but I don't know yet what it is you want from me.'

Silas could hardly believe it. 'News travels fast, it seems.'

'I'm afraid so. Especially *bad* news.'

'If you know all about it, you must also know why I'm here.'

'I thought as much.' The smile was arrogant, the voice condemning. 'He's been stupid enough to get himself into hot water, and now you want *me* to bail him out, am I right?'

Embarrassed by his shameful errand, Silas's hackles rose in defence. 'My father is painfully aware of the situation he finds himself in. Fortunately, he considers himself to have friends who might help.'

'And as he considers me amongst these "friends", he sent you here to ask me for money, is that it?'

'No, sir. That was *my* idea. I know that you and my father worked together for many years. I also know he helped you to start trading, when everyone else joined forces to keep you out.'

'And do you think your father made me what I am . . . is that what you're saying?'

'Every man needs that first helping hand, and my father gave you yours.'

'My God!' The big man's laughter shook the room, then he was yelling, 'Do you realise what you're saying, you young pup? I'm a wealthy man, with more money than you or your father will ever see in your lives. I have trading partners all over the globe . . . huge warehouses filled with merchandise ready to be shipped to the far corners of the earth. I employ two hundred men and control many more.' Dropping his voice to a menacing whisper, he gave Silas a shrivelling look. 'And you dare to imagine all that came about because he allowed me to use his grubby little office?'

When he stood up, as he did now, Frederick Carstairs was formidable. 'I paid your father for the privilege of working in that cramped dungeon he called an office!

I paid for every consignment that went through his premises, and he made sure he took a handsome share of the commission. The truth is, he saw in me a serious rival. He knew it was only a matter of time before I set up on my own and gave him a run for his money.'

Enraged, Silas held his fists tight by his side, desperate to resist the temptation to smack that grinning face. 'My father was never afraid of competition!'

'He was afraid of *me*. He took me in so he could keep an eye on what I was doing. It wasn't a generous gesture, it was shrewd and clever, and I might have done the same, given the circumstances. But he gave me nothing for free. Nobody did! I'm my own man . . . always have been. I don't owe them *anything*. Not your father, not anybody!' Spent of rage, the big man fell into the chair. 'Now get out!'

'When I've had my say.' Standing tall, his dark eyes blazing, Silas's voice was calm. 'It's common practice to pay rent for the office you use, and he would have been a poor businessman if he hadn't taken a commission for the goods that passed through his establishment. But I don't have to tell you all that, because you already know it.'

His voice hardened. 'You have every right to refuse him now. But you have *no* right to belittle the kindness he showed you all those years ago. Whichever way you say it, he was a friend when you needed one.' His smile was deadly. 'But then you wouldn't know about friendship, would you?'

He paused to let his words sink in. 'What's more, if

I should hear that you've been spreading his business to all and sundry, you will answer to me.'

'Are you threatening me?' Red in the face, the big man scrambled to the door and wrenched it open. 'Get out of here, damn you! Before I forget myself and do something I might live to regret.'

As he went to leave, Silas turned back. 'You know, from a distance you're a big man with a fearsome reputation, but close up . . .' He shook his head. 'You're just a little man after all.'

Out in the hallway he heard the door slam behind him. Taking out his pocket-book, he drew a line through Carstairs's name. 'One down, two to go,' he muttered, and ran down the steps, eager to be done; eager to be home with Cathleen. He glanced at the church clock, 'Three o'clock.' There was time yet, he thought.

One man had turned him down. But hope was not lost.

<hr />

B Y FIVE O'CLOCK, however, all hope was gone. He had fared no better with the other two businessmen than he did with the first. 'I only wish I could help,' one had said, 'but I have too many commitments of my own.'

The other was more truthful. 'Your father got himself into this mess . . . he'll have to get himself out. I want no part of it. You tell him that, and tell him he's been a bloody fool!'

Bill Trimble was never far away with the carriage, and when he saw Silas making his way down the steps from the last office he noted the stoop of his shoulders and the look of devastation on his face. 'Summat's gone badly wrong,' he muttered. Though he had an idea what this errand was all about, he didn't know the full extent of it. Nor did he want to.

Climbing into the carriage, Silas saw how tired the old fella looked. 'Sorry, Bill,' he apologised, 'it's been a long day, and I've sadly neglected you.'

Weary though he was, Bill would hear none of it. 'Think nothing of it, sir,' he answered kindly. 'I expect you've had a lot on your mind.'

'Are you hungry?'

'Ravenous, sir,' he admitted, 'but I can wait.'

'You'll do no such thing.' Knowing his age, and realising with a shock how long Bill had waited about for him, Silas put his own troubles aside for the moment. 'Let's go and find an inn,' he said. 'We'll fill our bellies with beef and ale before we start the long drive home.'

'Not too much of the ale, I'm thinking,' Bill chuckled. 'We don't want to end up in the nearest ditch.'

The inn they found wasn't too far away; two streets in fact, straddling the corner and looking as welcoming as Bill had ever seen. 'By! Me throat's parched as a watchman's brazier,' he said, licking his lips. 'I must admit, sir, a jar o' best ale will go down a real old treat, so it will.'

Inside the inn it was warm and cosy, with a fire roaring up the chimney despite the July day and a group of merry men singing out of tune. 'Don't mind them,' laughed the fat landlord. 'Another half-hour and they'll be too drunk to stand up, never mind sing.' He took their order and went away, chuckling.

When the ale and bully-beef was served, Bill tucked in, but Silas seemed miles away. 'If you don't mind me saying, you'll feel a lot better if you eat that.' The old fella pointed to the plate of food. 'It won't do no good, you shoving it round the plate with a fork.' Lowering his voice, he confided, 'I've allus found my troubles didn't seem half so bad with a good meal inside me.'

Surprised, Silas looked up. 'Is it *that* obvious?'

Tearing a chunk of bread off with his teeth, Bill nodded. 'I've had my own share o' troubles, sir, and I know the signs. This morning there was a light in your eyes and now it's gone. Got dimmer as the day went by, it did.'

'Tell me something, Bill.'

'Ask away.'

'Do you know what's going on – at Fenshaw House, I mean?'

Knowing his place, Bill grew wary. 'In what way d'you mean, sir?'

Silas had never seen himself as any different or more important than his fellow beings, and it showed now in his reassuring smile. 'You know what I'm saying, Bill. You know what's going on, don't you? With my father, I mean.' Sensing the man's reluctance, he told him, 'Look, Bill, we're away from it all here. I want us to talk, man to man. Nobody else will ever know what's been said between us.'

'I understand, sir.' Trusting him implicitly, Bill confessed, 'There have been rumours. As a rule I don't pay no mind to rumours of any kind, but . . .' Wrapping his two fists round his jar of ale, he made no attempt to raise it to his mouth. Instead he fidgeted uncomfortably.

'Go on, Bill,' Silas urged. 'Tell me.'

'Well, I'm sorry to say it, but I know there's a measure o' truth in this partic'lar rumour because I were in the garden the other day when the master and his business partner, Mr Turner, were having the most fearful row.' Blowing out his flabby cheeks, he gave a little whistle. 'Going at it hammer an' tongs they were. By! It were fearful, sir. I've never heard the like.'

In a strange way, Silas was relieved. 'How much did you hear?'

Wishing he'd kept his mouth shut, Bill took a great swig of his ale. 'I'm sorry sir,' he said, wiping the froth from his moustache. 'It's none of my business, and I swear to God nobody will hear none of it from me.'

'Bill!' Leaning forward, Silas persisted, 'Listen to me.'

'Yes, sir?'

'Tell me *exactly* what you heard.'

'I'd rather not, sir.'

'Did you hear that my father and his business partner had split up?'

'Aye, that's what I heard, and I don't mind telling you, I were very sorry.'

'So you must know the reason for it?'

After three long deep gulps of his ale, Bill was beginning to lose his guard. 'From what I recall, your father bought some land while his partner were away drumming up business. The land cost a pretty penny, so I understood, but it turned out to be worthless. When Mr Turner got back from his trek there was hell to pay!' Closing his mouth round a chunk of beef, he smacked his lips and winked at Silas. 'That's the measure of what I heard, sir. But you needn't worry, 'cause my lips are sealed.' And he promptly opened them again for another drink of the amber liquid.

'Bill?'

'Yes, sir?'

'Is that *all* you heard?'

The old groom cast his mind back. 'Aye,' he nodded his head. 'That's all.' Horrified, he was struck by a sudden thought. 'By!' Staring at Silas wide-eyed, he asked in stumbling tones, 'Gawd Almighty! Is he having to cut back? Is he planning to get rid of me, is that it? Is that why we're talking, you and me?'

'No, of course not!' Anxious to allay his fears, Silas explained, 'It has nothing to do with cutting back, or getting rid of you,' he said. 'It's more to do with *me*.'

The fear gradually ebbed from Bill Trimble's eyes. 'By! You had me worried there for a minute. I don't know what I'd do if I didn't have my work, and who would want an old bugger like me, eh?'

'That's one thing you need never worry about.' Reaching out, Silas grabbed the man's shoulder, telling him kindly, 'There'll always be work for you with a Fenshaw . . . whether it be with me or my father. And that's a promise.'

'Bless you, sir, 'cause you've put an old man's mind at rest.' To celebrate he raised his jar and emptied the dregs. When he replaced it on the table, he looked at Silas with curiosity. 'You said it had to do with *you*,' he recalled. 'I know it's none of my business, but I've watched you grow up from a likeable young lad to a man I could trust. So, if there's summat troubling you, and that being the reason for us sitting here when we should be on our way home, then I'd be proud to help, if I can?'

Thanking him, Silas gave a half-smile. 'I *am* troubled,' he quietly confessed. 'More than I've ever been at any time in my life. The truth is, Bill, there's nobody who can help me now.'

Looking up at the old fella, he saw the wrinkled face and the eyes that betrayed goodness and honesty, and he knew he had a friend he could open his heart to. 'When we set out today, I had high hopes that everything would come all right, but as you shrewdly noticed, the hope dimmed as the day went on, and now there's nothing else I can do.'

Bill knew there had been something gnawing at Silas, and now he could only guess at the enormity of it. 'Surely to God it can't be all that bad,' he said encouragingly. 'In my long experience there's a solution to every puzzle.'

Silas gave a sad, wry smile. 'Oh, there's a solution all right,' he answered. 'But it's a wicked thing, and one that will wreck two lives from the outset.'

Studying Silas's face for a minute, Bill noticed how those naturally smiling eyes were now hollowed with sadness, and his heart went out to him. 'Look, son, you've come this far, so tell me everything, why don't you?' Having drunk a pint of good ale and warmed to the troubles of this young man of whom he was very fond, Bill forgot that he was the servant and Silas the master, and spoke to him as he might speak to his own grandson. 'Sometimes an old head is wiser than a younger one. Why don't you trust me with the full story, and we'll see what can be done, eh? What d'you say?'

As briefly as possible, Silas told him everything. He confirmed the rumours Bill had already heard, and the conversation he had witnessed between the two men involved. He explained how, by demanding immediate return of monies owed, together with due interest and compensation, Turner had it in his power to destroy his father. Moreover, if his father took it into his head to fight Turner in court, the outcome could not be guaranteed, and if it went badly for him, not only would he still have to meet Turner's demands, he would have to settle the ensuing crippling court costs into the bargain.

'The worst thing of all,' he concluded, 'is that my mother would never get over the shock of it. Her health is frail, as you know, and only last night she suffered a collapse. Everything she treasures would be lost.' He paused, his mind and heart in chaos. Cathleen or his mother; which one must he hurt?

Raising his eyes, he looked at the old man. 'My mother's life is in that house. It's in the paintings and the furniture. It's woven into the very fabric of the walls. If it was all snatched away, it would be the end of her.' Dropping his gaze he spoke so quietly, his voice was almost inaudible. 'What sort of son would I be if I let that happen? How could I do that to her?'

Throughout Silas's outpouring, Bill Trimble listened with increasing horror. 'As God's my judge, I had no idea!' he exclaimed. 'But I don't understand why you're laying blame on yourself. It weren't *you* as brought all this down on your heads.'

'No, but I can put a stop to it whenever I like. The debt would be wiped out, Father would be released from any threat, and Mother would never know of it. Turner would agree to all this, but first I have to say the word.'

Intrigued, Bill asked, 'What word is that, son?'

Silas quietly explained. 'The word is "yes". You see, Bill, Turner has promised to suffer his losses silently – but only *if I agree to marry his daughter*.'

'What!' The old man was visibly shocked. 'That's like selling yourself – unthinkable!'

'Unthinkable or not, there's no other way out.' Pushing his untouched food aside, Silas sat back in his chair. 'So you see, I'm trapped,' he murmured, 'hopelessly trapped.'

'And have you no feelings for Turner's girl?'

'Huh!' Silas's expression hardened. 'Oh yes, I have feelings all right,' he said. 'Feelings of hatred and disgust. Feelings that if I'm made to marry her, I might end up throttling her.'

'Have you spoken to her?'

'It wouldn't do any good. I went to see her father and he told me as much. He enjoyed it too, telling me how she'd set her heart on a husband, and I'm it. If you ask me, he just wants rid of her. He's stuck with a vicious bitch and now he wants somebody else to take over the responsibility.' He gave a small, mirthless laugh. 'I have a choice, that's what he said, and it's this: either I marry Helen Turner or my parents are thrown to the wolves.'

'By! What sort of a man is he to do such a terrible thing?'

'Desperate, that's what he is. Desperate to get his daughter out of his life and into mine.'

Shaken by the animosity of Silas's remark, the old man felt out of his depth. 'It's monstrous. Blackmail of the worst kind!' Flattening the palms of his hands he wiped them over his face. Silas seemed in the depths of despair. 'Look son,' he said, gently tweaking the sleeve of his jacket, 'you know I want to help you. But the top and bottom of it is . . . I don't know how. Sadly, I'm past my prime or I'd beat the living daylights outta the heartless bugger. By! I'd make him see sense, I can promise you that. And if I had money enough you'd be welcome to it, so you would. But I've never had money . . . never wanted it neither. As far as I can see, it brings its own troubles. No, I've been content living at Fenshaw House, with enough for my needs, a bit o' baccy for my pipe, and a warm fire to curl up to. That's all I've ever wanted.'

Deeply impressed, Silas regarded him with admiration. 'I saw three men today,' he told him. 'Three very powerful men who, in some way or another, my father has helped over the years. Today the tide turned and I went to them, cap in hand, ready to beg for their help. But they turned me away.' Dropping his gaze, he slowly shook his head. 'Every manjack of them has more money than he knows what to do with, but not one would put his hand in his pocket for my father. Then there's you, Bill, living hand to mouth with no money put by for your old age, and nothing much to call your own, and yet here you are, ready to do whatever you can to help.'

Pausing a moment, he gestured for the landlord to bring two fresh pints of ale, and when they were on the table, he raised his glass. 'Here's to you, Bill,' he said, taking a long, deep drink. 'And I'll tell you what, my friend. You're a better man than I've seen today, and a better man than I'm likely to see in a long time to come.'

Chinking his glass with Silas's, the old man replied softly, 'Thank you, son. That's a grand thing to say. And here's hoping everything will come out for the best.' He winked, a cheeky, cheery wink that made Silas smile. 'Sometimes, when you least expect it, life has a funny way of turning things about.'

They drank the toast and sat together in silence, reflecting on what had been said, and what must be done. After a while, Bill asked in a quiet voice, 'What about the lovely Cathleen?'

When Silas didn't answer, but stared into his jar of ale, the old fella leaned across to put his hand over Silas's fist. 'I'm sorry, son,' he murmured. 'You love the lass, don't you?'

Now, when Silas looked up, his eyes were dull with pain. 'More than you'll ever know,' he answered. Then, pushing aside both his drink and his emotions, he said,

'We'd best get on the road. We've a long way to go. You did tell the stablemen we need the fresh horses tonight?'

'Course I did, son,' Bill assured him.

As they got up from their seats, Silas dug into his coat pocket and drew out two silver coins; throwing them onto the bar he thanked the landlord for his good ale. While he was doing this, Bill made his way to the gents. 'I can't hold my ale like I used to,' he chuckled. 'But you go on, son. I'll catch up with you in no time.'

Neither of them paid much attention to the two ruffians seated at a nearby table.

'Did you see the cut of his jacket?' the younger one asked his bearded mate.

'I did.' He grinned, a wide open grin that showed off his blackened teeth. 'I'll tell you something else an' all,' he said, tapping the side of his nose. 'Just then, when he drew back the edge of his jacket, I spied a bulging little wallet, just waiting to be plucked.'

'Right! Let's be about it then!'

Swallowing the rest of their ale, they bade the landlord goodnight and slunk out, smiling at each other, the thought of that bulging wallet uppermost in their minds.

'Them two are up to no good, I'll be bound.' The landlord had seen their kind before. 'Mind you, so long as they settle their arguments outside these premises, what they do is no concern of mine.'

Making his way back to the carriage, Silas took a short cut through an alley. Deep in thought as he walked the few hundred yards, and taking his time in order to let the old fella catch up, Silas heard a sound. Believing it must be Bill, he turned to speak. Like shadows in the night, the two thieves were on him.

Taking him unawares, they wrestled him to the wall; the heavy, bearded man pinned his arms behind his back while the other frantically rifled through his pockets. Quickly finding the wallet he held it aloft. 'That's it, matey!' Flicking it open he licked his lips at the thought of spending the money within. 'This'll see us right for a day or two,' he laughed. As he looked at Silas, the smile slid away and in its place came a look of hatred. Tugging at Silas's jacket, he sneered, 'Maybe we should strip him of his fancy clobber, eh?' he asked his partner. 'Fetch a bob or two, these will.'

The big man stood back and grinned. 'And why not teach the bugger a lesson afore we go? A lesson he'll not forget in a hurry.'

'Now that's a good idea. I mean, we can't leave him to raise the alarm, can we now?' The other man continued to glare at Silas, who stood tall against the wall, his brain calculating the strength of the opposition, but his quiet face expressionless as he looked into the man's eyes. 'My mate here wants to tear you apart.' The ruffian's bad breath wafted over Silas, making him want to puke. 'Tear you apart and feed you to the dogs! What d'you think to that, eh?' He laughed insanely. 'Huh! You ain't got much to say, 'ave you? Cat got your tongue, 'as it, Lord Snooty?'

The bearded man cackled at that, and while the two of them were enjoying the joke, Silas made his move.

Fetching his knee up, he rammed it into the small man's groin. After that everything happened at once; the man reeled back and doubled up, groaning in agony and clutching his private parts, while the bearded man caught hold of Silas by the throat and, drawing his fist back, prepared to slam it into Silas's face. But he didn't get the chance, because with a speed that took the other man by surprise Silas caught him a hard blow to the head. The big man retaliated by slamming his whole weight into Silas, at the same time screaming like a banshee. Silas was sent crashing against the wall with such force that it split open his temple, sending a spray of blood down his face and into his eyes, quickly clouding his vision and giving the big man an opportunity to land a mighty blow to his stomach.

Momentarily dazed, Silas struggled to keep his balance, and soon the two of them were battling it out; it was a hard and vicious fist-fight, but Silas eventually came out on top, bloodied but triumphant. The two men took to their heels, speeding away through the alley and out of sight. They still had his wallet, but somehow that didn't seem to matter any more.

Bill had heard the commotion and came running. 'I'm all right,' Silas assured him. 'You recall the two rough looking men in the pub?' When Bill nodded, he explained, 'I'm afraid they must have caught sight of my wallet when I paid the landlord.'

'Waylaid you did they, the thieving bastards?'

Silas nodded. 'They got the wallet,' he said, then grinned. 'But not without a bit of a struggle.'

'I can see that, son.'

Taking stock of Silas's bloodied face and the raw, skinned knuckles, he knew there had been more than 'a bit of a struggle'. 'I can't take you home like that,' he said. 'Let's get you back to the washroom and clean you up a bit, eh?'

'No.' Silas was adamant. 'We've wasted enough time. Let's away home.'

'As you say, sir. But look, I've some old cleaning cloths up front of the carriage,' Bill told him, 'and I allus keep a bucket o' water for the horses. What say we make use of them?'

Silas could find no argument against that. 'Come on then,' he agreed. 'Let's be off, before some other rogue takes a fancy to the carriage and horses.'

Tutting and complaining about 'thievin' London swines who want stringing up,' Bill Trimble walked back to the carriage, where he promptly searched out a bundle of rags. Dipping one of them into the bucket of water, he handed it to Silas, 'And no argument!' he warned. ''Cause I ain't tekkin' you home lookin' like some old tramp off the streets.'

Before climbing into the carriage, Silas asked the old man not to repeat anything he had been told about his father and Turner's shocking conditions. 'I'll not breathe a word,' Bill promised. 'You can count on me.'

Knowing he could trust him to keep his promise, Silas had one last question. 'What would you do, Bill,' he asked quietly, 'if you were me?'

Bill thought about it for a minute, then he smiled a

sad sort of smile. 'I would do what *you* must do,' he said wisely, 'and pray to the good Lord for the strength to see it through.'

Silas knew what he meant, even though he hadn't spelt it out. 'Thank you, Bill,' he murmured. Then he closed the door and settled back for the long journey ahead.

Perched on the high bench above the carriage, Bill turned up the collar of his coat and pulled down the peak of his hat then, thinking that Fate could be a cruel master, he turned the pair of horses towards home and sent them away at a trot. 'We'll be there afore you know it,' he called over his shoulder.

But Silas wasn't listening. He was thinking of a life with a hard woman, for whom he had neither love nor respect. But mostly, he was thinking about Cathleen, and wondering how he might break the news to her. However painful it was, Bill was right.

He knew in his heart what he must do.

Chapter Seven

'FOR GAWD'S SAKE, sit down, lass!' Spreading the
shirt over the table, Jessie smoothed out the sleeves,
then the tail and the collar. 'Yer like a cat on hot bricks,
so you are!' she chided. 'Up and down, backwards and
forwards. Yer making me nerves bad, so ye are. And
where's your da and Robert got to, eh? Their dinner's
still in the pans, cold as charity.'

'Where can he be?' Cathleen had waited all day; now
it was almost ten o'clock at night, and still there was no
sign of Silas. In her heart of hearts she knew there must
be something wrong, but even now she daren't admit it
to herself. 'I've a good mind to visit the big house.' The
idea had grown with the day. 'I'll speak to the cook.
She's a kind old soul, and we get on really well. *She'll*
know. There's nothing goes on at Fenshaw without her
knowing.'

'You'll *not* go to Fenshaw House,' Jessie told her
sternly. 'Not if I have my way you won't.'

Cathleen was seated at the window, staring out at

the night. Now though, at Jessie's firm words, she swung round, a look of surprise in her blue eyes. 'I thought you were on my side?'

'Oh, I am, lass!' With an indignant glance, she told Cathleen, 'You're going about it the wrong way, so ye are. In my experience a lass doesn't run after the man – not if she wants him to think she's a cut above the rest.'

Silently mulling over Jessie's words, Cathleen resumed her vigil at the window. A minute later she was asking, 'What am I to do then?'

'You're to *wait*!' Turning away, Jessie wrapped a cloth round her fist and carefully lifted the iron from the hot coals. Holding it bottom-up, she spat on it. When the spittle sizzled and fried, she gave a satisfied grin. Slapping the iron onto the shirt-sleeves, she congratulated herself when they flattened and spread to perfection. 'One and six I paid for this rusty old iron,' she told Cathleen. 'Got it off the rag-a-bone man.' Clicking her tongue, she started on the other sleeve. 'Best bargain I ever had.'

Cathleen was still contemplating Jessie's advice. 'I can't wait for ever.'

'I never said you should.' Replacing the iron on the hot coals, Jessie swished the shirt over to its side. 'I said you shouldn't go after him. It doesn't look good.'

But Cathleen's mind was made up. 'I don't care what it looks like,' she said. 'If he doesn't come after me tonight, then first thing in the morning I'll have to go after *him*.' And she was determined that nothing would change her mind.

'Yer a stubborn little bugger.'

Uncurling herself from the window-seat, Cathleen came over to sit at the table, her sorry blue eyes raised to Jessie's. 'I'm worried, Grandma.'

Up until now, the old woman had tried to be firm, distancing herself from what she saw as a bad situation. She knew Tom bitterly regretted ever letting Cathleen get close to the Fenshaws. He hated the idea of his lass falling in love with one of what he called 'her betters'. And she knew that, however much she adored her daddy, Cathleen could never turn away from this young man, whom she loved with such a passion it was frightening.

But as she'd feared all along, Jessie believed the lass was in for heartache. Like Cathleen, she had an idea that all had not gone well at Fenshaw House. 'Look, lass . . .' Rounding the table, she sat beside Cathleen, one hand on her shoulder and the other fiddling with her grand-daughter's wild hair. 'I know yer worried, and I'm sure there's a good reason why he hasn't come to see yer, but . . .' Pausing, she let her gaze fall to the table.

'But what?' Looking into those wise old eyes, Cathleen saw her answer. 'You don't think he'll ever come back, do you?' she asked sorrowfully.

'Ey, I don't know, lass.' If she was ever to be honest, now was the time. 'If he *doesn't* come back . . . well, happen it might be for the best, eh?'

Without a word, Cathleen withdrew from her embrace. Returning to the window, she curled up close to the pane and stared out at the darkness. 'He'll come back,' she whispered. 'And when he does, everything will be all right, you'll see.'

Thinking it best if she didn't say any more, for now at least, Jessie carried on with her ironing. Every now and then she would glance at Cathleen, but the lass was lost in the darkness, watching and waiting, and for the next half-hour or so that cosy little room was filled with hope, and a small measure of despair.

At ten-thirty, just as Jessie was packing away her beautifully ironed shirts, Cathleen gave a cry and leaped out of the chair. 'Someone's coming up the path!' she cried, and as she ran to the door, Tom opened it to let himself in.

'By! It's black as a coal-pit out there!' he groaned. 'The cart threw a wheel some three miles along the lane. I'll have to leave it there till morning. It's a good job Robert is staying over at Lou's again.' Putting his arm round Cathleen, he said wearily, 'I've a spare wheel in the shed. Tomorrow I'll have the cart back on the road in no time at all.'

'Huh! Unless the gypsies take a fancy to it first.'

Jessie's remark made both Cathleen and her father smile, but it was Tom who commented, 'Come on, Jessie! You're not still harping on about that, are you? By! It must be two year since it happened.'

'Two year and four days this Sunday.' Jessie had never forgotten her run-in with the gypsies. 'It's coming to summat when a woman can't hang out her washing at six of a morning without finding it's been pinched afore she's even come back with the second basket.' Turning to put the kettle on, she continued to mutter, 'If them thievin' buggers would make off with a poor widow woman's smalls, they'd think nowt o' making off with your cart.'

Knowing how the incident had upset her, Tom tried not to laugh. 'Well, they'll not mek off with the horse,' he promised. ''Cause he's happily munching on his hay in the bottom shed, safe and sound till morning.' Taking off his cap and jacket, he gave them a little shake, sending a shower of flour to the floor and getting a telling off from Jessie for his trouble.

'Hey! I've told you afore,' she cried. 'You're to shake them outside.'

'Sorry.' He glanced down at Cathleen's smiling face. 'I'm so tired and hungry I forgot.' He promptly took them outside and gave them a thorough shaking. Then he came back in and hung his clothes on the nail behind the door. Giving Cathleen a kiss, he remarked, 'Summat smells good. I'm not sure whether it's you or my dinner.' Unlike Jessie, he didn't notice how quiet and thoughtful his daughter was. 'Well? How's my lovely lass then? I've never known you come home early before,' he told her. 'But how are you now, lass? Feeling better, I hope.'

Infused with guilt, Cathleen nodded. She hadn't been ill, she'd been fretting for Silas. 'I shouldn't have left Lou to finish the rounds,' she apologised, 'not when you needed him in the bakery.'

'Away with you! You'd already done the donkey's work.' Glancing at Jessie he gave a sly wink. 'Poor old Lou though, he was really down in the dumps after you'd gone. I reckon if I'd given him the nod, he'd have been up the hill after you an' no mistake.'

Discreetly interrupting, Jessie told him, 'I hope you're good an' hungry, 'cause I've made a pan o' hot-pot enough to feed an army. Mind you, it's a couple of hours past its best.' She hurried to put a generous portion in a clean pan and to heat it over the range.

Tom rubbed his hands together. 'Sounds wonderful!' He sat up, ready to tuck in. 'I've an appetite fit for a bull-elephant.'

Jessie wagged a finger. 'If yer want yer dinner, you'd best go an' wash them grubby hands first.' As he hurried out to the scullery, she whispered to Cathleen, 'Not a word. What he doesn't know won't hurt him.'

Cathleen had intended going back to the window to keep watch, but after Jessie's timely warning, she turned about. 'I'll serve the food,' she said, and decided to do whatever else needed doing to keep her mind off Silas.

When Tom returned and began his meal, he had no inkling of the secret between the two women.

An hour later, after the three of them had talked over the day's events and the crockery was washed and put away, Jessie took herself off to bed. 'It's been a very long day,' she chuckled. 'If I'm to catch meself a millionaire, I'd best get me beauty sleep.'

Kissing Tom goodnight, she remarked on how tired he seemed. 'Looks like somebody else is ready for their bed an' all.'

'It's been a tiring day,' he yawned. 'I dare say I'll be dragging meself up them stairs afore too long.' For now though, he was content to loll in the chair and smoke his battered old pipe.

On kissing Cathleen goodnight, Jessie whispered in her ear, 'Don't be long to bed, lass. And don't worry. Things are sure to sort themselves out in the morning.' Though which way they might be sorted out, she daren't imagine.

After half an hour, Tom got up from his chair and, stretching his aching limbs, he told Cathleen, 'Right, lass. That's me done for.' A moment later, he too went up to his bed.

Left alone, Cathleen made straight for the window. When she could see nothing, she went to the door and, softly opening it, walked down the path and peered every which way. There was no one about, no sound, nothing moving, and with every passing minute her heart sank a little deeper into her boots. She stood there for a few minutes, her eyes peeled as she looked this way and that, desperately willing Silas to appear out of the darkness. When the rain started, she lingered awhile, then, when it was plain he wasn't coming, she made her way back to the cottage.

By the time she got inside and took up her place at the window once again, the rain was coming down fast and hard against the glass. The wind had risen and suddenly, without warning, it had the makings of a bad night.

She thought of Silas. Was he out there in the wild weather, or was he at home, with his dogs by his side and a roaring fire to keep him warm? More importantly, why hadn't he come to see her? Could he be avoiding her? And if so, why? At the back of her mind was his father, and the idea that she and Silas would never have his blessing.

She recalled the direction in which he had gone that morning, and now she realised that one of two things might have happened; either his father had forbidden him to see her, and he was biding his time, or he really had gone to London, and he wasn't coming back. 'Don't desert me,' she murmured.

Like any woman who loved her man, she couldn't bring herself to believe the worst. Yet she had never felt so alone in her entire life as she did at that moment.

⟶●⟵

NOT TOO MANY miles away, another young woman was staring out of the window, her hard, glittering eyes betraying the excitement she felt. 'There's a storm brewing,' she said, turning to her father. 'If you ask me, it's long overdue.'

At the other end of the drawing room, Jack Turner was seated at the bureau, busily poring over some documents. He didn't look up. He had heard his daughter but was not in the mood for conversation.

Angrily raising her voice Helen persisted, 'Father! Did you hear what I said?'

Now he looked up. 'No.'

Tutting, she repeated, 'I said there's a storm brewing.'

'Really?' He bent his head to his work again.

Placing her sherry glass onto the mantelpiece, she strode across the room. 'What's wrong with you?'

'I'm busy, dear, surely you can see that?'

'It's about Edward Fenshaw, isn't it?'

'Is it?'

'You *know* it is. You shouldn't be feeling guilty, Father. He's the one who cheated. He's the one who took your money and used it for his own purpose.'

'Not quite true.' This time he sat back in his chair, quietly observing her. 'You do tend to get the wrong end of the stick,' he said. 'Edward Fenshaw is not a man to deliberately cheat anyone, my dear. He did take the money; he also used it carelessly and without my knowledge, but throughout, he believed he was buying wisely.'

'Then he's a damn fool! In my opinion, that's even worse than being a cheat.'

'We're all of us guilty of being fools at one time or another.'

'Not me!'

'No, dear, not you.' Regarding her as though she was a stranger, he noted the plain features and hard eyes and could only imagine the cruel heart beneath. Almost without meaning to, he muttered, 'If only you were more like your mother.'

'Huh!' Laughing in his face, she hissed spitefully, 'I'm glad I'm not like her. She had no head for business – you said that yourself, many a time.' And my mother was a whore, she thought silently, but without quite daring to say it aloud. She ran off with her lover, and left me, her only daughter, to grow up alone. The bitterness rose in her.

'Yes, and it was true. But she had a kind, loving heart, and a smile that shamed the sun, and if she couldn't do a kindness she would never do harm, not even to those who deserved it.'

The bitterness overwhelmed her. With her cold eyes boring into him, Helen burst out, 'Why do you hate me so much?'

'I don't hate you, my dear.' He felt something akin to disgust for her, true, but it wasn't hatred. No man could hate his own child.

'You're angry with me then? Because I made you trade with Edward Fenshaw?'

'Nobody makes me do anything.' He had his own reasons for going along with her wishes.

She smiled, a cunning little smile that made him shiver. 'Silas Fenshaw will have the best of the bargain,' she told him. 'Once he puts a ring on my finger, not only will he have rid his father of any debt owed to you, but he will have *me*, the daughter of a very powerful and influential man.'

'Will you make him happy?' Guilt coloured his every word.

'Well now . . .' Walking slowly around him, she placed her manicured fingers on his shoulders. 'Silas Fenshaw is a good-looking man, quite a catch in fact, and no doubt the peasant girl from the baker's cottage will hate me for snatching him away, but really, you should be asking if he will make *me* happy, not the other way round.'

Drawing away, she went to the mantelpiece and retrieved her drink. 'Things have changed, Father. The peasant girl lost and I won. I have him, and she hasn't. And if Silas Fenshaw doesn't like the way things have turned out, he must blame his father, not me!'

'God Almighty! How did you get to be so wicked?' Jack Turner grabbed her by the shouders and shook her hard. 'Silas Fenshaw deserves none of this! He's a better man than I am! God help me, if he agrees to take you off my hands it will be the best day of my life, and the worst day of his!' Thrusting her aside, he stared at her for a moment. 'You reek of greed! You have everything you could ever want . . . money, travel, this house. It will all be yours when I'm gone. What is it that you truly want? Is *all this* not enough?'

No! it could never be enough! Nothing could.

Seemingly contrite, she lowered her tear-filled gaze. 'I'm sorry, Father,' she whispered brokenly. 'You're right. I didn't mean to sound peevish.'

Seeing her like this, he began to wonder if he'd misjudged her. 'I'm sorry too. I was a bit harsh . . . too quick to anger these days, my dear.' Placing a fleeting kiss on her forehead, he collected his work from the bureau, before bidding her goodnight. 'Things to do,' he said, then he went on weary footsteps up the stairs and into his lonely bedroom, where he would stay and finish his work, then sleep awhile, ready for another busy day tomorrow.

Downstairs, Helen laughed softly to herself. 'Old

fool!' She poured herself another sherry and, holding it out towards the door, made a toast. 'Here's to me!' Gulping it down, she suddenly flung the glass across the room, where it smashed against the door. 'Bastard!' She thrust out her arms to encompass the room, her fists curling so tight, the nails dug into her skin and drew blood. 'You think I want all *this*?' Her voice shook with anger. 'Oh no.'

The rage left her as quickly as it had come on. 'What I *want* is more than you can ever give me. Something that will make people sit up and take notice of *me*, Helen Turner!' Going to the mirror, she began preening herself, her mental instability taking over as she whispered low, confiding in some imaginary figure. 'I can be someone through Silas Fenshaw.' Sourness distorted her voice. 'I'm more suited to him than she is! What does it matter if he loves her? He's mine!'

Looking up, she grew calm. 'You were wrong, Father. You should never have promised Edward Fenshaw that he could keep his house and possessions, because, you see, I can't let that happen.'

Admiring herself from every angle, she smirked. 'Silas is lucky to have you.' With exaggerated movements she patted her hair and straightened her collar. 'You'll make a fine mistress of Fenshaw House,' she murmured wickedly. 'And once you've taken over, you must never allow yourself to be cheated, not like your father. Oh, and you mustn't tell him of your plans or he might get squeamish.' Her smile was awful to see. '*After all, murder is a very serious business.*'

Gazing at her image, she said over and over, 'Helen Fenshaw, Mistress of Fenshaw House.' It sounded right somehow. As though it was meant to be.

Chapter Eight

CATHLEEN KEPT HER sad vigil by the window as she heard the clock strike midnight, then one o'clock; still there was no sign of Silas.

Curled up on the window-seat, her limbs grew cramped and sore, but she wouldn't leave, not yet. Not until all hope was gone.

She napped and woke and stared through the glass into the darkness beyond, and her heart ached to see him. But he didn't come, and she was beginning to think he never would.

At half past two, Jessie came down and saw her there, folded into herself like a mouse, fast asleep. 'Oh, lass!' Gently waking her, she scolded, 'Whatever are ye doing, child? Go to yer bed.'

'He told me he'd be here, and he's never lied,' Cathleen said passionately and, unable to persuade her to leave, Jessie returned to her bed. But she didn't sleep. Instead, she lay there, thinking about that dear lass downstairs, knowing in her heart it would never come right. 'You've lost him, lass.' A solitary tear ran down her face. 'God help us, he were never yours to keep.' Tired as she was, she closed her eyes and was soon dozing, but she did not sleep. How could she sleep when Cathleen was down there, watching and waiting for something that would never happen?

———❖———

THE CLOCK STRUCK four, waking Cathleen from a fitful sleep. In her dream she saw Silas walking away; she reached out her arms to hold him, but he was always out of her grasp. '*Silas!*' Her voice sounded like that of a stranger.

Groaning, she sat up, her eyes going instinctively to the window. *And there he was!* She rubbed her eyes and looked again, thinking it might be a remnant of her dream. But it was no dream, and her heart leaped. 'He's here!' She could hardly believe it. Drenched to the skin, he stood at the bottom of the path, looking up at the house. He hadn't seen her, she was sure of it.

In a minute she had opened the door and was running down the path. The rain quickly soaked her hair and clothes; it was slippery underfoot, but she didn't care. All she could think was that Silas had come to see her, just as he had promised.

When he saw her coming towards him, Silas ran to meet her. 'I came straight here,' he told her, catching her into his arms. 'I didn't know if you'd be watching. I didn't . . .' She stopped him with a kiss, and the touch of her lips against his, the feel of her body close to his own, washed everything else away. 'Oh, Cathleen!' He held her at arm's length, looking at her lovely wet face, those bright blue eyes that glowed like sapphires in the dark, and his love for her was a beacon inside him. 'I've missed you so.'

Laughing with joy and relief, she held on to him. 'I waited,' she told him. 'I couldn't sleep. Where did you go? What did your father say?' She had to know.

He grew quiet. How could he tell her? Yet tell her he must, even though it would break his heart, and hers. 'The news is bad,' he said; the words clogged in his throat and he could say no more. He fought to find a solution but there was none, so, like a desperate man, he caught her to him, savouring the moment, knowing it must end.

Sensing his turmoil, Cathleen drew away. 'Tell me now,' she said softly. 'I have to know.'

And so, there in the pouring rain he told her how his father was deep in debt to Turner, and how his parents' salvation lay in his own hands. 'He wants his daughter married and he wants me for a son-in-law, that's the price he demands.'

Numbed by the news, Cathleen stared up at him, her voice almost inaudible. 'No! That's monstrous. How can he do that?'

'Look at you.' Roving his eyes over her, he grew frantic. 'You're wet to the skin. Come and sit in the carriage. We'll talk there.'

Struck to the heart, Cathleen would not be persuaded. 'If you refuse to marry her, what could he do?'

Taking off his jacket he wrapped it round her. 'He means to ruin my father. And, if he does that, what would happen to my mother? She's so frail, Cathleen, and to lose her home and everything in it would kill her.' Taking her by the shoulders, he said desperately, 'Do you understand what I'm saying? Do you see how I can't let that happen?' His voice shook. Raising his eyes to heaven, he paused, cut to the core by the shock on her face. 'What am I to do, Cathleen?' he groaned. 'How can I live without you?'

Grabbing her to him, he buried his face in her hair. 'I'm lost,' he wept, 'I don't know what to do, and yet I know I have no choice. I don't matter in all of this. It's you and Mother, but mostly you. Yet what sort of a man would I be if I snatched at my own happiness at the cost of my mother's life? She's had so much pain and worry these past few years, and now we've had the news that she hasn't but a year to live. How could I let them take away everything she treasures? How could I live with myself if anything happened to her because of me?'

Now, as he held her at arm's length, Cathleen looked up to him, her sorry gaze seeking his out. Deeply moved by the pain in his stricken eyes, she knew he was right. 'You can't let it happen,' she murmured. 'I understand that.'

Taking a moment to recover his composure, he told her frantically, 'I tried everything. I went to Turner but it was no good. I've been to plead with my father's so-called friends in London, but they won't help, and the little money I have is nowhere near enough. I'm at my wits' end.'

Cathleen could only imagine what he was going through. 'Do you love her?' The question was simply put, but it might have been an earthquake for the effect it had on him.

'Dear God!' Shaking his head as though warding off something evil, he told her, 'It's *you* I love, Cathleen. I'll love you to the day I die, you must know that.' Holding her, one hand on each of her small shoulders, he looked down into her face and his heart turned over. 'Tell me something,' he asked. 'If I was to refuse Turner's demands . . . if I asked *you* to make the decision, what would you say? If you and I were to get married, could you be happy, knowing what would follow?'

'No.' Now Cathleen felt the entire weight of his burden, and it was more than she could bear. 'Your mother is a good, kind person, and I love her almost as much as you do. Protect her, Silas. Don't let her suffer unnecessarily.' As she spoke, the tears rolled down her face, mingling with the rain. 'You're right, Silas. Against all of that, you and I don't matter.'

They stayed awhile, oblivious to the rain, holding each other close, knowing it was all over. From the carriage, Bill watched and felt incredibly old. 'Life's a cruel bastard!' he said, and wiped away a tear.

Presently, Silas walked her back to the cottage. 'Remember what I told you,' he said. 'Whatever happens, I'll never stop loving you.' His voice broke. Lingering one precious moment longer, he let his gaze rove her face . . . the tip of her nose, the full, rich mouth that had laughed with him, and kissed him, the long, wet hair draping her shoulders, oh, and those wonderful eyes, so blue, so honest, and yet not laughing now like he remembered. Instead, they were quiet, and filled with a sorrow he had brought to her and for which he would never forgive himself. All of this he drank in, as though branding it on his mind for all time.

Taking off the jacket he had wrapped around her, she now draped it round his broad, strong shoulders. 'Take care of yourself,' she whispered.

Silently, he took her two hands in his. A kiss, the gentlest of smiles, then he was gone, leaving her alone, her life now a cold, empty place.

She watched the carriage as it moved down the lane, and when she could see it no more she ran to the gate and caught sight of it again, and her heart was broken. Crumpling to the ground, she let her emotions swamp her. Racked with sobs and not caring whether she lived or died, she called his name.

But he was gone, and he was never coming back.

——————⟶◆⟵——————

UPSTAIRS IN HER bed, Jessie felt cold. Shivering, she drew the bedclothes about her, but it didn't make any difference. Unsettled, she sat up, suddenly feeling Cathleen's pain as though it were her own.

Quickly now, she scrambled out of bed and ran to the window. Her eyes were drawn straight to the small hunched figure by the gate, and she was afraid. 'Oh, dear God!'

Throwing on her robe, she hurried downstairs. The back door was wide open, and she knew at once why she had felt so cold. Grabbing two long-coats from the back of the door, she put one on, and carried the other with her. 'What's to become of her?' she mumbled as she fled down the path into the night. 'Dear God, what's to become of her?'

Stooping to help her, Jessie wrapped the coat round Cathleen's shoulders. 'Come away in, lass,' she pleaded, 'you'll catch yer death o' cold, so ye will.' The wind was driving the rain mercilessly, with Cathleen already ice-cold to the touch.

Through her tears Cathleen gave a shattered smile. 'He came back, just like he promised.' She didn't need to say any more, because Jessie saw the harsh truth in her face. 'I know, lass,' she answered softly. 'Let's go inside an' ye can tell me all about it.' Without any delay, she covered Cathleen with her arms and hurried her away into the cottage.

Once inside, Jessie put the big pan onto the fire and the kettle on the hob, and while Cathleen took off her dripping wet clothes, she emptied the boiling water into the tin bath, topping it up with cold water from the bucket.

When, a moment later, Cathleen slithered into the water, Jessie took up a soft-bristled brush and a bar of carbolic and scrubbed her back until it sang. 'Here, lass!' Handing her both brush and soap, she instructed, 'Do the same all over and we'll soon have the blood flowing again.'

Meanwhile, Jessie boiled another pan of water. By the time Cathleen was glowing and clothed in a clean nightgown and robe, Jessie had the tea on the table and a fire up the chimney. 'Now then, lass.' Settling herself at the table, she regarded Cathleen with the fondness of a mother. 'How are yer?'

Reaching out, Cathleen laid her hand over Jessie's. 'Thank you,' she said, and it was enough.

'D'yer want to tell me what yer were doing out in such terrible weather?'

With her mind still following the carriage, it was a moment before Cathleen spoke. 'Silas was here.'

'Aye.' Jessie had already guessed as much. 'An' what did he want?'

Again, Cathleen was slow to answer. Instead, she kept her gaze averted, studying her teacup as though the answer to all her problems might lie there. 'It's all over between us.' They were the hardest words she had ever had to utter.

'I see.' Nodding resignedly, Jessie was not surprised. She knew it had to be something bad to have kept Cathleen out there like that; something crippling to have taken the sparkle from that lass's bright eyes. 'D'yer want to tell yer ol' grandma about it?'

Cathleen drew comfort from the old woman, just as she had done when she was a child and had needed someone to talk to. 'It isn't his fault,' she began, and told her exactly what Silas had confided.

Jessie listened until Cathleen was finished, then she rubbed her hands over her face and sighed, long and hard. 'It's a bad thing,' she said. 'Oh, I've heard of such an arrangement afore, but never amongst the gentry. Usually it's a thing that happens in the back-streets, between two men who are no better than the rats round their feet. Sell their childer for tuppence so they would!'

'It's not the same though, is it?' Cathleen had never heard of such a thing before, and never wanted to hear of it again.

'I'm not sure about that. All right, so Silas Fenshaw isn't being *made* to do it; he's agreed to wed this Turner woman in order to save his father from shame and ruin, and his poor mother from a nightmare not of her making and an early grave. He has no choice, as I can see. And neither do the young 'uns who are sold for the price of a pint and a wad o' baccy so, when yer get right down to it, there ain't a lot o' difference between one and the other . . . except one comes of gentry, and the other comes of poorer stock.'

Cathleen gave that some thought, concluding, 'How must he feel? I'll have a life to live, though it won't be a happy one without Silas. But what about him? How will he get through the days and . . . ?'

Jessie voiced what Cathleen had been loath to say. 'Aye, an' the nights.' To her wise old mind, there was nothing worse than keeping a bad thought inside and letting it fester. 'The best thing is for you not to think on it. Happen he'll be in one room and her in another, and happen they'll tolerate each other with a degree of kinship, an' happen they'll hate the sight of each other for as long as they live. But one thing I *do* know, and it's this . . .' Taking both of Cathleen's hands in her own, she said firmly, 'You mustn't torture yerself. Put it as far to the back of yer mind as yer can, and pray to the good Lord that you find a man who'll love you, the same as Silas did.'

When Cathleen looked away, the old woman got out of her chair and came to hug the lass she so adored. 'Aw, lass! I know yer hurting like the very divil, but there's nothing yer can do. Silas Fenshaw is shouldering his burden like the good man he is, and for his sake as well as yer own, you *must* forget him as quick as yer can. D'yer understand what I'm saying, child? Find the courage, just as he's having to do. Look to the future, and I swear to God it will all come right. You're only young, with so much to look forward to.'

When she paused, Cathleen looked up at her. She didn't comment. Instead she waited, knowing Jessie had not yet said her piece.

Swallowing hard, the old woman cupped Cathleen's face in her hands. In a small, tight voice she told her, 'You have to do all that, lass. Because if ye can't, then I might as well have left you out there in the rain to die.' Harsh words, cruel even, but they had to be said.

For what seemed an age, the two of them clung together. There were no more words. Only the sound of Cathleen's quiet sobs. She knew that everything Jessie had said was true.

Silas was lost to her now; that much she knew. Jessie had said she must forget him.

Even though, in her heart, she knew she never would.

S ILAS DIDN'T GO to bed. His mind was in such turmoil that sleep was impossible. *Life* was impossible.

For a long, lonely time he sat at the kitchen table, staring at the grain in the wood and seeing only Cathleen's face. 'God forgive me,' he whispered. 'What else could I have done?' And he knew there was nothing.

As the hours ticked by . . . four o'clock . . . five o'clock . . . the clothes dried on his back, and he didn't even notice.

I N THE LIBRARY, Edward Fenshaw stirred. Like Cathleen, he had kept a lonely vigil for Silas, and when he grew cold and tired he had sat down on the sofa, meaning only to nap for a few minutes. But the worry of these past days had taken its toll, and he slept for three hours. It wasn't an easy sleep; chased by monsters and faced with impossible obstacles, he found his life threatened at every turn.

When the watery sun played through the window and woke him, he opened his eyes with the idea of suicide once more on his mind. 'But if I did away with myself, what would it solve?' he asked himself. And back came the answer, 'It would solve *nothing*' He laughed gruffly. 'In fact, it would only prove me to be even more of a coward than I already am.' He had no illusions about his own part in this terrible state of affairs.

He had made a bad judgement, and it had come back to haunt him.

The idea of selling his son to save what was left of his own life did not sit easy on his shoulders. But, with everything against him, he was desperate enough to accept the unthinkable, if only for his wife's sake.

With the day came a new round of anxiety. Going straight to the window he peered out. Through the arch, he could see the carriage parked in the courtyard. 'He's back!' Excited, he rushed out of the room, going swiftly down the corridor and across the hallway, searching in every room as he went, but there was no sign of Silas.

When he came to the kitchen, he was shocked to see his son seated there, lying forward with his head on the table and his arms for a pillow.

Choked with emotion, he sat opposite him, waiting, hoping, and giving up a prayer to God that all was well, and that Silas had secured the loans to save them.

After a while, Silas stirred. Haggard and worn, he stared up at his father, and the look in his eyes said it all.

'They wouldn't help, would they?'

Silas shook his head. 'I'm sorry, Father, I did all I could.'

'Bastards!' The tremor in his voice broke into a sob. 'They turned you away, after all I've done for them over the years?'

Slowly waking, Silas sat up, his eyes swollen with tiredness, his limbs pained by the cuts and bruises he had suffered in the fight, though they were nothing to the pain inside. For a while he just looked at his father and, for the briefest of moments, he felt a fleeting sense of hatred.

Edward saw it and was broken. Closing his eyes, he shuddered and moaned, and with his two hands over his face, he sobbed like a baby. 'I'm sorry, son,' he kept saying, 'I'm so sorry.'

Ashamed of that fleeting emotion, and that his father had witnessed it, Silas went to him. Grabbing his father's bent shoulders, he drew him to his side. 'It's all right,' he told him gently, 'I'll do the honourable thing by you and Mother.'

With silent gratitude, Edward looked up at him. In that moment, Silas saw the face of a very old man. 'It's all right,' he assured him again. 'Your worries are over.'

But his own weren't, he thought bitterly.

And nor were Cathleen's.

Chapter Nine

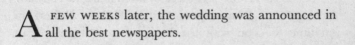

A FEW WEEKS later, the wedding was announced in all the best newspapers.

Jack William Turner of Kildalton Manor is pleased to announce the wedding of his only daughter, Helen, to Silas Fenshaw, son of Edward Fenshaw.
The service will take place at 3 p.m. in St Peter's Church, Blackburn, on the 21st of October, 1900.

All other details were reserved for the private invitations:

. . . and afterwards at the Riverside Hotel, Salmesbury.

On the morning of the announcement, Jessie saw the notice and showed it to Cathleen. 'If I don't tell you, somebody else will,' she said, and, thanking her, Cathleen took the newspaper and sat in the window-seat, head bent and heart aching, as it had ached since that awful night.

Standing at the sink, Jessie watched her. She saw her grand-daughter's knuckles whiten as they closed around the newspaper; she saw how Cathleen momentarily closed her eyes and knew that this wedding was a hard thing for the lass to come to terms with.

After a while, Cathleen gently folded the newspaper and, returning to the table, laid it by her father's plate. 'I'll call him,' she told Jessie and, running up the stairs, she knocked on Tom's door. 'Breakfast is on the table!' she told him.

There were only the three of them living at Fenshaw Cottage now. In a desperate attempt to get Robert up on time to cope with the bakery's early hours, Tom had made an arrangement with Mrs Matheson, Lou's mother, to have him as a properly paid-up lodger. The new arrangement suited them all.

Coming back to the kitchen, she took the dish of six sausages from Jessie and began sharing them out between the three plates: two for Jessie, three for her father, and one for her; the same with the six rashers of bacon. When the tomatoes were cooked, she scooped half onto Jessie's plate, and the remaining half onto her father's. 'By! Is that all yer having, lass?' Jessie believed in a big breakfast to start the day. 'You'll not get far on one sausage and a rasher o' bacon.'

With ruffled hair and unshaven face, Tom called out from the door, 'Leave the lass be, I expect she's saving a little space for the muffins we'll be baking later.' Though he knew Cathleen wasn't interested in the muffins. The only thing on her mind these past weeks had been Silas Fenshaw and how he had thrown her over for someone else. Though he had been delighted by the news, it riled Tom to think that the young pup had encouraged Cathleen, then gone off and promised himself to one of his own kind.

Over breakfast, Cathleen saw him pick up the paper and wondered what he might have to say. It wasn't long coming. 'Well, I never!' Peering at the two of them over the top of the paper, he tutted and shook his head. 'Have you seen this?' he asked indignantly.

'Seen what?' Winking at Cathleen, Jessie sliced a huge piece of bacon and shoved it into her mouth.

Shaking the paper, he persisted, 'This announcement of Fenshaw's wedding to the Turner girl.'

Jessie nodded. 'What about it?'

'Well, what d'you think?'

'It's a *wedding*.' Feigning indifference, Jessie took another chunk out of her bacon, this time squashing it onto a generous slice of sausage before forking it into her mouth. 'There's a few other weddings announced, if yer look further down,' she mumbled.

Knowing he would get no change out of her, he addressed Cathleen, this time a little gentler. 'Did you know about this, sweetheart?'

'Yes, I knew about it.' Taking a ribbon from her skirt pocket, Cathleen tied back her hair. 'And I wish him well.' What she truly wished was that it was her about to walk down the aisle with Silas.

Unaware of the reason for Silas and Cathleen parting, Tom spoke his mind. 'I think you're well shut of him,' he declared, 'and I hope you never set foot on that property again. They're all the same, that sort. All I can say is, I'm glad you didn't get in too deep, thank God. By! I don't mind telling you, lass, I were worried about you.' He winked. 'But now he's about to be wed, and I for one am not sorry.'

Cathleen's reply was quiet and heartfelt. 'I'll miss him,' she answered, and looked away.

Stunned by the intensity of her voice, he glanced at her, then at Jessie. 'Is there summat going on here that I don't know about?'

'What d'yer mean?' Jessie was a hopeless liar, but this was an emergency. 'It's only natural the lass should miss him,' she retorted. 'They've been friends since they were bairns. And here he is getting wed. It's no wonder our Cathleen is feeling a bit low. She's lost a friend, 'cause it's a fact this new wife of his won't want him messing with the peasants!' Wiping the crust round her plate, she mopped up the juices and rammed it into her mouth. 'By! There's nowt like a good breakfast!' she declared, casually asking Tom if he would like, 'A nice, fresh brew afore you leave for work?'

'Hmh!' He glanced at Cathleen, who was already beginning to clear away the breakfast things. 'I'm sorry if I were a bit harsh just now,' he told her. 'You both know how I feel, and it's just as well you might never see him again. Bear in mind, he were only your friend because you had no mammy, and Lucy Fenshaw took pity on you. She let you run about the garden and pal up with her son, and at the time I were grateful for that. But them days is long gone, and rightly so.'

'Come on, Tom!' Jessie held the teapot aloft. 'D'yer want a brew or not?'

Seeming not to have heard, he continued to study Cathleen. She was such a lovely, homely creature, and he adored her. Looking at her now, with her long fair hair and cornflower-blue eyes, he thought himself the luckiest man on God's earth. 'Look, lass, I hope I've not upset you. But there you are, it's said. I'm glad you've seen the back of him, and now I never want his name mentioned in this house again.'

An awkward silence descended on the room, with Jessie holding her tongue, and Cathleen on the verge of telling him the whole truth. Instead, she said quietly, 'You won't hear his name again. Not from me, you won't.' In that moment she was suffused with anger. Yet he didn't know, couldn't know that, if Silas were to walk in now and ask her to go with him, nothing on this earth would stand in her way, not even the family she loved and trusted.

Something in her voice, the look in her eye, made him pause. Then, pushing aside his chair, he stood up, glancing from one to the other before going out of the room and up the stairs without a word.

'By! For a minute there I thought an almighty row was brewing.' Jessie was relieved. 'I was sure he suspected summat underhand.' Leaning forward, she lowered her voice. 'Look, lass, don't yer think he should know what's happened?'

Still bristling with anger, Cathleen was adamant. 'It won't serve no purpose,' she answered. 'He's taken against Silas and nothing will ever change that.'

In truth, Jessie had to agree.

THE TWENTY-FIRST OF October was a Friday, and the significance of it was branded into Cathleen's mind. Since six o'clock that morning she had busied herself, looking for work that wasn't hers, going over paperwork and washing floors that had already been twice scrubbed to perfection – anything to keep her mind off what was soon to happen in St Peter's Church, which was just five minutes away from the bakery.

'What's ailing yer, lass?' Taking out the last tray of scones, Tom stood by the big ovens with his sleeves rolled up and a look of consternation on his flushed face. 'You're making me dizzy just watching you!' he declared. 'Flying about all over the place, wearing yourself to a frazzle. Anybody'd think the devil were on your heels!' He'd completely forgotten about the wedding.

To Cathleen, that was exactly how she felt . . . as though the devil was on her heels, making her want to run and run, until she was far enough away not to know what was happening. 'I need to work,' she answered. 'I don't like being idle.'

Lou had something to say about that. 'Idle, is it?' He clicked his tongue. 'Huh! I've yet to see the day!' He looked a comical sight; his face was red where he'd been feeding trays into the back oven, and there was a dollop of dough squashed into his hair. But there was no doubting the love that shone in his warm brown eyes. 'You never stop!'

Tom didn't know what to make of it. 'Anyway, you'd best get off and deliver that big order to the Riverside Hotel. Sounds to me like somebody's either getting wed or getting buried, the amount of food they've ordered.'

Cathleen was glad he'd forgotten the date, and its meaning. But *she* hadn't forgotten; it had been on her mind all day long. 'Can't Lou do that delivery?' She didn't have the heart to go. Besides, what she couldn't see, she couldn't grieve over.

But Tom refused. 'Sorry, lass, you'll have to manage on your own for that one. Lou and Robert have got their work cut out here with me. There's them two big functions tomorrow in Accrington, and half-a-dozen little shops down King Street . . . fair size orders every one.' He gestured to the front of the bakery. 'On top of that, we've to open the shop in an hour.' Raising his eyebrows, he told her sternly, 'Everything has to be done in double-quick time today.'

Wiping his floury hands down his overall he added, 'You've no need to worry, lass. There's sure to be somebody at the other end who'll help you off with them trays.' Gesturing to Lou, he instructed, 'Help Cathleen load the cart, then get back in here, sharpish.' And, as always, Lou was at Cathleen's side, even before Tom had finished speaking.

It took twenty minutes of toing and froing before the

cart was loaded. 'There's nothing I'd like better than to be sitting up there beside you.' From the front of the cart, Lou looked up with adoring eyes, his thick mop of fair hair sweated to his temples. 'Make sure you ask for somebody to help offload this lot, though.' Reaching out, he fleetingly touched her hand. 'I know you,' he said. 'You're proud and stubborn. You'd turn the world over before you'd ask for help.'

Squeezing his hand, Cathleen thanked him. 'You'd best get inside,' she said with a grin, 'before Dad comes looking for you with a rolling pin.'

Reluctantly, Lou did as she said, though he stood at the doorstep watching her until she was out of sight. 'One day . . .' His brown eyes clouded over. 'One day I'll make you mine, Cathleen Roe,' he murmured, then fled inside at the double when Tom's voice boomed out, 'LOU, WHERE THE HELL HAVE YOU GOT TO NOW?'

———◆◇◆———

CATHLEEN LOVED THIS time of the morning. Perched up there on her lofty bench, peering over the hedges and witnessing the glories of nature, it was a wonderful feeling. Alongside the canal, the ducks played and squabbled, and beyond that the field was alive with hares and rabbits, leaping and running and hiding as only they could.

The lane before her was littered with leaves, laying a carpet before the horse, whose great hooves made a shuffling noise as he went along, clippety-clopping, two feet down, two feet up. It made a unique kind of rhythm, echoing into the world, as if he and Cathleen were the only two living things.

Suddenly the rhythm changed, and when the horse began throwing his head from side to side, Cathleen knew there was something wrong. Drawing the cart to a halt, she went to the front. 'Let's have a look at you.' Bending to the belly of the horse, she lifted his feet one by one until she found it – a stone the size of a marble, embedded in the rim of his shoe. 'I'll have it out in no time,' she told the patient creature.

It took a minute to find a stout enough twig, and another minute to gouge out the stone, then all was well. 'There you go.' Ruffling his mane, she planted a kiss on his rubbery nose. 'We'd best go a bit faster now, to make up for lost time.' She climbed back into the seat, took up the reins and away they went.

Altogether, the ten-minute journey took half an hour.

———————

T HE RIVERSIDE HOTEL was a grand old place, built in the 1800s and situated in prime position beside the River Ribble. With a reputation for good food and pampering, it was mainly frequented by the gentry, though now and then a bold gambler might treat himself after a night of winning. He'd come back to the pubs with his tales of pretty things in aprons, and how 'A shilling buys her for the night.' He'd talk about 'Amazing food served under silver canopies, and fish made to sit up on the plate and smile at you.' And everyone would listen with wide eyes and tongues hanging out.

Outside, Cathleen sat a minute, wondering which way to go. 'I'm not even sure if they're expecting me,' she told the horse. 'I'd best go and see, eh?' She left him waiting patiently at the kerbside.

As she went cautiously through the great entrance, it wasn't pretty things in aprons she noticed, it was the plush red carpets and the long, heavy curtains hanging from ceiling to floor. 'By! They must have cost a man's wages for a year!' she whispered. Big fluted columns flanked her either side, and great mirrors made the whole area seem enormous; there were long marble tables with grand things upon them, and a sense of luxury she had never encountered before, even in Fenshaw House. It was a brand-new experience, and one she would not forget in a hurry.

Overawed by her surroundings, she found herself instinctively tiptoeing over the carpet, fearful that she might have carried some of the flour-dust in on the soles of her boots, and looking back to reassure herself that she hadn't. At reception a smartly uniformed young man stopped halfway through his yawn at the sight of her. 'Hey! What d'you think you're doing in here?' Noting her well-worn long-coat and wild mop of hair roughly bunched into a frayed blue ribbon, he knew she didn't belong there. 'Get out, before I call the manager!'

Standing tall before the high counter, Cathleen told

him proudly, 'I've a delivery outside.' She didn't like his attitude. He looked to be in his late twenties, but carried an air of superiority far beyond his years. 'If you don't want it, I'll take it away. Happen *you* can explain to the manager why he hasn't got fresh bread and rolls for the wedding reception this afternoon – *and* why he won't get them back once I turn that cart around!' With that she swung away, smiling to herself, sure he would follow.

'Hey!' Running round the counter, the young man barred her way. 'You're a stroppy little bugger, aren't you?' Amazed by her beauty, he thought she should be dressed in silk, not an old long-coat that was twice too big for her. 'What's your name?'

'None of your business.' Tall and lanky, with straight dark hair and a cunning smile, he was a little too sure of himself, Cathleen thought. 'Do you want it delivered or don't you?' For some inexplicable reason, maybe the black probing eyes that seemed to see right through her, she had taken an instant dislike to him.

'I go by the name of Jake,' he said. 'Jake Brewer.'

'Well, Mr Brewer, it will take me two minutes to walk out of here and another one to climb on the cart. If you want the delivery, you'd best decide before I take up the reins, because after that there'll be no stopping me.' Giving her cheekiest smile, she added, 'It's the old horse you see . . . he's not what he used to be. Once he's turned around, he makes straight for home and there's not a thing I can do about it.'

Laughing out loud, he was about to answer when out of the corner of his eye he spied another, older man in a dark suit making his way across the foyer towards them. 'It's the manager!' Grabbing her by the shoulders, he pushed her into the shadows. 'Look, take it round the tradesman's entrance,' he told her. 'I'll make sure there's somebody there to help you offload.'

Without wasting any time, Cathleen manoeuvred the cart round the back and through the narrow tradesman's entrance and, as good as his word, Jake Brewer had positioned someone at the back doors to meet her. Cathleen was surprised when it turned out to be a girl. She had short brown hair, was aged about sixteen, and was almost waif-like, with big scared eyes and a nervous smile. 'I'm stronger than I look,' she told Cathleen in a pretty Welsh accent. 'It's my job to help offload the deliveries.'

Jumping down from the seat, Cathleen held out her hand in friendship. 'I'm Cathleen Roe.' There was something about the girl, about the big eyes and the nervous way she kept shifting her gaze, that made Cathleen think she'd been through a rough time.

When the girl smiled she was surprisingly attractive. 'I'm Megan,' she said, shaking Cathleen by the hand. 'I've been here two months, but I don't think I'll stay.' Glancing towards the door, she seemed uneasy.

Before Cathleen could comment, the girl had already offloaded one tray and was hurrying inside with it.

Between the two of them they soon had the cart emptied. 'It's a big society wedding,' Megan told her. 'There's flowers brought in specially, and every guest is to have a present . . . silver for the women, pewter for the men. Oh, and there's to be musicians and everything.' She sighed dreamily. 'It's like a fairytale and it must be costing a fortune. But that nice Mr Turner doesn't seem to care. He wants his daughter to have the very best, that's what he told me.' She gave a little giggle. '*And* he gave me a two-shilling tip.'

Cathleen was surprised. 'That's very generous.' Somehow she had come to think of Helen Turner's father as being some sort of a monster.

'I've put it with my other tips,' Megan confided. 'I hide it all in a sock, then I push the sock up the chimney.' Suddenly she gave a gasp and flattened her hand to her mouth. 'I should never have told you!' she cried. 'That's the first time I've ever told *anyone*.'

Cathleen quietened her. 'Your secret's safe enough with me,' she said, and Megan instinctively felt she could trust her.

'You're nice,' she told Cathleen, and with a sideways glance she added, 'Not like *him*!'

When Cathleen asked who she meant, Megan clammed up. Instead, she lowered her voice to an excited whisper. 'Do you want to see the cake?'

Thinking of Silas, Cathleen shook her head, but then curiosity got the better of her. 'All right, but we'll have to make it quick,' she said, nervously following the girl through the long winding corridor. 'I've to get back, you see.'

'Wait here. I'll make sure there's no one about.' Inching open the big wooden door, Megan peered inside. 'It's all right.' She beckoned Cathleen forward. 'They've gone now.' And she threw open the door for Cathleen to see. 'It's magic!' she sighed. 'Fit for a princess.' She grimaced. 'The bride's no princess, though. She was here early this morning and ended up yelling at everybody. Nobody likes her.' She smiled shyly. 'Silas Fenshaw is lovely though.' Clasping her hands together, she rolled her huge eyes. 'I wish he was marrying *me*.'

The mention of his name tore at Cathleen's heart. 'Can I go in?' she asked. 'I've never seen the layout for a society wedding before.' Against her deeper instincts, she found herself driven by a kind of morbid curiosity.

Afraid to be seen, Megan glanced up and down the corridor; it was all clear. 'Yes, of course you can . . . only a minute or two though. If they find us here we'll be for the high jump.'

Following Megan inside, Cathleen was open-mouthed with astonishment, her startled gaze going round and round the room. 'Oh my God!' Just as Megan had said, it really was like magic.

The ceilings were festooned with silk, and every wall fitted end to end with long tables, each covered in a white damask cloth; silver and crystal chandeliers hung over it all. Enormous silver tureens and dishes of various shapes and sizes were set ready on one side to receive the soups, fish and many meat dishes which would undoubtedly be carried to the tables the moment the guests arrived.

Other tables, large and round, were placed about the room, every one set with the very best of silver cutlery and crystal glasses. There were blue china plates, and on these were displayed napkins of a deeper blue, made to look like oriental wands. On each table was the most exquisite and extravagant arrangement of imported flowers and, beside each setting, a box tied with ribbon, containing a present for every guest.

Standing there, overawed by what she could see, Cathleen found it difficult to imagine Silas being part of all this; and yet she knew he was, and always had been. Strange, she thought, how only now did she understand how far apart they really were.

'That's the head table,' Megan's voice whispered in her ear. 'That's where the bride and groom sit . . . and there look, that's where the Maid of Honour sits . . . and there the bridesmaids, and over here the parents of the newly-weds. Do you see?'

Cathleen didn't want to see. She wanted to get out of there as quickly as her two feet would carry her. With a muttered apology, she took to her heels, fleeing along the corridor and out of the back door, straight into the arms of Silas Fenshaw.

Shocked and delighted, Silas held her at arm's length. 'Cathleen!' His smiling gaze enveloped her.

Breathless from her escape, and now completely startled at seeing him there, Cathleen couldn't speak. Instead she stared up at him, a great well of emotion rising inside her.

Before either of them could recover, Megan was there. 'Why did you run off like that, Cathleen?' Bursting onto the scene, she saw the two of them together and guessed how they'd collided at the door. 'Oh, Mr Fenshaw, sir!' Colouring up, she began to stutter, 'Is everything all right? I didn't know you were coming in this morning. Can I help you? Is it the manager you want? Only, this is the tradesman's entrance, sir.' Embarrassed and shy, she looked from one to the other, an impossible idea crossing her mind when she saw how distressed he appeared to be, and how his gaze kept going back to Cathleen, who kept her head down, her whole manner subdued.

Sensing her curiosity, Silas was quick to distract her attention. 'There's no need for the manager,' he answered with a charming smile. 'And yes, you *can* help, if you will.' He went on to remind her how, the previous evening, he and his mother had visited the hotel. 'My mother so wanted to see the banqueting room before the event,' he said. 'As you will recall, she and I were alone. I pushed her in her wheelchair.' He glanced at Cathleen as he said this. 'The thing is, she's lost her handbag, and I have an idea she might have left it there, in that room.'

Megan shook her head. 'I don't think so, sir,' she told him. 'There have been all kinds of people in and out of that room only this very morning, and I'm sure if a handbag had been found, someone would have sent it straight over to Fenshaw House.' Glancing at Cathleen, she then returned her attention to Silas. 'I'll go and have a look, if you want?' she offered discreetly. 'Or you can look yourself, sir. There's nobody who'll mind.'

Silas was quick to accept her offer. 'If you would just have a quick look around for me,' he told her. 'And you mustn't worry anyone else. If it isn't there, then it must be somewhere else. If it *is* there, I'm sure you'll find it.'

Eager to please, and certain there was something going on between Cathleen and Silas, Megan hurried away. 'I'm not daft,' she muttered to herself as she went. 'I saw the way he was looking at her, and I saw how she couldn't bring herself to look up at him.' Megan wasn't a gossip, and she had taken to Cathleen like she had never taken to anyone else. 'It's an odd thing and no mistake,' she concluded. If there was an opportunity, she might ask Cathleen about it because, as sure as night followed day, she meant to keep in contact with her. 'She's a lovely girl, that Cathleen, and I've a feeling the two of us might end up being good friends.' The thought brought a happy smile to her face.

Outside, Silas was telling Cathleen how seeing her had brightened the worst day of his life. 'When I woke up this morning it was like I had to prepare for the hangman,' he confessed. 'And now, seeing you . . .' Looking down on her, he thought he would never see anything more beautiful than her shining face. 'You've no idea,' he whispered. 'Not a minute goes by when you're not in my mind. God knows, I think of you all the time.'

With all manner of emotion running through her, Cathleen was loath to look him in the eye, but she couldn't help herself. 'I have to go,' she murmured. The sight of him had turned her whole world upside down. She wanted to run from there, but her feet wouldn't do what her head told them to.

With great tenderness, he took her in his arms. 'Stay with me, Cathleen. Let me hold you,' he pleaded, and, feeling as she did, how could she refuse?

She felt herself being pressed to him, then he brought his warm mouth down on hers and her heart raced with joy. Then Megan could be heard coming down the corridor and the moment was lost. Ashamed and afraid, Cathleen tore herself away. 'Goodbye, Silas,' she told him resignedly. 'You belong to *her* now.'

Without looking back, she ran to the cart and climbed up. Collecting the reins, she urged the horse on and was swiftly gone, leaving Megan and Silas staring after her; one sensing something sad and wonderful and wondering what had happened between the two of them, the other knowing and hating himself for it.

Driving the horse on at greater speed through the narrow lanes and on towards the bakery, Cathleen sought to put as much distance between herself and Silas as possible. When she couldn't see for the blinding tears, she drew the horse to a halt and gave herself a moment to recover. Closing her eyes, she let his image flood her senses. She could still feel his kiss burning on her mouth. Tenderly, she touched her fingers against her lips.

Then she wiped away the tears and was on her way again. She was calmer now, ready to face anything.

———◆———

T HAT VERY AFTERNOON, her resolve was put to the test.

With her work done, she took to the fields, walking the rough paths that skirted Blackburn town. At the top of the hill she paused, her gaze reaching down towards the lovely church of St Peter's.

The wedding was already underway, with myriad people queuing in the grounds; there were drivers in top hat and tails waiting beside their shiny black carriages, and a photographer setting up his equipment, ready to record the momentous occasion.

Then the church bells rang out and the service was over. The congregation began to spill out, followed by the happy couple; Helen Fenshaw resplendent in her magnificent white gown, and Silas incredibly handsome in his grey suit and tails.

A short time later, as they hurried through the heightening breeze to the carriages, Silas must have felt her presence, for he glanced up in her direction. It was as if his heart was calling her.

'Be happy, my love,' Cathleen whispered. Then, holding back the sobs that threatened to engulf her, she walked away.

The dream was over.

Drawn by the past that still held them together, she glanced back, just once. He was still there, his gaze raking the hills, searching for her. Turning away she began to run, and the faster she ran, the more the loneliness came on her.

There was something else too. Something she dared not even think about, though at some point in the future, God help her, she would have to face it, together with the consequences that would surely follow.

Chapter Ten

❦

'IT'S A FUNNY kind of autumn, don't you think?'
Manoeuvring the cart down the narrow cobbled alley,
Lou opened the neck of his shirt. 'Last month we had
days like winter, with the rain and wind, and now here
we are, almost at the end of October, and it's like summer
all over again.'

Holding onto her seat as the cart leaped and dipped
through the deep ruts, Cathleen glanced at him; she
noted how his face was red and his temples sweating,
and beneath his jacket peeped a thick layer of clothes.
'That's the quickest way to catch flu,' she chided.

'What – the weather, you mean?'

'No, I mean *you*.' Turning back the lapel of his
jacket, she revealed the thickness of his clothes. 'How
many jumpers have you got on?'

'Only two.'

'It's no wonder you feel uncomfortable. You've been
in and out of a hot bakery, fetching and carrying to the
shops, and up and down God knows how many stairs.

And all the time you've been wearing two woollies under your jacket.'

'It were cold when I left home this morning.' Drawing the cart to a halt outside Clayton's yard, he declared quietly, 'Here we are then, Cathleen.' His voice and his smile were half-hearted. 'The last delivery before we make our way back.' It was a Saturday, the day he dreaded, because it meant he wouldn't see her again until the Monday morning.

Getting down from the cart, Cathleen gave a sigh. 'It's been a long day,' she commented. 'I won't deny I'm ready for home.' Normally the day could be as long and hard as it liked and she'd still be as fresh as a daisy at the end of it, but since that afternoon at the church, when Silas had sought her out with his dark eyes, nothing was the same. One day ran into another, and none of them meant very much. It was morning, then it was night, and then it was morning again.

'Here, let me do that.' Following her to the back of the cart, Lou snatched the end of the sheeting and threw it back. Gesturing to the trays of pork pies, he confessed, 'I put two extra in . . . one for you and one for me. Or, if you're hungry, you can have them both.'

Cathleen smiled; he was such a considerate person. 'Thank you, Lou, that was thoughtful of you, and normally, as you know, I'd be wolfing one down, but . . .' She looked at the tray of freshly baked pies with the gravy still warm on top and the pastry flaking at the edges, and her stomach turned over. 'I couldn't eat anything just now.'

'Are you all right?' Lou had watched her all day and

thought her unusually quiet. Now he saw how the colour ebbed from her face, and he was concerned.

Cathleen was quick to reassure him. ''Course I'm all right.' Only she wasn't. She was ill and worried, and frightened, too. 'I'm a bit tired, that's all. Like I said, it's been a long day.'

He didn't believe her. 'Look, Cathleen, if ever you need someone to talk to, I make a good friend.' Taking her by the shoulders, he gazed at her with his honest brown eyes, and in them she saw his longing to be more than just a friend. 'I'd do anything to help, you know that, don't you?'

She nodded. 'I know.' But on this occasion, Lou was the last person she could talk to. 'I'm grateful,' she said, 'but there's no need to worry. I'm all right, really.'

'Cathleen?' With his trembling hands gripping her shoulders, he looked down on her, his face burning and his heart going thirteen to the dozen. 'I just . . . I mean . . .' Gulping, he fought to keep his composure.

Realising what he was striving to say, Cathleen put a tender finger over his lips. 'Please, Lou,' she murmured, 'I think we'd best get to work, don't you?' She didn't want to hurt him, nor did she want to encourage him; he was a nice enough bloke, and she did like him as a work colleague and a friend, but that was all.

With no choice but to accept her gentle refusal, he backed off. 'Think on though,' he persisted. 'If you need me, I'm never far away.' At the back of his mind he suspected she was still fretting over Silas Fenshaw. But the tide was turning *his* way now, and with Fenshaw safely wed, all he wanted was half a chance with Cathleen and he'd be there.

For the next half-hour they were too busy for conversation. With fourteen trays of pork pies, two crates of muffins and a box of barmcakes to deliver, they had their work cut out.

'No, dear, the barmcakes go on the shelf.' Ma Merry stood at the door, directing them here and there, her voice ringing out when Cathleen made for the counter display. 'I keeps the inside counter for pork pies, and the top for muffins . . . all set out pretty in dishes with doilies.'

When she laughed she shook, like a jelly half set. 'The juicy pies will make their mouths water, and their big eyes will finish off with a muffin,' she cackled. 'Afore they go, their consciences will force them into buying a teacake for the wife, and before you know it I'll have sold each man one of everything. I'll open shop at half past seven tonight, just as they're mekking for the pub, and by the time they come rolling out some hours later with their bellies rumbling for food, they'll remember the sight o' them goodies in my window and they'll be in here like dogs after a rat.'

Full of herself, she promised grandly, 'Mark my words, afore I go to bed tonight, the shelves will be empty and the till full to bursting.' Folding her fat little arms over her chest, she continued to give instructions. At the end of it, when everything was set out and covered to keep moist, she paid the bill without batting an eyelid. 'Off you go then,' she winked, 'and no canoodling on the way.'

Lou thought wryly a chance would be a fine thing, but wisely made no comment, while Cathleen was intrigued as to what gave Ma Merry the idea that she and Lou might want to 'canoodle'.

'Like a bloody sergeant-major she is!' Lou grumbled as they made their way to the cart. 'She's a hard little bugger an' no mistake.'

Clambering onto the cart before he could offer to help her, Cathleen came to the little woman's defence. 'She's *had* to be sharp.' Ma Merry had gone through bad times, everyone knew that.

When Lou seemed surprised, she went on, 'Don't forget how it used to be – lazy husband, shop open till all hours, and hardly any business coming in. I mean, the shop isn't in the best spot, hidden away down this side street. Poor thing, when her husband got run over and killed, she was left destitute.'

Clicking the horse on, Lou recalled how it was. 'You're right,' he agreed. 'Any other woman might have pulled up sticks and moved on, but not her. She saw how, of an evening, the men allus took a short cut past her shop and into the pub, and so she shut the shop during the day and opened it at night. By! It were a canny move, 'cause she ain't never looked back.'

There was little else said during the journey to the bakery, though Lou was aware of Cathleen, and she of him; the one wondering what was playing on her mind, the other afraid he might have guessed her secret. Who could she share it with? she wondered frantically. Who could she trust enough to confide in? A kind of quiet came into her heart. 'Jessie!' Oh, but how? That was the thing.

Now, as she murmured Jessie's name, her voice was the merest whisper, but the heartfelt cry did not escape Lou. 'Talking to yourself now, is it?' he asked curiously. 'You know what they say about folks who talk to themselves.'

Cathleen smiled but said nothing. Instead, she kept her gaze straight ahead. Not once after his light-hearted remark did she look at him, nor he at her.

But the undercurrent between them was intense.

———❖———

It was Sunday evening when Cathleen had no option but to confide in Jessie.

Seated by the fire, with her sewing in hand and concentration on her face, Jessie finished mending the apron, then darned the socks, and now, as she stretched her back to ease the ache, she saw Cathleen curled up in the window-seat, her arms round her knees and her head down.

There was something about her that struck at Jessie's old heart. 'Will yer look at that.' In a whisper, Jessie voiced her concern, 'She ain't well, poor little bugger . . . nor has she been these past weeks.' Sighing, she got out of her chair and started over to her. 'What she needs is to get right away for a complete change of scene. I'll speak to Tom about it, so I will.'

Coming to the window, she stooped to see Cathleen's

face, and sure enough the lass was sleeping; though when Jessie fetched a coat to put round her, she woke with a start. 'Hey! Easy, lass. It's only me.'

Sitting up, Cathleen put her two arms round the old woman's neck. 'I was dreaming,' she said.

'Huh! More of a nightmare I'd say, judging by the way yer almost leaped out of yer skin when I woke yer.'

'Sorry.' Kissing the old woman on the cheek she noticed how tired Jessie looked, and said so. 'Why don't you go and have a lie-down,' she suggested. 'You've been busy all day, cooking and washing, and now the sewing. You're too hard on yourself.'

'Oh, and what about you, eh? You've not sat still for two minutes. Every time I've gone to do summat, it's been "Let me do that, Grandma", "Sit down, Grandma".' Shaking her head, she chuckled heartily. 'I reckon if anybody should have a lie-down, it's you!'

Swinging her feet to the floor, Cathleen put on her shoes, 'D'you fancy a brew?'

'Go on then. I can see I'll get no peace till I say yes.'

Fighting the butterflies in her stomach, Cathleen made her way to the scullery.

A short time later, when they were seated by the fire, each with a mug of steaming-hot tea, Jessie casually glanced up and straight into Cathleen's worried blue eyes. 'Whatever is it, lass?' She saw the fear on Cathleen's face, and the guilt, and above all that, the desperate need to talk with her.

Cathleen took a deep breath. 'I've got something to tell you.'

Putting down her mug, Jessie moved to the edge of her chair. 'Go on, lass, I'm listening.'

When Cathleen glanced towards the stairway, Jessie understood. 'It's all right,' she assured her, 'yer father's having a snooze. There's nobody here but you and me.'

Afraid and unsure, Cathleen didn't know where to start.

'Go on, lass,' Jessie urged. 'Unless you've changed yer mind?'

Unable to sit still with Jessie's eyes on her, and knowing she was about to break the worst news possible, Cathleen got out of the chair and took to pacing the room. After a minute, she came to sit on the rug next to Jessie. 'I don't know what to do,' she murmured, 'I'm so afraid.'

In that moment, Jessie knew; she looked into those deep blue eyes and she knew. 'Jesus, Mary and Joseph!' She slowly shook her head, not wanting to believe it, but losing the last semblance of doubt when she saw the tears falling down Cathleen's sorry face. *'Yer with child, aren't yer?'*

There was a fleeting moment when Cathleen was tempted to deny it; to protest how she was a good girl and knew the difference between right and wrong. But she was no longer a girl, and there on the island she had crossed the line between right and wrong, but she didn't regret it. For as long as she lived and however hard the consequences, she would *never* regret it. Inside of her was a tiny, living soul; Silas's baby. Last night she had even imagined she felt it move. 'I think I'm into the third month,' she said, and it was as if the weight of the world had been taken off her shoulders.

'Oh, lass!' Instinctively reaching out, Jessie caught her tight. They stayed like that for a while, held together by a bond that would never be broken on this earth, with the warmth of the fire in their faces and their love for each other warming their hearts. 'Does Silas know?' It was the first question that came into Jessie's troubled mind.

Cathleen shook her head. 'No, and I don't want him to.'

Jessie didn't argue with that, but said, 'Yer realise your father will have to know?'

'What will he do?' It was her father's reaction she was afraid of.

'I'm not sure, lass. He'll be furious. Ashamed too, I've no doubt.'

'Will he go to Silas?'

'Happen he will, aye. And yer can't blame him if he did.' Jessie was not going to hide her feelings. 'When all's said and done, Silas Fenshaw took advantage of you.'

'That was not the way it happened.' She would never be able to live with herself if she let Silas take all the blame.

Jessie was shocked by Cathleen's outburst. 'What are you saying, lass?'

Embarrassed but not ashamed, Cathleen told her, 'I wanted us to be together. It was *my* idea to go to the island.'

'Then more's the shame!'

'There's no shame, Grandma.' Only love and respect

and a precious memory that would carry her through. 'Don't tell Father. He's grown so bitter towards Silas.'

'He has to know, lass. Surely you can see that?'

'Not yet.'

'A thing like that . . .' Torn by divided loyalties, Jessie protested, 'Yer can't keep it from him.'

Persistent, Cathleen asked again, 'Promise me you won't tell him.'

'I'll promise, but only if *you* promise to tell him yourself.'

Cathleen played for time. 'I'll tell him when the time is right.'

Stewing the whole business over in her mind, Jessie couldn't see a way out of it. 'We've plans to make,' she said. 'There are things to be done. In the morning, you and me will take a little trip to the doctor's. Happen yer not with child at all. More experienced women than you have made mistakes.'

Jessie knew she was clutching at straws, but what Cathleen had told her was something that would change all their lives, and she wished with all her heart that it had never happened.

Glancing at Jessie's ashen face, Cathleen knew she had shocked the old woman to the core. Only then did a sense of shame engulf her, for she loved Jessie too much to hurt her. 'Grandma?'

'What is it, lass?'

A pause, then, 'I'm sorry.' Simple, heartfelt words.

With a well of love spilling over for Cathleen, who could have no idea of what lay in store for her, Jessie cupped her gnarled old hands round that uplifted face and whispered, 'I'm sorry too, child. Sorry you thought to give yerself away like that, without a ring on yer finger, and with a man you must have known could never be yours. It hurts me to think you kept this to yerself for almost three months, worrying and fretting and no one to turn to.' She blamed herself, too, for she had seen Cathleen lose her appetite, and just the once she had heard her retching in the washroom. Also of late, she'd noticed how the lass seemed to think twice before lifting heavy crates and such.

But then, she had never in a million years thought it could be a bairn, not even though she had been concerned about Cathleen and Silas growing too close. Now though, she knew what the lass must have been going through, with the wedding, and now a bairn on the way and no father to love it. 'Most of all,' she concluded, 'I'm sorry you've been denied the man you love.' Blinking away the tears, she promised, 'I'll tell yer this though. That little bairn o' yourn won't go short of love, nor will it ever know hard times, and neither will its mammy – not while I'm here to watch over the both of yez.'

Feeling incredibly old, and needing to be alone with her thoughts, she kissed Cathleen goodnight. 'I'm tired, lass,' she said, and in a moment was climbing the stairs, leaving Cathleen to reflect on their conversation.

When the stairs door closed behind the old woman, Cathleen was quiet for a moment. Then she climbed onto the sofa, where she let her thoughts drift back to that day on the island; it seemed a lifetime away, but the consequence of what had happened there would be with her for another lifetime. Yet she welcomed it, for it meant Silas would never be far away.

Sitting there on the sofa, warm before the fire in this cottage that was home, and with two people upstairs who loved her, she felt secure. Then she thought of Silas and his new wife, and herself and the bairn, and the awful loneliness came back with a vengeance.

———⊰•⊱———

I T WAS TEN o'clock when Robert arrived at the cottage with a friend, rather late for his usual Sunday visit. Drunk out of their minds, the two of them struggled in through the front door, giggling and chattering. 'Be quiet!' Robert urged. 'Or you'll get us both thrown out.'

Coming into the parlour, the friend noticed Cathleen fast asleep on the sofa, her skirt twisted about her legs and her face upward against the cushion. 'Hey!' Inching forward, he looked down on her sleeping face. 'Who's this little beauty then, eh?'

Falling into the nearby chair, Robert guffawed. 'That's my sister, Cathleen,' he said. 'Pretty, ain't she?'

'Best I've seen in a long time.' Some eight years older than Robert, the other man was tall and thin with a heavy mop of black hair, and glinting eyes that betrayed his every emotion; right now they were riveted on Cathleen. 'How much?' Jiggling from one foot to the other, it was all he could do to keep his hands to himself. But he knew Robert and the kind of temper he had, so he bided his time. 'I never knew an ugly bugger like you might have a sister like this.' His greedy gaze roved her perfectly shaped legs, the soft, pink skin glowing in the firelight. His voice was low, his smile evil. '*How much?*' Looking round, he grinned at the other lad. 'Come on! You know what I mean!'

Robert knew exactly what he meant, and the thought of Lou being cheated appealed to his warped sense of humour. 'She's yours if you want her.'

The other man was taken aback. 'You're even more of a bastard than I thought.'

Shrugging his shoulders, Robert answered sullenly, 'What do I care? She ain't *my* responsibility.'

Stooping, the other man gentled her skirt back; he saw the lace on her petticoat and the curve of her thighs and it was enough to set him going. Opening his trousers, he let them slide to the floor. In a minute he was on her, one hand over her mouth and the other fumbling at her clothes. In the background Robert's drunken giggles smothered the other man's groans as he fought desperately to keep her still while he got on top of her.

Jolted out of a troubled sleep, Cathleen woke, her blue eyes wide with terror when she realised what was happening. Fighting like a wild thing, she pitted her strength against her attacker's, but it only excited him more.

From the corner of her eye she could see Robert, slouched in the chair, his face contorted with laughter, and, on top of her, the beast tearing at her clothes, his hard member jabbing at her through her drawers.

Suddenly, from out of nowhere, a pair of huge hands grabbed him by the throat and tore him away. The fist came down like a hammer and the man was flying backwards, there was a lot of swearing and shouting, and now, as she crouched on the sofa, clutching her torn clothes about her bruised body, Cathleen felt herself being dragged to her feet, her arms twisted behind her back and her brother's fingers round her throat, crushing the breath inside her.

'*It wasn't me!*' Beside himself with fright, Robert whimpered like a baby, one minute staring down at his friend out cold on the ground, the next pleading desperately with Tom, who threatened to tear him apart. '*Get away!*' he screamed. '*Get away, or I'll break her neck!*'

Standing his ground, but careful not to antagonise his son too much, Tom warned, 'You were here. You saw what he was doing and you left him to it.' Disgust coloured his voice. 'What kind of a brother are you?'

'Let me go. I don't care what you do with him.' His scared eyes looked down on the other man. 'It were *him*, I tell you. You've no right coming after me.' He squeezed Cathleen's throat until, grey with pain, she began to feel the life going from her. 'HURT ME, AND I'LL HURT HER!' In fear for himself, he had no mercy.

Suddenly another voice cut across the room. 'Robert, NO! She's with child!' In the heat of the moment, Jessie forgot her promise; her only thought was for Cathleen's safety.

In the wake of Jessie's frantic cry, a hush settled over the room. Shocked to his roots, Tom turned to stare at

Jessie. His son grabbed his opportunity and, dropping Cathleen to the floor, fled from the room, unable to resist a spiteful comment as he went. 'Happen you should have let him have the slut! Nobody else will want her, that's for sure!' The sound of his laughter echoed through the night, and Tom's agony was tenfold.

Going to Cathleen, Jessie lifted the girl into her arms. 'It's all right, lass.' But it wasn't, and Cathleen knew it. With haggard eyes, she looked to her father; and was distraught when he turned away.

Satisfied that Cathleen was recovered enough from her ordeal, Jessie gently escorted her to the door. 'Go to your room, child,' she urged, 'I'll be up presently.'

When Cathleen was out of earshot, Jessie turned her attention to Tom. 'Listen to me,' she pleaded. 'What Robert said isn't true. Cathleen is no slut.' Trying desperately to make amends, she asked him to look at her. 'It's not what it seems. The child belongs to—'

Startling her with his sudden movement, Tom grabbed her to him, his face almost touching hers as he said in a shockingly quiet voice, 'I don't want to know who it belongs to. I can't stay in this house if she's here. I want her out before I come back. She can have an hour, possibly two, but I want her gone from here.' With a long, shuddering sigh, he finished on a whisper, 'For as long as I live, I never want to see her face again. D'you understand what I'm saying, Jessie?'

Hardly able to see for the tears swimming in her eyes, Jessie murmured, 'She's your daughter, Tom, don't turn on her now.'

He gave a soft laugh. 'I *had* a daughter,' he said, 'and I had a son. But they both shamed me, and now I have no children. That's how it is, Jessie. That's how it must be from now on.' The cold rage in his voice struck her dumb; she had known this good man long enough to realise how deeply this had affected him.

Collecting the man from the floor as though he weighed no more than a bag of flour, Tom carried him shoulder-high to the door, where he threw him out on to the ground. When the man opened his eyes to see Tom standing over him, he scrambled to his feet and was quickly away.

Covering his face with his two hands, Tom began to sob, gently at first, then deep, racking sobs that echoed into the house and up to the stairs where Cathleen waited, hoping he would forgive, wanting to go to him, but not daring to.

Her father's cries tore at her heart until she could stand it no more. Running to the door, she saw it was too late; already he was striding from the cottage, his weary frame disappearing into the night.

He would not come back, she knew that.

Not until she was gone.

UP IN HER room, Cathleen washed and changed, then packed just enough for her to carry. 'Underwear, a clean nightie, a change of day clothes and my toiletries, that's all I need.' One by one she placed the items into her tapestry bag, and while Cathleen busied herself, Jessie followed her round the room.

'Don't go,' she pleaded, 'I'll talk to him. Oh, he were all riled up at Robert, and then I let the cat out of the bag about you an' the bairn. Don't yer see? It were one shock after another. But he'll come round. Once he's walked in the fresh air and seen how cruel his words were, I'll make him understand.'

Turning to face her, Cathleen was adamant. 'He'll *never* understand. He set his heart against Silas, and now he's set his heart against me.'

Knowing Cathleen could be as stubborn as her father, Jessie stopped arguing. Instead she suggested, 'Let me go with yer.'

Cathleen shook her head. 'I know how worried you are,' she said, 'but be honest, Grandma. Would you be happy away from here?' When Jessie hung her head, Cathleen took her into her arms. 'You've been my only friend, and I love you dearly, but now I have to go, and you're not to worry.'

'Oh, lass, where will yer go?' Jessie's voice trembled. 'How will I know what's happening to yer?' To lose sight of that darling girl would surely kill her.

'I have money saved,' Cathleen confided. 'I had hoped it might be for a wedding dress and such, but now, well . . .' Pausing, she smiled a wistful smile. 'It'll be for me and the bairn.' Seeing the doubt in the old woman's eyes, she told her, 'Tonight I'll find a respectable boarding house on Preston New Road. In the morning I'll be up early to make my way out of

Blackburn. Happen I'll go to Liverpool. I'm told there's plenty of work for the taking.'

Jessie was even more worried now. 'If I don't get word from you by the end of this week, I'm coming after you!'

'Soonever I'm settled, I'll get word to you.' Cathleen wouldn't let her down.

'I wish you'd wait till yer father gets back.'

Cathleen shook her head. 'He won't come back until I'm out of the way,' she said. 'He's probably stood at the edge of the spinney now, watching the cottage . . . waiting for me to leave.' Picking up her tapestry bag, she gave Jessie a last hug. 'I'll be fine,' she assured her. 'Don't worry.'

'What about when the bairn comes?'

Cathleen hadn't thought that far ahead. 'It'll be all right. We'll be safe, God willing.'

Subdued, Jessie went with her to the front door. 'See?' Gesturing to the spinney, Cathleen pointed out the solitary figure in the moonlight. 'Like I said, he won't come back until I'm gone.'

Jessie's expression hardened. 'God forgive him!' she snorted. 'He'll live to regret this day.'

'Don't be too hard on him,' Cathleen murmured regretfully. Her father might never find it in his heart to forgive her, but she had already forgiven him. 'He did what he thought was right.'

Amazed, Jessie asked, 'Look at me, lass.' When Cathleen turned, she told her in a quiet, surprised voice, 'Yesterday you were just a darling young girl. Now you've grown into a woman, and I'm that proud of you.' The tears had trembled on the edge of her eyes and now, as she smiled, they fell like raindrops, dancing down her homely old face. 'God go with yer,' she whispered, and when her breath caught in a sob, Cathleen held her fast.

'I'll get word to you,' she promised, 'I *will*!'

From the spinney edge, Tom watched them hold each other; he saw Cathleen say her goodbyes and Jessie wave her down the lane. He felt Cathleen's sad glance on him as she turned the corner, and his heart was unbending. 'You shame me,' he kept saying, over and over. 'You *both* shame me!'

When Cathleen saw him turn away, she held her head high and kept on walking, her heart breaking but her step determined. One day, who knows, he might forgive her. He might even come to love his grandchild.

———⇒•⇐———

THAT NIGHT, CATHLEEN booked into a boarding house on Park Street. 'I don't normally allow boarders in at this time of night.' The landlady was a sour old puss. 'But you look decent enough to me – though why a young lady such as yourself should be wandering about alone at this hour, I'm sure I don't know! However, I'll make an exception this time. How long will you be wanting to stay?'

'Just the one night,' she said, and was shown to her room by a tired-looking girl who came scurrying out of the kitchen. 'This way, ma'am.' It made Cathleen uncomfortable to be addressed as 'ma'am' by a girl not much younger than herself.

The room was clean and spacious and would serve her purpose. 'Thank you.' Fishing in her purse, Cathleen brought a smile to the girl's face by handing her a threepenny piece.

'D'you want anything?' There were no frills and fancies about this young woman.

'No, thank you.' All she wanted was to lie down and reflect on the day's traumatic events.

''Night then.'

'Goodnight.'

Left on her own, Cathleen was soon undressed and in bed, though the mattress struck cold to her flesh. Lying there, in the quiet darkness, her mind soon turned to Silas. 'I wonder if you'll ever see your bairn?' she whispered.

In her heart, she believed he never would.

⁂

IT WAS NINE-THIRTY when Cathleen took a cab to the railway station. 'Yes, miss?' The red-faced ticket-officer looked her up and down and, obviously appreciating the sight of a fresh young thing at his window, gave her a cheery smile. 'And where might you be going, my dear?'

Cathleen had made up her mind. 'London. I'd like a one-way ticket to Euston, please.'

There was a half-hour wait for the train. On the platform the wind was blowing and there was a cutting edge to the morning air. Spotting a sign to the waiting room, Cathleen made her way there.

Inside was a small fireplace, a cheery fire burning within. There were two other people: an old man and what appeared to be his daughter. 'We're going to Birmingham.' The tired young woman latched onto Cathleen, as if she was desperate to talk to someone. 'Faither's deaf as a post . . . not been well. He's a handful, I can tell you. I'm taking him to my aunt's in Birmingham – let her look after him while I have a rest.'

After a few minutes, their train came and they ambled away, leaving Cathleen alone again. Not long after the two had gone, she was warming her hands by the fire when she thought she heard someone come in the door behind her, but when she turned there was no one there. Shrugging her shoulders, she went to the bench and sat down, anxious for the train to come, yet dreading it at the same time. Leaving her beloved Blackburn was a hard step to take.

Above her head the big clock ticked noisily. 'Ten minutes,' she observed, 'then I'm on my way.' She thought about her destination, and wondered if she was doing the right thing. In all her life, she had never been to London. She had no idea where to go or whom to trust, even whether she would like it enough to stay. One thing was certain, though. The way things were, her life had to take a different direction, whether she liked it or not.

Going to the window, she watched for the train to

arrive. After a minute, something caught her attention. As well as the clock and its giant tick, she could hear what sounded like someone crying. Curious, she traced the sound; it seemed to be coming from the ladies' cloakroom.

There were two WCs in the cloakroom, and the sound of crying was coming from the farthest one. 'Hello!' Standing by the door, Cathleen called out, 'Is everything all right?'

'Go away!' The voice filtered through the sobs.

Cathleen persisted, 'Please, come out and talk. It sounds as if you've got troubles – well, so have I. Maybe we can comfort each other.' She knew what it was like to be all alone and afraid.

The sobbing stopped, and after a moment the door opened, and out came a young woman. One eye and the side of her face were badly swollen, with an angry red weal running from ear to chin. 'My God!' Cathleen could hardly believe her eyes. 'MEGAN!' It was the girl from the Riverside Hotel, where Silas and Helen Turner had held their wedding party. 'What happened to you?'

Recognising Cathleen, Megan told her, 'It was Jake.'

'Jake?' Cathleen recalled the name. 'He's from the hotel, isn't he?' She hadn't liked the look of him then, and now she knew why.

Megan nodded. 'I have to get away from him.'

Leading the girl to the wash-basin, Cathleen bathed her wounds with cold water. 'Why would he do this to you?'

Nervous, Megan glanced towards the door. 'Thanks

for your help,' she said, pulling away, 'I have to go now.'

Aware that Megan didn't want to discuss the matter of why Jake had attacked her, Cathleen changed the subject. 'Where will you go?' She saw the small portmanteau standing by the door.

Megan answered in a furtive whisper, '*Anywhere*, as long as he can't find me.'

The porter opened the door to announce, 'London train arriving!'

'Come with me, Megan,' Catheen urged. 'We can help each other. What d'you say?'

The young Welsh girl shook her head. 'Me and Jake Brewer used to work in a hotel down there. London's the first place he'll go looking for me.'

'They tell me London's a big place. How could he find you?'

'Oh, he'll find me all right.' A look of fear marbled her eyes. 'He wants to kill me!'

From outside, the call came for everyone to get aboard. 'You'd better hurry or you'll miss your train,' Megan said. 'Go on. I'll be all right.'

Cathleen didn't like leaving her like this. 'I'll stay with you,' she offered. 'I can always catch another train.'

Megan was adamant. 'I've already got my ticket to Manchester,' she said. Taking it from her purse, she showed it to Cathleen. 'There's only a few minutes to wait then I'll be gone from here.'

'If you're sure?' Cathleen was still reluctant to go.

'I'm sure, but thanks all the same.' She gave a smile. 'You've been very kind. I won't forget you.'

A moment later, Cathleen was boarding the London train. Megan stood by the waiting room while the conductor walked along the platform, closing the train doors one after another. There was a whoosh of steam from the engine and Megan was quickly lost from sight.

Unsettled, Cathleen sat herself by the window. The whistle blew, and suddenly came a cry and the sound of running feet. When she looked out the window it was to see Megan running up the platform, frantically boarding the train only seconds before it drew away.

'I must be mad!' Megan burst into the carriage. 'I just couldn't let you go without me.' They fell into each other's arms, laughing and crying.

In that brief moment, when for the time being all troubles were forgotten, a wonderful friendship was made.

Chapter Eleven

———⟫•◦•⟪———

JESSIE THREW THE invitation aside. 'Damned cheek! What makes the buggers think we'd be interested in seeing them stuff their faces with turkey and such. I'd rather watch pigs swilling, so I would.'

Feet up by the fire and smoking his old pipe, Tom peered over his newspaper. 'Now then, Jessie!' he scowled. ''Tain't no use you blaming them. It were *her* fault as much as his. She were brought up good and now she's turned bad. If she had a spark of decency in her, she'd know how to conduct herself with any young man, Silas Fenshaw included.'

'Yer can think what yer like, but I'm not going to their Christmas Eve do, tradition or no tradition!'

Sitting up in the chair, he folded his newspaper and, putting it aside, told her sharply, 'I don't suppose they've any idea that that lad o' theirs made her with child.' His anger growing, he shook his fist threateningly. 'By! I wish to God I hadn't made that promise to you, 'cause I'd like to go up there right now and tell them a thing or two about their precious son!'

'Oh? And then what?' Taking her hot cocoa to the fireplace, Jessie sat herself down and waited for an answer.

'I don't know what y'mean.' There were times when his mother-in-law talked in riddles, and he couldn't make head nor tail of her.

'Think about it, Tom,' she urged. 'There was a very good reason for me asking you to promise you'd never say anything about our Cathleen's predicament.'

'Huh! To tell you the truth, I don't care one way or the other, 'cause like I say, it takes two to make a bairn, and one of them were my daughter, sod and damn her!'

'Mebbe, but if, by whatever means, Lucy and Edward Fenshaw should discover there's a grandchild on the way, do you think they'd just sit back and do nothing?'

'What *could* they do now? It's too bloody late. The damage is already done, more's the pity.'

Jessie sighed. 'Just like a man. No, what I'm saying is this: the rumours are that poor Lucy Fenshaw hasn't long on this earth. Edward dotes on her, as yer well know. And there's nothing he wouldn't do to make her happy.' Now that she could see Tom was beginning to realise what she was saying, Jessie outlined it for him. 'If Edward Fenshaw knew that Silas had fathered a child, he'd turn the world upside down to find it. Money talks, Tom, don't ever forget that. Against them, our Cathleen would be helpless. Oh, and don't forget either, if the truth should come out, there's Silas himself to be reckoned with. The child is *his*. He has the same rights as our Cathleen. You'll not get round that, whichever way yer turn.'

'I thought I told you I never wanted to hear her name in this house again?' Leaping to his feet, he threw the newspaper down. 'As far as I'm concerned, they can *have* the little bastard! Aye, an' its mammy an' all, 'cause I have no claim on her, not any more I haven't. And nor do I want to!'

As always, Jessie was saddened by his bitterness. 'You don't mean that, Tom.'

'Oh, don't I?' Slamming his fist down on the table, he sent the teapot leaping into the air. 'All I can say is, I'm glad your own lovely daughter's not alive today, 'cause it would break my Mary's heart in two if she could see how her childer have turned out! Good for nothing, the pair of 'em! And now they've both cleared off, and good riddance to them!'

Ever since the terrible evening of the near-rape, Robert had continued to work at the bakery and to lodge at Mrs Matheson's house, but he and his father never exchanged a word apart from essential work-related matters. A terrible atmosphere of mutual dislike and suspicion hung in the air between them.

As he went out of the room cursing and swearing, Jessie murmured under her breath, 'She'd have understood better than you ever will. Robert may have a bad streak in him, and God only knows where it's come from, but our Cathleen is right enough. It were *you* who pushed her and Silas together when you let them be playmates all those years ago. Well, they fell in love, just as I thought, and now she's the one suffering for it.'

She stared a moment into the flames of the fire, her heart sore at the turn of events. 'I'm sorry, Tom, I know you've been a good father – the best. But just when she needs you most, you've let your beloved daughter down. You've turned the lass out of house and home, and here she is, with a bairn on the way. But, for all that, she's a happy little soul. She has a part of Silas with her now, and that's only as it should be.'

Dipping into her pinnie pocket, she took out a letter dated a week ago. She proceeded to read it in a whisper.

Dear Grandma,

Well, I'm settling down in my new job. Mr Trent says I'm not to worry about my job when the baby comes, because he'll keep it open for me. He's even given me more responsibility, and a small rise in my pay-packet, so I am very pleased. Me and Megan have made our room in the bakery look really lovely, and oh, she's so happy now.

London is really exciting. There are theatres and street cafés, and wonderful big shops. The markets are full of noise and colour, and everyone rushes about like there's no tomorrow.

I've been very well, considering I'm almost five months now. But I miss you so much. I miss Father too. You never write about him, so I expect he doesn't want to know how I am, but if you get a chance, please tell him how much I love him.

I'll write again soon,
Your loving grand-daughter, Cathleen
X X X
P.S. Have you seen Silas? Does he ever ask after me? I
know I shouldn't, but I think about him all the time.

Jessie continued to stare at the letter for a few minutes. 'I ain't seen hide nor hair of him, lass,' she murmured, 'but I know he must rue the day he wed that Turner woman, 'cause the word is she's making his life a hell on earth.'

Carefully, she folded the letter and put it safely away.

———◦———

Lucy Fenshaw loved the Christmas Eve party. It was a tradition within the family and, as with other years before, everyone was invited, including family, old friends and close neighbours.

All day the kitchen had been a hive of activity; even now, only two hours before the guests would begin arriving, not all the food was ready. There were joints of pork turning on the spit, succulent pork pies cooling in the pantry, bacon and sausages done to a turn, and the biggest turkey you ever saw, hanging over the grill, with the juices running into the channel beneath, ready to make the gravy.

Cooling on the trays were plump mince pies and sweetmeats, and there, standing proud in the centre of the old pine dresser, was a huge Christmas cake, piped with icing and decorated with a smiling Father Christmas, carrying a sack filled with goodies.

At the doorway, Lucy sat in her wheelchair and clapped her hands. 'You've done me proud,' she told the cook, and the fat little soul beamed from ear to ear.

'I does me best, ma'am,' she said, and went away, happy in her work.

With Silas pushing her about, Lucy conducted a tour of the house, to make certain everything was as it should be; clean towels in the bathrooms, new soap at the basins, and the curtains all tied just so.

'You're an old fusspot,' Silas teased, and she agreed with a smile.

'All done,' she said. 'You can take me back to the hallway now. I need to check the Christmas tree before the guests start arriving.'

On the way they called in on Edward, who was behind the bar, knee-deep in bottles. 'I must be sure there's enough to drink,' he laughed, and Lucy warned him not to get too merry all on his own.

'He's drinking too much of late,' she confided in Silas. 'Ever since you got married he's been different ... quieter, more secretive, as if he's troubled about something.'

Silas sought to put her mind at rest. 'You're imagining things,' he chided. 'I'd know if he was troubled.'

'Is the business all right?' she queried. 'Only when I ask, he changes the subject.'

'Business is the same as always.' Silas had to be

careful how he phrased it. 'A bit slow at the minute, maybe, but it's the same for everybody at this time of year.'

'So he has nothing to worry about?'

Silas shook his head. 'No more than usual. With land and property, you learn to take the rough with the smooth, that's the way it is.'

His mother appeared to be satisfied with his explanation, because now she was more concerned about the Christmas tree. Grabbing Maggie as she went by with an armful of napkins, she told her, 'The tree . . . I'm sure it's leaning. Just give it a tug on that side, dear . . . that's right. No, the other way . . .'

Totally confused, Maggie tripped over her own feet and fell, arms out and legs astride, like a lead weight against the wall. 'Oh dear! Get up, Maggie, before you hurt yourself.'

While Maggie fumbled her way up, hair all messed up and her hat dangling from her ear, Lucy couldn't help but smile up at Silas, who had gone to help and was silently chuckling.

As Maggie collected her napkins which had scattered far and wide, Lucy told Silas in an undertone, 'The poor dear, she's accident-prone. Every day she falls over or into something.' And as Maggie returned with her napkins under her arm, Silas had to turn away or let her see him laughing, because his mother had never said a truer word. Yet, like Lucy, he had a real soft spot for the maid.

'Sorry, ma'am.' As usual, Maggie was all of a fluster.

'It's all right, dear,' Lucy told her. 'You're not hurt, are you?'

'No, ma'am.' Though she did wonder if her arse was skinned, 'cause it stung like merry hell!

'You go on and do what you were doing, and Silas will see to the tree,' Lucy told her gratefully. 'Thank you, dear.'

Convinced that the tree was now leaning the other way, Silas wisely made no mention of it. Instead, he offered to take his mother for a brandy, and, being Lucy, how could she refuse. 'That would be a real treat,' she said, and happily chatted all the way to the library.

When she was settled with her brandy and Silas with a measure of whisky, Lucy told him to come and sit beside her. 'I've been wanting for you and me to talk,' she said, 'and as there's no one here but us, this is as good a time as any.'

Accepting her invitation to sit beside him, Silas was curious. 'You seem serious.'

'I *am* serious. What's more, I want you to be honest with me.'

'Aren't I always?' There were times when he might be economical with the truth, but only to save her any anxiety.

Regarding him with concern, Lucy realised how he had changed over these past weeks. The light had gone from his eyes, he was slower to smile, and where once he walked with a spring in his step, now he looked like a man under sentence. 'Are you happy, son?' It was a simple question, born of a mother's instinct.

'In what way?' He had to keep the truth from her at all costs.

'With Helen . . . your marriage. Are you content?'

He smiled. 'Do you hear me complaining?'

'No, but then you wouldn't, would you?' Knowing him as she did, Lucy sensed something here that she didn't like.

'Look, Mother, I'm happy enough,' he lied. 'Helen's father has taken me on as his right-hand man. He trusts me enough to handle large sums of money, and I've rewarded him with handsome profits already. I enjoy my work, and I get on with Jack far better than I imagined I would.' That had been the biggest surprise of all. Jack Turner had forced him into a marriage with his petulant daughter; he had threatened to ruin his father; and now, after witnessing the situation between father and daughter, Silas had come to realise so many things. He had come to like Jack Turner, and to pity him.

'And Helen, what about her?'

'She's my wife, and as far as I can tell, she's very content. As for me, I'm like any other husband. I go to work and I come home. I'm not neglected, and she's always pleased to see me.' Waiting like a vulture, he thought bitterly, asking questions, suspecting him of seeing other women, and making his every waking minute unbearable. 'So, everything's fine. You're worrying for nothing.'

Lucy was not so easily fobbed off. 'You've gone all round the mulberry bush, about your work, and about Helen. You've told me how content *she* is,' she said softly. 'Now tell me about you. I asked you to be honest with me.' Pausing to let him think about that, she asked again, 'Are *you* happy, son?'

Taking a gulp of whisky, he stole a moment to think, to weigh up the situation. This was the moment when he could set her mind at rest, or turn her whole world upside down. He either had to be honest and destroy what peace of mind she might have, or tell a lie to save them both.

Given such an impossible choice, he silently uttered a prayer for forgiveness, and chose to lie. 'I'm very happy,' he answered. 'Helen and I are even talking of starting a family.' Delivered with the brightest smile, he was totally convincing. Yet, in a way he had not misled her, because he *was* 'happy' – when away from Helen . . . happy as he could be without Cathleen. And they *had* talked of starting a family, but it was mostly Helen talking. The discussion always ended in argument. She wanted to consolidate their marriage with children, and he did not. *Would* not. And so far, no bairns had come along.

Lucy took him at his word, and soon they were heading back to the kitchen. 'Leave me here, son,' she said, 'I must talk to Cook.'

Relieved to be out of the house, Silas walked around the gardens. He needed to clear his mind, to assess his life as it was, and to nurture some semblance of hope for the future. 'Where are you, Cathleen?' he whispered. Gone, he thought sadly. She's gone and I'm here, and I miss her more than she'll ever know.

The biting air sliced through his clothes, then the rain started, but he hardly noticed. Instinctively, he made his way to the gardener's hut, where he stood a moment in the doorway, his mind going back over the years to when he and Cathleen would play here, laughing and chasing, despite the gap in their ages.

A smile lifted the corners of his mouth. 'You brought me alive,' he whispered. 'You *kept* me alive, and now you're not here and I'm dying inside.'

He stayed awhile in the musty hut, seated on an upturned wheelbarrow and smiling at his memories. Now, as the rain began to ease, he recalled a certain, wonderful day.

They had been racing up from the spinney in the rain; he in front and Cathleen behind. When he got to the verandah he sat on the step and waited for her. Suddenly the rain stopped, and the largest, most beautiful rainbow he had ever seen streaked across the sky. Cathleen called with excitement, 'Look, Silas! Look at the rainbow!' She pointed up, and for one wonderful, unbelievable moment, it seemed as if she was part of that incredible rainbow.

He had never forgotten, and he never would. The image was etched in his mind for all time.

Presently, his thoughts came back to the day when he and Cathleen had made love for the first and only time. Driven by the memory, he walked on to the jetty where the little boat was tethered; the same boat that he and Cathleen had taken to the island on that wonderful day last summer. He remembered how it was; he climbed into the boat and sat there quietly, hearing her laughter, seeing her face, so real it was almost as though she was there with him. He felt her presence, and she brought a kind of peace to his lonely heart.

From the library window, Edward Fenshaw followed his son's every move. 'What have I done to you?' he murmured thickly. 'What kind of man am I to have taken away your life . . . all your dreams?' Lately, it had haunted him and now, as it weighed unbearably on his conscience, he began to whimper, like a small, lost child. Head down and his heart breaking, he curled up on the floor, moaning, 'God forgive me.' Over and over. 'God forgive me.'

This was how Silas found him, drunk and distraught on the floor. Helping him up, he led him to a chair where he sat him down. 'What's happened to you?' he asked softly. 'Why do you torture yourself like this, drinking from morning till night? Do you think Mother hasn't noticed? She's becoming worried about you. What is it, Father? Why do you drive yourself to distraction like this?' But he already knew, and there was little consolation he could give.

Instead, he put away the drink, at the same time reminding his father, 'The guests will be arriving in less than an hour. I'll fetch some black coffee.' Pity mingled with disgust. 'You stay where you are. I don't want Mother seeing you like this.' Irritation coloured his voice. 'This is *her* day, you know that.' It may even be her last Christmas, he added silently.

At the door, his father called him back. 'Tell me something, son.'

'What is it?' He had lost respect for Edward long

ago, but the love still remained. He was his father, after all.

'Do you hate me?'

Made guilty by his own feelings, Silas walked back to him. 'No, Father, I don't hate you,' he said softly. 'I could *never* hate you.' Looking down on that tearful face, made haggard by the turn of events, Silas was deeply moved. Instinctively, he put one arm about the once broad shoulders, now stooped with care. 'Don't torment yourself,' he murmured, 'there's no need.'

'I did a terrible thing to you.' With bloodshot eyes he looked up at Silas and, grabbing his hand hard, he held it for a minute, his voice making a low, grating sound. 'I know how she treats you. She's the devil incarnate!'

'You mustn't think like that, Father.'

'She'll destroy you.'

Silas gave a small, hard laugh. 'Never!'

'Promise me.' Gripping Silas's hand until it ached, Edward demanded, 'Promise me you won't let her destroy you!'

'You have my word.'

Satisfied, Edward let go of his hand. He seemed peaceful again. 'You've been a good son,' he said. 'I couldn't have wished for better.' His smile was serene. 'Get the coffee now. It's time I made myself presentable.'

When Silas had gone, Edward scribbled a short note. After leaving it by the blotter on his desk, he got out of the chair and went to the door, turning to rove his gaze round the room he knew so well. He smiled, momentarily closed his eyes, then pulled the door to. Making his way down the hallway, he was careful not to let anyone see him. 'No goodbyes,' he murmured. 'No tears.' He left the house silently by the side door.

It was a moment or two later when Silas returned with a tray containing a large pot of black coffee, two cups and saucers and a small plate of Rich Tea biscuits. 'I'll join you,' he was saying as he came into the room. 'Coffee and biscuits, just what the doctor ordered.'

Closing the door, he turned, surprised to see the room empty. 'Father?' Seeing the open door to the walk-in stationery cupboard, he assumed his father to be in there, sorting out his papers. A quick inspection told him he was wrong.

'He's probably gone to tidy himself up,' he chuckled. 'It wouldn't surprise me if Mother hasn't been and carted him off.'

With little else to do but wait, he crossed the room to the window and stared out at the darkening skies. He caught a sudden movement . . . someone going at a fast pace towards the spinney. He recognised his father almost immediately. 'What on earth is he playing at?'

For the life of him he couldn't imagine why Edward should be wandering about outside when, any time now, the guests would be knocking at the door. 'I'd best go and fetch him in, before somebody sees him drunk out of his mind!'

Rushing past the desk, he paused when the flap of his

jacket brushed a piece of paper onto the floor. Quickly stooping, he picked it up and was about to fling it back on the desk when some instinct made him stop and read it. The words filled him with horror, and he found himself reading them aloud.

Those of you who know me for the coward I am, please remember me as I was, not how I became.
Forgive me, Lucy. No man could ask for a better wife.
I love you still, but I cannot live with myself any more.
I pray to God that those who care for you now will protect you always.
God bless and keep you,
Edward.

For one brief moment, Silas refused to believe what the letter was telling him, but then the awful truth rippled through his brain. Frantic, he glanced at the window, but there was no sign of his father now. 'NO!' The cry tore from his lips as he ran down the hallway and out of the front door, racing towards the spinney. Calling his father's name he ran until he thought his chest would burst open. But there was no answer to his cries, only the muffled sound of his footsteps as they sank into the wet grass.

Behind him, Lucy had heard his cry and seen him run out of the house. She was beside herself. 'There's something terribly wrong! Go after him! Please, oh please, go after him!' While the servants fled over the lawn after Silas, she called for Edward, but he couldn't hear. *Not any more.*

In the gathering dusk, Silas saw his father, knee-deep at the edge of the water. '*Father, no!*' Oblivious to his son's cries, Edward pushed on, deeper and deeper, until the water carried him off his feet. 'FATHER!'

It was only minutes before Silas was there. Throwing off his jacket, he dived into the ice-cold water. He saw his father go under, and went down after him into those murky depths, searching this way and that. Three times he came up for air; three times he went back down, swimming wide, losing hope by the second.

On the last dive he found him, arms up, eyes open, his hair waving in a gentle movement as Silas swam towards him. Grabbing him by the armpits, Silas drew his father to the surface.

It was only minutes, but it seemed like an age. When the servants arrived on the scene, they found Silas on the bank, his arms about his father, cradling him tight, rocking him back and forth, like a mother might rock her child. 'I was too late,' he said brokenly, 'too late!' Stroking his father's quiet features, he buried his face against the old man's and his cries were terrible to hear.

The quiet air round that beautiful lake was quiet no more. The sound of Silas's anguish rent the air and touched everyone's hearts. Making the sign of the cross on herself, Maggie cried, and so did Edna, the cheeky little cockney; they had loved Edward too, as had the others, for he was a kindly man, despite his formidable appearance.

The truth seemed too shocking to bear. Edward Fenshaw had taken his own life, and now, like Silas, they could do nothing.

———◦———

LATER, WHILE A local bobby turned away inquisitive guests, Lucy was being comforted by Silas. When he gave her the letter, she took it with trembling hands, and what she read only compounded her terrible grief. 'But . . . what did he mean?' In a whisper she read out part of his letter. '"I pray to God those who care for you now will protect you always".' She couldn't understand. 'Protect me from what?'

Silas knew but couldn't tell. 'From loneliness,' he said heavily. 'I expect that was what he meant.'

He had puzzled over the meaning himself, but now it was clear. His father was asking Jack Turner and Silas to protect Lucy from the awful truth; that the husband who adored her had sold his son. Silas knew, and so had Edward, that if Lucy were ever to discover the truth, it would destroy her.

Chapter Twelve

'You'll *never* be free of me!' Helen spat out the words. 'If you think your father's death has set you loose, you'd better think again!' Her cruel eyes focused on Silas. Standing by the window, looking out and seeing only a lifetime of loneliness, he cut a forlorn figure.

Swinging round as she came into the room, he addressed her with a quiet dignity. 'What vicious scheme are you brewing now?'

Sauntering into the room, she looked stunning; dressed in black and with a row of pearls at her throat, she had her hair coiled into a scarlet ribbon, and her lips painted the same colour. 'Are you a good son, Silas?'

'Better than I am a husband,' he conceded.

'A good son wouldn't leave his mother all alone in that big house.'

He shook his head in disgust. 'I wondered how long it would take you to come round to that.' From the day they laid his father to rest, he knew she would soon want the mantle from his mother's shoulders. 'Can't wait to be lady of the manor, is that it?'

'Really, Silas, is that fair?' Cunning to the last, she excelled at feigning innocence. 'I'm only thinking of your mother. You must admit, she's been through so much; her health has worsened since we buried her husband, and last night I heard you telling Father how lonely she seemed, in spite of you going round there every day before you come home to me!' The last few words were added with bitterness.

'Go on. Tell me what you're thinking . . . as if I can't already guess.' He had come to know his wife very well, and didn't like what he had learned. Helen Turner was without heart or compassion; she had no thought for anyone but herself. Thanks to her habit of using people to further her own ambitions, she had won many enemies, and was despised even by the staff who attended her.

She sat down on the cream sofa, boldly displaying her legs like treats in a shop window, knowing he was not interested, yet goading him all the same. 'I'm not as hard as you make me out,' she said sulkily. 'Though you choose not to believe it, I really *am* thinking of your mother. Lucy Fenshaw is a fine woman. She was always a good friend to me and my father, and I have great respect for her. If you think I intend to undermine her position at Fenshaw House, I can tell you now, you've got it quite wrong.'

He didn't believe a word of it. 'Really? You do surprise me.' Walking over to the fireplace, he stood, hands in pockets and legs astride, with his back to the flames. 'No doubt you have a plan?' He had learned to play her at her own game. 'Or have I got that wrong as well?'

Rising gracefully from the chair, she went to the dresser, where she took a cigarette from the silver box and lit it with great deliberation. 'It's a pity you have such a bad opinion of me, Silas, because, as you already know, I happen to be *very* fond of you.' Walking towards him, she blew a trail of smoke before her. 'I haven't been a bad wife to you, have I?' Sidling up to him, she fondled his tie. 'I could be even better if only you'd let me.'

When he didn't answer, but drew away from her, she doggedly pursued him across the room. 'I know you resent the manner in which you were made to marry me, but the end justified the means. And I mean it, don't imagine you can walk out on me now your father's dead. Don't think his debt died with him, because it didn't. If you leave me, I'll tell the world what he did. Your mother won't last two minutes if she finds out about your father selling you to buy off his debt. All of that will come out. So, nothing changes, Silas. If anything, the debt is even larger now.'

Shaking with anger, he reached for the door handle. With her voice shrill in his ear, penetrating his brain, he wanted to kill her. Incensed now, because he was almost out the door and still hadn't acknowledged her, she raised her voice. 'Damn you, Silas! You should be grateful my father didn't have Edward Fenshaw put in jail for the common thief he—'

She didn't go on, because suddenly he had her by

the throat, his face dark with fury, his voice low and threatening. 'I was taught to treat a woman with respect,' he rasped, 'but you're less than a woman . . . less than a human being. My father was no thief, and well you know it. You were never fit to wipe the dirt from his feet, never mind utter his name!'

Realising she had gone too far, Helen turned on the tears. 'I'm sorry, Silas. It was a bad thing to say. Forgive me . . . say you'll forgive me?'

Far from forgiving her, he hated her just that bit more. 'You disgust me!' Throwing her aside, he flung open the door and, standing there, looking shocked to the core, was Jack Turner.

Sensing an ally, Helen's voice cut the air. 'Tell him, Father,' she cried. 'Tell him I didn't mean it.'

There was an awkward moment when each man was unsure of the other, but then Jack spoke and the situation was saved. 'Can you spare me a minute or two?' Jack asked Silas. 'I'd like a word.'

Convinced he was about to plead on her behalf, Helen drew away, silently congratulating herself.

'Well, Silas?' Jack saw the hostility in the other man's face, and knew he was about to refuse. 'We need to talk.'

Silas nodded. Jack turned and Silas followed him into the office.

'Close the door,' Jack instructed. 'Sit yourself down.'

When Silas was seated before the desk, Jack Turner eased his own frame into the leather chair. 'I heard you just now . . . and *her*,' he said. 'It's a good job the servants are on their night off or they might well have had something to gossip about, and we wouldn't want that, would we, eh?'

Ashamed that he'd allowed himself to lose his temper, Silas apologised. 'Sometimes she pushes me too hard.' He wasn't sorry for turning on her, though. He was only sorry she had a hold over him.

Jack Turner understood only too well. 'She's a hard bitch,' he said. 'She might be my daughter, but there have been times when I could have throttled her with my own bare hands. More so since I all but forced you to put a ring on her finger.' There was a note of regret in his voice. 'You paid a hard price for what your father did.'

Silas saw his chance and he took it. 'Look, this marriage isn't working. I have no feelings for your daughter and I never will. I want out. Let me pay you the debt back out of my earnings. I've made profit for you already. You know I'm good at the buying and selling . . . I'll work all the hours God sends.' As if he didn't already, he thought, just to get away from her. 'Let me end this sham of a marriage. I have a sick mother who needs me, but I swear I won't let you down. Give me enough time and I'll repay my father's debt. You know I'm as good as my word.'

'No.' Leaning back in his chair, Jack Turner regarded Silas, wishing with all his heart he had a son like him. 'You *are* good at what you do, and I'm sure you get your business acumen from your father, because there was a time when no one could come anywhere near him for wheeling and dealing. But I also like to think

I've taught you something since you've been working with me.'

Silas was hopeful. 'So, you'll agree?' he asked eagerly. 'You'll let me carry on working with you, and give me time enough to repay the debt?'

'I can't do that, I'm sorry.' Realising he was little better than his daughter, Jack explained. 'The debt isn't the issue here, not altogether. You've seen what she's like. I've had years and years of that, and I was at my wits' end. Your father gave me the opportunity to be rid of her once and for all.' He gave a knowing smile. 'I'm sure you guessed as much.'

Silas felt all hope slipping away. 'You and her . . . you're as bad as each other.'

'Maybe, but since you've taken her off my back, I've had time to breathe . . . time to live.' He drew in a long, withering sigh. 'It's been a long, *long* time since I felt like that.'

Pushing back his chair, Silas stood up. 'I can see there's no use me talking with you, but I'll tell you this: one way or another I'll find the money to repay you, and when I do, nothing on earth will keep me here.'

'You may pay off the debt in time. But, even then, if you were to leave her I don't know how you might stop her from spreading malicious gossip. Look, Silas, if you want to protect your mother, as your father asked, then you have to dance to Helen's tune, I'm afraid. Of course, when your mother passes on, and let's pray it won't be for some long time yet, *then* you might be free, who knows?'

When Silas remained silent, lost in thought, he went on, 'You hate it here, don't you?'

Silas looked up, a twisted smile on his handsome features. 'You can't know how much.'

'You don't have to stay here if you don't want to.'

'What?' What trick was he up to now?

'Go home, Silas, where you belong. Pack up here and go back to Fenshaw House. As you so rightly said, you have a sick mother who needs you.' A look of compassion came over his features. 'I'm not a monster. I've known Lucy for many a year now, and a better woman never lived. She lost her husband because of me and what I did. It isn't fair that she should pay a price as well as you. Look, Silas, we all know Lucy isn't one to ask for help, but she must be feeling unbearably lonely. Go to her. Take Helen with you. Maybe, God willing, some of your mother's goodness will rub off on her.'

Silas couldn't believe his eyes. This man, who had held him to ransom, this big, ruthless businessman was close to tears. And though Silas's heart was hardened by experience, he felt a surge of pity for him.

'I'll do what I think is right,' he murmured, and made his way out of the office.

Outside, he closed the door and leaned on it, his mind in turmoil. 'I wonder . . .' Something of what Jack Turner had said *did* make sense. And oh, it would be so good to be at Fenshaw House again, to be there when his mother needed someone to talk to. It would be good for him too, to have a friendly face in a hostile world.

And it was true, he had always considered a fleeting visit after work to be more cruel than kind to her.

What should he do? He had to think. Yes, of course. After work tomorrow he would talk it over with his mother. Like Jack Turner said, she would never ask for help, but she was honest enough, and would tell him the way of things.

>=•0•=<

IT WAS THE last appointment of the day. The prospective purchaser was a southerner by the name of Joseph Woodley. A jolly fellow, with a face like a moonbeam, he was just up from London and looking to buy land for investment.

After showing him several possibilities, Silas had taken him to the site of an old warehouse down Fielden Street. 'It's prime land,' he told him, 'smack in the centre of town and reasonably priced . . . for the moment. Give it another year and you won't be able to buy it for love nor money.'

After walking over the site several times, Mr Woodley scratched his beard, pursed his lips, and thought for what seemed an age. Then he said, 'Very well. I'll think about it.'

'Fair enough.' Silas had come to recognise every man's ploy; some said nothing and went away promising to come back, others, like Mr Woodley, would act casually, go away, then come back with an offer of sorts.

It was a game, and Silas could play it as well as any

man. 'Don't take too long thinking about it though,' he warned the man. 'Land like this doesn't wait. I've already got two others interested in it – with money waiting.'

Smiling, Joseph Woodley suspected it was a bluff, but couldn't be certain. This was a delicate matter. If he hesitated and there really *were* other buyers, he'd lose probably the best development site in Blackburn. On the other hand, if this enterprising young man was bluffing, it was a very convincing act. *Too* convincing to take a chance. 'All right,' he answered. 'If we can reach the right price, you may consider it sold.'

'State your offer and I'll tell you if it's acceptable.' There were no other buyers, and the price *was* in fact negotiable, but having learned a hard lesson from his father's one mistake, Silas gave nothing away.

'Hmh!' Mr Woodley was impressed. 'I've a bloody good mind to make *you* an offer,' he said, 'never mind the land. I've been looking for somebody to head the southern end of my business, and from what I've seen these past two hours, I reckon I wouldn't go far wrong with you.'

Silas thanked him for the compliment, but said firmly, 'I'm not for sale.' Not on this occasion, he thought, and never again.

'Pity.' There was something very special about this man . . . young and dynamic, with an open, honest nature, and just enough ruthlessness to keep a customer on his toes. Oh, yes, he had the makings of a top businessman. 'You're wasted here,' Joseph Woodley told

Silas. 'You should be down south where the money is. You should be with *me*!'

But Silas would not be drawn. 'It's here in the north where the newer opportunities are,' he answered assertively. 'There are still considerable areas of good land available, but suddenly it's going fast . . . mostly to your developers in the south. As it becomes scarcer and scarcer, the prices will rise. Every prime site, such as this one, will demand a premium.' His eyes lit up when he thought of the exciting challenges ahead. 'When that happens, I want to be part of it.'

Deeply impressed, the older man shook his hand. 'You'll go a long way,' he said. 'I'm only sorry you've turned down the offer of joining my company.'

'I'm not ungrateful for your offer,' Silas was quick to assure him, 'but I do have commitments.' What he *had* in fact, was a millstone round his neck in the shape of Helen Turner.

'I don't doubt that.' The more Silas refused, the more Joseph wanted him on his team. But slowly, slowly, catchee monkey, he thought with a smile. 'You have my name and address back at the office,' he persisted. 'Let me know if you change your mind. A week, a year . . . whatever. There'll always be a place in my company for someone like yourself.'

'Meanwhile, we have business underway here,' Silas reminded him.

'What figure do you have in mind?' Woodley pursed his lips, waiting.

'You already know the figure.'

'I never pay the asking price.'

'You'll need to come pretty close or I'll have to offer it elsewhere.'

'You're a sharp one, I'll say that for you.' Someone had taught this young man well, Woodley thought. Someone had also made him bitter; even when he smiled, it was there in his dark eyes, the look of a haunted man.

There and then the deal was done. An offer made and refused, a counter offer and some adjusting, and they reached an agreement. 'You don't let the grass grow under your feet, young fella, I'll give you that.' Shaking Silas by the hand, Joseph Woodley bade him good day. 'I'll be in your office first thing in the morning to sign the papers, but the deal is done, and by God I've never done a deal so quick in my life, nor been held so close to the asking price.' His good opinion of Silas strengthened by the minute. 'Remember what I said. If you should change your mind . . .'

Parting company, Mr Woodley returned to his waiting carriage, while Silas volunteered to walk the short distance back to the office. As it was already five-thirty, he intended locking up without delay, and making his way to Fenshaw House where he would take stock of the situation and decide what to do.

<hr />

LUCY WAS AT the kitchen window when she saw her son striding up the garden path. 'It's Silas!' she cried, her face beaming with joy as she turned to the cook. 'Call

Maggie will you, please? Tell her I must get back to the drawing room.'

'Of course, ma'am.' Though she addressed Lucy in a formal manner, they had come to know each other very well. It was a rare and wonderful friendship between two lonely women, albeit from different backgrounds.

In a minute, Cook was rushing out of the room, and was back again a minute later with Maggie at her heels. Yet another minute and there was Silas himself. 'I thought I'd find you down here,' he chided, going straight to Lucy. 'Bothering Cook, when you know perfectly well she's busy baking me one of her marvellous apple pies – that's if she hasn't forgotten?'

Winking at Cook, he smiled when she went a deep shade of pink. 'Away with you, Mr Fenshaw, sir.' She had known him since a bairn, and loved him like her own. 'How could I forget your apple pie?'

'Custard too, I hope?'

'Lashings of it.' Chuckling, she turned away to take the pie out of the oven; in an instant the whole room was filled with the most wonderful aroma.

'Hello, son.' Raising her face for a kiss, Lucy's heart took wing, as it always did whenever he came to visit.

Manoeuvring up the shallow ramp, Silas wheeled her into the hallway. 'How are you today, Mother?' She looked peaky, he thought, and not for the first time today, his conscience pricked him.

'I'm well,' she lied. 'I've been chatting with Cook. She made fresh teacakes and we shared a pot of tea together. She's such a dear soul, you know. She tells me tales of her life in service. My! You'd never believe some of the things she used to get up to!'

It was only then, in that moment when she laughed out loud, that he realised how lonely she really was. Settling her beside the fire, he asked curiously, 'How often do you go down to the kitchen?'

There was a pause before she confessed in a quiet voice, 'I like to go down every day. Cook is a *real* person, not like the vultures who call on the pretence of bringing sympathy. All they want is a look at the inside of Fenshaw House, and to impress me with their cruel, nonsensical gossip. They talk and cackle and smile sweetly, and never have anything worthwhile to say.' Her features softened. 'Cook and I understand each other. The only difference between us is that I've been more fortunate in life than she has.'

Seated across from her now, Silas wondered how she could say that, when only a short time ago her beloved husband had taken his own life. Now, here she was, a woman in constant pain; she had a quick mind and so much to offer the world, and in less than a year her life would be ended. He daren't even think about it.

While she made herself comfortable, he studied her face, the high cheekbones and that proud way she had of holding herself. She was beautiful and kind, with no airs or graces to cloud her vision. She loved people for what they were, not for what they had.

Inevitably, his thoughts flew to Cathleen. They were so alike these two women, he thought. That was why he loved them so.

Almost as soon as they had settled, Maggie arrived to tell them their apple pie and custard was served in the dining room. 'For heaven's sake!' Lucy laughed. 'There's only the two of us, and we have a table in here, though I admit it isn't as grand as the one in the dining room, but we'll manage, I dare say.'

Maggie couldn't believe it. 'You mean you want me to fetch the food in here, ma'am?' With eyes like saucers and her mouth wide open, she stared from one to the other. 'Cook won't like that.'

Such was the look of horror on Maggie's face that Lucy had a change of heart. 'Oh, all right, dear. We'll make our way to the dining room. Tell Cook thank you.'

In such a hurry to relay the message to Cook, Maggie tripped twice, once over the edge of the rug, and again as she went out the door. 'Sorry, ma'am,' she cried, and promptly knocked into the hall dresser, sending a vase into the air, but catching it with a show of skill that had the other two full of admiration.

Lucy laughed out loud. 'She should have been in the circus.' Recalling the many times Maggie had entertained them with her frantic antics, Silas had to agree.

The apple pie and custard were delicious. 'I must say, I've never tasted pastry like that in all my life,' Lucy admitted, laying down her spoon. 'It deserved a proper setting at the table, don't you think?'

Throughout the meal, Silas had watched her and worried. 'Shall I tell you what I *really* think?' he asked softly.

Knowing he had seen through her light-hearted charade, Lucy sighed. 'If you must.'

'I think I'd like to sit by the fire and talk, just the two of us.'

'About what in particular?' As if she didn't know.

'About *you*.' Getting out of his chair, he went round the table and, helping her into the wheelchair, asked Maggie to 'Bring a pot of coffee to the drawing room, would you, please?'

Taking his mother along the hallway, he wondered how he might broach the subject of her being lonely. She was a very private and independent woman.

As it happened, when the coffee was served and the door closed against the world, it was Lucy herself who opened the subject. 'I miss your father,' she said, and desolation hung heavy in her sigh. 'Fenshaw House isn't the same without him.'

Thinking it best to let her talk now she had opened her heart to him, Silas made no comment. Instead, he busied himself pouring the coffee, and handed a cup to her.

'I miss you too,' she murmured. 'All at once I've lost you both. Oh, I know you visit most evenings and I'm grateful for that, but sometimes the house is so empty . . .' Her voice tailed off. 'I'm sorry. It's unforgivable of me to worry you like this.'

Leaning forward in his chair, Silas took hold of her hands. 'I'm glad you confided in me,' he said. 'I realise how lonely you must be, and it's played on my mind all day. I have a proposition to make.' It was plain to him now that both Helen and her father had been right; his mother needed him there, for now at least.

Lucy hoped it was what she thought. 'What proposition is that, dear?'

Just as she spoke, the door pushed open and in walked Helen. Hurrying across the room, she came straight to Lucy and pecked her on the cheek. 'Edna let me in,' she said sweetly, while Silas groaned inwardly. What the devil was *she* doing here?

Since Helen had become Silas's wife, Lucy had made every effort to like her, although she sensed a certain friction between her son and this woman that concerned her deeply. 'Hello, Helen.' Her ready smile gave nothing away. 'How kind of you to come and see me.' Inviting her to join them, she watched with interest when Helen sat down beside Silas, and Silas seemed to shift away. 'You were saying, Silas?' Lucy had no real cause to believe they kept secrets from each other.

Silas came straight to the point. 'You were telling me how the house seemed empty these days,' he reminded her, 'and I was thinking—'

Before he could explain, Helen's voice piped in, 'I think he's trying to ask if he and I should move in with you.'

'Helen!' Irritated by her interference, Silas covered his true feelings by quickly gentling his tone, suggesting, 'The coffee's gone cold, see if you can rustle up a fresh pot, will you? And we'll need another cup.'

Giving him a daggered look, she flounced out of the room, enraged by his coolness towards her but compensated by the fact that her dearest dream was about to be realised. Once she moved into Fenshaw House, it would take nothing short of an earthquake to get her out.

She looked about her at the richness of her surroundings. *This* was something different. It had tradition, history, a sense of place. It was somewhere she would be someone to be reckoned with at last. People would talk about her in the streets, and bow their heads respectfully as she went by. She murmured her name. 'Helen Fenshaw, *Lady of Fenshaw House*.'

With a kind of madness, she put out her arms and spun joyfully round, as if gathering to herself the entirety of her surroundings. Then, breathless and slightly dizzy, she clung to the bannister. 'It isn't mine yet though,' she muttered, her face darkening to a scowl. 'It can't be mine yet.'

Not for the first time, the idea blossomed in her evil mind. *Not while Lucy Fenshaw is still alive!*

She was impatient. And when Helen Turner was impatient, nothing was allowed to stand in her way.

PART TWO

January 1901

MAKING A NEW LIFE

Chapter Thirteen

IT WAS THE dream that woke her; the same unsettling dream she had experienced time after time. She and Silas were swimming in the lake and suddenly a dark shadow fell over them. They tried to climb out onto the bank, and each time the shadow reached out and pushed them back. It was a beautiful day, but whenever the shadow appeared, the sun went in and everywhere was cold. 'Go back, Cathleen!' Silas cried. 'Get to the island,' but she couldn't leave him. If he were to die then she wanted to be with him. The shadow grew larger and larger and, as always, she could hear Silas screaming, 'Go back, Cathleen. For God's sake, *go back*!'

It was at that point she always woke.

She woke now to see the day dawning, the world bathed in bright winter sunshine. During the night, the January wind had spent itself, and now there was a wonderful calm everywhere; except in Cathleen's heart, for she had not known peace of mind or heart since leaving behind everything she knew and loved.

Tiptoeing out of bed, she glanced across at Megan, snoring loudly as usual, and hanging out of her narrow bed as though she might tumble onto the floor at any minute.

Smiling, Cathleen made her way to the kitchenette, a small alcove behind a curtain where they made tea and prepared meals. Dark stains on the wall showed where every now and then Megan had set the stove alight.

Large enough for the two women to have their own space, yet cosy too, the room was long and narrow, with a tiny bathroom at one end and the kitchenette at the other. A wide window at the front overlooked George Street, a busy East End thoroughfare flanked by small factory units – a signmaker, an ironworker, a strange little shoemaker who turned out the best shoes in the whole world, and a blacksmith. From morning to night, all manner of people and vehicles paraded up and down outside. It was a constant procession, and the accompanying noise was never-ending. But Cathleen loved it. She never tired of watching the comings and goings.

The other main window was at the back of the room, with a far-off view of the river. There were also two tiny windows that didn't open, one in the bathroom and the other in the kitchenette.

Cathleen and Megan had gasped with horror when they first set eyes on the room. Previously used for storage, it had smelled damp, and there were huge patches of fungus creeping over the walls. 'It's yours if you want it,' Mr Trent had told them. 'It's this or nothing.'

So they took it with thanks and set about making it into a home. The fungus had been removed, the room well aired and the walls covered with two fresh coats of whitewash. Now there were pretty curtains at the windows and colourful rugs on the floor. Jessie had sent Cathleen a picture of a little thatched cottage with a garden in front, which she had hung over the fireplace; now, whenever she looked at it, she thought of home.

Half asleep, she filled the kettle and set it on the gas ring. She then prepared a cup; one heaped spoonful of tea and half a spoonful of sugar. Every morning the same – a cup of tea, a slice of bread and jam, and half an hour at the table to get her thoughts in order before Megan woke with her questions and queries. She had never come across anybody with so much to ask.

Walking out of the kitchenette to the table, she almost leaped out of her skin when Megan sat bolt upright in bed. 'Did you make *me* a cup?' she called in a shrill voice. 'My throat's that parched I could drink the sea dry!'

'Have mine,' Cathleen told her graciously. 'I'll make myself another.'

When, a few minutes later, she returned from the kitchenette, Megan was bent over the table, yawning into her teacup. 'Why didn't you tell me it was only half past six?' she groaned.

'You never asked.' Sitting opposite her, Cathleen sipped at the hot tea. 'Anyway, I thought you wanted to be out early.'

'I did! . . . I *do*!' She yawned again.

'Go back to bed for an hour if you're that tired.'

Cathleen took in Megan's baggy eyes and unkempt hair, and chuckled. 'You look like something the cat dragged in,' she teased.

'Huh!' Megan regarded Cathleen's pretty face and bright eyes, and the mass of fair hair that fell naturally into deep shining waves; for a moment she envied her. Then she thought of how Cathleen was the kindest person she had ever met. She recalled how, when they first came here, she had often caught Cathleen crying, and how, many times of late, she would wake from a nightmare, covered in sweat and shaking like a leaf. And she wasn't envious any more.

'Right then, Megan, what would you like to do today?'

Only now realising it was Saturday morning, Megan was suddenly awake. 'Yippee! With Norman Trent having the whole place scrubbed and painted, we've got the entire weekend ahead of us!' She was like a dog with two tails.

Cathleen laughed. 'So what have you got in mind?'

'Just think, Cathleen,' she urged with a grin, 'we can browse round Petticoat Lane to our hearts' content, with not a sight or sound of our Mr Trent.' She giggled at the little poem she had created and then mimicked him to perfection. 'MEGAN! How many times have I told you? You've burnt the bloody scones again! And the ovens are bleedin' filthy. If the customers were to come in 'ere now, I'd lose half my business overnight.'

Cathleen laughed again. 'You're as bad as each

other,' she said. 'He yells at you, then you yell at him; I don't know which one of you is worse.'

Throwing herself back in the chair, Megan chuckled. 'Aw, he's not a bad old stick really.'

'He's a godsend,' Cathleen remarked. 'I don't know what we'd have done if he hadn't happened to be meeting his auntie at King's Cross and seen us looking lost and bewildered. He took us under his wing then and he's done us proud ever since.'

'Truth is, I really like him.' Suddenly, there was a twinkle in Megan's eye that hadn't been there before.

'It's *more* than like,' Cathleen observed shrewdly. 'I think you *fancy* him. And I'm sure he feels the same way about you.'

Megan blushed all shades of pink. 'Don't be daft! He's fifteen years older than me.'

'That makes him, what? Mid-thirties? Hardly past it, is he?'

'Cathleen?'

'What now?' Megan was always whittling and fretting over one thing or another. But Cathleen loved her like a sister, and looked after her the same way.

'Why do you think Norman never married?'

'He already told you, he's been too busy building up a business.'

'He does work hard. We come away of a night and he's still working, and when we get up of a morning, he's already knocking and banging and moving about down there. He'll work himself into the ground if he's not careful.'

'That's how it is with a bakery.' If anyone knew, Cathleen did. 'You have to work late to prepare the next day's batch, then be up early enough to turn on the ovens for the baking.' Nostalgia washed through her, making her homesick.

'Do you miss it – the bakery . . . your family and all that?' Megan had seen how these past weeks, as she grew larger with child, Cathleen also grew quieter in herself. 'Do you ever wish you were back there, in Blackburn?'

Cathleen nodded. 'Sometimes.'

In fact, she missed it *all* the time, more than she could say. Her home, her father, Jessie. And Silas. Oh, how she missed *him*. With every passing day, his baby grew and stretched inside her, and though it gave her some measure of comfort, nothing could compensate for losing Silas, and along with him, her future, and that of the innocent bairn.

Megan's voice interrupted her. 'So you think he likes me, then?'

'Hmh?' Cathleen was miles away.

'Norman Trent. Do you *really* think he likes me?'

'I've seen the way he looks at you, and I'm as sure as I can be that Norman Trent has taken a definite shine to you, and well you know it.' Cathleen had seen how Megan had blossomed since being in London. Her face was plumper, she smiled more often, and her confidence had come on in leaps and bounds. It was good to see, and Cathleen was glad for her. 'He might yell at you and threaten to send you packing if you don't buck yourself up, but he never would.'

Megan gave a coy little smile. 'Maybe not.'

Now, when Cathleen stood up and began to make her way across the room to fetch a robe from her bed, Megan noticed how, these past few days, she had seemed to show with child more than ever. Being small, Cathleen wouldn't be able to hide it like some women. Concerned, she asked, 'Has he said anything yet, about you, and . . . ?' Pointing to her friend's swollen belly, she asked, 'When is it due?'

Cathleen was already ticking the days off on the calendar. 'Dr Armitage reckoned it up for me the last time I went to see him. He says the bairn should arrive about the end of April.'

'How long will it be before you need to stop work?'

'Not for some time yet.' Although it was a worry to Cathleen. 'I should be able to work up to about four weeks before the bairn is due.'

'Then what will you do . . . after the baby is born, I mean?'

'I'm not really sure, that's why I'm hoarding every penny I can. I desperately want to spend three months with the bairn, but my savings won't last for ever so I'll need to get back to work soon after that. If only I can find a clean, reliable woman to look after her.' It was all 'ifs' and 'buts', and if she were to tell the truth, Cathleen didn't really know how it would all turn out. Even with Megan to talk to, she felt isolated and alone. It was a hard thing to be with child, in a strange place, with your man in someone else's bed and your own father a stranger. Never a moment went by when Cathleen was not afraid.

When Megan chuckled, Cathleen wanted to know, 'What's tickling *you*?'

'You said "her".' She was like a child discovering a secret. 'Just now, when you spoke about the bairn . . . you said "her"!'

It was odd, but Cathleen had always thought of her baby as being a girl. 'A slip of the tongue,' she said. 'Girl or boy, it won't matter as long as it's got all its fingers and toes, and is handsome like its daddy.'

'You never did tell me who its daddy is?'

'Happen it's best you don't know.'

'I can guess.' Megan was a devil for guessing.

When Cathleen didn't encourage her, Megan said it anyway. 'It's Silas Fenshaw, isn't it? I saw how you looked at each other that day at the hotel. *He's* got you in the family way, hasn't he? Took advantage of you, then threw you aside like they all do. The bugger's had his way with you, and now he doesn't want to know, and that's why you've run away.'

Shocked into silence, Cathleen concentrated on drinking her tea.

'I won't tell anybody, if that's what you're worried about.' Megan thought the world of Cathleen, and wouldn't hurt her for anything. Now, seeing her friend's disheartened face, she wished she'd kept her mouth shut for once. 'Look, I'm sorry. It's none of my business.'

'It's all right, Megan,' Cathleen answered kindly, 'but it wasn't the way you think. Silas and I loved each other . . . we still do. Only it was never meant to be, with us coming from different backgrounds and such.' She wisely made no mention of the deal that had forced Silas into an unhappy marriage. 'Even my own father was dead set against it. He threw me out of the house . . .' Choked with emotion, she paused. 'It's a long story.'

'I've got time if you want to talk about it.'

Cathleen shook her head. 'Best not, eh?' It wasn't that she didn't trust Megan, because she did. It was too early, it went too deep, and she hadn't yet come to terms with it all herself.

They were quiet then for a time, sipping their tea and waking up with the day. Megan broke the silence. 'Have you told Norman you might be away three months after the bairn is born?'

'Not yet.'

'Will he keep your job open, do you think?'

Cathleen hoped so. 'You remember I told him about the bairn when he offered me that promotion, and he said I wasn't to worry? Well, since then I haven't had a chance to discuss it with him again.' But she had thought about it long and hard, and it was a source of great concern to her. 'I'll talk to him again on Monday,' she promised. 'Make sure he still means it. I'm sure it'll be all right.'

And with that the subject was closed.

⋙━◆━⋘

A N HOUR LATER, washed and dressed, they put away the clean crockery, made their beds, tidied the room and were ready for off. 'Have you got everything?'

Cathleen remembered how many times Megan had to run back because she'd forgotten something.

'Oh, my purse!' Diving across the room, Megan grabbed it and *then* they were ready.

Locking the door, Cathleen noticed a small-built man dressed in a pin-stripe suit; he was standing on the pavement looking up at the building. 'It's Norman,' she teased. 'He's pretending to look at the paintwork, but he's really hoping you'll give him a smile as you pass.'

'Give over!' But Megan smiled all the same. 'Good morning, Mr Trent,' she said, sticking out her tiny breasts and blushing root deep. 'We're off to do some shopping.'

'Oh, that's nice.' Neat and plain, Norman Trent was not very good with women; a kindly soul, he was alone in the world and lived only for his business. Not once had he thought of himself as ever being wed, but since meeting Megan, he lived in hope.

'Checking on the paintwork, are you?' Cathleen said mischievously.

'That's right.' He pointed upwards. 'I weren't thinking of spending good money on the outside, but look at that there.' Drawing their attention to a dark patch where the rendering had fallen off the wall, he said, 'I reckon the whole place might as well be done up while they're at it.' Suddenly swinging round to Megan, he asked, 'What do *you* think, Megan?'

Caught unawares, Megan was flustered. Stuttering and stammering, she gabbled, 'I'm sure I've no idea about walls and paint and such.'

Delighted with her answer, his little face beamed at her. 'That's how it should be,' he said masterfully. 'Paint and suchlike, well . . . it *is* a man's business after all.'

'We'll be off then.' Cathleen thought she'd best make a move before Megan started swooning. 'We'd best hurry if we're to catch the early tram.'

Touching his trilby hat, he nodded. 'Mind you don't spend too much, or I'll be thinking I'm paying you over the odds.' He watched them go, and would have given anything to have gone with them . . . or at least with Megan. Switching his attention, he called the painter out from the bakery. 'See that wall up there? I'm of a mind to have the whole face done again,' he confided. 'But I'm not made of money, so don't give me no silly price or I'll get somebody else in.' Wagging a finger, he warned, 'There's more bleedin' painters in London looking for work than there are loaves in my ovens.'

While he argued with the painter, Cathleen and Megan were looking forward to their day. 'Petticoat Lane look out, here we come!' Cathleen laughed, and the pair of them went off down George Street like two children on a trip to Wonderland.

Clambering off the tram at the top end of the market, Megan urged Cathleen to, 'Get a move on, or we'll miss all the bargains!'

Cathleen had to remind her that she was not as slim and agile as she was six months ago, and Megan promptly apologised. 'Mind the dogs,' she warned, spotting a pack of strays some way ahead. 'They'll leg you up sure as eggs is eggs if you don't look sharp.'

No sooner had she finished speaking than a big black mongrel shot out of a side street and knocked her sideways. 'See what I mean?' Losing her footing, she trod straight into a dollop of dog muck. 'Aw! Filthy devils!' Disgruntled, she set about scraping the sole of her boot against the kerb.

The incident was soon forgotten when they arrived in the thick of things; all around them the market came alive, with men shouting their wares and women pushing and shoving as they surged from one stall to another. There was a band playing and a man juggling oranges in the middle of the street. 'It's like feeding time at the zoo!' Megan laughed, while Cathleen thought she hadn't enjoyed herself so much in an age.

It was two o'clock when they made their way to the tea-shop, loaded down with fabrics and fruit, a piece of pork for Sunday lunch, and a pair of cosy slippers for Cathleen. 'They're like the ones my grandma used to wear,' Megan teased. 'You wouldn't see me *dead* in them things!'

'I might!' Taking off her shoes, Cathleen rubbed her feet until the blood flowed back. 'If you were nearly six months gone and had a friend who dragged you all round the market until your feet swelled like two balloons.' To tell the truth, Cathleen was glad of a sit down.

Ashamed, Megan volunteered to fetch them both a drink. 'You've got a face as red as one o' them tomatoes in your bag,' she said, delivering a big pot of tea and a rockcake each. 'Are you sure you're all right?'

Refreshed and rested, Cathleen's smile was mischievous. 'What would you do if I weren't?'

Taking a huge bite out of her rockcake, Megan settled herself. 'What?'

'You asked if I was all right,' Cathleen reminded her. 'What would you do if I wasn't?'

'Run away and leave you.'

'I bet you would too!'

'Naw.' Winking, Megan gestured to a fat, balding man at a nearby table. 'I'd sell you to him for a shilling.'

They laughed out loud and the man looked over. 'Nice day?' Megan said boldly. When the man shook her by replying in a foreign accent, Cathleen had to look away so he couldn't see her smile.

'One of these days you'll get yourself in trouble!' she warned after the man left. 'When I first met you, you were a scared little thing, and now look at you . . . mad as a hatter and twice as cheeky.'

Megan laughed. 'It's the company I keep,' she chirped, and what could Cathleen say to that?

By three o'clock, they decided to make their way home.

They were wending their way back through the stalls to the tram-stop when, seemingly out of nowhere, a carriage swept by at high speed, catching Cathleen's basket and knocking her to the ground.

As it happened, she wasn't hurt, just shocked and shaken. Megan helped her up. Some way up the street the carriage stopped and a big, kindly faced gent emerged from within.

'You could have killed her!' Megan shook her fist as he hurried towards them. 'She could have lost the bairn and everything!'

Cathleen's basket was upside down and the fruit lay bruised and broken. 'I'm all right,' she told the man, brushing herself down. 'But Megan's right. You shouldn't be travelling so fast here, not with the market nearby and children running about.'

He was filled with remorse. 'Are you sure you're not hurt?' he kept asking, and Cathleen kept reassuring him. 'Look, I'll take you and your friend to where you're going,' he offered. 'Let me do that much at least?'

Cathleen was all for going on the tram, but Megan had seen the cut of the carriage and it was grand. 'He *could* take us home,' she urged, and between the two of them, Cathleen was persuaded.

Having settled them in the back of the carriage, the stranger called for the driver to take them back in the direction of the market. 'And go slowly,' he warned. 'Wait for me here, ladies. I'll only be a few minutes,' he told them, and was as good as his word.

When he returned, he was carrying a basket crammed with fruit. 'With my apologies,' he said, and set it at Cathleen's feet.

'Thank you, but you needn't have done that.' For some reason, and in spite of his carriage having knocked her down, Cathleen had already taken a liking to him.

In no time at all, they arrived on George Street. 'Is this where you live?' Climbing out of the carriage to help the two women down, he looked up and down the street. 'But there are no houses.' Instead, there were horses and carts, fetching and carrying goods. There was the sound of the blacksmith at his anvil, and somewhere else two men were involved in an argument about the price of iron.

'We live upstairs, over the bakery,' Cathleen told him.

'And we work *downstairs*,' Megan chipped in. 'Our employer, Mr Trent, is a lovely man.'

When they parted company, the stranger told them, 'I've taken the liberty of putting my name and address in the basket. If you ever want anything, let me know.' And with that he was gone, smiling and waving as though he'd known them all his life.

Once inside, Cathleen and Megan set about unpacking their baskets. 'Look!' Megan found the envelope. 'Here it is.' Opening it, she gasped aloud. 'There's *money* in here! A lot of money!'

The sum amounted to two guineas. 'We can't keep that.' Cathleen was loath to accept such a large amount, and from a complete stranger.

''Course we can.' Megan was all for spending it on some new crockery and some posh cushions for the sofa. 'There'll even be enough left to buy that lovely cradle for the bairn. You know,' as if Cathleen needed reminding, 'the one we saw in that shop window.'

'No, Megan.' Cathleen would not be dissuaded. 'We have to send the money back. We don't know this man from Adam. He could be anybody, and now he knows where we live. I wish we'd come home on the tram.' Though she would have given a week's wage for his being a genuine person.

Megan thought she was wrong and said so. 'He's not about to murder us in our beds, is he?' she scoffed. Dipping into the envelope she found a business card. '"Joseph Woodley,"' she read. '"Prime land and Property always available."' She read on. 'His office is situated on Liverpool Street.' Laying the card down she told Cathleen, 'There you are. He's a businessman, not Jack the Ripper.'

Cathleen had stopped listening, her attention elsewhere. Just now, when Megan had thrown the envelope down on the table, it had flipped onto its back, and there, amongst the hasty scribble, was a name that struck her to the heart.

Picking up the envelope she turned it around to make sense of the words. 'It's *Silas*!' Frantic now to decipher the message on the back of the envelope, she read falteringly, '*Meet Silas Fenshaw . . . two o' clock . . . Blackburn office of . . .*' The last two words were almost illegible '. . . *Jack Turner . . . Turner . . .* NO!' Astonished, she glanced up at Megan. 'It's Jack Turner.'

'Who's Jack Turner?'

Excited, Cathleen explained, 'It all makes sense. Jack Turner is a land and property agent in Blackburn. The man who knocked me over, Joseph Woodley, he's in the same business, here in the south. He must have gone north to buy land or something. According to this scribbled note, he made an appointment to meet Silas in Jack Turner's office.'

Delighted, she laughed out loud. 'Oh, Megan! He had business with Silas. That man we met today, he met Silas . . . he *knows* him!' She had to sit down. 'I can't believe it!' A wonderful thought came into her mind. 'He'll be able to tell me how he is. Oh, Megan! I must see him, I must ask after Silas.' Her voice broke. 'I need to know what he's doing, how he is . . . whether he's happy.'

Choked with emotion, she grew quiet. 'In her last letter, Grandma told me she'd heard how he was working with Jack Turner, but she didn't know much more than that.' She didn't know how his marriage to Helen Turner was faring, Cathleen mused silently. Or whether he still thought of her, in the same way she thought of him.

If Megan had needed any proof of who Cathleen's lover had been, there was no doubt in her mind now. 'So I was right after all?' she murmured. 'Silas Fenshaw *is* the bairn's father?' When Cathleen looked up she insisted, 'You can't deny it, Cathleen. It's there, in your eyes, like a mirror to your soul.'

Reluctantly, Cathleen nodded.

Clapping her hands, Megan cried, 'I *knew* it!' On seeing Cathleen's anxious look, she assured her straight away, 'You can trust me not to say anything.'

'Thank you.' The last thing Cathleen wanted was for Norman Trent, or anyone else, to know her business.

What had gone on between her and Silas was too precious to be talked about amongst strangers.

➤◆◄

THE WEEKEND WAS busy. 'We should spring-clean while we have a chance,' Cathleen suggested. 'Once the painting is done and Norman Trent has us back at work, we may not get another free weekend for a long time.'

Megan wasn't too keen. 'Whoever heard of spring-cleaning in January?'

'It's almost February,' Cathleen reminded her.

'Same thing!'

But when Cathleen began stacking chairs and pulling their beds out from the wall, Megan was soon on her feet and rolling up her sleeves. 'You're a slave-driver!' she protested.

Too full of energy to argue, Cathleen part-filled a bucket with cold water from the jug, and topping it with warm water from the kettle, she handed it to Megan. 'You start from the window and I'll start from the door,' and she slapped a dishcloth into Megan's hand and left her to it.

By Sunday evening, every surface was washed and dried; the floor was given the same treatment, and, finally, all the furniture that could be wiped down was, and the rest of it polished until it shone.

Worn out and weary, the two stood back and couldn't believe how hard they must have worked. 'I thought this was meant to be a quiet weekend, when we could catch up on some sleep!' Megan wailed.

'Next time,' Cathleen promised. Tired but happy, she remembered the note on the envelope. Tomorrow, she would find out about Silas, and she couldn't wait!

That night, in spite of being bone-tired, Cathleen couldn't sleep. She got up, then she sat down, then walked about the room, and when Megan moaned, 'Go to bed, you're keeping me awake!' she lay down and stared at the ceiling for an age. Finally, in the early hours of the morning, her exhausted body gave itself up to sleep.

The morning was cold but bright. At seven o' clock Megan and Cathleen reported for work. 'My God!' Shocked by the deep hollows under Cathleen's eyes, Norman Trent feared she would drop the baby there and then. 'Go back to bed!' he told her. 'We'll manage without you for today.'

'There's nothing wrong with me!' Worried he might think she was not capable of doing her work, Cathleen put on a good act. 'I'm a bit tired, yes, but I'm not ready to be put out to grass, not by a long chalk. Although I *was* hoping you might let me go half an hour earlier this afternoon.'

Realising she must grow tired easily these days, he agreed, with one condition. 'I want to see you bright-eyed and bushy-tailed when you come in tomorrow. You and me must have a little talk.'

Cathleen's face dropped. 'Do you intend to finish me?'

'Tomorrow,' he said, and would not be drawn any further.

The day was frantic as usual. Cathleen never ceased to be amazed at the volume of custom there was here, compared to her father's bakery in Blackburn. The queue never ended . . . vans one after the other came to collect constant deliveries to shops and outlets all over the East End. There wasn't a moment to relax.

When, at half past three, Cathleen brought the invoices for Mr Trent to sign, he regarded her approvingly. 'The best thing I ever did was to put you in charge of the office,' he told her. 'Since you've taken that side of it off my back, this place has run like clockwork.'

He nearly said he would be sorry to lose her, but decided to save it for the morrow, as arranged. 'You do look washed out though,' he commented, returning the papers to her. 'Finish what you're doing and get off upstairs. Have a lie down, take it easy, and I'll see you in the morning.' It was a prospect he dreaded, but it had to be done.

Ten minutes later, Cathleen left. 'I expect you're off to see that Mr Woodley, aren't you?' Megan whispered. 'I've a good mind to ask Norman if I can go home early an' all. You shouldn't be going there all on your own.'

Cathleen assured her she was all right, and there was 'No need to fuss!'

'All right then, but go easy, and take a cab instead of the tram.'

Cathleen told her a cab was an unnecessary expense. 'Besides, you know I'd rather be with people than stuck in a cab all on my own,' Cathleen reminded her. 'I'm not the only woman ever to have been with child, and I'm sure I won't be the last.' Recalling how Megan had had a job to keep pace with her last night, she chuckled. 'Besides, you said yourself, I'm strong as an ox.'

'Hmh!' Megan knew it only too well. But Cathleen was small-built and seemed to be carrying the child hard. In spite of that, she always pushed herself to the limit. Lately, she hadn't been sleeping, and it was beginning to show. 'Go on then. I'll cadge some hot pies and muffins off Norman. By the time you get back I'll have the tea on the table.' Knowing the reason for Cathleen's errand, she winked. 'I'll be waiting to hear all about it . . . though I still think you're crazy to return that money!'

<hr />

J OSEPH WOODLEY WAS delighted to see her. 'My goodness! It's Cathleen, isn't it? Come in, come in!' Opening the office door wide, he was anxious when he saw how pale she looked. 'Sit down, my dear.' Gesturing to the red leather armchair, he waited until she was seated, then he hurried to the fireplace where he stoked up the coals to send the flames up the chimney. 'You're sure you're warm enough?' he asked, and when she assured him she was perfectly comfortable, he said, 'Now what brings you here? Oh, I do hope you haven't come to tell me we caused you any serious harm the other day?' Seating himself in the partner chair, he quietly regarded her. 'It couldn't have done you much good, my carriage knocking you down, especially in your condition. I had to have a long talk with my driver. He is, naturally, extremely sorry.'

Taking the envelope out of her bag, she handed it to him. 'You're very kind,' she said, 'but we couldn't possibly accept it.'

He protested, but she stuck to her principles. 'We're not destitute,' she explained. 'We have a nice room, and jobs, and manage well enough.'

He smiled wryly. 'And I've struck a blow against your independence, is that it?'

'No, but it's a great deal of money, and we really don't need it. Besides, it was an accident, and I've already accepted an apology. If it's all right with you, I think that should be an end to it.'

'Whatever you say.' Glancing at the sideboard, he offered, 'A glass of sherry then, to warm you up?'

Cathleen thought him such a gentleman, and after returning the money, how could she refuse? 'I'm not a drinker,' she confessed, 'but yes, just a wee drop.'

He poured Cathleen a small glass of sherry and himself a whisky. 'When you've drunk that, I'll run you home – that is, if there's nothing else you want to discuss?'

'There's no need to run me home, Mr Woodley, because I've got a return tram ticket.' But she thanked him all the same. 'However, there *is* something I'd like to ask, if I may?'

'Of course. Ask away.'

She pointed to the envelope on the sideboard. 'There's a message,' she began, 'scribbled on the back of the envelope.'

His eyes widened with surprise. 'A message? Is there really?' Getting out of his chair, he collected the envelope from the sideboard and turned it over. 'You're right!' he exclaimed. 'But it's of little consequence now. The deal is done, signed and sealed. I remember now, I made the note on my way home in the carriage – to remind me, you understand?' He chuckled. 'I'm afraid I have a memory like a sieve.'

'The man you mention . . . Silas Fenshaw . . .' She hesitated. 'Do you know him well?'

'Not really. His office had land to sell, and I was looking to buy. But I do recall him very well . . . offered him a top job, in fact, which sadly he turned down. He was a quick-minded and very shrewd young man.' Laughing aloud, he admitted, 'To tell you the truth, he played me at my own game and cost me a few hundred guineas more than I intended paying.'

Cathleen was saying it before she hardly realised, and in a voice that might have betrayed her feelings if only he had been listening closely. 'Was he well?'

'Oh yes, and do you know, he's a very lucky man. I had occasion to return some papers to Fenshaw House. Beautiful place – oh, and there's a lake . . . and an *island*, would you believe? He showed me from his window. Absolutely magnificent! We were talking in the office afterwards when his wife came in; very attractive woman, she positively dotes on him.' He grew curious. 'I didn't realise you knew him,' he remarked. 'It's a small world so they say.'

'It was a long time ago.' A lifetime, it seemed.

With her task done and his answers weighing heavy in her heart, Cathleen thought it time to go. 'Thank you for everything,' she said. 'I hope you weren't offended by me returning the money.'

'Disappointed,' he answered, 'not offended. But look, I *do* feel upset about the accident, and if there is ever anything I can do to make amends, you will let me know, won't you?' He thought her a charming creature, but lonely and sad in a quiet way. Now though, as she smiled up at him, he was shocked by her loveliness. Those blue eyes were made for smiling, he thought.

Watching her walk away down the street, he wondered about her. Where did she come from? Where was her family? And why was she here, heavy with child and no husband to take care of her? 'If she were *my* daughter, she'd want for nothing,' he murmured. But she wasn't, and there was nothing he could do about that. As he returned to his work, he had no idea of the effect his words had had on Cathleen.

On the tram, she sat by the window, a woman and child immediately in front, laughing and chatting. Every now and then the child would turn and play peep-bo with her. 'She's taken to you,' the woman told Cathleen. 'It's not everybody she takes to.'

Cathleen made the child laugh and found herself laughing with her. When they got out two stops down, they waved goodbye and Cathleen was alone again, with time to reflect on what Joseph Woodley had told her about Silas. 'I'm glad he's content,' she whispered. 'I wouldn't want him to be locked in an unhappy marriage.' But she had never needed him more than she did at that moment.

Gentling her hand over her bulging stomach, she felt closer to him and, as always, it brought a measure of comfort to her.

Megan was as good as her word. The aroma of fresh-baked bread and hot pies assailed Cathleen's nostrils as she opened the door. 'It smells wonderful!' Taking off her coat, she looked at the table, with its pretty cloth and places set for two, and in between a selection of muffins and pies and a dish of boiled potatoes, dressed with carrots. 'It all looks very special,' she said. 'What's the occasion?'

'There's no occasion,' Megan assured her. 'It's just that you've been looking tired lately and it's always you who gets the food. So, I thought I'd give you a treat.'

Smiling, Cathleen looked her in the eye. 'Are you sure that's the real reason?' she asked mischievously. 'You're not keeping something from me, are you?'

'Like what?'

'Like Norman paying you a special compliment, or asking you out to the music hall?'

Blushing bright pink, Megan confessed, 'Well . . .' She began to giggle. 'I was in the pantry and he came in to get some flour and, well, he kissed me – only quick like, but oh, Cathleen, he *does* like me, he really does!'

Laughing, Cathleen told her how she'd known that all along. 'Did you kiss him back?'

Megan shook her head. 'He kissed me then he ran off, and I stayed in the stock cupboard for ages. After that we daren't look at each other.'

'You're a crazy pair and no mistake! Him running off, and you hiding in the stock cupboard – what a carry on!' When Cathleen put it like that, it seemed so comical that Megan had to laugh with her.

When they were seated and enjoying their meal, Megan asked her how she had fared with Mr Woodley.

Cathleen told her everything; how he was disappointed about her taking the money back, but had accepted it and offered them a helping hand should they ever need it.

'Did you ask him about Silas?' Having forked a heap of hot pie into her mouth, Megan almost choked. 'Ooh! Ah . . . whew!' Wafting her hand in front of her open mouth, she cooled her burning throat before, quickly recovering, she asked croakily, 'What did he say about the message on the back of the envelope?'

'It was a business appointment,' Cathleen explained. 'Apparently he and Silas did a deal regarding some land. In fact, he was so impressed with Silas he offered him a job here in London, but Silas turned it down.'

'He must be mad! Why would he do that?'

Cathleen took her time in answering, because she was loath to put into words what Mr Woodley had told her.

Impatient, Megan banged her spoon on the table. 'Cathleen!'

Cathleen looked up, her blue eyes betraying a mixture of anger and regret. 'Silas didn't take the job because he's far too content to up sticks and move away.'

'Did Mr Woodley say that?'

Toying with her food, Cathleen shook her head. 'No, not in so many words, but he might as well have.'

'So, what *did* he say?' Helping herself to another potato, Megan smothered it in brown sauce.

Taking a deep breath, Cathleen let it out in a rush. 'It seems that Silas is lucky to have such a charming and attractive wife, who absolutely dotes on him. When they got wed, he and Helen went to live with Jack Turner . . . her father, and the owner of the land agency. Now though, according to Mr Woodley, Silas has taken her to live at Fenshaw House.'

'And how do you feel about that?'

Cathleen wasn't really sure about her feelings any more; except that she loved him and always would. But one thing she did know. 'I wouldn't want him to be unhappy. What happened was not his doing, but he was the one made to pay. Awful things happened, and now he has to make the best of it.'

'What awful things?'

'This is between us?'

Spitting on her finger, Megan crossed her heart.

'There was a debt to be paid, and no money to pay it. Because of it, his father committed suicide. His mother is ailing, with little time left, and Silas has carried the weight of it all on his own shoulders.'

'My God!'

'What's more, Mr Woodley is wrong about Helen Turner. She's *not* attractive and charming . . . she's a vicious, dangerous woman who gets what she wants and doesn't care who she destroys along the way.'

Megan understood. 'I only ever saw her once – before the wedding – but I didn't take to her at all. She seemed a thoroughly nasty piece of work.' Something of what Cathleen was saying fermented in her mind. 'Are you telling me that Silas was made to marry her because of this debt?'

Afraid to say any more, Cathleen warned, 'No one knows about it, except those involved. No one must *ever* know. You do understand that, don't you, Megan? I'm confiding something in you that must never be repeated outside these four walls.'

'I won't tell,' she promised. 'But if he's taken Helen Turner to live with him at Fenshaw House, does that mean he's come to love her after all, d'you think?'

The same thought had occurred to Cathleen, and it was a hurtful one. 'Maybe so,' she conceded. 'But I'd like to think he's gone home because of his mother. Losing her husband like that must have taken its toll on her.'

A quiet smile shadowed her face. 'Lucy Fenshaw is the loveliest person, Megan. When I was small, she used to play with me in the garden. We'd have picnics and games, and when my mother died Lucy was always there to make me smile. Silas too.' In her mind's eye she could see his face, the unruly mop of dark hair and those deep, dark eyes that could turn her upside down with just one loving glance. She finished in a whisper, 'Silas was *everything* to me.'

The two of them chatted a while longer; about Fenshaw House, then about Norman Trent. Megan outlined her dreams for the future. 'I want lots of children,' she said, 'and a house with a proper kitchen, and a garden where we can sit of a summer's evening.' And Cathleen said she hoped Megan's dreams would come true, although when she added, tongue-in-cheek, that she hoped their children wouldn't all look like Norman, Megan mimicked him to perfection again and they laughed until their sides ached.

While Cathleen cleared away and washed the dishes, Megan fell asleep by the fireside, her mouth wide open and snoring 'like a good 'un', as Jessie would say. 'I hope Norman doesn't find out how you snore until *after* you're wed,' Cathleen chuckled, and shut her ears to the awful sound as she went about her work.

In the middle of washing the plates, she was gripped by an urge to go to the window. There she looked out on a clear dark sky, like a carpet to heaven, it was. For a long, precious moment she closed her eyes and imagined herself and Silas on a certain island, on a beautiful, unforgettable day.

'Whatever happens to me now,' she whispered, 'and if I never see you again, my love . . . no one can ever take my memories away.'

Chapter Fourteen

Norman Trent never enjoyed doing what he was about to do, but as he saw it, he had no alternative.

When the workers first began to arrive, he was too busy delegating to have that 'quiet' word with Cathleen, and somehow the morning went by too quickly. Then it was lunchtime and he had to visit a customer, and didn't return until two o'clock, by which time Cathleen was on pins.

She didn't know why he wanted to see her, and was afraid to guess. In fact, as the day wore on, she began to hope he had changed his mind and didn't want to see her after all.

As it turned out, her hopes were short-lived.

At two-thirty, while she was dealing with a customer, Norman peered in at the office door. 'Cathleen, when you've finished, we'll have our little chat, shall we?'

'Sounds like trouble, gal!' The woman was round and amiable, and like every other customer she had taken a liking to Cathleen from the first minute she clapped eyes on her.

Making no comment other than a smile, Cathleen continued to write down Maisie's order.

Not realising how close to the truth she was, Maisie told her light-heartedly, 'If he gives you the push, gal, there's allus work down the market.'

'There you are then, Maisie.' Handing her the docket, Cathleen was careful not to get caught up in *that* sort of conversation. 'I've entered your order for delivery to the stall at eight o'clock on Saturday morning, same as usual. Oh, and,' she lowered her voice, 'I've thrown in two crusty loaves and half a dozen muffins, on the house.'

Maisie was delighted. 'You're a pleasure to do business with.' Leaning forward, she intimated softly, 'When that babby's ready, I know just the person to fetch it safely into the world – Sally Newton from Argyle Street. She fetched all ten o' mine in and never a worry.'

Cathleen thanked her, but said, 'I'm attending Miss Burton's.'

Maisie was surprised. 'What? Her from the clinic?'

'She makes you see the doctor once a month,' Cathleen informed her. 'I don't want to take any chances, that's all.' Not with Silas's bairn she didn't.

'Blimey, gal! I bet that's costing yer a bob or two an' all?'

'It's a shilling a visit, and I only go twice a month,' she explained, 'but I already had a few savings, and I'm earning a wage, so it's all right.'

'I'm glad to hear it.' Maisie gave her a little hug, as

she always did on leaving. 'If you change your mind, Sally's only a shout away. What's more, she only charges a tanner a visit, and a threepence more to deliver.'

That said, she went away, whistling like a navvy.

From the bakehouse Norman watched her leave. A moment later he was in the office. 'You know how to please the customers,' he said thoughtfully. 'You know how to run this office too.' He glanced about the room, with its new shelving and proper files standing all in a line, like little soldiers complete with name tags. 'Everything in its place and a place for everything,' he said proudly. 'Business up and overheads down. I don't mind admitting, you've made a real difference to this place.'

'But?' Cathleen sensed there was more to come.

'Hmh!' He sat down some distance away, then got up and paced the floor, before coming to the desk and sitting opposite her. 'It's not easy for me to say this, Cathleen,' he began. 'I've nothing but praise for you. You've earned the respect of every customer and brought them flocking to this bakery, more than ever before. You're a hard worker and you've a quick mind; you could run this business with your eyes tight shut . . .' He would have gone on, but she stopped him.

'You're finishing me, aren't you?'

Startled by her intervention, he hung his head. 'I'm sorry, gal, but yes – you'll be given your cards by the end of the week.' Now that she'd guessed, there was no other way to say it.

'Can I ask why?' Even though she'd suspected it since

yesterday, it still came as a shock. 'You've only just got through telling me how I've helped the business grow. So, what have I done wrong? Is it the bairn? You did tell me I needn't worry about that. Are you afraid I won't be able to do my work, because, one way or another, I *will*.'

Somehow, all of a sudden, her work was desperately important to her. 'Miss Burton says I'm strong and healthy, and so long as I'm not lifting heavy stuff, there's no reason why I can't work right up to the end, and come back soon after that, if I find someone suitable to look after the bairn.'

Then, feeling ashamed and humiliated, she forced herself to stop gabbling. 'I'm sorry,' she said falteringly, 'I'm sure you must have a good reason for finishing me.'

He almost leaped out of the chair with excitement. 'That's just it!' he cried, 'I *do* have a good reason.'

Looking furtively out of the office window he made sure Megan was out of earshot. 'It's Megan,' he said, and his whole face lit up. 'I was wondering . . .' Under the brim of his trilby his face coloured like a ripe tomato. 'Er, I was wondering – I mean, I really like her, and well, I wonder if . . . I mean . . .'

Cathleen put him out of his misery. 'You want to know if she feels the same way about you, is that it?'

Giving a silly little giggle, he went all sheepish. 'Something like that, yes.'

It did Cathleen's heart good to know he had real affection for her pal. 'I think you mean a lot to her, if that's what you're asking.'

It was *exactly* what he was asking. 'Whoo!' Making a noise like a bird, he puffed out his little chest and rolled his eyes, blinking and grinning, and looking as if he might fly out the window at any minute. 'Did she tell you that?'

'More or less.' It was all she could do not to look through the window and wink at Megan, who was suddenly covered in flour when she stepped back from peeping into the office and collided with Harry, who was shifting the flour onto the shelf. Poor, startled Harry lost his balance and dropped the sack of wheatflour, which promptly split wide open to send up a white fountain, which showered the pair of them.

Another time Cathleen would have laughed out loud, but this was no laughing matter: there was still the matter of her job here, and why he was getting rid of her. 'I don't understand why you have to finish me, though,' she queried. 'I won't come between you and Megan, if that's what you're worried about. Oh, I know you're a bit older than she is, but anyone can see you think the world of each other. And that's much more important than any difference in age.'

'My sentiments exactly!'

'All I can say is, I'm thrilled to see her so happy, and I know you'll be good to her.'

'Oh, I will, I *will*!'

'So how does all this affect me?' It didn't make sense. 'There has to be another reason why you're giving me my cards. You say it's not my work, so what is it?'

In a hushed whisper he told her, 'I haven't told anyone this, not yet ... except, of course, the people who need to know, but I've been made a cash offer for my property. It's such a good offer I'd be crazy not to take it.'

Fidgeting with excitement, he went on, 'I've always said when I retired, I'd travel the world. But I've been too busy, always rushing here and there, and of course, I'm still much too young to think of retiring. However, I wouldn't mind taking a year or so out. After that, I could start up again somewhere else, maybe go into something different, I haven't really thought about it.'

Cathleen was amazed. 'You told me you've been in the baking business all your working life. I know how important it is to you.'

'Not as important as Megan. She's the best thing that's ever come into my life.'

'I understand how you feel, but can you really turn your back on it all just like that?' All thoughts for herself were now swallowed up in her very real concern for him. 'It's not a job, it's a way of life, and like you said yourself, you're much too young to retire.' She suspected he was letting his heart rule his head. 'Don't make a mistake you might regret,' she suggested kindly. 'Why can't you have both your business, *and* Megan?'

A look of determination spread over his features. 'I have more money than I know what to do with, and thank God I have my health. If Megan would only consent to be my wife, I'd lay the world at her feet. My mind's made up. I've never done what I want, and I've never had anyone else to consider but myself. If she says no, then that's a different matter, but I'm praying she'll say yes and make me the happiest man alive.'

Knowing what she had found and lost with Silas, Cathleen understood every word he was saying. Deeply moved by his heartfelt confession, her eyes filled with tears. 'You're right. Nothing is more important than spending the rest of your life with someone you love.' No one knew better than she did what it was to find true love and then to lose it. 'I wish you all the happiness in the world,' she said, and meant it.

'I'll make you a promise,' he told her. 'When the property changes hands, I'll write it into the deal that you be given first refusal on renting that room upstairs. Moreover, because I value what you've done for me here, I mean to pay you two weeks' wages in front, with a handsome bonus to tide you over.'

'You're a good man,' she said, 'but I don't want you to risk losing the sale by making conditions regarding me. When you've signed the deal, let me know, and I'll start making plans right away.' She didn't refuse his generous offer of wages and bonus because she had an idea she might well need every penny.

'I appreciate that.' He was obviously relieved. 'To tell you the truth, I don't imagine the buyer *would* be too pleased to have conditions written into the deal, but I will insist if you want me to. It's the least I can do for you.'

'No, I don't want that. Thank you all the same.'

'You're a considerate woman, Cathleen,' he told her, 'and the best friend Megan could ever have.' He knew nothing of her background, other than that she came from the north and knew the bakery business inside out. 'I've no idea who the father of your child is, or why he isn't with you, but I'll tell you this . . . he's lost out on both counts, you *and* the nipper.'

Cathleen smiled in that quiet, thoughtful way she had. So many times she had agonised over whether she should have told Silas she was expecting his child, and each time she came to the conclusion that it would only add to the heartache.

Norman Trent's whispered plea invaded her thoughts. 'You won't tell Megan, will you? If she asks what we were talking about, you won't let on?'

Cathleen promised she wouldn't. 'Though she'll want to know why you asked to see me. I'll just tell her you're concerned that I'm overdoing it, shall I?'

Norman thought that was a very good solution.

The next few hours flew by, with no opportunity for Megan to quiz her, and besides, Norman was toing and froing like a cat on hot bricks.

'Are you all right?' Megan asked him worriedly.

'Never better,' he said, and gave her such a wonderful smile she went weak at the knees.

'What did he want with you?' she asked Cathleen immediately after tea. 'You were in the office long enough . . . heads together and talking as if you were planning a secret of sorts.'

'We were!' Cathleen knew she suspected something, so had to distract her from asking too many questions. 'We're planning to run off together. He's madly in love with me, and can't wait to get me on my own.'

At first, Megan didn't know *what* to believe, then she saw the twinkle in Cathleen's eye and burst out laughing. 'You little devil!' she chided. 'You really had me going there for a minute.' The conversation concluded, 'There you are then, Cathleen. I told you so.' Megan was delighted she'd been right. 'He wasn't intending to finish you after all.'

Rather than tell a deliberate lie, Cathleen merely nodded and concentrated on sipping her hot malt drink.

'I think there's something going on with Norman.' Megan had been puzzling over it for the past hour or so.

'Why's that?'

'I'm not sure. It's just that he was so full of himself this afternoon, smiling and pacing about . . . peeking at me all the time.'

'That's 'cause he doesn't know how to keep his eyes off you.'

'Do you really think so?'

'I'm sure of it.'

'Oh, Cathleen, I do wish he would ask me out!'

'Oh, he will, any time now – you'll see.'

With that amazing thought in her mind, and a desperate need to dream of her precious Norman, Megan got ready for bed.

Half an hour later, the sound of her contented snoring filtered through the air. 'Poor Norman,' Cathleen softly laughed. 'He doesn't realise what he's in for.' All the same, she was happy for them. 'You and Norman belong together, Megan, like two peas in a pod.'

When, a moment later, Megan fidgeted so much the blanket fell from her, Cathleen tiptoed across the room to cover her again. 'He'll take good care of you,' she whispered. 'And it's no more than you deserve.'

———⋙•⋘———

THE FOLLOWING MORNING a letter arrived from Jessie.

Dear Cathleen,

I was so pleased to receive your letter of last week, and am glad to know you are still well. I do worry about you being so far away from home, where I can't keep an eye on you. Still, and all, you are a sensible lass, so you are, and I thank the Good Lord for that.

I know you won't come home because of your father. I know you're worried that he's still hard-hearted towards you, and maybe he is, and maybe he isn't, I can't really tell. But what I will say is this: he seems almighty lonely.

Only the other day, he said as how Lou Matheson was asking after you. I think it was just an excuse for himself to find out how you were. Mind you, I have to say, that young man is forever stopping me in the street, asking all manner of questions about you. 'How is she?' he says. 'Does she ever mention me in her letters?', and, 'Is she not thinking of coming home?' So you see, I think he really does care for you.

Mind you, my little darling, I can't help wondering the

*same myself. When are you coming home? And I think
the sooner the better. It worries me that you'll be having
the bairn all by yourself, and without me at your side.*

Pausing a while, Cathleen held the letter on her lap.
'She's so concerned about me,' she told Megan, who
had been listening to her read the letter aloud. 'I wish
she wouldn't fret. It makes me feel so guilty.'

'Finish the letter,' Megan urged. 'What else does she
have to say?'

Cathleen continued:

*'I don't suppose you know, but Silas and his new wife have
moved into Fenshaw House. I think it's a big mistake, because
if you ask me, that dreadful Helen Turner means to get her
feet under the table good and proper, so she does!*

*Mind you, I've an idea Lucy may well have been taken in
by her devious charm, because the other day I saw her and
Lucy seated together in the carriage, like they were the best
of pals. It just goes to show, doesn't it?*

Oh, I do miss you, Cathleen, lass.

*Please, for the sake of an old woman, will you not come
home?*

*I know how the leaving was not your fault, but a lot of
water has gone under the bridge since then, so it has.*

*Now I believe with all my heart that your father is missing
you badly enough to welcome you with open arms. But he
won't be drawn, so, hand on heart, I can't promise he's
altogether forgiven you.*

I know you've got your friend Megan, and I'm very glad of

*that. But you're far away from your family and home, and
I think there must be times when the loneliness touches you.
I say a prayer for you every night, asking the Good Lord to
keep you strong and well.*

*I only wish I was a younger woman and could travel easier.
But I mean to come and see you soon, so I do, when the
weather improves.*

*Till then, God bless you, lass. Give my love to Megan. As
always, I shall look forward to your next letter.*

From your loving grandma, Jessie.

XXXX

There followed a moment when the two young women
thought about the letter, which had made them each feel
lonely in their own way. 'I wish I'd met her,' Megan said
presently. 'She sounds such a lovely person.'

Not for the first time, Cathleen told her about Jessie,
and the more she talked, the more she missed her.

'Will you ever go home, do you think?' Megan
asked.

'Sometimes I wish I could, but,' Cathleen knew her
father too well, 'it's not my decision to make.' In her
troubled mind, she saw that cosy little cottage, her father
in his chair reading his newspaper, Jessie bustling about
over the fire-range. So far away, yet so close, as in that
moment her heart soared over the miles between them.

'Maybe she's right,' Megan wondered aloud. 'Maybe
if he sees you again, your father *will* welcome you with
open arms.'

Cathleen shook her head. 'I wouldn't count on it,'

she answered with a wry little smile. 'My brother Robert has been a constant heartache to him, so he always looked on me as being the reliable one. When he found out I was with child, he took it badly. He's a proud man and I shamed him, you see.' When she said it like that, out in the open, it sounded a shocking thing. 'He threw me out, and to tell you the truth I can't blame him. Like Grandma always told me, you make your bed and then you have to lie on it.'

And that was what she must do, she thought. Yet it was a sad situation, and one which gave her many a sleepless night. There were times when she couldn't help wondering where it would all end.

---

*C*ATHLEEN COULDN'T KNOW *it, but already there were things underway that would change the course of her life yet again.*

Chapter Fifteen

I T WAS HALF past five when Megan burst through the door, her face alight with happiness and her arms up in the air as she rushed to hug Cathleen. '*He's asked me to marry him!*' she cried, and danced round the room. 'Oh, Cathleen, Norman asked me to marry him, and I've said yes!' Laughing and crying all at the same time, she said, 'That's why he kept me back . . . and I thought I'd done something wrong. But, oh, I can't believe it! I just can't believe it!'

Cathleen had known it was coming, but was thrilled all the same. 'I'm very happy for you,' she said sincerely. 'You and Norman are so right for each other.'

When Megan calmed down and the two of them were discussing the happy event, Megan told her how Norman had been concerned about having to lay off all the staff thanks to the impending sale of the property. 'Especially you,' she said. 'He's worried about you.'

'There's no need to be,' Cathleen assured her. 'I can look after myself.' She chuckled at the thought, but said,

'If it came right down to it, I could always work with old Maisie on her market stall.'

'You can't do that!' Megan was horrified. 'She's always burping and trumping, and that awful snuff she takes smells like dead sheep.'

'I was joking,' Cathleen confessed. 'But, aw, she's harmless enough is Maisie. I could do worse than work on her stall.' The laughter welled up again. 'As long as I stood downwind of her, I'd be all right.'

Megan stifled a giggle. 'Do you remember the time she insisted on climbing the ladder to inspect the flour? Norman nearly had a fit when one of the lads said he saw her bare arse, 'cause she had no drawers on.'

Cathleen remembered as though it was yesterday. 'And what about when she spent half an hour in the office giving Norman a right telling-off because he'd sent two muffins short. After she'd gone, he came running out like his tail was on fire . . .'

Megan concluded the tale. 'Poor Bill Bentley was sent in to open all the windows because the smell was so bad . . . And he came out red in the face where he'd been holding his breath!' Cathleen exploded. Now she couldn't hold back the laughter, and neither could Megan. 'We shouldn't laugh, it's wicked,' she chided, and through the sound of their hearty laughter, Megan agreed.

Later, when the meal was over and everything cleared away, Megan got herself ready for her date. 'He's taking me to the music hall in Bethnal Green,' she said, dabbing rouge all over her cheeks. 'Tomorrow, he says we can go and choose a ring.' Overexcited, she dabbed the rouge in her eye. 'Oh! *Now* look what I've gone and done!' Then she got some on her jacket and began wailing, 'What do I look like? What's he going to think of me, eh?'

'He'll think you're daft as a brush, and he'd be right,' Cathleen teased. But she took charge and soon had Megan pretty as a picture. 'Go off and enjoy yourself,' she said, 'and don't come back two sheets to the wind.' She'd seen Megan a bit tipsy once before, and it was a sight to behold.

Right up to the minute she went out the door, Megan was full of it. 'He's selling the property soon as possible, then he's taking me travelling. But first we're getting wed. I'm to have a big wedding dress, with oodles of lace and a long train, and we both want lots of children. Will you be my maid of honour, Cathleen?'

Cathleen told her she'd be proud to. 'As long as you don't mind me waddling down the aisle with a belly like a barge,' she laughed.

Megan said she didn't care because, 'You're my best and only friend, and anyway, you'll look lovely, big belly or not.' With that, and a twirl to show off her new black skirt and matching jacket, she went on her way.

Drawing back the curtains, Cathleen saw her climb into the waiting carriage. Afterwards, she sat on the sofa and took stock of her own young life, and the future ahead. It didn't seem much, she thought.

But the news of Megan's coming wedding, and all

her exciting plans, put a smile on Cathleen's face. At least *one* of them had got it right.

———◆◇◆———

JAKE BREWER HAD been in a foul mood all day.

With only ten minutes before he was off-duty he paced the foyer of the Riverside Hotel, nervously smoking and watching the clock as it ticked the minutes away.

'Right, I'll take over now, Jake.' The new receptionist was a long thin streak, with a pasty face and a personality to match. 'Quiet tonight, ain't it?' he said, yawning lazily.

'It's just as well!' Jake snapped. 'I'd hate to see you cope with a rush.' Snatching his coat, he was out the door and away.

'Off down the pub, are you?' the man called behind him.

'None of your sodding business!' Jake snarled.

Twenty minutes later, after pushing his way through a bitter cold night, he burst into the pub, puffing and blowing and rubbing his hands to get the blood flowing. 'It's bloody freezing out there!' he told the landlord. 'Give us a pint and a chaser.' Throwing his money down on the counter, he asked in a gruff voice, 'Has anybody been asking after me? Jake Brewer's the name.'

Taking an instant dislike to him, the landlord served him his beer with a chaser to follow. 'There's nobody been in here asking after you,' he answered equally gruffly. 'And I should know seeing as I've been serving at this 'ere bar for the past two hours.'

'A little man with a tache,' Jake insisted. 'Wears a long coat, grey neb cap . . . kinda dips when he walks.'

'Nope!'

'Have you been serving here on your own, or is there a barmaid?' He and the man in question had arranged to meet here at this time on this day, and now, with no sign of him, Jake was on edge.

'Look, matey!' The landlord knew Jake's sort and didn't encourage them into his premises. 'There's no barmaid, and there's been nobody here of the kind you mention. So, if you don't mind, I've got my regulars to serve.'

Taking stock of the landlord, a big man with a neck like a bull and a chest that could lift wagons, Jake nodded. 'All right, all right! Just asking.' If the odds had been even he might have hit out, but he was no fool. There was no use getting a bloody nose if you could avoid it. Besides, he had someone to meet who he hoped would bring news of that little bitch Megan! No woman ever got away from him without paying the price. So! Here he would stay until the bugger turned up, even if he had to sit out on the pavement after closing time.

Taking his drinks, he turned round to find a table. There were a few men propping up the bar, and a man playing the piano in the background, but no sign of his mate. 'Damn it!' Finding a table near the door, he sat down and kept watch, his bad temper thickening with every passing minute.

It was half past ten when the man he'd been waiting for finally showed up, and no sooner was he through the door than Jake grabbed him. 'Where the hell have you been?' Propelling him to the table, he sat him in the nearest chair. 'D'you think I've got nothing better to do than hang round pubs with folks gawping at me? Have you any idea how long I've been waiting for you?' Giving him a shake for good measure, he hissed, 'Well? Have you got summat for me or not?'

Nervously searching through his coat pocket, the little man shook like a leaf. 'I'm that cold I can't feel my fingers!' he protested bravely.

'You'll feel the end of my fist in a minute!' Jake threatened. Like the coward he was, he could handle them when they were smaller than himself. 'Well? Did you find her?'

Breathing a sigh of relief, the little man drew out a small pocket-book. 'I've got it! It's here – her address and everything.'

Flicking through the pages he almost leaped out of the chair with fright when Jake grabbed the book from him. 'It's all there, like I said. She's renting a room with another of Norman Trent's workers. But there's summat else. You'll not be best pleased, I'm thinking.'

He fell silent when Jake flicked open the right page and began to read, crying out after a minute, 'The cheating little whore!' Dropping the notebook on to the table, he sat quite still, his eyes narrowed and mouth drawn tight. Twice he picked up the notebook, and twice he seemed not to believe what was written there. 'I'll skin her alive, so help me I will!'

'I said you wouldn't like it.'

Gathering courage, the little man verified what was written in the book. 'You didn't give me a chance to tell you,' he said. 'She's tekken up with the boss and they're planning to wed. The word is, he means to take her travelling. Selling his business so he can be with her he is. By! I've seen them together; besotted with each other, like two kids in a bloody toy shop they are!'

Now, as Jake grabbed him by the throat, 'It ain't *my* fault,' he pleaded. 'I'm only telling you what I found out. You paid me to track her down, and that's what I did. You can see that, can't you, Jake? You can see it ain't my fault!'

'HEY!' The landlord's booming voice drew their attention. 'If you want to fight and argue, take yerselves outside, afore I *put* you out!'

Releasing the little man, Jake raised the palms of both hands to the landlord. 'Just a small disagreement,' he said, 'soon settled.' Suspicious, the landlord went about his business, one eye on his customers, the other on Jake and his friend.

Taking a sip of his ale, Jake pushed his third chaser over to the other man. 'Here.' He was calmer now. 'You done good.'

Immensely relieved, the little man took a deep swig of the warming spirit. 'By! That's better,' he chuckled, his voice scraping like wire in his throat where Jake had almost throttled him.

Leaning forward so no one could hear, Jake asked,

'What did she look like?' He grinned. 'Still as pretty as ever, is she?'

Surprised, the little man humoured him. 'She's a good-looking lass,' he answered, but he didn't really think so. Oh, she was passable, but not pretty exactly. If anything, it was her pal that was pretty. Beautiful, she was, and fat in the belly from some man who appeared to have tasted the goods then made off before he had to pay for 'em.

'She's not what you might call a real raving beauty,' Jake admitted, 'but she's good in bed, and knows how to please a man, if you know what I mean?'

The little man shook his head. 'Can't say as I do,' he answered in a sorry voice. 'I've not been so fortunate in that quarter.'

Jake sniggered. 'With the money I'll be paying you, you should scour the streets and find yourself a woman afore it shrinks to nowt!'

'This woman . . . Megan?' Wisely ignoring Jake's nasty little taunt, the man asked, 'If you still had a hankering for her, what made you let her go?'

'I didn't let her go,' Jake snapped. 'The little cow ran off. We'd had a row and I smacked her one. I can't understand it. I'd hit her afore and she'd never run off like that. I thought she'd come creeping back with her tail between her legs, but two days went by, then a week, and still there was no sign of her. I searched high and low. For two whole weeks I scoured everywhere I could think of, but there was no sign of her anywhere. That's when I brought *you* in.'

'She weren't easy to find, I'll tell you that.'

'Hey! Don't imagine I'm paying you more than we agreed, 'cause I'm bloody not!'

It had been on the little man's mind to ask for a bonus, but he saw the danger signs in Jake's eyes and changed his mind. 'I wouldn't dream of it,' he lied. 'We had a deal. I've done my bit and now I'm here with the goods so you can do yours.' He held out his hand, but Jake seemed not to notice.

Instead, he rambled on about his precious Megan. 'She's *mine*!' He slammed his fist on the table, making the little man glad he wasn't in Norman Trent's shoes. 'I'll get her back, you see if I don't!' Winking, he took another swig of his ale. 'We had an understanding,' he said. 'Me and her meant to make it legal one of these days, only she frightened me off with all her silly ways and airy-fairy ideas. She wanted a house and a garden, and so many kids it scared the hell out of me! I *had* to hit her – oh yes, she needed keeping under, did that one!' He started giggling like he was insane. 'I'll smack her when I see her, all right,' he whispered. 'Have to teach the little lady who's boss, you see?'

There was something about Jake's manner that really frightened the agent. 'I'd best be going,' he muttered. 'If you'll settle up with me now, I'll be on my way.'

'I put her in the Infirmary once, did you know that? No, you wouldn't, would you? Well, anyway, I broke two fingers on her right hand. It was her own stupid fault. She shouldn't have put up her hand to stop the blow, should she, eh?'

'Can you settle now? I've a tram to catch.'

'Another time, I gave her a hiding and locked her in the stock cupboard. I turned out the light and left her in the dark. She didn't like that . . . poor little sod, she's scared of the dark. But I let her out in the morning, before the workers arrived. We made love right there and then. She didn't like *that* either, but it didn't make no difference to me. If I want it, I take it, that's the way it is.'

'I'd best have my notebook back.' Realising he had been dealing with a madman, he was anxious to get away. 'There are things in there I need. Other clients, you understand.'

'I've a mind to break her bloody neck for what she's put me through!'

'Look, I've other business to attend to. You know what it's like. A man has to earn a living.'

Suddenly, Jake had him by the wrists. 'You haven't heard a word I've been saying, have you, matey? Oh, that won't do at all.'

Startled, the other man was amazed at how his mood had swung back again. 'I've got cloth ears,' he said with a nervous little smile. 'Oh, and a terrible memory. Funny, but I forget everything except the money I've earned.' It was not a very subtle reminder, but he was desperate.

Reaching into his pocket, Jake drew out a handful of coins and slapped them on the table. 'Will that do?'

The man counted them into the palm of his hand, surprised to find that it was more than enough. 'I'll be off then.'

As he got up, Jake began to laugh. 'Did I tell you she snores like a pig?'

The little man shook his head.

'Oh, but she does! I've often threatened to throttle her in her sleep,' he bragged. 'Sometimes she were that frightened, she wouldn't even go to bed.'

Suddenly the laughter stopped and his face darkened. Reaching out, he took hold of the other man's sleeve, trapping him there. 'If she doesn't mend her ways, I might just *do* that . . . throttle her, I mean. That would be a pity, don't you think? Especially as you've gone to so much trouble to find her for me.'

As he left, the little man heard Jake's manic laughter. 'Dear God, what have I done?' he murmured, as he walked slowly down the street. 'I'm paid to find somebody, and I can't be held responsible for what happens after that, can I, eh?' A sense of panic took hold of him as he thought of Megan. 'Poor kid. The man's a raving lunatic! Happen I'll give it up and look for other work.'

As it happened, it would be a long time before he did any work at all. In the early hours of the morning he was found in the alley behind the public-house, badly beaten, with his pockets emptied and all his fingers broken.

When they asked him who did it, he said he didn't know.

He daren't tell. Not with Jake Brewer's warning still ringing in his ears.

Chapter Sixteen

THE DAYS WERE flying by.

Megan was caught up in a whirlwind. 'It's only two weeks since Norman asked me to marry him, and already he's signed the deal on the bakery. We've set the date for the wedding and I still haven't got my ring, or been fitted for my dress!'

Cathleen had been washing her hair at the sink. 'Megan, pour the water over my head, will you?' Blinking out of one eye, she kept her head bent to the bowl. 'Hurry up! I'm getting soap in my eyes.'

Megan rushed across the room, where she picked up the big jug and poured half its contents over Cathleen's wild mop of hair. 'Is that enough?' It would have been for Megan, but Cathleen's hair was thick as a forest. 'Hang on, you've still got soap,' and she poured the remainder of the water over her. 'That'll do.' Handing her friend the towel, she sighed forlornly. 'If only I had my ring I'd not be so worried about Norman changing his mind. And what about my dress? What if it's not made in time?'

'Oh, Megan, do stop worrying!' Cathleen peeped at her from under the towel. 'You'll get your ring, and you've already been measured for your dress; you've got your first fitting tomorrow, and it's been promised in plenty of time.'

Megan gave a shy smile. 'Isn't Norman wonderful?' she cooed. 'He found me the best dressmaker in London, bless him.'

'Well, there you are!' Wrapping the towel round her head like an oversized turban, Cathleen put the kettle on. 'He's been chasing his tail ever since you agreed to marry him. He's sold his business in record time, he's been God knows how many times to the solicitor, then the bank, and in between he's been keeping an eye on the bakery and taking time out to find you a dressmaker.' Washing the dregs from the teapot, she rinsed it round with hot water. 'He's hardly been into work, and I know, because he puts me in charge every time he has to go out.'

'You're right.' Megan was convinced. 'He's not about to change his mind, is he? Not when he's gone to so much trouble.'

'No, he's not!' Pouring the tea, she put milk in both and a spoon of sugar. 'So stop worrying, before you drive us both insane!' Handing Megan her cup, she sat down with her own. Curling her legs under her, she settled awkwardly into the chair. 'You'll get your ring soon, I've no doubt.' She smiled knowingly at Megan.

Megan noticed and was instantly suspicions. 'What's got into you?'

Making a face, Cathleen teased, 'Shall I let you into a little secret?'

Sensing something to her own advantage, Megan grinned. 'You'd better!'

'I happen to know he's been talking to a jeweller.'

Megan gave a little squeal. 'How do you know that?'

'Because there was a letter for him from *Pontefract & Son, Jewellers of Distinction*. That's what it said on the envelope.'

Megan gasped. 'That's the one down Regent Street. Oh, Cathleen, it's all posh, with flowers in the window and all that.'

'You're not to say anything, or he'll think I've been snooping.'

Megan promised she wouldn't breathe a word. 'I expect he means to surprise me, eh?'

'So, now will you drink your tea so we can get off to the shops and find you some fancy underthings?' She laughed. 'And a saucy lace nightgown that's sure to make him turn tail and run.'

'Hey! Stop it, you.'

'All right then, a red one with feathers.'

Megan burst out laughing. 'D'you want me to look like a chicken? He *would* turn tail and run then, and who could blame him, eh?'

But Cathleeen had seen the frantic look on her face. 'You're not worried are you, Megan?' she asked. 'About you and Norman and . . . well, you know what I mean.'

Megan knew all right, and it had been playing on her mind. 'I am a bit worried,' she confessed. 'You see, we haven't . . .' a wave of bright pink spread over her features making them glow '. . . *done* it yet, so I don't know what it will be like.'

'You never told me you were a virgin.' Cathleen thought it strange, because she and Megan had already discussed all that.

'I'm not a virgin,' Megan confided sadly. 'But the only man I've been with is Jake Brewer, and he was a terrible bully.'

'Jake Brewer?' Cathleen fought to recall the name. 'He's the one at the hotel where you worked?'

Nodding, Megan told her, 'He used to hit me bad. Once, he even locked me in the stock cupboard overnight. It was awful! There were spiders and everything.' She shuddered.

Cathleen was shocked. 'Sounds to me like you're well shut of that one!'

'Norman won't turn out like that, will he?'

'I don't think Norman's got a bad bone in his body.' Cathleen had worked with him long enough to know he was a man of principles. 'What's more, he worships the ground you walk on.'

Blushing fiercely, Megan twittered and fussed. 'Do you really think so, Cathleen?'

Finishing her tea, Cathleen heaved herself out of the chair and came to give her a hug. 'You *know* I'm right. If anybody was to hurt one hair on your head, he'd do for them without a second thought.'

Megan looked up at her. 'You're so good to me,' she said tearfully.

Another hug, then, 'I'm glad you're smiling at last. Honest to God! You've been driving me mad, with your ring and your dress and wondering whether he'll change his mind. It'll all come right in the end, you'll see.'

Megan was a lot happier. 'I wonder when he'll tell me about the jewellers?'

'Hey! That's enough of that. No more fretting.' Slipping her clean drawers on, she took off her nightie. Catching sight of herself in the mirror, she groaned, 'Look at me! I get bigger by the minute.'

Looking across the room, Megan envied her. 'You're beautiful,' she said. Cathleen was so lovely, she thought, with her wild hair and her ripe, mother-to-be breasts; her skin was a fine, silky texture that seemed to shine out. 'I can't wait to be carrying Norman's baby.'

Cathleen smiled. 'It's not all roses,' she warned. 'You can't lie comfortable in your bed; you get heavy and tired, and sometimes you think it will never end.' Her smile deepened. 'But it's wonderful too. When you feel the bairn move inside you, and you know that soon you'll hold a real, living person in your arms, and that person is part of you and someone else. It's a miracle, there's no denying it.' As always, Silas was strong in her mind.

'You miss him real bad, don't you?'

Cathleen nodded, her heart breaking. But she knew the way things were and was trying to come to terms with them. Forcing a bright smile, she told Megan, 'Get yourself ready 'cause we've some shopping to do. Like silk drawers and fluffy slippers and long sheer stockings . . .'

'Hey! I'm not wearing all that, not even for Norman.'

'All right then, so we'll get thick flannelette knickers like Grandma wears, and as it's winter we'd best find some Winceyette nighties and a few pairs of them long thick stockings, you know the sort, all ribbed and wrinkly.'

Megan giggled. 'Behave yourself, you wicked thing!'

Arms out and tripping like a mannequin, Cathleen glided through the centre of the room, bowing this way and that, and putting an edge to her voice. 'Oh, and here we have some comfortable, flat black shoes and a long dark skirt sweeping the floor. Then of course you simply *must* have a green woolly hat that pulls right over your face.' Taking the cushion out of its cover, she drew it down over her head. 'Oh, and we mustn't forget the grey shawl, dear me, no!' Whipping off the tablecloth she wrapped it round her shoulders. 'This is the look for a new bride, and isn't it just wonderful!'

With Megan screaming and laughing in the background, she danced and twirled round the room, holding her aching sides when the baby objected. 'That's another thing,' she said, falling into the nearest chair. 'You can't leap about with a baby inside you.'

An hour later, they were ready for off, dressed like working girls, with Megan in her red coat and Cathleen in a warm, loose-fitting coverall, which stretched across her bulge whenever she moved.

'It's the only thing I can get into these days,' she said as they went out the door. 'I could get another coat but it hardly seems worth it now.' Especially as she was saving all her spare cash for that rainy day which loomed closer by the minute.

When she turned to lock the door, one of her buttons popped off. 'Happen I'll have to get myself a big grey shawl,' she said, and for a minute Megan actually believed her.

Fumbling in her bag for a safety pin, Cathleen secured the gap. 'Why not go back and stitch the button on?' Megan suggested.

'We've no time,' Cathleen reminded her. 'It's eight o'clock on Saturday morning. You know how the trams get packed, *and* the shops. If we don't get off now, we'll have a long wait at the tram-stop.'

Megan didn't need any persuading. 'Well, I for one don't fancy waiting about in the cold,' she said, and was soon out on the street. 'Blimey! It's freezing!'

Linking arms, they pushed against the wind. 'It cuts right through your clothes,' Cathleen said, and had to stop now and then to catch her breath.

JAKE BREWER FOLLOWED behind at a safe distance. He wasn't about to lose Megan now. Nor did he intend going back to Blackburn without her.

AROUND MIDDAY, THE wind dropped and a clear bright sunshine filtered through. 'That's better.'

The woman in the West End department store smiled on her two unlikely customers. 'It's so much nicer when the sun shines,' she remarked politely, 'though, being February, we can't expect too much, I suppose.'

Looking first at Cathleen then at Megan, she thought them both out of place and common. At first she wasn't sure which one to address, but on noticing how Cathleen was heavy with child, she decided her best bet was Megan. 'I understand from the store manager that you're soon to be married?'

'That's right.' Megan felt uncomfortable in such plush surroundings.

'And that you have a letter of introduction from Mr Norman Trent?'

'Yes.' Taking the letter out of her purse, Megan handed it to her meekly.

'A moment.' Putting on her spectacles she began perusing the letter, until Cathleen interrupted. 'Excuse me?' She did not like the woman's superior attitude with regard to Megan. 'The manager has already seen the letter and said it was perfectly acceptable. He was the one who sent us up here, so my friend could see if there's anything she wants from this particular department. If you're not satisfied with that, happen we'd better go back down and tell the manager?' It was a veiled threat and the woman knew it.

At once she was all smiles and apologies. 'Of course I'm satisfied,' she insisted. 'Mr Trent is a valued client here. If he wants you to buy on his account, that's all right with me.'

Placing the letter in a drawer beneath the counter, she made a wide circle with her arms. 'Please. Feel free to look round. If you need any help, just let me know, and I'll be right there.' In the meantime she intended keeping a close eye on them. She had encountered many a shoplifter in her time, and they were far better dressed than these two ragamuffins!

For the next hour the girls had a whale of a time. With the help of an assistant, Megan tried on countless outfits, from a dark blue two-piece to a dazzling scarlet dress. 'It's not really me,' she told Cathleen, who had fallen in love with it. 'I haven't got the confidence to wear something like that.' Instead, she settled for a cream-coloured dress and jacket and a pair of shoes to match. 'It's perfect for evening,' she said, and Cathleen agreed.

'Is that all?' Packing the outfit, together with a brown silk scarf and a pair of silk stockings, the woman pointed out, 'I noticed in Mr Trent's letter that you were to spend any amount up to four guineas. You've hardly spent a quarter of that.'

'It's all I want.' Megan signed the acquisition with trembling hands, grabbed her bag and purchase, and led the way out at such a pace that the woman was convinced they were thieves after all. 'Did you see how they ran out?' she said, hurrying down to tell the manager of her suspicions.

Regarding her ample bosom and wide mouth, the manager had long fancied her. 'Mr Trent took the trouble to come in and verify all of this yesterday morning,' he answered, 'so I can assure you it's all in order, and they are not thieves as you suspect.' It was the first time he had seen her blush and he thought it very fetching. 'Miss Tucker?'

'Yes, sir?'

'Would you care to join me for lunch? I had intended going out, but we can stay in the office and have sandwiches brought in. We won't be disturbed if we lock the door.' He twitched a smile. 'Only if you want to, that is?'

'Ooh, yes, sir!' It was like all her birthdays in one. 'I'd like that very much.'

<hr />

THEIR NEXT STOP was the café opposite. Cathleen bought them each a cup of cocoa and a ham sandwich. 'I know how you feel,' she said.

'I don't know what you mean.' Megan had been subdued ever since they came out of the department store.

'I think you didn't buy anything else in that store because you didn't want to take advantage of Norman's generosity.' When Megan simply looked up with cow eyes, she went on, 'If you want my opinion, for what it's worth, I think you did right. I would have done the same myself.'

Megan's face brightened. 'Honest?'

Putting her sandwich down, Cathleen crossed her heart. 'Hope to die.'

Happier now, Megan explained, 'I must admit, I didn't feel comfortable in that place.'

'Neither did I,' Cathleen confessed. 'I don't belong in them posh places, and I don't suppose I ever will.'

'Me neither.'

Raising her cup of cocoa, Cathleen made a toast. 'Long live Bellamy's and the market-place.'

'Where's Bellamy's?'

Cathleen had surprised herself. The name had rolled off her tongue almost without her thinking about it. Now the nostalgia rushed in, making her smile wistfully. 'It's a little corner shop in Blackburn. It's run by a darling little woman called Maggie Bellamy. She sells it all . . . from reels of cotton to working boots, and everything in between.'

'Here's to her, and all like her.' Megan drank her cocoa. 'Ooh, I'm dying to pee,' she said as they prepared to leave. Truth to tell, so was Cathleen.

'It's the baby,' she whispered. 'It weighs on me in all the wrong parts.'

The woman at the counter was very helpful. 'We *do* have a latrine,' she said, 'but I don't know if it's working. The damned thing has fits and moods, just like my old man!' Cackling at her own joke, she recovered enough to explain, 'You'll have to go out the back and down the passage. It's the first on your right, but there's only the one, so you and your mate will have to take turns.'

Cathleen insisted on Megan going first, while she herself chatted to the owner. 'When's it due?' the woman wanted to know.

'I was told to get ready for the third week in April.'

The woman did a quick count on her big, podgy fingers. 'Six or seven weeks, eh?' She regarded Cathleen's belly with awe. 'Looks like you might be carrying half a dozen in there.'

Cathleen laughed. 'It feels like it an' all.'

'Got any names picked out yet?'

Cathleen hadn't quite decided. 'One or two,' she confided, 'but I'm not rushing it. If I set my heart on one particular name, the baby might not suit it, so I'd rather wait and see.'

'Not me! I've got six kids, and all their names were taken from a hat.' She chuckled. 'I've even got one called Oakley, 'cause the name of the hat-maker fell out and was mixed up with the others.'

She and Cathleen got on like a house on fire, and before they knew it they were caught up in a lengthy and interesting conversation about babies and children, and how they turn out. 'Some come out right, some wrong, and it don't matter how you raise 'em neither.'

Cathleen found herself confiding her fears for her brother Robert. 'A "bad apple", my father says.'

'Like I say, it *can* happen.' And she ushered Cathleen to a table where she proceeded to tell her all about her own mother. Pursing her lips she made a whistling noise, 'Now, *she* were a bad 'un if ever there was one . . .'

———⟫•⟪———

NEITHER OF THEM had seen Jake Brewer sitting hiding behind a newspaper in the corner by the window.

Having followed Megan and Cathleen for most of the day, he had waited for his moment, and now here it was, like a gift on a plate.

Discreetly, he watched where Megan had gone, then he waited a while until the women were chatting obliviously before sneaking away, following in Megan's footsteps. As he rounded the corner he muttered, 'A door at the end of a passage.' That's where she'd be.

But not for long, he vowed, because that little slut was going back with him, whether she liked it or not!

———❧◦❧———

MEGAN HAD FOUND the lavvy halfway along the passage. Rusted and stuck, it took a minute or two to get the door open, and when she did, the smell of damp and the cold took her breath away. 'Not exactly the Ritz, is it?' she chuckled as she went in. 'But I'm not royalty neither, so needs is as needs must.' Picking up her skirt, she dropped her drawers and sighed with relief.

A few minutes later she tidied herself and pushed her way out. 'Best warn Cathleen about this,' she murmured, negotiating a half-hidden step the other side of the door.

When he stepped out of the shadows, her heart leaped to her throat. 'JAKE!'

Leering in that sly, familiar way she had come to know and fear, he stepped forward. 'By! You've run me a pretty chase, I'll say that for you.'

Making a frantic effort to dash past him, she cried out when he slammed her against the wall. 'So! You thought you'd run out on me, did you?'

'We were neither of us happy, Jake,' she gabbled.

'If I hadn't left, you would have ended up killing me, I know it.'

'Happen I would, happen I wouldn't, but that don't alter nothing.' Pushing his face close to hers, he dropped his voice to a rasp. '*Nobody runs out on Jake Brewer, especially you!*'

Fear drove through her like a knife. 'Let me go, Jake,' she pleaded, 'I've made a new life. I'm happy now . . . happier than I've ever been.' But looking into his evil eyes, she knew there would be no mercy. 'Please, Jake, don't hurt me.'

Softly laughing, he wiped away her tears. 'Good is he, this Norman Trent? Makes you feel like a woman, does he?'

'How do you know about him?'

Raising one eyebrow, he studied her face. 'Can't see why he'd go so far as to marry you,' he said cruelly. 'You're no looker. You'll do for me though.' Lowering his head he kissed her full on the mouth, wiping away a trail of saliva as he parted from her. 'Your gadding days are over, my lady,' he said thickly. 'You've had your fling and now you're coming home with me!'

When she struggled, he slapped her hard round the mouth. 'Bitch! I've spent good money and time searching you out. Give me half a reason and I'll whip the devil out of you.' Raising his hand he laughed when she cowered from him. 'That's right,' he fondled her breast painfully with the palm of his hand. 'That's the old Megan . . . the one I've been missing.'

Twisting her arm up her back, he propelled her down

the passage. 'If you're thinking of crying for help, *don't!*' he warned, 'or I might have to deal with your friend, and that slimy little bugger you think you're marrying!'

Knowing he had it in him to hurt both Cathleen and Norman, and anyone else who got in his way, Megan had little choice but to go with him.

Yet, as they came to the door, she prayed that somehow he might be stopped.

———⋙◆⋘———

W AITING IN THE café, Cathleen began to wonder where Megan had got to. 'If she's fallen down the lavvy, it's likely she'll never be seen again,' the woman joked.

But Cathleen had the strangest feeling that something was wrong. As she turned to go outside and look for her friend, an elderly couple came in out of the cold.

'Two teas, please,' the woman requested. 'If you ask me they should be locked up and the key thrown away,' she went on, pointing to the street outside. 'Any man who hits a woman is a downright coward.'

Her husband suddenly cried out, 'Look! They've got the bugger.' With Cathleen behind him, he rushed to the door. 'G'arn you bleedin' coward! What kind o' scum are you, to thrash a woman like that?'

When Cathleen saw two policemen with Jake Brewer arm-locked between them, she couldn't believe her eyes. As they loaded him into the Black Maria, her thoughts went straight to Megan. Taking to her heels she ran down the street, oblivious to the pain in her side and all the eyes staring in her direction. 'Megan!' And there she was, safe in a policeman's arms, weeping on his shoulder, her hair unkempt and her face bleeding.

At a run, Cathleen wrapped her two arms about her. 'Dear God, what's he done? However did he find you?' She had never been so frightened.

'It's all right, missus,' the policeman told her. 'She's taken a bit of a beating, but there's nothing broken.' Handing her into Cathleen's tender care, he asked her a few questions – address and such – the answers to which he wrote into his pocket notebook.

'We'll need you to come down to the station when you're up to it, miss,' he told Megan. 'Routine, that's all, to help put the record straight. For now though, that young man is going to be locked up, and he'll stay there until you decide whether or not you want to press charges.'

'Well of course she does!' Cathleen was sure of it.

But Megan knew it was a decision that might cost her dear. 'Take me home,' she begged Cathleen, 'I'm all right, really I am.'

But Cathleen would have none of it. 'You're *not* all right!' she said. 'You're trembling like a leaf and your face is covered in blood. I'm taking you to the nearest hospital.'

'Please, Cathleen, no.'

Something about her voice, the way she suddenly seemed to have grown up, surprised Cathleen. 'Is that what you really want, Megan?' she asked gently. 'To go home?'

One nod from her friend was enough to convince her. 'All right. But let's get inside and clean you up first. You'll need a hot, sweet drink too, for the shock.' The first-aid instruction she'd received from her father had come in useful after all, she thought.

Back at the café, the kindly woman sat Megan down and bustled about making her the tea. 'There's some wicked bastards about today,' she ranted on. 'Cut off their balls, that's what I say. That'll stop 'em!'

Making certain Megan was fit enough to be left, Cathleen recovered her shopping from the passage. 'It's all right,' she assured Megan when she got back. 'Still in its wrapping, and come to no harm.'

After the tea came the cotton wool and warm water. 'I'll put in a drop of paraffin shall I?' the woman said. 'There's nothing like paraffin for cleaning out a wound.'

Megan and Cathleen looked at each other in astonishment. 'No offence,' Cathleen said, 'but we have to go home on the tram, and we don't want to go up in smoke if someone should decide to light his pipe.'

'Just warm water and salt,' Megan said. 'If it's no trouble?' She didn't want her skin stripped off.

'No trouble at all,' the woman replied.

Ten minutes later, Cathleen and Megan were on their way, slightly the worse for wear, the shopping bags somewhat crumpled, but on the whole intact.

'Do you think they'll keep him inside?' Megan was like a cat on hot bricks.

'He'll stay there until you go down tomorrow and press charges, or not, as the case may be.'

'I'm frightened.' Megan was still trembling. 'He knows . . . about you, and about Norman and the wedding . . . *everything*!'

'He can't hurt you if you press charges, Megan.'

'Do you think I should?'

Cathleen had no doubts. 'You *must*!' she urged. 'You have too much to lose if you don't.'

Chapter Seventeen

C ATHLEEN GATHERED UP her few personal belong-
ings and dropped them into a small bag. 'Well,
that's that,' she exclaimed, walking out of the office. 'The
desk is cleared and ready for the next occupant.' There
was a kind of sadness in her smile. 'I've enjoyed my time
here,' she told Norman Trent. 'It'll be strange getting up
in the morning and not coming down to work.'

'I know how you feel.' Norman glanced at Megan,
who was strolling round the empty bakery. 'It'll be strange
for all of us,' he said quietly. 'But I'm glad I managed
to get you another six months in the room upstairs. It
would have been on my conscience if I hadn't, and it
will give you plenty of time to find somewhere else after
the baby's born.'

'Thank you for that,' she said again. 'And for the list
of people you've recommended.'

'They're all respected landlords,' he promised. 'I'm
sure one of them will find you a room, when you're ready.
Oh, and don't forget Mr Bartholemew. His accounts clerk

is leaving in June, and he'll be looking for somebody reliable.'

'I'm very grateful, thank you.'

Cathleen's gaze was drawn to Megan. 'You've made her so happy,' she said. 'All she talks about is the wedding, and how you mean to move west when you get back, setting up a new business in Cornwall, was it?'

'Nothing's been decided,' he told her. 'It was just one of a few ideas I've been toying with.' He smiled wistfully. 'You see, I'm a Londoner born and bred. I'm not altogether sure I could live outside the city. But I'm not ruling *anything* out.' His smile broadened. 'I've a wedding coming up, and a new life. Things are bound to change one way or another.'

Cathleen laughed. 'With Megan, there'll never be a dull moment, I can promise you that.'

'I'm beginning to realise that,' he chuckled, then fell silent before, to Cathleen's surprise, posing a question. 'How has she been with you these past weeks?'

'In what way?'

'I'm not really sure, but she seems a bit quiet like. Ever since that dog went for her and she fell over.' Sighing heavily, he confided, 'It gave me a terrible shock when I saw her all hurt and bleeding like that.'

'It gave us *all* a shock.'

'Damned dogs, roaming the street and tripping people up like that. It's a disgrace!' Quieting himself, he asked again, 'Has she been all right though? I mean, whenever we go out now, she seems nervous . . . looking over her shoulder all the time.'

'Well, she's bound to be nervous, isn't she?' Cathleen didn't want to lie to this lovely man, but he must never find out about Jake Brewer. 'I expect she's frightened that some dog or other might come charging out of nowhere.'

'Hmh.' He smiled at Megan as she came towards them. 'I had thought of getting a dog myself, but we'll have to see now, won't we?'

'It's a bit eerie here now!' Megan said, glancing back at the vast, empty space. 'All open and echoing.'

Norman found it upsetting. 'Come on, then. The sooner I lock up, the sooner I can put it all behind me.'

Outside on the pavement, while Norman locked the door, Megan asked Cathleen, 'I saw the two of you talking. You didn't tell him about Jake, did you?'

'Of course not!'

'I don't ever want him to know.' She shuddered.

'Well, he won't hear it from me.'

Norman couldn't get away quick enough. 'Right, all done. I'll take the keys to the agent, and afterwards I've an errand or two to make.' Giving Megan a fleeting kiss, he told her and Cathleen, 'Like me, I expect you two have a lot to do, so we'd best get on with it.'

Gazing at Megan he told her, 'It won't be long now before you're Mrs Trent.' With a silly grin on his face he turned away. 'See you later then.'

Upstairs in their room, Megan paced the floor. 'He'll come after me again, I know it!'

'He can't if he's locked away,' Cathleen argued.

'Besides, he'll have Norman to deal with if he ever tries it on again.'

Coming to the kitchenette where Cathleen was rinsing her cup, Megan said, 'You could be right. Jake's a coward through and through. Maybe he wouldn't attack a man where he would a woman.'

'There you are then. And don't forget the police know all about him now. They'll be watching him, I bet you. If he so much as takes one step out of line, they'll be onto him.'

'Do you really think so?'

'Look, Megan. When Jake Brewer comes out of prison in six weeks' time, he'll be labelled an ex-convict, and you'll be Mrs Trent. The picture will have changed altogether.'

Megan grew excited. 'Of course! I'll be a married woman, and he wouldn't dare try anything.'

'That's what I've been trying to tell you.' Cathleen was glad to see her friend begin to relax again. 'Now then, there's something I want to ask *you*.'

'What?'

'I want you to think again about having me as your Maid of Honour . . .'

'No! I've told you before, I won't change my mind. I need you by my side when I marry Norman. I've lost touch with my family, so they won't be there. Cathleen, if you refuse, it will ruin what should be the best day of my life.'

'But look at me, Megan.' Cathleen stepped back for her to see. 'I'm as big as a house. It's your day, Megan

. . . yours and Norman's, and everyone will be looking at me instead of you.'

'Please, Cathleen. I really want you with me,' Megan pleaded. 'I've spoken to Norman, and he said if it's what I want, he's happy.' A thought struck her then. 'Are you embarrassed, is that it?'

'No.' In a strange way, she was looking forward to her little moment of glory. 'I've never been a Maid of Honour before. It's just that I don't want to embarrass you both, that's all.'

'Well, you won't. So *please* don't let me down. *Please!*'

It was agreed; Cathleen would be Megan's Maid of Honour, and that was an end to it.

———◈———

FIRST STOP WAS the clinic. 'You're doing well,' Miss Burton told her. 'The baby hasn't dropped yet, but then you've still got three, maybe four weeks, to my reckoning. I'll make you an appointment with the doctor for the week after next, then we'll see.' Handing her the appointment card, she said, 'I hope you've got the necessary all to hand for when the baby decides to arrive?'

Cathleen recounted, 'I've got everything together in the pillow-slip as you said: baby things, sheets and towels, and your address if I need to send a runner.'

Miss Butler reminded her, 'And money put aside for a cab if I'm not at home and you need to make your way in?'

'Yes, it's all there.'

'Good girl! There's nothing else worrying you is there, m'dear?'

'No.' She looked at Megan and grinned. 'Apart from Saturday, when I'll be standing at the altar looking like the back end of a tram.'

'Go on with you!' Miss Burton retorted. 'You're not *that* big. I've seen women the size of wrestlers when they're only four months gone. It's 'cause you're small, that's why you feel bigger.'

'I've told her that,' Megan butted in, 'but she won't believe me.'

———◆◆◆———

N EXT STOP WAS the dressmaker for their final fittings.

First, Cathleen. 'I hope it hides my bulge,' she said, following the dressmaker into the back of the shop.

'Oh, I think you'll be well and truly pleased with what I've done.' Fanny Truman was short and thin, and wore the tiniest pair of spectacles on the end of her nose. 'Slip it on and we'll see.'

The dress slithered over Cathleen's head like silk. 'It feels really comfortable.' Delighted with her image in the mirror, she could hardly believe it. 'The way you've gathered it high makes all the difference.' Turning every which way, she felt like a princess. 'I can't wait to show Megan!'

Throwing back the curtains, she came out to where her friend was waiting impatiently. 'What do you think?'

Megan's eyes widened with astonishment. 'Oh, Cathleen, you look beautiful!' The dress was the loveliest blue, like Cathleen's eyes. Slim at the shoulders and neck, it was drawn together above the bust by means of tiny pleats, then, cleverly disguising Cathleen's condition, it fell softly downwards to a full hem just above Cathleen's pretty ankles.

'You were right!' Megan gasped. 'They *will* be looking at you instead of me, but not because you're with child. They'll be looking because you're the most beautiful thing they will ever see.' She meant every word, but it didn't matter if they *were* looking at Cathleen. All that mattered was having Norman on one side, and her best friend ever on the other.

Next it was Megan's turn.

When, after a while, she came out fully dressed for the occasion, Cathleen was speechless.

The ivory dress was the best money could buy. Sheer silk and lace, it was slim in the waist and full in the skirt. The sleeves were close-fitting, with ruffs of lace at the wrist and the same at the neck. A cascade of silk train followed behind, and the veil was long and figured, with a coronet of pink silk roses to hold it in place.

'Oh, Megan, it's just perfect,' Cathleen whispered. Overcome with emotion, she fought back the tears. 'I was wrong,' she smiled. 'All eyes will be on you, not me, and rightly so.' Laughing and crying at the same time, she said, 'They won't even notice I'm as big as a barge!'

The instructions were taken for delivery the following day, and then there was only one more call to make.

————◦◦◦————

THE FLORIST ALREADY had the order; now all that remained was to choose the flowers. 'Being March, there's less choice than in the summer,' she told Megan. 'Describe the dresses and headwear to me, then I'll know straight away what's needed.'

When Megan finished explaining, the woman took a moment to consider, then with a smile from ear to ear she declared, 'I have it! For the bride, I think, lily of the valley and tiny white chrysanthemums, with green fern leaves trailing over a blue ribbon, to tie in with the Maid of Honour's dress.'

Megan thought that would be lovely. 'And what about Cathleen?'

'For the Maid of Honour, I think, *cream* chrysanthemums and pink roses . . . the chrysanthemums to complement the ones in your own bouquet, and the pink roses to highlight the silken roses in your coronet.'

Buttonhole flowers were ordered for Norman, his best man – a long-serving worker from the bakery – and Mr Joshua Collins, a valued customer who had kindly offered to give Megan away. Instructions were taken for delivery, and at last everything was ready for Saturday.

On the tram on the way home, Megan opened her heart to Cathleen. 'I wish I had a decent father to give me away,' she confided. 'Mr Collins is a nice enough man, but it isn't the same, is it?'

Cathleen knew the story of how Megan's parents had split up and gone their separate ways. 'Can't you find out where he is?'

Megan hadn't seen hide nor hair of her parents for three years. 'Norman offered to pay for a detective to find them,' she said, 'but I've thought about it and decided I don't want either of them here. They'll only mess up my wedding day. All they ever did was argue and fight. If I invited one and the other found out, there'd be hell to pay, and if I invited them both, they'd probably end up killing each other.'

'That's a shame. And Grandma can't be here either.'

Megan understood. 'Bless her old heart, and she was so looking forward to coming, wasn't she. But she can't help being laid low with that bad bout of flu.'

'Well, we're a right pair, aren't we, eh?' Cathleen couldn't help but smile. Putting on her best cockney accent, she chirped, ''Ere's you, gal, with no family to see you wed, and 'ere's me with nobody to see me in that dandy frock bought by your intended.'

'You're mad as a hatter!' But Megan loved her all the more for it.

Cathleen linked her arm with Megan's. 'Look on the bright side,' she said in a more serious voice. 'You've got your fella, and I've got my baby.' Tapping her bulge, she said, 'I wonder if she knows what's going on?'

Megan tutted. 'There you go again, calling it a she.

You could be in for a bitter disappointment if it turns out to be a boy.'

Cathleen winked. 'We'll have to wait and see, won't we?'

———⋙·◦·⋘———

ON FRIDAY EVENING, when the flowers were delivered, the dresses hung on the picture rail, and all the paraphernalia for the big day was spread across the sofa, Megan couldn't keep still. 'That's six times you've been to the lavvy,' Cathleen chided. 'You'd better calm down or they'll have to carry you up the aisle tomorrow.'

'I'm sorry, I can't help it. I'm that nervous.'

Cathleen made her sit down. 'I'm making us a mug of cocoa before we go to bed,' she said. 'Don't move from that chair!'

Out of sight in the kitchenette she dropped an extra spoonful of cocoa in Megan's drink. 'That should make you sleep well,' she murmured, and as a second thought, added another half spoon.

'This tastes a bit strong,' Megan complained.

'Stop moaning and drink it down,' Cathleen urged.

'I'm telling you, Cathleen, I won't sleep a wink tonight.'

'You will if I knock you out!'

'What's in this cocoa? It tastes really odd.'

'Poison. I'm trying to kill you so I can get some peace.'

Laughing, Megan took a long, deep slurp of the liquid. 'Best get it over with quick then.'

The evening ended with the pair of them recalling all manner of funny things that had happened at the bakery. 'I'll miss that place,' Cathleen remarked with a sigh.

'So will I,' Megan replied, 'when I'm on that cruise ship, drinking champagne and being waited on hand and foot.'

'Monster!' Cathleen threw a badly aimed cushion at her; the cocoa went flying, and it took them half an hour to clean it up. 'Well, I'm buggered!' said cockney Cathleen on her knees. 'This is a bleedin' good start, ain't it, gal?'

And they laughed so much they couldn't get up.

Chapter Eighteen

J ACK TURNER WAS not a happy man.

Seated behind his desk, he looked through the dividing window into the cubicle where Silas sat beavering away, head down, intent on his work as always.

He watched for a few minutes, then took another glance at the clock. Unsettled, he leaned back in his chair and regarded Silas again. 'God help us, I should be hung, drawn and quartered for what I've done to him!' He had seen Silas change from an outgoing young fellow to a quiet, serious man, with too much on his mind. He didn't smile any more. He worked like a dog until all hours, earning more money for the company than Jack did himself.

The clock struck nine. It was pitch black outside and still there was no sign that Silas would end for the day. Unable to stand it any longer, Jack got out of his chair and hurried across the room. 'Keep on like this and you'll drive yourself insane.'

Looking up, Silas told him, 'I've nearly done.'

'You're out on your feet, *that's* what you are! In here

at seven of a morning, out selling till five or six, and then back here until all hours. For God's sake man, are you trying to kill yourself or what?'

Silas didn't answer. Instead, he made an entry into the ledger and closed it up. Pushing back his chair, he stood up and replaced the ledger into the filing cabinet and turned the key. 'I'm not the only one working late,' he said. 'You're always here when I arrive, and you're still here when I leave.'

There was a brief span of silence while the older man looked at Silas; at the dark shadows under his eyes, and the haggard look on his face. *He* had done that, and it was a hard thing to live with. 'How can you not want to kill me?' he murmured.

Silas smiled sadly. 'I might,' he answered, 'if I thought it would solve anything. But it won't, will it?'

Silas knew how Jack was haunted by what he had done. He was haunted by Edward's untimely death and by the chains he had put round Silas's neck. He was haunted by a daughter who was the devil incarnate, and by the fact he could do nothing about the shocking circumstances he himself had created.

Taking his long-coat from the peg, Silas put it on. 'Goodnight,' he said, 'I'll see you in the morning.'

'Wait a minute.'

Silas turned. 'Yes?'

Jack took a deep breath. 'I've decided.'

Silas waited, hoping against hope it was what he thought. Now, when he spoke, his voice was calm, belying the mounting excitement inside. 'I'm listening.'

'The company is yours if you want it – at the price you mentioned.'

Silas was elated. 'What made you change your mind?'

'I want out. I need to get right away . . . as far away as I can.' He closed his eyes, his mind filled with the image of Edward Fenshaw. 'There's nothing to keep me here any more.'

Silas was pleasantly surprised. 'I didn't think you would ever come round to agreeing to my offer.'

The other man smiled. 'I can afford to choose now.' He laughed, a harsh, bitter sound. 'Ironic, isn't it,' he said. 'Your father almost ruined me, and now you've turned this business round in no time at all. You've made me a rich man, Silas. If ever there was a debt to pay, you've paid it over and over. You've given me my freedom.' He paused, his voice breaking. 'I only wish to God it was in my power to give you yours.'

'Honour has a price,' Silas answered quietly. His 'price' had been Cathleen, he thought bitterly.

'So? Are you still interested in buying me out?'

'You know I am.'

'Then we'll lose no time. I'll make an appointment with the solicitor first thing Monday.'

And the two men shook hands on the deal.

⸻※◈⸺

HELEN WAS WAITING for him as Silas came in through the door of Fenshaw House. 'I thought you'd never come home.' Her voice was sweet, while inside she was enraged by the fact that he'd rather be at work than with her.

Throwing his coat over the back of a chair, Silas noticed that she was dressed in the flimsiest of nightgowns, cut low enough at the neck to reveal the better part of her breasts, and clinging to her body like a second skin. 'Is Mother asleep?'

'As far as I know.' *As soon as she could fix it, his mother would be lying in her grave!*

Crossing to the dresser he poured himself a measure of whisky. 'I've told you before, Helen, you've no need to wait up for me.'

'There *is* a need,' she murmured, sidling towards him, '*I* have a need.'

'Go to bed, Helen.' As she came towards him, he walked away.

She paused, her eyes blazing. 'Look at me!' she hissed.

Wearily, he raised his gaze to her, a coldness in his heart that crippled him.

'Am I ugly?' she asked, almost pitifully.

Knowing what she wanted, he looked away. 'You know you're not.' Strange how she had grown from a plain thing to a creature with something to offer. With her hair tumbling over her shoulders, and a figure of good proportion, any man might fancy her now. But she meant nothing to him. He had never made love to her and never would. A repulsion crept into his soul. Slamming his glass down, he brushed past her. 'Goodnight.'

'Silas!' Reaching out, she caught hold of his sleeve. 'I'm your wife. Doesn't that mean anything to you?'

He shook her off. 'You'll never be a wife to me,' he said vehemently. '*Never!*' He turned to look at her, the hatred alive in his dark eyes. 'You knew that from the start.'

In that moment, as she returned his gaze, Helen knew she might have him trapped, but she would never own him. 'I love you,' she whispered. 'You should know that.'

He gave a small laugh. 'You don't *love* me!' His voice rose with anger. 'You need to break me, but you can't. I won't give in to you, and you don't know how to deal with it. You've never been refused *anything* before, have you? You only had to ask and you got. But that's over now. To the outside world we're husband and wife, but in here, where I can still be master, we know the truth, don't we? This marriage is a sham, Helen. It was never anything *but* a sham. I don't love *or* want you. I never have. I never will.'

'You'll be sorry.'

He gave a half-smile. 'I'm sorry already.'

'You're a bastard!'

'I'm what you made me.'

As he closed the door, he heard her calling after him, 'Do you think I don't know why you can't love me? It's *her* you want, isn't it . . . your precious Cathleen? Well, she's gone and I'm here, and whether you like it or not, I'm your wife! I'll get what I want in the end, I always do. *Bastard!*' There was the sound of something being thrown, then silence.

As he went up the stairs he let the familiar surroundings quieten his senses. He never meant to hate her, but he did, and with all his sorry heart.

Upstairs, Lucy lay awake. Not for the first time, she heard raised voices and was saddened by the fact.

'Mother?' Silas opened the door and peeped in, his voice gentling towards her. 'Mother, are you awake?'

'It's all right, son,' she replied, 'Come in.'

As always, he sat on the edge of her bed and told her of his day's work. 'I've clinched three big deals today,' he said. As well as one he didn't want her to know about. Not yet anyway.

'You work too hard,' she sighed. 'Your days are too long.' She stroked his face. 'You look so tired, son.'

He turned the tables. 'You're a fine one to talk,' he smiled. 'I expect to find you fast asleep, and here you are, wide awake, with not an ounce of sleep in you.'

'I've rested on and off all afternoon,' she told him. 'Maggie took me for a walk across the garden.' She paused. 'Silas, is everything all right between you and Helen?'

'Of course.' He hated lying to her. She was the only sane influence in his life.

They chatted a while longer, about the ordinary, important things, then Silas said, 'Try and get some sleep, Mother.' When she closed her eyes, he kissed her goodnight and left quietly.

For a long time, Lucy lay there, her mind churning over and over. She couldn't settle. More than ever now, she was convinced there was something going on. 'There's something wrong,' she mused. But what?

She had a plan. In the morning, she would take a little trip and see what she could find out.

***

A FTER HIS EVENING meal, Tom settled down at the fireplace as usual, his newspaper stretched out before him and his eyes glued to it. This was the time of day he liked best, especially on a Friday.

'Tom?' Jessie's voice invaded his thoughts.

Slightly irritated, Tom looked up. 'I'm reading the paper, lass,' he said. 'Can't it wait?'

'No.' Laying down her sewing, Jessie was determined. 'No, it can't. I've been waiting to ask you summat all evening, and now you've got your head stuck in that paper!' She sighed. 'Listen to me, will you, just for a minute?'

Folding the paper, he looked at her and knew what was coming. 'If it's about our Cathleen, I don't want to know.'

'Then you're a bigger fool than I took you for, Tom Roe!'

'Mebbe! But I mean what I say. I've no childer, and that's an end to it.'

'Oh, and what about *grandchilder*?'

'Don't want no bastards, neither!'

'Cathleen's bairn is due to arrive in a matter of weeks now,' she persisted. 'Why can't you forgive her?' Jessie never stopped trying. 'You know in yer heart she's not a bad girl.'

In a surge of anger he leaped out of the chair. 'Not a bad girl! What is she then, eh? I thought I'd brought them two up to be decent people. There's Robert, up to all manner of shady tricks, mixing with bad 'uns, sullying my name across the county; it's only a matter of time before he's put in jail. God help us, Jessie, how can I call him a son of mine? Tell me that!'

His voice broke. 'Then there's Cathleen. I would have died for that lass.' A smile crept over his features. 'Right proud of her I was,' he said. 'Then, hardly afore she's got the cradle marks off her arse, she acts like a tart with the first man who comes along. Next thing we know, she's in the family way.' Running his hands through his hair, he groaned like a man in pain. 'Nobody could have tried harder with them childer than I did, Jessie. But they turned out bad and that's the truth of it.'

Storming across the room, he snatched his jacket from behind the door. 'I've *no* childer,' he cried. '*No* childer, and *no* grandchilder. And the sooner you get that through your head, the sooner we might get some peace in this bloody house!'

The slamming of the door jarred Jessie's nerves. 'Dear God, Cathleen,' she sighed. 'I've done me best, lass, but it's no use.'

Wearied by her recent illness, she dragged herself across to the scullery where she made herself a cup of tea. 'I'll wait up for him,' she decided. Though her loyalty would always be with Cathleen, she deeply regretted the way she and Tom had rowed. 'Happen when he gets back, he'll be in a better mood.'

She glanced at the clock. 'Half past nine. He'll have gone down the pub.' Settling herself in the chair, she raised the cup of tea to her lips and let her old mind wander. As always her thoughts flew straight to Cathleen. 'I wish I could have been there tomorrow, lass,' she murmured, 'I'd have loved to make sure you were all right.' She chuckled. 'By! I bet you and that Megan will look a treat in all your finery.' Tutting, she shook her head. 'All the same, it's a pity it ain't *you* getting wed tomorrow. That might bring your father back to the fold. As it is, I'm not sure if he'll *ever* forgive yer!'

It was a long, long time since she'd been to a wedding, and it would have been a real treat. Mostly, though, she needed to see for herself how Cathleen was. In spite of the reassurances in her letters, it was hard having her so far away, and Jessie so longed to see her grand-daughter again.

Finishing her tea, she pushed the chair back and forth on its rockers. Lulled by the gentle rhythm, she fell asleep in minutes.

Unbeknown to Jessie, Tom wouldn't be home for some long time yet, and when he did return it would be with news that would shock her to the core.

L OU STOOD BACK and let Robert do the work, his face leering with satisfaction when the younger boy collected the money from the girl. 'I've done what you said.' Robert delivered the money to Lou. 'They never even questioned my authority.' It was the first time he had executed Lou's business with the prostitutes and he felt ten feet tall.

'Well, they *wouldn't* question your authority,' Lou explained, 'not when I've already told 'em how you're my right hand from now on.'

'Did I do all right then?' Robert was eager to know. 'Were you pleased with the way I handled things?'

Lou patted him on the back. 'I'm proud of you,' he said. 'In fact, I think I'll treat you to a drink. Come on!' He led the way to the bar, feigning astonishment when the landlord told him, 'Look 'ere, sunshine! The next time I see you pair doing business in my pub, you're barred.'

'What "business"?' Lou laughed. 'I'm sure I don't know what you mean.'

'Is that so?' Stretching a long, sturdy arm over the counter, the landlord grabbed Lou by the collar. 'I wasn't born yesterday.' Lifting him clear off his feet, he warned, 'I run a clean pub here. I don't want no rozzers closing me down on account o' rubbish like you two. Do I need to say more?' Dropping Lou like a sack of potatoes, he glared at him. 'Well?'

'All right, all right!' Straightening his shirt, Lou's smile had lost some of its arrogance. 'Understood,' he said. 'We'll give you no trouble, will we, Robert lad?'

Robert shook his head. 'We don't want trouble.'

'There you go.' Clamping his arm round the boy's

shoulder, Lou said, 'All we want is a quiet pint, ain't that right?'

Again Robert nodded. 'That's all, Lou. Just a quiet pint.'

The landlord smiled back. 'That's what I'm here for,' he declared warily. 'To serve pints and please the customers.' With that he drew two good pints, dark and rich, with rivers of white froth running down the sides.

Lou thanked him and paid.

Afterwards, he and Robert retired to a corner table where they set about planning their future. 'I'm sick of playing a mug's game,' Lou confided. 'I reckon there's more money to be made out there on the streets, using the girls and selling your arm to the hard men.'

'What d'you mean exactly?' Robert was fascinated. Lou and he had become real mates, now he was living at the Mathesons' full-time.

'What I mean is this . . . you and me, we're working at the bakery for a pittance when we could earn ten times as much by using our brains. Look at what them girls took tonight, and half of it's mine!' Leaning forward, he lowered his voice to a whisper. 'I could earn twenty guineas tomorrow for half an hour's work . . .' He clicked his fingers. 'Just like that.'

Robert was astounded. '*Twenty* guineas!'

'Shut up, you bloody fool!' Lou hissed. 'If it got out, we'd *both* be for the hangman!'

Robert backed away. 'Hey! What's all this about?' Talk of the hangman put the fear of God in him.

Beckoning for him to lean forward, Lou explained,

'There's this posh bitch – got more money than you and me could earn in a lifetime, she has.' He was speaking so quietly, Robert had to bend his head closer. 'She wants me to do a job for her.'

'What "job" could be worth twenty guineas?'

Lou's face was wreathed in smiles. His answer was to run a pointed finger across the width of his neck, at the same time making a whistling noise.

The colour drained from Robert's face. '*You mean she wants you to slash somebody's throat?*'

'That's right! An old biddy . . . halfway to heaven already, only she ain't going quick enough for this lady.'

'I don't want nothing to do with it!' Prostitutes were one thing; murder another.

'Come on, it's the easiest job in the world,' Lou said. 'Money for the taking.' He chuckled. 'Besides, you know her.'

'Who?'

'The one she wants rid of. It's Lucy Fenshaw . . . your Cathleen's old friend.'

Swallowing hard, Robert could hardly talk. 'My God! Who wants rid of *her*?'

'Who d'you think?'

'Who is it, Lou? Who could possibly want her murdered?'

Biting his lip, Lou glanced about. Satisfied they couldn't be overheard, he whispered, 'It's that rich tart, Helen Turner that was. The one as married Silas Fenshaw.'

'Bloody hell!' Falling back in his seat, Robert was

dumbfounded. But not for long. Bending his head over the table again, he asked, 'Will you do it?'

'I might,' Lou's grin was evil. 'If she doubles the offer.'

'*Forty guineas!* She'll never do that.'

'I've already told her . . . it's *my* neck on the line, not hers, I said. The price is forty guineas or I'm not interested.'

'What did she say then?' Robert was becoming excited. 'D'you think she'll fork out?'

'She says not, but give her time and I reckon she will.'

'You're an evil bastard!'

'Are you in or not?'

Robert took a minute to think about it. 'I'm in,' he said. 'But only if I get half.'

Lou shook his head. 'I don't give nobody half.'

'A third then?'

'That's better. Now, all we have to do is wait and see what the bitch comes back with.'

———————⟶◦⟵———————

As Tom came in the front door of the pub, Lou and Robert went out the back. 'There goes a right pair o' bad buggers.' The landlord served Tom his pint. 'Running prostitutes from this bar they were, until I put 'em straight. "This is a clean bar," I said, "I don't want no rozzers closing me down on account o' scum like you two."'

With half a mind on his pint and half a mind on Jessie, Tom supped his ale and pretended to listen.

'They skulked in the corner over there, planning God knows what. The young lad, well, 'e weren't much older than what? Sixteen? By! What's his father thinking of, to let him hang about with that one, eh? That's what I'd like to know. That Lou's a bad 'un, an' no mistake!'

Suddenly, Tom was listening. 'Lou, you say?'

'Aye, that's what the lad called him, right enough.'

'What's he look like, this Lou?'

The landlord described him. 'Thick-set bloke, fair hair, sallow complexion, like he must work inside or summat.'

The other man at the bar had minded his business so far, but now he had something to say. 'Or he's just got out o' prison.'

'Hey! You could be right an' all.'

Tom had another question. 'The lad with him. I don't suppose you caught *his* name, did you?'

The landlord shook his head. 'Can't say as I did. Why?'

The stranger included himself in the conversation. 'The lad's name were Robert.'

'*Robert?*' Slamming his drink down, Tom was engulfed by rage.

'Aye. He collected the money from the street-girls, and paid it over to this Lou.' He sniggered. 'Being trained in the art of pimping, he were, and Gawd only knows what else. Like the landlord says, they sat in that

362

corner, whispering and planning like they were talking to the devil.'

'Where did they go?'

'Through there.' Pointing to the back door, he said, 'It leads onto the alley, and from there to the street.'

The landlord laughed crudely. 'Happen they've gone to check on the girls . . . making sure they're not keeping their legs together for too long at a time.' Bandying other obscene comments, the two of them were carried away with laughter.

When next they looked up, Tom was already out the door.

Outside, he looked one way then the other, and at first he couldn't see a hand in front of his face. About to turn away, he was alerted by the sound of a man's voice. 'For Chrissake get a move on, will you? We've things to do.'

It was Lou!

At once, Tom took off down the alley after them. Not a man for running, he seemed not to notice the physical effort. Instead, driven by the row he and Jessie had just had over Cathleen, and the dreadful things he had learned about Robert, his feet took wing. 'ROBERT!' His angry voice carried down the alley.

'Bloody hell!' Having finished his pee against the wall, Robert fumbled to fasten his trousers. 'It's me da!'

Lou was frantic. 'Quick! This way!' Taking to his heels, he ran like the coward he was.

Robert wasn't as quick. 'You filthy little bastard!' Taking him by the lapels, Tom shook him hard, his breathing erratic and his eyes out on two stalks as he slammed his son against the wall. 'Will you *never* stop shaming me? D'you think I don't know what you've been up to?'

Never in his life had Robert seen his father as he was now, and it filled him with a strange kind of horror. 'I don't know what you're talking about!'

'*Liar!*' For a brief moment Tom looked on this young man and saw a child he had once loved; a boy who he had hoped would grow into a man he could be proud of. Instead, here was a thing of the dark, a creature who was already learning to prey on others.

Now, his sadness coloured his quiet words. 'God only knows I've been as good a father as I know how, and still you've turned out bad. You're like a rat in the sewers.' His voice sharpened with disgust. 'You and the other one . . .' His chin trembled as he struggled to force the word out. 'PIMPING! My own son using women like that! And *Lou*! My God, is there nothing decent any more? Can none of you be trusted?'

'Let him go!' Lou had not gone far. Now, he came back to help his partner in crime.

'Let him go, Roe!' Brandishing a piece of iron he'd picked up from the rubble, he threatened, 'I don't want to hit you, but I will, unless you let him go, NOW!'

Tom's answer was to go for Lou. There was a struggle, a cry, and suddenly the older man was slumped against the wall, his head covered with blood. 'I warned you!' Terrified by the turn of events, Lou glanced up and down the alley.

It was then that Tom sprang on him again and, like a madman, Lou retaliated. 'No, Lou!' Robert tried to drag him off, but there was no stopping him now.

'He started it!' Lou cried. 'Now he'll get what's coming to him!'

The fight was short, but fierce. In the end it was Tom who lay on the ground, with Lou standing over him, panting but triumphant. 'He started it,' he kept saying. 'It were Tom as started it!' Grabbing Robert by the arm, he urged, 'Come away! He'll be all right. Somebody's sure to find him.'

With Lou's persuasive voice in his ear and the sight of his father lying on the ground looking up at him, blood oozing from his head, Robert had never been more frightened.

When Tom struggled to get up, he stepped back a pace, his eyes wide and terrified. 'Filth!' Tom's broken voice issued through a wall of pain. 'You shame me . . . *you*! Your sister with . . . Fenshaw's bastard . . . shames me.' Falling back, he rolled his eyes and was silent again.

'What was that he said?' Lou had heard and was beside himself. 'About Cathleen and "Fenshaw's bastard"? What did he mean?'

'I don't know.'

Shaking Robert hard he demanded to know, '*What did he mean? Was she with child when she went away? Did Silas Fenshaw get her with child?*'

'I don't know anything about it!'

Suddenly the air was filled with the screech of police

whistles, and when they heard the sound of pounding footsteps coming down the alley, the two of them ran for their lives.

When they paused a few streets away to catch their breath, Lou took hold of Robert. 'One word about what's happened tonight, or one whisper of what we've discussed, and it'll be *your* throat for the chop.' Making the same awful gesture that he'd made in the pub, he warned, 'You're in with the big boys now.'

As they quickened their footsteps back to Lou's place, Robert's mind went back to the alley, and his father. The words he'd uttered had left a deep impression in the boy's mind. 'You shame me . . . you and your sister.'

Suddenly, the thrill of being 'different' was not so exciting any more.

JESSIE WAS DESPERATE. 'Where in God's name can he be till now?' For the umpteenth time she looked up at the clock. 'Seven o' clock in the morning and still he's not home.' She recalled the row between them the previous night. 'Row or no row, he's never stayed out all night afore.'

Still tired from a restless sleep, she wandered about like a lost soul, into the parlour, back to the kitchen, then out to the door, where she would peep up and down the lane. But there was no sign of Tom.

It got to be eight o' clock, then nine, and she was growing angry. 'Stay away then, you bugger! See if I care.' But she *did* care, and now she wanted to tell him so. 'It's my fault for going on,' she muttered. 'But it haunts me, so it does, with him set agin the childer the way he is. Oh, I can't say as it's his fault altogether, 'cause it's not, but . . .' Easing her aching limbs into the rocking chair, she laid her head back and closed her eyes. 'To see you and the childer friends again, Tom, that's all I want before the Good Lord takes me.'

When she heard a noise outside the door, she jumped up, sure that it was her son-in-law.

Flinging open the front door, she was astonished to see Lucy Fenshaw in her wheelchair, large as life, with Bill Trimble behind her. 'Hello, Jessie.' Through Cathleen, Lucy and Jessie had known each other a long time. 'Is it all right for me to come in?'

Flustered by Lucy's appearance at the cottage door of all places, Jessie stammered, 'No, er, what I mean is . . . I'm just getting over the influenza. It's not wise for you to come in here.'

Eyeing Bill, she asked, 'What is it yer want anyway?' Her nervousness made her sound hostile. 'I mean, what brings you here so early, and on such a cold day?' While she stood there, Jessie felt a blast of icy wind through her bones.

Lucy dismissed Jessie's fears. 'Since when have I been wise?' she asked wryly. 'Besides, if you stand there with the door open for much longer, we'll *all* end up with pneumonia.'

Standing aside, Jessie opened the door wide. 'You'd best come in.' She regarded the bulky wheelchair.

'Though I'm not sure if you'll get that contraption through the door.' Eyeing Bill she added, 'He'd best come in an' all, out of the cold.'

They were soon inside, without too much difficulty, though Bill had to shove a chair out of the way in order to wheel Lucy by the fireside next to Jessie.

Feeling more sociable, Jessie told him, 'Sit yerself down, and I'll get us all a brew.'

Lucy intervened. 'Bill has an errand to do for me,' she explained, 'but he won't go short, you have my word. He has my permission to stop off for a pie and ale at the pub before he returns to collect me.' She smiled up at the man. 'Isn't that right, Bill?'

The old man's smile in return betrayed his obvious affection for her. 'That's perfectly true, ma'am, yes.'

'You're not to be cold,' she ordered. 'Make sure of that, won't you?'

'I will, ma'am, thank you.' With that, he took his leave.

While Jessie bustled about, Lucy chattered away. 'My, but you've made this cottage lovely,' she observed. 'Such a pretty place – I'd forgotten.'

'It's a cosy home,' Jessie answered, fetching the tea and muffins. 'A bit empty though, without our Cathleen.'

Accepting her tea, Lucy sneaked a look at the old woman; because of her disagreement with Tom last night, and then his non-appearance this morning, Jessie looked fraught. 'Are you all right?' Lucy was concerned.

'You mentioned just now that you were getting over the influenza.'

'It wasn't a bad bout, but enough to put me in bed for a few days,' Jessie explained, handing her a muffin. 'I don't suppose these are as good as your own cook might bake, but they're from the bakery, and Tom has a reputation for his muffins.'

Lucy laughed. 'Now then, Jessie,' she chided. 'You know very well how Cook always buys from your Tom, muffins and all. She might be a wizard at most things, but she still hasn't mastered the art of making the best bread and muffins.'

Jessie chuckled. 'Aye well, we can't none of us be good at everything!'

Taking a bite on her muffin, Lucy glanced round the room. 'How is Tom anyway?'

'Ah, sure he's not very happy with me at the minute.' Jessie found it good to have someone like Lucy to talk with. 'We had a row last night and he hasn't been home since.'

'Is that usual – not coming home I mean?' She found Jessie so easy to talk to; it was as if they'd known each other all their lives.

Jessie shook her head. 'He's never done it afore. When I heard you outside just now, I thought it were him.' Her sorry gaze went to the parlour door. 'It's not like Tom to have me worried like this. I don't know what to think, I'm sure.'

Lucy put her mind at rest for a time. 'I expect he's gone straight to work. We all know how particular he is where the bakery's concerned. He's probably gone to check on something . . . an oven or whatever, and found himself caught up with another matter.'

Which brought her back to the reason for her visit. 'And it's another matter altogether that's brought me here today, Jessie.'

Jessie gave a knowing look. 'Sure I didn't think you'd come to pay a social call, not with you being no better in health than I am.' Jessie didn't waste time mincing her words. 'I thought it must be summat important, to fetch you out on such a day.'

'It's Silas.'

'Silas, eh? And what's wrong with him?' Jessie guessed the root cause, but knew enough to keep her own counsel.

'He's desperately unhappy, Jessie. I wondered why he ever married Helen Turner, and then I got to thinking, well, maybe he and Cathleen grew out of love with each other.' She shook her head. 'I found it hard to believe even then, and now I suspect there must have been another reason why he and Cathleen parted company.'

Jessie shrugged. 'People fall out of love all the time,' she replied innocently. 'It's the fashion so it is.'

'No.' Lucy knew different, and so did Jessie. 'Right from the start, those two were made for each other. It's strange too, because not long before he and Cathleen went their separate ways, Silas all but confided in me. All he talked about was Cathleen. I really believed he wasn't far away from asking her to marry him.' She clapped her hands in delight. 'Oh, Jessie, nothing would have made me happier!'

'Nor me.' And that was the truth.

Lucy's smile slid away. 'Soon after that, he told me how he and *Helen* were to be married. I didn't understand it then, and I don't understand it now.'

'Have you asked him about it?'

'As far as I can, without being a nuisance. I asked him only the other day if he was happy, and, as usual, he avoided giving me a straight answer.' Clasping one hand over Jessie's she pleaded, 'Tell me what's going on, Jessie. *Please!*'

Embarrassed but cagey, Jessie fobbed her off. 'What makes yer think there's summat going on?' she queried. 'Moreover, what makes yer think *I'd* know?'

'Why did Cathleen go away?'

'She's a young lass. Yer know what they're like. They can't sit in one place for too long.'

But Lucy was on to her. 'You *do* know what happened,' she accused gently. 'Please, Jessie. I have to know or I'll go insane.'

Jessie couldn't answer straightaway. Instead, she hung her head and thought on what this dear lady was saying. If only she could tell her, she would. But she had promised Cathleen to keep her secret. It was a God-given promise, and one she had vowed never to break. 'I can't tell you anything,' she replied softly.

'Just tell me this . . .' Leaning forward in her chair, Lucy looked deep into Jessie's troubled eyes. 'Do you ever *hear* from Cathleen?'

'Every week.' There was no harm in telling her that much at least.

'Does she mention Silas?'

Again, Jessie could see no harm in admitting it. 'In almost every letter, aye, she does.'

'Does she still love him, Jessie?'

Having gone so far, Jessie now clammed up. 'You'll have to ask the lass herself, so yer will.'

'I see.'

For a long awkward minute, the two women sat quietly sipping their tea, each acutely aware of the other, and the unbearable tension between them.

Presently, Lucy spoke, slowly and surely, as though she had given it a great deal of thought. 'You say I must ask Cathleen herself?'

'That's right.'

'You'd rather I did that, would you?'

'Indeed I would.'

'Then you'll be kind enough to give me her address, will you?'

Startled, Jessie sat up. 'Sure, I can't do that!'

'Then how am I supposed to ask her?'

'Look, I'll tell yer what,' Jessie began. 'The very next time I write to the lass, I'll pass on the business of why you came to see me. I'll ask her to write to yer, so I will. After that it's between the two of youse.'

Convinced she was right now, Lucy persisted. 'Something happened between Cathleen and Silas – and if I'm not very much mistaken, Helen Turner was involved.'

'I'm saying nothing.'

Lucy continued, 'My son and your grand-daughter are still very much in love, I'm sure of it. They meant to marry, and something, or some*one*, put a stop to it.'

''Tis *you* said that, not me!'

Lucy had guessed. 'Cathleen made you promise not to tell, didn't she, Jessie? For some reason she feels she must protect someone . . . is it herself, or is it Silas? You know, Jessie, and you *want* to tell, but you gave your promise, isn't that so?'

Jessie shook her head. 'There yer go again!' she sighed. 'Putting words in me mouth when I ain't looking.'

'It *was* Helen Turner, wasn't it, Jessie? Trust me, if you can. You won't be doing Cathleen any harm, I promise. I'm on their side, can't you see that?'

Just then, and much to Jessie's relief, there came a knock on the door. 'It's your man come to fetch yer!'

Clambering out of the chair, Jessie almost ran to the door. 'She's all ready,' she said, ushering Bill in. 'Make sure she's well wrapped up against the cold afore yer take her out.'

As Lucy was wheeled across the room, she asked Bill Trimble to wait outside a minute. 'Jessie?'

'I'm sorry.' Jessie would not be drawn. 'I've told yer all I can.'

'Do you love Cathleen?'

'Well, that's a silly question. O' course I love her, more than anything.'

'More than a promise?'

Jessie knew exactly what she meant. 'Honest to God, I can't say no more.'

'Then think on this, Jessie,' Lucy said, 'I have a son who is torn apart by something you know of and I don't. Can you imagine how that makes me feel?'

Not for the first time, Jessie hung her head.

Lucy was not about to give up now. 'If Cathleen is the same way . . . unhappy and pining for Silas the way he is for her,' she drew in a deep breath, 'then for pity's sake, Jessie, don't you think you and I should help them?'

Jessie felt the same, but said, 'I'm a woman of my word.'

'All right, but think on what I've said.' Giving the signal to Bill that she was ready to leave, she told Jessie, 'You know where I am if you change your mind.'

PART THREE

March 1901
HOPE

Chapter Nineteen

'STOP FUSSING!' CATHLEEN had gone through every-thing, time and again, and still Megan was a bag of nerves. 'The carriage will be here any minute,' she told her now. 'Maisie here will help you down the stairs with your train. She'll see you into the church and, just as you asked, she'll stay close behind us while the ceremony goes on.'

Megan wouldn't be consoled. 'What if I drop my flowers? What if the vicar's late? I wonder if Norman remembered to give his best man the ring? What about *you*? Will you be all right? Maybe it was selfish of me to insist on you being Maid of Honour . . .' On and on she went, making everybody as nervous as her-self.

'For goodness sake, Megan, it will all go to plan, I'm sure.' Cathleen went through the actions. 'Look! You'll walk down the aisle, I'll be right behind you. Maisie here will slip into the front pew, and Norman will be waiting at the altar.' Waving her arms and taking dainty little steps, she walked up and down the room, stopping at the table. 'When you get to the altar, the vicar will have his book open, ready to start the service.'

'That's right,' Maisie agreed. 'That's the ticket!'

'So calm down,' Cathleen pleaded. 'We've been through it twice with the vicar, and God knows how many times here. If you don't know what you're doing by now, you never will!'

Turning to Maisie, she said, 'You've been so good. Are you sure it's all right for you to leave your stall? We know Saturdays are your busiest time.'

'It's no trouble at all,' Maisie answered. 'I've got our Pauline to stand in. She eats half the fruit, but that's all right. I'll just take it out of her wages.'

'You do look lovely,' Cathleen observed. 'I've never seen you dressed up before.' She was impressed with the way Maisie had done herself up. Scrubbed clean and scented with lavender water, she wore a simple but elegant brown two-piece and little veiled hat, and was smarter than either Megan or Cathleen could remember. 'You've not got a bad figure either.' Though she was plump, Maisie had managed to squeeze herself in very well, she thought.

'Away with you!' their guest chuckled. 'It's me corsets, and they're killing me. I'm fat as a barrel, whichever way you look at me.'

Wisely ignoring the comment, Cathleen said, 'I don't know what we'd have done without you.'

'Oh, I'm enjoying it,' Maisie assured her. 'It's been

years since I've attended a proper wedding.' Lowering her voice she confided, 'Our Betty got wed last year, but it were a quick do in a back-street registry. Eight months gone she were . . . much like yourself.' Pointing to Cathleen's large belly, she remarked with surprise, 'D'you know, that dress hides it really well.'

'Thank you, Maisie, I think so too.' Laying the flat of her hand over her stomach, Cathleen groaned, 'Though the little monkey is kicking and shifting and making me feel queasy.'

In the middle of trying on her head-dress, Megan swung round, almost knocking a vase of flowers over. 'Oh, my God, Cathleen!' she cried. 'What if the baby decides to come right in the middle of the service?'

'I'll ask the vicar to bless it there and then,' Cathleen retorted, and Maisie laughed so much she burped and let rip all at the same time, making Megan pull a face and Cathleen snigger into her hand.

'I'll go out and see if there's any sign of the carriage,' Maisie said. 'We've still got time.'

The minute she turned her back, Megan ran to open the window. 'If she does that in church, I'll just *die*!' she said indignantly.

'If she does that in church, we'll *all* die,' Cathleen answered with a grin.

When Maisie returned, the two of them were helpless with laughter. 'What's tickled *your* fancies?' she asked, and set them off again. 'Bleedin' lunatics!' Poor Maisie had no idea of the chaos she caused wherever she went.

A T HALF PAST one, Megan's escort arrived. Joshua Collins was a quiet, gentle fellow, a loyal customer at Norman's place for a good many years. 'My, but you do look sweet,' he told Megan, his soft, slow voice and mild manner seeming to calm her where no one else could. 'I'll be proud to walk down the aisle with you,' he beamed.

In the street he helped all three ladies into the carriage, taking extra care with Cathleen, who found it difficult to climb up the steps without treading on the hem of her dress.

He climbed in beside her. 'It's a lovely day to get wed,' he remarked, glancing out at the watery March sunshine. 'I remember when me and the missus tied the knot, it poured all day and the wind was that bad we could hardly stand up.'

'There you are,' Cathleen said to Megan, 'I told you it would all go to plan.'

Set against the canal, with its colourful barges, the church was old and very beautiful. Its many spires reached up high towards heaven, and the narrow windows were studded with magnificent pictures of Christ on His journey to the Cross. 'I'm so lucky, aren't I?' Megan whispered as they climbed out of the carriage.

Cathleen kissed her fleetingly on the cheek. 'Just keep

remembering that,' she replied softly, 'and everything will be perfect.'

Suddenly, people came from everywhere – the men from the barges with their wives, families of all ages, children who skipped round Megan and Cathleen as they walked the few steps to the church, and all kinds of ordinary, wonderful people – young couples in love and girls of a certain age who came to see a bride in her gown and dream of the day when they too might walk down that same path.

As they marched slowly up the aisle, Megan with her escort in front, Cathleen slightly behind, the other people filed in to take their seats; strangers or friends, each one softly wished them well.

It was a moment to cherish.

Overawed by the magnificence of the occasion, Cathleen felt hot tears scald her eyes. It was all so wonderful. But how much more wonderful it would all be if only it were she and Silas kneeling before the altar.

When Megan turned to seek reassurance, Cathleen gave it with a smile, and all the love in her gentle heart.

<hr />

THE WHISTLES ECHOED through the night; from the moment he slipped the net, all diligent officers searched high and low. 'How could he have made his getaway so quickly?' they asked. 'It was only a second or two while we transferred him from one block to the other.'

The streets outside the prison were combed inch by inch, but still there was no sign of Jake Brewer. 'He's a dangerous bugger,' the governor said. 'Take no chances.'

But Jake was long gone. And as he loped along the streets, he knew exactly where he was going.

He knew what day it was, he knew the place, and he meant to be there.

With wickedness on his mind, he stuck to the alleys, hiding in the shadows. Determined he would not be caught again.

———◆———

THE SERVICE WAS over. The bells tolled and the newly-weds emerged into the sunshine to the cheers of a happy crowd. 'Well, Mrs Trent?' Kissing her soundly, Norman held her tight. 'Any regrets?'

Smiling, Megan turned to answer him but the words froze in her throat, for suddenly, out of the crowd, she saw him running towards them, a look of madness in his eyes. '*Jake!*'

Her scream echoed through the air as he grabbed hold of her. 'She's mine!' he cried. When Norman moved towards him, he backed away, taking her with him, frightening every heart there.

Shocked to his roots, Norman knew nothing of what had gone before. All he knew was that Megan was in mortal danger. 'Hurt her and I swear to God I'll kill you!' His voice trembled as he came closer, arms outstretched. 'Let her come to me . . . *please* . . . don't hurt her.'

Cathleen pleaded too, and Megan, but Jake was beyond reason. 'She's mine,' he kept saying. 'She's *mine!*' Only in that moment, when he had seen her, a beautiful woman in all her finery, with another man at her arm . . . only then did he realise how much he loved her.

Suddenly, having tracked him down, the police were everywhere. *'He's got the woman!'* one of them cried, and a circle of uniformed officers moved in.

'Get back!' he warned, and they waited, afraid to move, unsure of his intention.

Quickly now, they moved the people back. Twice Norman broke away, and each time they held him back. 'He's a madman,' they said. 'Leave him to us.'

Horrified and helpless, Cathleen stood by. She saw how white and afraid Megan was, and her heart turned over. 'Dear God, don't let him hurt her,' she prayed.

The officer talked to him, and, as he talked, he moved closer; each time, Jake Brewer stepped back a pace.

There was a moment when the officer believed he had persuaded Jake to give himself up. Then, to everyone's horror, Jake laughed aloud. 'If I can't have her, nobody else will!' And without any warning, he lifted Megan into his arms and, running the last few yards to the canal edge, *he threw himself in,* taking her with him. 'NO! MEGAN!' Norman's scream mingled with Megan's as she hurtled through the air.

Panic gripped everyone. Covering the distance quickly, the officers made for the canal. Norman followed, unable to believe what he had seen with his own eyes, and desperate to find her alive.

In sudden, terrible pain, Cathleen fell to her knees. 'Dear God help her!' she cried over and over. But it was she herself who needed help.

'Jesus, Mary and Joseph! The baby's coming!' Maisie had watched the whole incident unfold with increasing horror, and now, seeing Cathleen collapse, she knew straight away that she was in labour. 'The baby's coming early!' she cried, and others quickly came to help.

While they carried Cathleen back inside the church, all efforts were being made to save Megan from a watery grave. Fanning out, the police went in every direction, down the bank and across the bridge to the other side.

From the canal edge they could see Jake in the water below. 'You're too late!' he screamed gleefully, and already Megan seemed lifeless in his arms. With no thought for himself, Norman finally broke free of the officers restraining him and, diving over the edge, he sliced into the icy water below, only feet away from where Jake Brewer held Megan.

Removing his heavy boots, the senior officer followed. While Norman made for Jake, the officer made for Megan, and from the top everyone watched in hushed silence.

Completely insane now, Jake Brewer dragged Megan under, holding her there. Suddenly he was snatched away. Filled with hate and terror, Norman fought with equal force. All he could think was that Megan must be saved.

Three times the men went under, and three times those who watched thought it was the end. When Norman surfaced for the last time, with Jake floating beside him, a great cheer went up. It was over. The attacker had got what he deserved.

On the bank they tended the limp woman, for a moment thinking it was too late. Then she opened her eyes and they gave up a prayer of thanks. Norman took her in his arms and they held each other, crying and laughing, while only a short distance away, the police recovered the body of the man who had almost destroyed them.

'Look!' Someone pointed to the canal, and there, caught in an overhanging bough, was Megan's beautiful bouquet of flowers. They watched it break free and float away. Somehow, it had a calming effect on them all.

———❖———

INSIDE THE CHURCH, Cathleen was resting after her short, violent labour. Worry about Megan mingled with joy as the child was put into her arms. 'It's a girl,' Maisie said. 'A bonnie little girl.'

At that moment, someone opened the door and called in, 'She's safe!' Looking up to the crucifix, Cathleen murmured a thank you. She gazed at the child nestled in her arms, and couldn't hold back the tears. The feel of that tiny newborn against her heart was like no other sensation she had known. 'Oh, Silas, if only you could see your daughter,' she whispered. 'If only you were here to hold us.'

Later, when Megan came to her, they held each other and cried. 'She's beautiful,' Megan told her, and through a haze of tears, Cathleen looked down at that tiny face, at the dark hair and familiar features. 'Like Silas,' she murmured. And he had never been closer to her than he was in that moment.

Outside, the people talked of a day that would never be forgotten. They talked of the madman who had tried to kill the new bride, and they marvelled at Cathleen, giving birth under God's roof. 'She'll be a lucky child all her life,' they said. 'Born with God's blessing.'

'One in, one out!' said an old woman, and everyone understood.

Chapter Twenty

THE FOLLOWING WEEK, Tom was well enough to be discharged from the Infirmary.

Excited and impatient, Jessie had been watching for him all morning. She saw the ambulance as soon as it turned into the lane, and by the time it got to Fenshaw Cottage she was waiting at the door, face beaming and arms open as he came slowly up the path. Her heart went out to him, so pale and worn he looked. 'It's good to see you home,' she said, enfolding him to her.

From the way he clung to her, it was obvious that he was glad to be home.

Coming into the parlour, he saw the fire crackling up the chimney and the box of baccy on the arm of his chair. It looked as if she'd bought him a new pipe an' all, he thought. He sniffed the air. 'Bacon dumpling?' he asked, and she nodded.

'There's apple sponge for after, and a dollop of fresh cream from the farm to go on top.'

'By! You've done me proud, Jessie,' he said. 'What would I do without you, eh?'

'You'd do all right,' she said, helping him to the chair.

She could have said how he might do even better with Cathleen close at hand, but she recalled how that particular argument had resulted in his being beaten senseless in some dark alley. 'Have they still not caught the devils who beat you up?' she asked, settling him with his newspaper and pipe. 'They should be strung up and left to rot, so they should!'

When he went very quiet, Jessie blamed herself. 'I'm sorry,' she apologised. 'I should have had more sense than gabbling on about it like that.'

'Sit down, Jessie.'

'What's that you say?' Something about his manner made her nervous. 'Yer not feeling bad, are yer?' she asked. 'I ain't upset yer have I, with me big mouth?'

'No, you haven't upset me,' he answered. 'I just want a word, that's all. Sit down a minute.' He gestured to the chair opposite. 'There's something you should know.'

Shaking with apprehension, Jessie did as she was told.

When she was still, her eyes on him and her hands folded in the usual manner, he told her, 'That night, when I was attacked . . .' He paused, taking a deep breath, because what he had to say would be as much of a shock to her as it had been to him . . . more perhaps, because she was an old woman.

'Everything's all right with you, ain't it?' she asked

anxiously. 'The doctor told me when I came to see you on Friday to keep you fed and warm and then you'd be better in no time, that's what he said.'

'Jessie, be quiet. Please!' When again she was paying close attention, he quickly allayed her fears. 'It's just as the doctor told you. Apart from the cuts and bruises, I'm mending quickly now.'

'So?'

'Like I said, it's to do with the night I was attacked. It wasn't ruffians looking for my wallet, as I told the police. It was . . . something else. I haven't told you because I didn't know how to . . .'

He looked at her, his eyes alive with anguish, and like a flash in her mind it came to Jessie. 'It was Robert, wasn't it?' When he nodded, she seemed to shrink before him. 'Oh, dear God above!' With wide scared eyes, she looked up. '*Why?*' Shaking her head in disbelief, she asked again, 'Why would he do such a terrible thing?'

'I've been blind,' Tom told her. 'I've been too trusting. I left him in the charge of a man older than himself, someone I thought might mend his ways, when all the time it was he who was corrupting him.'

He didn't have to say the name because Jessie had already guessed. '*Lou?*' Another shock. 'Are you saying that Lou was with him . . . that he and Robert beat you up and left you there for dead?' It was a hard thing for her to take in.

Painstakingly, as though to cleanse himself of a bad memory, Tom conveyed the happenings of that night.

And when he was finished, Jessie simply asked, 'How can you ever forgive him now?'

'I can't forgive *myself*,' he confessed, 'for being such a bloody fool! All along I've pushed him in Lou's direction, believing I was doing right, when all the time Lou was using him . . . moulding the boy into a copy of himself.'

'You weren't to know,' Jessie told him gently. 'None of us were.'

He gave a bitter laugh. 'Ironic, isn't it,' he muttered. 'If Cathleen hadn't resisted, I'd have married her off to him an' all. God Almighty! It doesn't bear thinking about.'

While Jessie set about getting the dinner, they each had their own private thoughts.

Afterwards, when the meal was over they sat a while at the table, going over all that had taken place these past few months. Jessie had a confession of her own.

'Lucy Fenshaw came here,' she revealed.

'Why would she do that?'

Reluctant to get into another argument about Cathleen, Jessie couched it in so many words. 'She said Silas is desperately unhappy, and would I give her the whereabouts of a certain person. She seemed to think I knew something she didn't, which of course I do.'

He gave her a strange look. 'You're a deep bugger, Jessie.'

'Sometimes you have to be.'

'And do you know something *I* don't?' He had always suspected it, but was never really sure.

'About what?'

'About why Silas Fenshaw threw Cathleen over to wed a hard-faced bitch like Helen Turner?'

Jessie nodded. 'I've wanted to tell you many times, but you've been so angry.'

'I'm not angry now, Jessie. So tell me.'

And she did. It was time to tell Tom everything.

She told how Edward Fenshaw had got himself into terrible debt and faced ruin. She explained how Turner had given him an ultimatum, and how Silas had been placed in an impossible position. 'Cathleen understood,' she said, 'but it didn't stop her from breaking her heart; nor hc his.'

For a long moment Tom sat there, head forward, his hands covering his face. 'Why didn't she tell me?' But he knew why. He hadn't given her a chance.

'You know Silas is the father?'

He nodded. 'Does Lucy Fenshaw know she has a grandchild on the way?'

'She knows nothing.' Jessie was unsure how he might react if she were to tell him that the baby had already arrived – a beautiful little girl.

'Why didn't you tell her?'

'I was sorely tempted, but I made a promise, and I can't go back on it, not without asking Cathleen.'

'Have you heard from the lass?'

Delighted that he was finally showing an interest, she told him, 'I had a letter only this morning.'

'Can I see?'

Thrilled, she hurried to the drawer and, taking out the letter, handed it to him. 'There's been terrible things happening,' she warned, 'but it all came out right in the end. And, oh, there's some wonderful news, too. I didn't have nobody to tell, and I'm that chuffed!'

Even now she was so excited she could hardly keep a limb still.

Opening the letter he laid it out on the table before him. He took a quick glance at it, before handing it back. 'My eyesight's been a bit hazy since that night . . .' He couldn't bring himself to say it. 'Read it for me, will you, Jessie?'

''Course I will, and be glad to.'

Putting on her tiny spectacles, Jessie settled herself to read.

Dear Grandma,

I've so much to tell you, I don't know where to start. Jake Brewer, Megan's old boyfriend, turned up at her wedding last Saturday and there was a terrible scene. He snatched her from Norman's arms and threw himself and her into the canal.

Norman was a match for him though. He dived in and they fought like lions. Jake Brewer drowned, but you can't feel sorry, not when he almost drowned Megan as well.

It turned out that he had escaped from prison, so thankfully the police were there very quickly, and soon dealt with the situation.

Now to some happier news.

The shock of it all brought the birthing on. In the church, with Maisie from the market and the vicar tending me, I gave birth to the most beautiful baby girl, who I've already called 'Bonnie'. Oh, Grandma, she looks so like Silas, with her dark hair and eyes that smile right through you.

But I miss you. I miss being at home, and I miss the open fields. Everything in London is so close, I sometimes feel I can't breathe.

Megan's been gone over a week now, and it's very odd without her here. She sent me a card from Paris. It seems she enjoys being a married woman, and says she's having a wonderful time.

I've been offered a job and a place to live. I can take the baby and, as you know, Grandma, I won't be able to stay here for ever. Not with the building already sold.

Don't worry though. If I decide to move, I'll let you know where I go.

Until then, please take care of yourself. I wish Father could forgive me and we could be friends again. I know he thinks Silas is far above me, but he doesn't know how much Silas and I love each other. Father has his pride though, and I can understand that.

Lots of love to you all,

Cathleen. XXXXX

Tom sat very still, his eyes closed, his face gaunt with regret. 'I've been all kinds of a fool, Jessie,' he said, and ever so softly he began to cry; a smothered sound at first, then a great well of emotion seemed to swallow him whole.

As Jessie held him, his body shook with deep, crippling sobs. She didn't say anything, there was no need.

Instead she let him cry, her own eyes swimming with unshed tears.

Shocked and relieved, she let her gaze rest on the folded letter. In all the years she had known this man, he had never once shown his deeper feelings. Now, his sorrow and regret were laid bare for the world to see.

Through her letter, Cathleen had touched his heart.

⟶❖⟵

T HE RUINED HOUSE at the bottom of Derwent Street was a favourite meeting place for villains.

'Remember what I told you!' Deep in the bowels of the cellar, Lou wagged a finger at the young man. 'If you want to be with me, you do as I say, is that clear?'

The young man, Arnie Williams, sniffed and coughed, and shrugged his bony shoulders. 'It's all right with me,' he muttered. In the candle-light, his shifty eyes took the measure of Lou. He wasn't so big he couldn't be taken if necessary, he thought. 'Just so long as yer don't chuck me out the minute yer cowardly mate Robert shows his face.'

Lou smiled. 'Yer don't like him, d'yer?'

'He chickened out, didn't he?'

'That's not for you to worry about,' Lou warned. 'I'll deal with that, if and when the occasion demands.'

'So? What's this business you mentioned then? Why are we here? Meeting somebody of importance, are we?'

In the half darkness, Lou glared at him. 'Like I said,

I'm the boss here. I do the business and you listen. Then, you do what I tell yer. Afterwards you get paid, then you bugger off and keep your mouth shut.' Leaning forward in the candle-glow, he looked monstrous. 'Understood?'

'Whatever you say.' But Arnie had his own plans, and Lou was not a part of them.

Eventually they heard footsteps. 'Right!' Standing up, Lou kept his eyes glued to the opening in the wall. 'You sit and you listen. Nothing more than that.'

Gesturing for the other man to stay where he was, Lou made his way to the opening. 'In here!' he called.

Guided by the candle-light, Helen Fenshaw picked a path through the rubble, occasionally crying out when her ankle scraped over a brick bat.

Eager to get his hands on the money, Lou guided her in. 'Don't worry,' he said, 'I'll escort you out when we've done.'

'Why did we have to meet here?' Startled to see another man in the shadows, she grew nervous. 'If I'd known it was like this, I would never have come!' Wrinkling her nose in disgust, she protested, 'It stinks to high heaven!'

'Look, missus, we're talking *murder* here. What would you rather do – stand out under a street-lamp so the whole world can see us?' Impatient, he got to the point. 'You want the old biddy done away with, right?'

'That's right.'

'I want half the money now and half when the job's done.' Holding out his hand he waited.

'Do it properly.' Opening her bag, she took out a

wad of notes and counted them into his hand. 'I don't want any half-measures.'

Stuffing the notes into his jacket pocket, Lou asked her for details. 'Just so as I don't get the wrong woman,' he laughed.

Made nervous by the other man's eyes on her, Helen replied with a question. 'How do I know I can trust you – *either* of you?'

'Oh, you can trust us all right. We'll do the job nice and neat. Keep your part of the bargain just as we agreed, and afterwards you won't hear a word from us.'

'We won't blackmail you, if that's what you're worried about,' Arnie Williams sneered.

Enraged, Lou took a swing at him. 'I told you to shut it!'

His fist landed true on Arnie's head, making him leap to his feet. Grabbing Lou by the throat, he growled, '*Nobody* raises a hand to me!'

Already frightened by what she was planning, and then by Lou's insistence that they meet down here in this unsavoury basement, Helen was horrified when they started fighting. 'Stop it!' she yelled, but they were too intent on slaughtering each other. Falling and scrambling, they tore at each other like two wild animals.

Terrified, she turned to run, but just then Lou swung a half-brick at Williams who, seeing it coming, ducked. Helen Fenshaw took the full force of it on her temple. There was a crunching thud, then a jolting silence, and realisation set in. 'Christ Almighty, you've killed her!' Arnie breathed.

For a split second they stared down at her lifeless body, the blood oozing from her head looking like treacle in the half-light. 'Jesus!' Lou's mind flew back to the night when he had left Robert's father for dead. 'Wait a minute. Happen she's still alive.'

Stooping, he touched her shoulder; she didn't move. He looked into her eyes and they stared back, glazed in death. 'Jesus!' He said it twice, and then he was away. 'Keep your mouth shut!' he warned the young man. 'Or I'll have to come looking for you!'

Alone in the cellar with her, Arnie Williams sniggered. 'Took you for a wad o' notes and didn't do the job, eh?' he said, stroking her outstretched leg. He raised her skirt to peep. 'We could have had some fun, you and me,' he murmured. 'Shame!'

Her staring eyes cooled his ardour.

Quickly he felt for her bag. A furtive look inside told him he had been right to stay. 'This little lot will keep me in comfort for some time to come,' he chuckled.

He took her fob-watch, her bracelet, and tore the earrings from her ears. Stuffing them into his pockets, he took another moment to look at her. 'Didn't work out right for you, did it, missus?' he said in mocking sympathy, then he went away at a stroll, as if he had all the time in the world.

With a bit of luck she wouldn't be found for some days, maybe even a week.

By that time he would be miles away.

Chapter Twenty-one

FOR A WHOLE week, no one knew where Helen Fenshaw might be.

Silas had dutifully informed the authorities of her disappearance. 'Did you have a disagreement?' they asked. 'Did she take any clothes? What about money? Was there a large amount withdrawn from the bank account?'

All these details were checked. No large sums had been taken from the bank, although Helen always had access to her own private cash box at home. Soon it became clear that she had not left home with intent to stay away.

The search was underway.

It was an old tramp who found her. White-faced and shaking, he ran along the street to tell someone.

On the third day after the discovery, the authorities made an arrest.

Silas protested his innocence, but the circumstantial evidence was overwhelming.

———❧◦❧———

LIKE EVERYONE ELSE, Jessie was shocked. Coming in with her shopping, she put her basket on the table and, as usual, went to give Tom a kiss. 'How are you feeling today?' she asked. 'You look better,' she observed. 'There's more colour in your cheeks an' all.'

'I'll be back at work on Monday,' he told her. 'Ted Mason's been brilliant, but it's time I were back at the helm. I'm ready now. Fit to tackle anything.'

'I'm delighted to hear it.' Taking off her scarf and coat, she hung them on the nail behind the door. As always, her first thought after trudging round the shops was to get home and brew a nice cuppa. She set about that now. 'I bumped into Edna at the butcher's – you know, the little parlour-maid from Fenshaw House?'

'Oh aye?' Tom only knew her from when she came into the bakehouse. 'Did she have anything to say about this awful business with Silas and his wife?' He lowered his voice as she came back into the room. 'Did she say whether he were still in custody?'

'She said it were looking bad. According to Edna, the authorities set themselves up in the house and questioned everybody, one after the other.' Tutting, she shook her head forlornly. 'It seems they were made to tell the truth, about the rows that went on behind Lucy Fenshaw's back. They had separate rooms and hated the sight of each other, that's what Edna told me, and I've no doubt it's what she told the police.'

Tom took a minute while it all sank in. 'After

what you told me, I'm not surprised he hated her. Any man would.'

'He didn't kill her, though, I'd stake my life on that!'

'Are you sure about that, lass?' Without his work, Tom had had plenty of time to think. 'I reckon if I'd been forced into marriage with a woman I'd no feelings for, it might well drive *me* to murder.'

'No!' Jessie was adamant. 'You would never take somebody's life, in any circumstances. And neither could Silas. Somebody out there knows the truth. *They* know Silas isn't the guilty one.'

'What I can't make out is what she was doing in that cellar.'

'Rats keep company of other rats, that's what I say!' When Jessie took a dislike to anybody, it went beyond the grave. From the kitchen she voiced her deeper fears. 'It's our Cathleen I'm worried about now,' she said. 'How will I tell her? It'll be a terrible shock, I know that much.'

'I've been thinking . . .'

Returning with two mugs of tea, Jessie passed him his, then sat before him with her own. 'What's that then, Tom?'

'It's not the sort of news you give in a letter,' he answered thoughtfully.

The same thought had been on Jessie's mind. 'I couldn't agree more.'

'Has the lass moved yet?'

'I've not heard, so no, I shouldn't think so.' Gasping when she took a sup of the scalding tea, Jessie slid it on the fender, where it would soon cool. 'You recall how she said in her last letter that she'd let me know soonever she got a new address?' Curious, she quizzed, 'Why, Tom? What's on yer mind?'

'I think the two of us should go and see her.'

Jessie's old heart danced. 'D'yer mean that?'

'Aye, lass. I reckon I've a few bridges to mend.'

The sigh rose up from her boots. 'Oh, Tom, you don't know how glad I am.' Yet since he'd asked her to read Cathleen's letter to him, Jessie had hoped and prayed.

'A few days,' he said. 'I'll be strong enough for London by then.'

Chapter Twenty-two

L UCY WAS DISTRAUGHT.
        'I have to keep strong,' she told Dr Leighton.
'For Silas.'

Finishing his examination, he sat beside her. 'All this is draining your energy,' he explained. 'I'm surprised you can keep going the way you do.'

Lucy smiled. 'You never had children, did you, Matthew?' They had known each other a long time.

'No,' he answered, 'I was never that fortunate.' Or unfortunate, he thought wryly. However, he hid his personal feelings. 'I understand what you're saying, Lucy, but please don't overdo it.'

'I won't,' she promised, secretly vowing that she would do what must be done, whatever the cost to herself.

An hour later, she was helped into the carriage. 'You know where we're going,' she told Bill Trimble, settling herself into the seat. 'While I'm there, you take yourself off wherever you fancy. Give me half an hour. They won't let me stay longer than that.'

At the prison gates, the warders recognised Lucy immediately. Even among the guards there were mixed feelings. 'He did it all right,' the old one said, but there were enough to argue that they didn't think so.

The routine was the same each time. Bill would wheel Lucy to the gates, there would be questions and delay, then, when they had gone through the rigmarole of checking her visitor's pass and stamping it on the back, she would be allowed through. Bill, though, was allowed only as far as the main doors, when a warden would take Lucy from him. Then he was made to return through the gates and into the street beyond. He was always relieved when the gates clanged shut behind him, and always ready for a pint of ale to calm his nerves.

With that in mind, he would get into the carriage and make for the pub as fast as the horse would take him. 'Make it quick,' he would tell the landlord. 'There's summat about being shut in behind them gates that scares the living daylights outta me!'

<hr />

However low Silas was feeling, he always found a smile whenever Lucy came to visit. 'How are you, son?' she asked, wishing with all her heart that she could hold him to her.

'I'm all right,' he answered. 'It's only a matter of time before they find whoever did it, then I'll be out.' Yet he knew, as did Lucy, that they had stopped looking for anyone else. Silas was the man in the frame, and they were satisfied that he was the right one.

Like a mother, she asked all the usual questions. 'Are they feeding you? Is there anything you want?' Somehow, it was hard to say all the things that were in her heart.

She saw how drawn he was looking, and how his wonderful dark eyes had dulled. 'You shouldn't be in here,' she murmured, and then regretted having said it.

In that one revealing moment he knew the agony she was enduring. 'Look, Mother, I'm here because they think I killed Helen.' He had to make her realise she could do nothing, however much she might want to. 'They won't let me go until they're satisfied I'm innocent. You have to face up to that, or you'll make yourself really ill.' Being hard was being kind. 'It might be better if you don't come and see me any more.'

'Don't say that!' Lucy had let her guard down and he had seen the rawness underneath. 'I'm no fool, Silas. I know what they think, and I know why you're in here. All the same, I want you to know I'm doing everything possible to get you out.'

Silas looked at her tired face and the smile that flitted in and out of her pretty features, and he was deeply saddened. 'You're a stubborn devil,' he said, 'but I don't want you breaking yourself on lawyers and barristers and the like. Besides, Jack Turner came to see me yesterday. He's promised to fight my case, and I trust him, in spite of . . .' Horrified that he might reveal the truth of his marriage to Helen, he paused, just in time.

Lucy picked up on his reluctance to go on. 'In spite of what?' she asked curiously.

Silas skilfully covered up his slip. 'In spite of him being devastated by the brutal way his daughter was murdered. He knows I'm innocent. Look, Mother, somehow or another the truth will out. It's not as grim as you might think.' But it was, and they both knew it. The punishment for murder was the rope.

Soon it was time to go. 'Keep your spirits up,' Lucy whispered, tears springing to her eyes. 'I won't leave any stone unturned.'

'Take care of yourself,' he said, and made himself ready to be escorted back to his cell.

Silas had desperately needed to ask after Cathleen, but for obvious reasons, he had curbed his tongue. Besides, he reasoned, his mother knew nothing of his true feelings for Cathleen. Why should she?

⥇⊶⊷⥆

B ACK AT FENSHAW House, Lucy was lying on the settee, recuperating. Her mind was quick with thoughts of Silas and Helen, and how this situation came to be. She thought of Edward and the odd things that had happened before he took his own life.

Things like raised voices in the library whenever Jack Turner visited; whisperings when she came into a room. Unexpected little events that were out of the ordinary.

It was like a puzzle that wouldn't quite fit.

The quiet knock on the door startled her. 'Come in.'

The door opened and Maggie entered. 'It's a visitor for you, ma'am.'

'A visitor?'

'It's Mrs Butler, ma'am.'

'Oh, do bring her in, and ask Cook if we could have some of her wonderful flapjacks, and a pot of tea, please, Maggie.'

By the time Jessie was admitted, Lucy had swung her legs round and thrown her blanket aside, but she was too stiff and uncomfortable to get herself out of the chair; however, her welcoming smile flew across the room to Jessie.

'Jessie, oh, how lovely. It's so lonely here on my own, with no one to talk to, except of course the servants, but they don't want to hear a silly old fool like me babbling on, do they now?'

Lucy asked after Tom, and Jessie asked after Silas, and it wasn't long before the two women were deep in conversation.

'You asked me some questions the other day, which at the time I couldn't bring myself to answer,' Jessie reminded her.

Lucy had not forgotten. In fact, every day since she had hoped Jessie might come to see her, and now here she was.

'I've been waiting for you,' she confessed. 'I had a feeling you would come and see me.'

'I'm here to tell you how sorry I am, about Silas

and his imprisonment but, like I said to Tom only this very morning, he could never murder anyone, not in a million years.'

'Thank you for that, Jessie. I haven't given up hope. I can't. I *won't*!'

'There's something else, and I'm not sure whether it will help his case or go against him.' Jessie realised that if the authorities knew how Silas had been forced to marry Helen, it would be the most damning thing.

'Go on, Jessie. Tell me what's on your mind.'

'There's so much to tell,' Jessie started, 'about Silas and Helen and the manner of their marriage. Then there's Cathleen, and something you have every right to know.'

Realising that the knowledge that she had a grand-child would lighten Lucy Fenshaw's life, Jessie began . . .

PART FOUR

———◆▸◦◂◆———

April 1901

SUNSHINE
AFTER RAIN

Chapter Twenty-three

T HE WARM APRIL sunshine promised an early spring.
Having walked through the house to the back
door, Joseph Woodley looked out across the garden, his
face wreathed in smiles when his searching gaze alighted
on Cathleen and the child.

Hanging out the washing, Cathleen kept a wary eye
on her daughter, who was lying on a rug beside her.
'Who's beautiful then?' she murmured, laughing when
the child gurgled up at her. 'Who's Mammy's little
darling, eh?'

Joseph watched a moment longer, thinking what a
lovely sight they made; Cathleen with her long, wild hair
gently dancing in the breeze, and the child, sturdy despite
being premature, and as beautiful as her mother. It did
his heart good to see them.

Turning back into the house, he called the maid
and gave an order. 'To be delivered to the garden,' he
beamed.

Engrossed in her task, Cathleen didn't hear him

approach. 'You do right to be in the garden,' he said, apologising when she almost leaped out of her skin. 'I've taken the liberty of ordering us some fresh orange juice – that is, if you don't mind me joining you?'

'We'd be honoured, wouldn't we, Bonnie?' Reaching down, she took the child into her arms. Seating herself at the table next to him, she said, 'It's such a lovely day, I thought I'd get on and do the washing. There's nothing more satisfying than seeing the sheets and whites blowing in the breeze.'

Joseph Woodley tutted. 'You never stop, do you?'

Cathleen's mood momentarily darkened. 'If you stop you get to thinking, and if you get to thinking you become sad.' She smiled and the mood was gone. 'I'd much rather be working.'

'I can see that.' Joseph Woodley had never regretted giving Cathleen the position of housekeeper. 'My home has never been cleaner, nor has so much laughter echoed from its walls.' He wagged a finger. 'You're a bad influence on us.'

Cathleen looked around the garden; it was a beautiful place, with narrow walkways and hidden alcoves, and all kinds of colourful shrubs. 'I'm very content here,' she answered quietly. As content as she could be without Silas, she thought.

The maid arrived with the orange juice. Tickling the baby under the chin, she made Bonnie kick happily.

As she went, Cathleen gave her a grateful little wink, which did not go unnoticed. 'See what I mean?' Joseph laughed. 'A bad influence!'

Balancing the child on one knee, Cathleen poured the juice out for them both. 'I shouldn't really be lingering,' she said, 'I have a great deal to do.'

'Nonsense!' Clinking glasses with her, he cooed at the child. 'The name suits her,' he observed. 'She's Bonnie by name, bonny by nature – much like her mother.'

'It was Maisie who gave me the idea for her name,' Cathleen said fondly. 'When she was born, Maisie called out to me how she was a "bonny little girl".' She looked at her daughter, growing more like Silas every day. 'You're right,' she agreed. 'The name was made for her.'

He looked at Cathleen's mass of wild hair, and at the child, blessed with the same promise of thick, wayward curls. 'She'll give you hell when you start running a comb through that!' he laughed.

Cathleen chuckled. 'She already does.'

'Have you heard from your friend, Megan?'

'I think they're homesick now,' she told him. 'I got a postcard today. Megan tells me they're making their way home. Norman's talking of getting back to work.'

'I thought he'd sold his business?'

'He did, but according to Megan he's thinking of getting into something different.'

'Hmh! Perhaps he could talk to me. I might be able to point him in the right direction. There are all manner of opportunities for an enterprising man in the business of development.' He paused, something coming into his mind. 'Talking about that, I'll be leaving for the north first thing in the morning. I've been neglecting my affairs at that end,' he said. 'Unfinished business and all that.'

He stayed a few minutes longer, before hurrying away.

Left alone with her thoughts, Cathleen wished with all her heart that she could go with him. With every passing minute she grew more and more homesick, especially since she'd had Bonnie. 'One day, happen?' she mused, running her fingers through the child's curly hair. 'Oh, Bonnie, wouldn't it be wonderful to see Grandma and Father again?'

Silas came strong into her mind. 'I wonder if you'll ever know *your* daddy,' she said soulfully. 'I hope so. Oh, I do hope so!' But there didn't seem too much chance of it, as far as she could tell.

That reminded her. 'We haven't had a letter this week,' she murmured. 'When the work's done, we'd best put pen to paper . . . find out what she's up to.'

Chapter Twenty-four

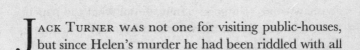

J ACK TURNER WAS not one for visiting public-houses, but since Helen's murder he had been riddled with all kinds of guilt.

Where he had once preferred to drink alone, he now needed the company of others; hearing their inane chatter helped to lift him out of his depression.

On this particular occasion he had gone to the pub at the top end of Argyle Street, as far away from Derwent Street as he could manage. The landlord was a friendly type. 'I haven't seen you in here before,' he said, handing over the jar of ale.

Passing over the money, Jack told him, 'I haven't been here before. I'm not a pub-goer, as a rule.' He didn't say who he was. There was too much talk and speculation in Blackburn already about the 'woman they found in the cellar. Battered to death she was,' they said.

But they didn't know.

Only the murdering bastards who did it knew what had really happened.

As the evening wore on, and the pub filled up, it was inevitable that the drink loosened tongues.

'She could have been a prostitute,' one man said. 'It's been known before, for a gentry to get her excitement from the likes of the common worker.'

'Aye, well, if she were then it's good bloody riddance,' said another. 'Give the place a bad name, they do.'

At this point, and the worse for drink, Jack was about to get up and slam him one, but the third fellow chipped in, 'Naw. She were no common prostitute! Helen Fenshaw came of a good family. From what the papers say, she'd been lured there by that swine of a husband. It were him as killed her, all right. There ain't no doubt about it!'

Another man had stood at the bar for most of the time Jack had been there. On hearing the heated discussion he came over, jar in hand and eyes glazed. As he walked, his lanky body swayed from the effects of booze. 'It weren't her old man as done it,' he said, laughing into his beer. 'I could tell yer who done it if yer like.'

They laughed at him. 'Oh aye, Blackworth? What fairy tale are you telling now, eh?'

Straddling the empty chair next to them from the rear he slammed his pint down on the table. 'It ain't no fairy tale,' he retorted angrily. 'If yer ask me, the rozzers should be talking to Arnie Williams.'

'Oh aye, an' how's that then?' Blackworth had a reputation for fantasising. They were used to humouring him.

'Tell me this then,' he said, repeatedly hiccuping.

'How come he owed me money, and try as I might I couldn't get a penny out of him, then all of a sudden, he turns up all excited, flashing a purse that looked like it cost a fortune, and money coming out of his ears.'

'You're making it up, you daft bugger! Talk like that could get somebody hanged.'

'Aye, well, he deserves hanging, 'cause he did it, I'm telling yer! Arnie Williams killed that woman, sure as eggs is eggs. How else did he come into that money?'

Suddenly the landlord was there, confiscating his pint. 'You'd best get out of here,' he said, 'if you know what's good for you.' With that, he booted him towards the door. 'And don't come back.'

Cursing and swearing, Blackworth left.

Keeping a discreet distance between them, Jack Turner followed.

Chapter Twenty-five

'So, what will she do?' Tom had heard all about Jessie's meeting with Lucy Fenshaw. 'Will she tell Silas – about the bairn, I mean?'

Jessie looked up from her darning. 'She says no. The way things are, it would be too cruel.'

'I can understand that.'

Jessie recalled how she had left things with Lucy. 'It came as a terrible shock to her, the business with Jack Turner and her husband, but she reckons she always knew summat were up. She just didn't know what.'

'And she were thrilled about the bairn?'

'Over the moon. But, like I said, she won't go to Cathleen. She says as how it might seem she was claiming the child.'

'She wants our Cathleen to come to her, eh?'

'Aye.' Taking out Cathleen's letter from her pocket, Jessie patted it lovingly. 'It's just as well this came today. I've given her Cathleen's new address, so she's about to write a letter, saying she hopes Cathleen will come and see her when she's next in these parts.'

'She'll not mention about Silas being in prison, I hope?'

'She said not.'

'When you write back, tell our Cathleen the two of us mean to come and pay her a visit quite soon, won't you?' He chuckled. 'It's time I met this little grand-daughter of mine, don't you think?'

As they beamed at each other, in that same moment, a knock came on the door. 'Who is it?' Tom called.

The door opened and there stood Robert, looking dishevelled and sorry for himself. 'Can I come home?' he asked, and hung his head.

Jessie thought it best to leave them to it. 'I've things to do in the kitchen,' she said, hurrying away.

From behind the curtain, she peeped out to see what was happening. 'Don't be too hard on the lad,' she whispered, looking at Tom, but he couldn't hear her and she knew that.

'You and that devil nearly bloody killed me!'

'It weren't me – I wouldn't do a thing like that. Anyway, I ain't seen him since.' His voice shook and his lip trembled. 'I've been away . . . living off the streets.'

'I can bloody see that with me own eyes – *smell* it an' all. Look at the state of you!' Getting out of his chair, Tom ranted and raved. 'What mischief have you been up to now, eh? Someone on your tail, is there? Got frightened, so you thought you'd come running home?' Remembering how he had nearly died, rage engulfed him. 'You're not welcome here. I don't want you. Go back to the gutter where you've come from. Go on. Get out!'

Without warning, the lad fell to his knees, tearful eyes uplifted, as he pleaded softly, 'Please, Dad, let me come home. I've learned my lesson and I'm sorry.' The tears fell from his eyes and rolled down his cheeks. 'I love you, Dad. I want my family back. I know that now.'

As he cried to his father, Jessie quietly sobbed in the kitchen, pleading on his behalf. 'Let him come home, Tom. Don't turn the lad away.' But she couldn't interfere. All she could do was watch and pray.

Her prayers were answered.

Seeing him like that, his own son on bended knees begging forgiveness, Tom did what any other father would do. 'Get up, son.' His voice was tender.

By the time Robert stood up, Tom had his arms round him. ''Course you can come home,' he said, his eyes glittering with unshed tears. Then, in a sterner voice, 'But I'll stand no more nonsense. I'll want you to choose your friends more carefully in future. Also, you'll work overtime whenever you're needed.'

Laughing, Jessie came out of the kitchen to hug Robert like she'd never hugged him before.

'All it needs now is for our Cathleen to come home,' Tom said.

And, to their amazement, Robert had some news to tell them that might just make that possible.

Chapter Twenty-six

ALL DONE UP in her Sunday best, Cathleen looked lovely. 'Where are we going?' The planned journey to the park had never been so long before.

'I'm taking you to a place I know,' Joseph said. 'I'm of a mind to buy it and I'd like your opinion . . . as a woman, I mean. Too often a man designs a house and the woman complains how it's all wrong. It's several hours away, I'm afraid. You don't mind, do you?'

Cathleen was delighted. 'Not if you don't mind your dinner being late,' she said.

When, much later, she and the baby awoke from a deep, refreshing sleep, Cathleen opened her eyes to a familiar landscape, and a country lane that, for her, was full of previous memories. Astonished, she looked at her employer.

'I lied, God forgive me,' Woodley confessed. 'It's a little treat I've been planning,' he told her. 'I know how your grandma's been ill and not able to travel, and I know how you're missing her, so I thought . . .

if your grandma can't get to you, I'll bring you to her.'

He pointed to Jessie, who was hurrying down the path as fast as her old legs would take her. 'And look! There she is.'

Laughing and crying, the two women hugged and cuddled, and the baby was made a fuss of, and then Jessie told her she could come inside, because there was no one there to object.

When Cathleen opened the door, a great cheer went up, amazing her. There was Jack Turner, Lucy in her wheelchair, and Robert and her father, all pleased to see her. 'Let me hold the bairn,' Tom said as he took Bonnie from her. 'You go and help your grandma make the refreshments.'

As they went into the kitchen, Jessie backed off and let Cathleen go in alone.

Cathleen turned, and there he was. '*Silas!*' Her mouth fell open and her heart turned somersaults, and when he caught her in his arms, kissing her and swinging her round, she laughed and cried and everyone came to see.

The whole story spilled out, about Helen's murder and Silas's arrest for it; and of how Robert knew of the plan to kill Lucy.

They told her how Jack Turner had overheard the man in the pub and followed him. Then, later, how he handed him in to the police to make a statement. Arnie Williams and Lou Matheson were now in jail, awaiting trial for manslaughter, and conspiracy to murder.

Silas took his daughter in one arm and Cathleen in the other. 'When the time is right, we'll be married,' he promised them all.

➤•◄

AND THEY WERE; on a lovely day in June, after a shower that made the flowers sparkle. The birds sang overhead and the sun shone on their love at long last.

'See that rainbow?' Silas pointed out.

Cathleen looked up. 'It's beautiful,' she said.

'I have a special memory,' he told her. 'It kept me sane while I was in prison.' And he told her of the day when she was a child, that it seemed as though the rainbow was all around her. 'You're my pot of gold,' he said, and he meant it with all his heart.

'Here! That's enough o' that billing an' cooing,' Jessie yelled. 'The man's waiting to take a picture!'

Headline hopes you have enjoyed RAINBOW DAYS, and invites you to sample the beginning of LOOKING BACK, Josephine Cox's compelling new saga, out now in Headline hardback . . .

Chapter One

'HELLO, AMY.' SOAKED to the skin, the stranger stood at the door, his face under the trilby hat oddly familiar to her. 'Look – I got caught in the rain.'

He smiled quickly, but it was a nervous, guilty smile. For almost an hour after the fierce summer downpour he had paced the streets outside, afraid to come in . . . afraid not to.

'It's been a long time,' he said, his steady gaze giving nothing away. 'I'm not sure you'll even remember me.' But he remembered her. 'Nineteen years,' he murmured fondly, 'and I'd still know you anywhere.'

At thirty-nine years of age, Amy Tattersall was still a good-looking woman, he thought admiringly, with the same thick, chestnut-coloured hair and pretty brown eyes. There was a time when those eyes had looked at him with love, but now they showed only bewilderment.

'Who are you? What do you want?' She stared at him for what seemed an age, while long-ago pictures spiralled through her mind. She thought she knew him, recalled that soft, persuasive voice. And there was something about his manner, the confident way he stood, with his legs astride, his hands in his pockets and his head cocked cheekily to one side. Recognition was slow to unfold, but when it did she gasped in amazement. '*Jack?*' Her voice trembled with emotion.

Taking off his trilby, the man revealed a thick shock of dark hair. 'I've still got my hair and all my own teeth. Not bad for a forty-year-old, eh?' He laughed, a low, musical sound that rolled back the years. 'What's more, I can still cut a fine figure on the dance floor.' He gave a little wink. 'Do you remember how we used to smooch till midnight down at the Palais?'

Still reeling in shock, Amy needed a moment for the truth to sink in. 'Jack Mason!' The ghost of a smile twitched at her mouth. 'I can't believe it!'

At first she had doubted her own eyes, but there was no doubt now. It was the same Jack the Lad! With the same, wonderful smile that lit his eyes and had taken her heart all those years ago. But what was he doing here? Had he no shame?

'Well, my beauty, are you going to ask me in, or what?' He took a step forward but stopped when she drew the door to, barring his way.

'Ah, don't turn me away, Amy. Not now, when I've come to make amends.'

He tugged at his clothes. 'I've been outside for ages plucking up the courage to knock on your door. Look! I'm soaked to the skin. Likely to get pneumonia if you don't let me in.'

A kind of longing washed over her, but fear gripped deeper. 'Soaked to the skin or not, you look like you've done all right for yourself.' Her glance swept past his disappointed face to the smart black car parked at the kerbside. 'Yours, is it?'

'Bought and paid for.' A sneak of pride coloured his weathered features.

'Hm!' His pride touched her deeply. 'Like I said, you've done well.'

He shrugged. 'Well enough.'

She noticed his expensive long overcoat and his smart clothes. Then she saw the confident gleam in his eye and her fears were heightened. 'All right, Jack – out with it. What do you want with me?'

'Trust me, Amy,' he pleaded. 'It's not like it used to be.' He gave a deep sigh, his gaze downcast for a brief second or two.

'All right, I've made mistakes, but I've learned the hard way. And yes, you're right,' he gestured towards the overcoat and the car. 'I've made a pot of money, but it's not been easy. I've been through the mill, gal. I've changed . . . grown up. Everything I've got was earned through my own sweat and tears.'

Amy felt herself weaken, but she persisted. 'You still haven't told me why you're here.'

'Can't you guess?' Reaching out, he touched her hand, seemingly oblivious to the turmoil he was causing in her emotions. 'I'm here for *you!*' His quiet gaze found hers. 'I'm here to put things right between us, to make up for what I did all those years ago.'

She wanted to believe him, but the fear was strong. 'Go away, Jack!' she told him. 'I don't want any trouble.'

He shook his head. 'I'm not here to cause trouble.'

She laughed – a hard, accusing sound. 'You were *always* trouble!'

The slight tug on her skirt made Amy look down; it was her two-year-old son, Eddie. 'All right,' she told the infant. 'Go to Lottie now, there's a good lad. Mammy won't be long.'

Looking backwards past Eddie, she saw the other children sitting on the stair. Beckoning to the oldest one, she asked her to take the little boy into the kitchen. 'I'll not be a minute,' she promised.

Returning her attention to Jack, she told him firmly, 'You'd best go. I've things to do. Besides, Frank will be home any time now. If he finds you here, there's no telling what he'll do!'

Jack's expression hardened. 'Still the same old Frank, is he? I'll lay good money you don't love him the way you once loved me.'

Guilt showed in his face. 'Believe me, Amy, I deeply regret the past.'

'So do I, but it's all water under the bridge now.' There was so much to regret, and he was only a part of it. Her voice fell to a whisper. 'Go away, Jack. Leave me be. *Please!*'

Jack's gaze went down the passage, to the children. Huddled together, wide-eyed and scruffy, they looked like pathetic little souls. 'How many are there?' His quick eyes went to the huge mound beneath her pinafore. 'Not counting that one?'

'Four little 'uns and the two older girls. Six altogether.' She rolled her eyes. 'Might as well be sixty, the way they drive me to despair.'

Horrified, and unable to take his eyes off the army of children, he asked, 'How do you manage?'

'I get by.' She laughed. 'I don't know how Frank will cope though, when this one arrives in a month's time. He doesn't know one from the other as it is!' Her laughter faded. 'He . . . likes a drink of an evening.' Seeing Jack's look of contempt, she was quick to add, 'He's no different from any other man in that way.'

Having done his homework, Jack knew her situation and so chose to ignore the comment. Instead, he brought his attention back to the children. 'Seven in all, eh?' His eyebrows rose in amazement. 'Good God, Amy! You're a glutton for punishment, I'll say that for you.'

A rush of guilt caused her to turn and smile at the children's upturned faces. 'Oh, they're not bad – as kids go.'

He sensed her warming towards him. 'I'm really soaked through, Amy. Summer showers are always the most penetrating, I reckon.' Shivering noisily, he huddled deep into the collar of his coat. 'A minute or two, that's all I'm asking. A hot drink and a warm at your fireside, then I'll be on my way.' He just needed to get his foot in the door.

'Why should I?' Forgiveness didn't come easily.

'Aw, come on. Amy. For old times' sake.' When he pleaded like that, she had never been able to refuse him anything. 'Besides, I've a proposition to make.' It was his sole purpose for being here. That, and a longing for her that had never gone away.

Her interest was aroused. 'What sort of proposition?'

'Let me in and I'll tell you.' He winked. 'I'm not leaving till I say what's on my mind.'

When she hesitated, he reminded her, 'Do you remember how I used to sing when I'd had a pint or two . . . and how you used to try and shut me up? "By! You've a voice to wake the dead", is what you used to say. Well, I can sing when I'm sober too. If you shut that door on me, I'll sing so loud the neighbours will all come running. Is that what you want?'

Opening his mouth he prepared to launch into song as Amy grabbed him by the shirt collar. 'You do, and I'll throw a bucket of water over you!'

'Let me in then?'

Fearful the neighbours had seen him, Amy glanced nervously up and down Victoria Street. It was a long, cobbled street flanked by tiny terraced houses, filled with ordinary God-fearing folk who had nothing and wanted nothing.

'Did anyone see you knock on my door?' she asked edgily.

'No, but if you don't let me in they will – I'll make sure of that.'

'You always were a rascal!' But the smile in her voice made him take heart.

Amy's busy eyes scoured the street. At the top end, Maggie Lett was arguing with the tiresome old man who lived next door to her. About halfway down, old Jimmy Tuppence was chalking his wonderful cartoons on the drying pavement, watched by a gang of snotty-nosed kids; and only two doors away, a young window-cleaner was scampering up his ladder and whistling to his heart's content.

Amy was relieved. None of them seemed to have noticed her visitor, thank goodness.

'Come in then!' Taking hold of his collar with both hands, she gave an almighty tug, jerking him into the passage and almost choking him in the process.

'Bloody hell, Amy!' Red in the face he quickly undid his shirt. 'There's no need to throttle me.'

'There's *every* need!' Quietly smiling to herself, Amy led the way down the passage to the back parlour. 'Five minutes,' she warned. 'I've got a fire on but, winter or summer, this house is never warm.'

As he came into the parlour she repeated her warning, 'Five minutes, and no more!'

Let It Shine

Josephine Cox

Ada Williams was once an ambitious woman who believed money and power would bring her happiness. But now, she is all alone in the world except for her greedy, bitter son Peter, who despises her and waits only for the day he will inherit her fortune.

Ada, however, has a different plan altogether.

Just a few miles away in Blackburn, the Bolton family may be poor – but the love they share, and the friendship of their neighbours, means they can overcome almost any adversity. But no one could foresee the shocking events of Christmas night, 1932, which split the family asunder, leaving young Larry crippled and the twins, Ellie and Betsy, in a foster home. Events that began many years ago, when Ada Williams was young and foolish.

Let It Shine is the heart-rending and poignant new tale from the *Sunday Times* bestselling storyteller Josephine Cox – the greatest living saga writer.

'Driven and passionate' *The Sunday Times*

'A Cookson by any other name' *Birmingham Post*

'As Warm and affectionate as an old chair in front of a coal-black range, and as satisfying as a Lancashire hotpot, Cox's talent as a storyteller never lets you escape the spell' *Daily Mail*

0 7472 6638 7

headline

The Woman Who Left

Josephine Cox

Riddled with guilt, she was far from being sleepy. Because even when he held her as close as any man could hold his woman, her mind was filled with thoughts of another man.

Louise and Ben Hunter have a happy, loving marriage, marred only by their unfulfilled longing for a child. Living and working with Ben's father, Ronnie, they quietly accept their uneventful but contented lives. But when Ronnie dies, their whole world changes.

News of his father's passing brings Ben's lazy brother, Jacob, back on the scene, in the mistaken belief that he stands to inherit Ronnie's small fortune. Added to which he means to have his brother's wife; though just as she did years before, Louise warns him off. Jacob, however, is not so easily dismissed.

When he realises it is Ben who will inherit everything, Jacob is beside himself with rage, and commits a terrible deed, one that threatens to destroy everything his brother and Louise hold dear – their home and their family, their friends, their marriage and even their very lives . . .

Praise for Josephine Cox's writing:

'Cox's talent as a storyteller never lets you escape the spell' *Daily Mail*

'Impossible to resist' *Woman's Realm*

'Driven and passionate' *The Sunday Times*

0 7472 6634 4

headline

Bad Boy Jack

Josephine Cox

Deserted by the two women in his life, Robert Sullivan is left to raise three-year-old Nancy and her seven-year-old brother Jack. Unable to cope, Robert is driven to abandon his children to those who he believes can provide them with a better life. However, he quickly has a change of heart and decides to go back for them. But on the way there, he is involved in a horrific accident.

Unbeknownst to him, Jack and Nancy are placed in the brutal regime of the Galloway Children's Home, where Jack's fierce devotion to his sister and fiery temper land him in more trouble. Clinging together, the two children find themselves at the mercy of the corrupt Clive Ennington, who splits them up and sells Nancy off to the highest bidder.

When Robert begins to recover in hospital he is determined to find and reunite his family. But he soon begins to realise the terrible consequences of his own cowardly actions.

Praise for Josephine Cox's writing:

'Cox's talent as a storyteller never lets you escape' *Daily Mail*

'Driven and passionate' *The Sunday Times*

Bad Boy Jack is also available in an audio edition.

0 7472 6640 9

headline

Now you can buy any of these other bestselling
books by **Josephine Cox** from your bookshop
or *direct from the publisher*.

FREE P&P AND UK DELIVERY
(Overseas and Ireland £3.50 per book)

Bad Boy Jack	£6.99
Jinnie	£6.99
The Woman Who Left	£5.99
Let it Shine	£5.99
Looking Back	£5.99
Rainbow Days	£5.99
Somewhere, Someday	£5.99
The Gilded Cage	£5.99
Tomorrow the World	£6.99
Love Me or Leave Me	£6.99
Miss You Forever	£6.99
Cradle of Thorns	£6.99
A Time for Us	£6.99
The Devil You Know	£6.99
Living a Lie	£6.99
A Little Badness	£6.99
More Than Riches	£6.99
Born to Serve	£6.99

TO ORDER SIMPLY CALL THIS NUMBER

01235 400 414

or visit our website: www.madaboutbooks.com

Prices and availability subject to change without notice.